UNTHINKABLE

ALSO BY CLYDE PHILLIPS

Fall from Grace
Blindsided
Sacrifice

UNTHINKABLE

CLYDE PHILLIPS

The characters and events portrayed in this book are fictitious. Any similarity to real persons, living or dead, is coincidental and not intended by the author.

Printed in the United States of America.

Published by Thomas & Mercer

PO Box 400818

Las Vegas, NV 89140

ISBN-13: 9781611098112

ISBN-10: 1611098114

Library of Congress Control Number: 2013901626

For Bill Glazer...

strong, deep and moving;

a timeless river of friendship.

And for Jane and Claire,

my wife and daughter.

Beauty, grace and possibility.

My dreams come true.

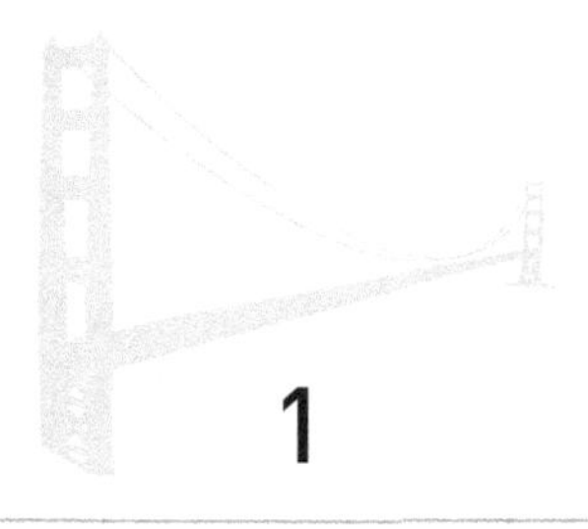

1

The wind gathered in the north hills, the California oaks bowing like geishas.

Moving in fathomless gusts, it squalled across San Francisco Bay, whitecaps bursting in silver-foam explosions. The suspension cables of the Golden Gate Bridge quavered like the strings of God's own harp. Drivers of the huge semis pressing north over the bridge struggled to steady their rigs, their wipers chattering against their windshields.

The masts of the sailboats at mooring in the marina tilted and dipped in unison, like a drunken marching band.

And still the wind pushed on, hour after hour, howling up the impossible inclines of San Francisco's storied streets.

People coming out of their houses and office buildings were forced back a sudden step or two before they realized that the morning's windstorm was still ripping up the mountain-steep canyons this late in the day. Bent at the waist, shoulders hunched, they trudged uphill like beasts of burden.

Terrence Unger hated San Francisco.

Sure it was beautiful, breathtaking even. Sure it was the ideal city in which to meet the ideal man. And sure he'd done just that a little over a year ago now. He always said that San Francisco would be paradise—better than that: paradise with great Chinese food. If it weren't for this damn wind.

Terrence Unger cursed it for churning up the dust from the endless construction on virtually every street in his neighborhood. And he cursed it for igniting his smoldering allergies. But mostly he cursed it for what it did to his hair. What little of it he had left.

He'd wash his hair every morning with a special shampoo he got from his stylist for twenty-two bucks a bottle. Then he'd blow-dry it, coaxing every remaining wisp to perform scalp-covering miracles. After that, he'd spray it to within an inch of its life—twelve bucks a can—and walk the three blocks to his office at UBS.

Two seconds out the door of the condo he shared with Charlie See, his new life partner, his hair would be all blown to shit.

Every goddamn day.

He leaned forward and tucked his head away from the wind. Then, everyone around him bending like mimes, he climbed Carmody Avenue, one of the city's most precipitous streets, toward Stella's.

As he got closer, the seductive smell of whatever Stella's put in their fast food made his stomach growl. He'd missed lunch again, while talking to the New York office. The time difference kept screwing him up. Good news was there wouldn't be much of a line at the counter. Usually, when he was able to take his lunch at a decent hour, the place was mobbed.

Terrence tugged open the front door and stepped aside as a slender black woman curled a purple knit muffler around her neck and maneuvered a baby carriage out of the restaurant. Patting his scattered hair back into place, he glanced down the street, worried that Charlie might spot him going in. But all he saw was Shanty Rourke, Carmody Avenue's own panhandler, crossing the street from his post near the main entrance of the

Staples. Shanty's body was side-slanted against the steepness of the hill, his left leg bent at the knee, his right leg straight as a stilt. He smoothed a wad of bills in the palm of his hand, rubbing them flat with his thumb.

Terrence checked his cell phone for messages. Charlie usually called this time of day to nag him. It was only last week that Terrence had been told by his doctor that his cholesterol was north of two-sixty, and Charlie was adamant about both of them going on diets. Must be an Asian thing. He caught his reflection in the mirrors over the booth where two teenage boys were huddled in conversation, fries and chocolate shakes between them. Sure, Terrence thought, I could lose a couple of pounds. Starting tomorrow, he promised Charlie in absentia.

Toni Salazar looked up from the cash register and smiled. "Hey, Mr. Unger. Blowin' like a mother out there, huh?"

"Blowing like…always."

"Tell me about it." Toni nodded. "Gonna have your usual?"

"And a chocolate shake," Terrence said, thinking what the hell, as he watched one of the kids in the booth poke his spoon into a frosted fountain glass.

Terrence Unger would be the first to die.

Shanty Rourke yanked open the door to Stella's and winced at the smell of cleaning fluid. He stepped inside, pulling the door closed before the wind could catch it, and looked around.

That fat faggot with the comb-over who was a stockbroker or something was turning away from the counter with a cheeseburger, onion rings, and a chocolate shake. Just what he needed, with a gut like that.

Crossing the room, Shanty nodded to the two boys in the back booth. The Mexican kid had laid a ten on him half an hour ago in front of the Staples. Usually kids didn't give him anything, but this one always seemed to have a fistful on him.

Shanty reached into the pocket of his old fatigue jacket as he approached the girl at the register. "Coupons still good this late?"

"For you, Shanty, anytime," Toni said.

Shanty liked this girl. Maybe she had a few more piercings than she should have, but she treated him like a human, letting him use the bathroom when the manager wasn't around. Shanty smiled—his teeth pocked and rotten from years of heroin, years of methadone, years of sugar to cut the jones—and smoothed the ten onto the counter. "Any chance I can get you to keep the change?"

"No can do. But thanks anyway...again."

Shanty took his food and looked for a place to sit. "S'all right. I'm having a good day."

He would be shot twice in the head.

Toni Salazar checked the clock.

Now that the lunch rush was over, all she could think about was walking up to Ashmont Street in this wind and catching the crosstown to SFCC. She was five units short of her secretarial degree; then it was bye-bye minimum wage...and bye-bye Sammy. Boy, had he been a mistake. This was the new, improved Toni. No more mistakes like that asshole.

Toni watched as Shanty Rourke took a seat near the front door, carefully draped his fatigue jacket over the back of a chair like it was a tuxedo jacket, and started in on his two-for-one.

Through the window just beyond Shanty, Toni saw Father Francis stepping up to the sidewalk, his hair whipping in the wind, his eyes squinting at the roiling dust. The poor guy looked so exhausted from all those hours working over at the AIDS

Hospice. Young man like him, Toni thought, ought to have more life in him.

Father Francis ate the same thing every day: veggie burger, apple turnover, and milk. The three most boring things on the menu. Maybe it was some kind of abstinence thing. Toni put in his order before he even entered. Save him some time, tired as he was.

Toni Salazar would be shot in the abdomen and the left side. She would live a few minutes longer than the others.

Liberty Street was so steep that only diagonal parking was permitted on its upper blocks.

SFPD Patrol Cruiser number 1534 pulled into a space by the fire hydrant in front of Art's Deli. The two patrol cops could feel their black-and-white shudder as a sudden gust of wind blasted up the hill from San Francisco Bay. The coffee in the thermos between the seats sloshed with the rocking of the car.

"Jesus." Patrolman Tommy Murphy looked down the hill. The west tower of the Bay Bridge loomed over the gray moving sea, its surface tweeding with whitecaps. "This ever gonna let up?"

His partner, Patrolman Rick Weymouth, shrugged. "It will or it won't." He crimped the squad car's wheels to the curb as Tommy grabbed the dashboard mic.

"4P99 to Dispatch."

"Dispatch to 4P99. Go, Rookie."

Tommy tossed back a smile. This was his third year on the force, but Melody, the dispatcher at Fifteen, still thought of him as a rookie. Not that anyone could blame her. The last time he went drinking with some of the off-duties, Tommy—who was in his midtwenties—was carded at the door.

"Murphy and Weymouth requesting 10-7M at Art's Deli on Liberty Street. Half hour tops."

"Roger that. Have a good lunch. Dispatch out."

The two cops pushed open their car doors as a construction crew, their own lunch break over, cranked up their jackhammers and went back to tearing up Liberty Street for a new fiber-optic line. The dust and dirt from the ditch they were grinding into the street spattered Tommy and Rick like shrapnel.

"Fuckin' urban uglification," Rick yelled over the racket as they ran across the sidewalk and into the deli.

Tommy held the door open. "S'why I live where I live." They slipped inside and he pulled the door closed, most of the construction din and the moaning of the wind fading away.

"Y'know what, buddy? You gotta make up your mind. Half the time you say livin' on your boat is heaven. Beautiful sunsets, no bugs, the occasional mermaid. The other half, all you do is bitch. Boat repairs, phone problems, sewage smells..."

"Yeah, well last night was a heaven night. In the mermaid department." Tommy started for the back of the restaurant. "Order me a Reuben and a Coke. I gotta pee like a racehorse." He waved to two California Highway Patrol motorcycle cops at the counter and made his way back to the restroom.

After nine hours in the almost pious stillness of the AIDS Hospice, Father Francis Cellucci welcomed the hum and hustle of Stella's.

He brushed the dust off his black coat and touched Shanty Rourke on the shoulder, nodding hello as he passed. Shanty looked up and smiled, mayonnaise dotting his stubble.

That Hispanic kid was in the back booth again. Something was going on with him—something not entirely kosher. Father Francis noticed these things.

"'Scuse me for saying, Father"—Toni handed him his veggie burger—"but you look like sh—Uh, you look beat. Don't they let you guys take vacations or nothing?"

"Actually they do," Father Francis said. "I've been thinking of a little whale watching down in Carmel."

"S'posed to be beautiful." Toni gave him his change.

"Supposed to be."

An elderly Vietnamese man rose from his booth, wiped it down with a paper napkin, and gestured for Father Francis to have a seat. As the Father started for the booth, Toni reached out and touched him on the elbow. "I hope you do it, Father. Whale watching, I mean."

"I will, Toni. That's a promise."

He would be shot in the hand, shoulder, and forehead.

Robert Farrier had told his mother he was out job hunting.

School had been over for a month and she'd been riding his butt pretty hard. It was easier to just leave the house, hang at Stella's, and come home to tell her no luck out there job-huntingwise.

He scraped the last of his chocolate shake out of the fountain glass and watched as that old Vietnamese guy who worked at the newsstand up the hill put his shoulder into the door and muscled it open. He stepped into the wind and turned right, quickly passing from view. "I'm gettin' another shake," Robert said across the table to the Mexican kid. He slid out of the booth. "You want anything?"

"Yeah," Nico Silva said, "a piece of that babe behind the counter."

Robert bumped fists with Nico.

Robert Farrier would be shot once in the face, just below the left eye, and once in the chest.

The back corner booth at Stella's was Nico Silva's office.

Stuff got done here. Not exactly legal stuff, but what the fuck. Victimless was how he saw it.

He watched as the white kid tried to work a hustle on Toni. But she was way ahead of that pimply-assed boy and shut him down like a slamming door. Then she looked over to Nico and kind of smiled at him. Just enough for a glimpse of her new tongue stud.

Coy was what you call it.

He was just pulling himself out of the booth to go talk to her when the killer walked in. Nico was the first one to know something was wrong. He could spot badness a mile away.

And this was definite badness.

Nico Silva would be shot once in the back, between the shoulders, and once in the side of the head.

He would have been twenty-one tomorrow.

Patrol Officer Rick Weymouth reached for his wallet as Sandy, the waitress, set the food down. She put her hand on his wrist and tilted her chin toward the deli owner, Art Kaplan. "On the house," she said. "Thanks for all you do for us."

Rick waved his thanks to Art and snatched a fry off Tommy Murphy's plate.

"If you can't trust your own partner..." Tommy said as he approached. He scraped back his chair and sat down. "Who can you trust?"

"Just tell me you washed your hands."

"To the elbows."

The CHPs at the counter finished their meal, waved to Rick and Tommy, and headed for the back door.

Hungry from a long shift, the two men fell silent for a moment as they ate. Then Rick took a long pull on his Diet Coke. "Mermaid, huh? Care to divulge?"

"I'll tell you what happened," Tommy said. "But you have to promise me one thing."

"Name it."

"When we get back to the station? You tell—"

"No one?"

"Uh-uh. You tell"—Tommy grinned—"everyone!"

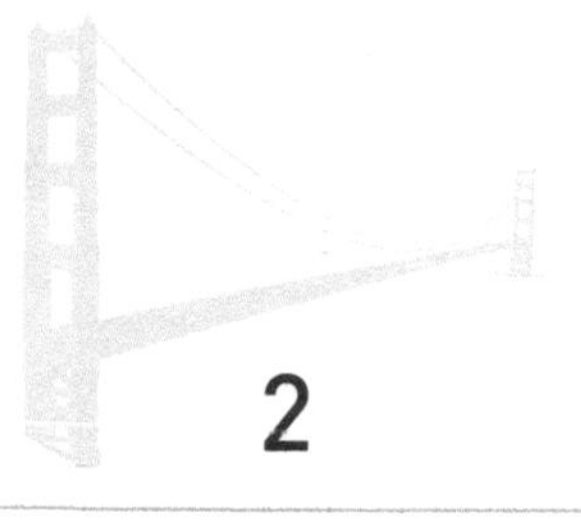

2

Homicide Lieutenant Jane Candiotti pushed up on her elbows, crouching forward on the exam table to get a better look at her fetus on the ultrasound screen. "I'll never get tired of looking at him."

"Or her." Her husband, Homicide Inspector Kenny Marks, leaned over to peer at the monitor. His eyes bounced with the light.

"Look at you," Jane said. "You've never been this happy in your life."

"Or this nervous."

"*You're* nervous? It's my belly they're going to poke like a voodoo doll." Jane brought his hand to her lips. She had turned forty this year and this pregnancy was the last thing in the world she had dared to hope for.

But here it was, real and vital, deep within her. Her dark brown eyes moistened, a tear slipping away.

"All I want," Kenny whispered, "is, boy or girl, that it looks like you." He brushed at her tear with the back of his finger. "I kinda like this Italian cheekbone thing you got going."

The door opened and Dr. Jason Berger stepped in. He was a handsome man in his early fifties with shaggy gray hair and soft blue eyes. Sharon, his nurse, followed with the amnio tray. Dr. Berger smiled at Jane and Kenny, then looked closely at the monitor. "There's plenty of fluid and the baby's in perfect position." He turned to Jane. "Ready?"

Jane nodded tightly. "Like you don't know."

"It'll all be fine," Dr. Berger said, pulling on a pair of latex gloves. "Still blowing out there?"

Kenny crabbed to the side to give the doctor some room. "Bakery truck blew over on Eight Eighty. S'why we were a little late."

"Better late than..." Dr. Berger didn't have to finish the sentence. He put a gentle hand on Jane's belly and smiled down to her. Then he tilted his chin toward the monitor. "See that little pulsating jelly bean? That's the heartbeat. I want you two to stare at it and think good thoughts. Keep that tiny thing beating forever."

The nurse peeled the sterile sleeve off a long needle and handed it to him. "Okay, deep breaths now."

Jane drank in a lung-filling breath and let it stream slowly past her lips.

Dr. Berger looked at Kenny. "I meant both of you."

Kenny glanced at the needle, then at the screen. He sucked in a deep breath between his clenched teeth.

Dr. Berger held the needle above Jane's belly, pressed her taut skin with the fingertips of his free hand, and watched the monitor. He touched the needle to a spot just to the right of her navel and pushed.

Jane gripped Kenny's hand as she felt the needle slip into her abdomen. Watching on the monitor, she could see the needle—an impossibly straight white line—penetrate the amniotic sac. The baby remained calm, drifting within its liquid pillow.

The nurse handed Dr. Berger three tubes. He quickly filled them, one after the other. "Okay, withdrawing. You're doing great." He tugged gently and the needle retreated, leaving the baby serene and undisturbed.

The nurse snapped a thick rubber band around the tubes and started for the door.

"Wait," Jane said. She held out her hand. "I want to see."

Sharon stepped forward and offered the tubes to her.

Jane took them in her left hand and held them up to the light. They were filled with a hazy amber fluid. The warmth of something so elemental, so primal, took her breath away.

She started to pass the tubes over to the nurse, but drew her hand back. Then she raised the test tubes, filled with information and promise and secrets...and she kissed them.

"Thank you," she said.

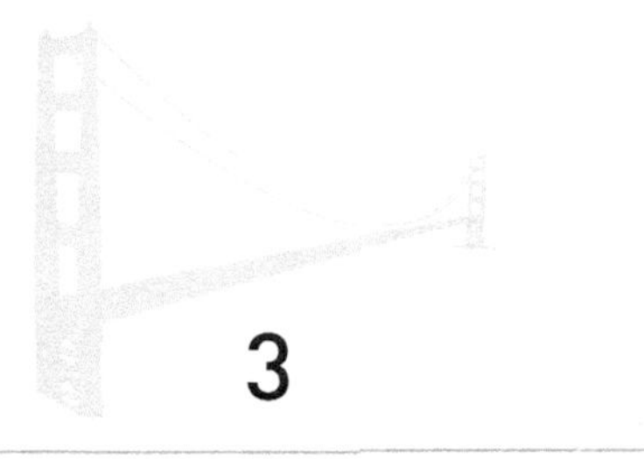

3

Isaac and Rodney Cooper, their hooded sweatshirts filling with the wind, grabbed the rails of their skateboards and cranked a hard left off Ashmont.

As they rumbled down the top of Carmody Avenue, Rodney's board side-slipped a little and almost whacked into the newsstand. The newspapers and magazines, held in place by heavy iron ingots, flapped in the wind like dying fish. Nguyen Bao shook his head in quiet disgust. Those damn Cooper brothers had been warned a thousand times not to ride their boards on these sidewalks.

With a deft pivot of his rear foot, Rodney corrected his board and caught up to Isaac. The slender black woman who had been in Stella's with her baby emerged from the fabric store and, her purple muffler unraveling in the wind, barely managed to get her stroller behind a parking meter as the boys screamed past.

Isaac and Rodney skidded to a stop at Stella's and kick-flipped their boards up into their hands. The manager always gave them grief about bringing their boards inside, but that girl Toni was usually pretty cool. Rodney peeled back his hood and scoped himself in the window. He let his eyes focus past his own reflection and into the restaurant, trying to get a glimpse of Toni behind the counter. "Looks all quiet in there."

Isaac peered through the glass. "Looks all empty." He pulled open the door. "Let's check it out."

The brothers entered the restaurant and stopped.

There was no one there.

Something else was different, too. The place usually smelled like that stuff their aunt used to clean windows. But now it smelled like burning metal.

They recognized Shanty Rourke's fatigue jacket draped over the back of a chair. A whole hamburger and a half-eaten one still on the table. Farther back, there was a veggie burger, an apple turnover, and a glass of milk in the second booth on the right. A chocolate shake was splattered on the floor in front of the counter. And there—half behind the counter, half in the open—the cash register lay on its side, pieces of its plastic cowling scattered nearby.

The cash drawer was on top of a litter of coins and checks. The paper money was gone.

Isaac looked to Rodney. "I don't want to be here." There was a tacit bridge of understanding between them. A robbery, plus violence, plus cops equaled a shit-ugly mix for two black kids.

"I'm with you, bro." Rodney turned toward the door.

Isaac was just about to join his brother, when an odd sound came from the back stairway. First there was a grunt, then a heavy thump like someone dropping something soft onto something hard. Over and over again: grunt-thump, grunt-thump. Rigid with fear, the Cooper brothers watched as something—at first they thought it was a black dog—finally appeared at the top stair.

As their eyes and their brains adjusted, they realized it was the black hair of a human being coming into view. Then they saw that it was the girl Toni who worked the counter and had always been so nice to them.

Toni struggled up one last step. Then, utterly spent, raised a bloodied hand to them. She pulled back her lips, sucking for air. When she could finally summon the breath to speak, a mist of red vapor blew out of her mouth.

"...police..." she gasped. Then she lowered her head onto the metal strip at the top step, as if falling asleep, and lay still.

Isaac and Rodney Cooper whipped out their cell phones.

An American flag had wrapped itself around a flagpole on the roof of the building across the way, the wind pulling at it as if trying to pry it loose.

Jane turned away from the window and looked at the wall behind Dr. Berger's desk.

A bulletin board with a mosaic of hundreds of baby pictures. Jane focused on the photographs, her emotions spinning.

Kenny touched the back of his hand to her cheek. "How you doing?"

Jane sat back. "The skin on my belly feels a little weird from the anesthetic. But I'm okay."

"Not a day goes by that I don't appreciate what you're doing for us."

Jane smiled at her husband. "Just promise me you'll still love me this much when I gain a thousand pounds."

"Where do I sign?"

"Right here." Jane leaned across and kissed him on the lips.

The door swung open and Dr. Berger stood in the doorway. "I could come back..."

"Tempting." Jane laughed. "But we have to get to work."

"Yeah," Kenny said. "Somebody has to keep this city safe."

Dr. Berger sat in his leather desk chair and dropped a file onto a stack of others. "Then I'm here to tell you to get out of here. I checked all the comparatives and your baby's right down the middle. No worries."

"What's next?" Kenny asked.

"We'll call with the results in a couple of weeks. Medically, everything should be perfect. Right now, your biggest issue is whether or not you want to know the gender."

"I do." Jane glanced at Kenny. "He doesn't."

Kenny shrugged. "We've got all this science and all this information. I want at least one surprise."

"And I want to know," Jane said, "for all the usual mother reasons."

Dr. Berger made a note on their chart. "Okay…Mom, yes… Dad, no…You got it. Jane, make sure you take your supplements, get plenty of rest, and eat whenever you're hungry."

Jane pushed her chair back and rose. "I can do that."

Kenny stood up to shake Dr. Berger's hand. "Thanks, Jason."

"It's always great to see you guys." Dr. Berger walked them to the door. "Look, I know it's hard with what you do, but try to keep your stress levels down as much as possible."

Jane picked up her purse, feeling the heft of her service pistol, walkie-talkie, and police badge. "It's been a quiet couple of weeks. Let's hope for a couple more."

Kenny reached into his jacket and pulled his Glock 19 from the inner pocket. He slipped it into his shoulder holster and held the door for Jane.

Jane Candiotti was his wife…and his superior.

Dr. Berger took a new file from his desk, prepping for his next patient. "Stay safe, you guys."

Patrol Officer Tommy Murphy tapped the bottom of his glass until the last piece of ice slid into his mouth.

"It's so not like that," he said, chewing on the ice. "Her father's boat is a couple down from mine. She was home from college. The wind knocked out the dockside power. She saw my lights and came over to ask if I knew how to help tap into the auxiliary." He wiped his mouth with a napkin and dropped it onto his plate. "Two things led to another…"

Rick Weymouth looked at his partner over his coffee cup. "Just like that?"

"Yup." Tommy beamed. "Just like—"

Their radios crackled. "All units vicinity Carmody and Ashmont. Shots fired. Possible multiple casualty situation at Stella's Restaurant, sixty-seven Carmody Avenue, one down from Ashmont."

Tommy snatched his walkie-talkie off his belt. "4P99 to Dispatch. We're at Eighty-Two Liberty. Couple blocks away. Rolling in one."

Melody's voice came on. "Dispatch to 4P99. Location is *not* secure. Perp or perps may still be on site."

Tommy and Rick threw back their chairs and raced for the front door of Art's Deli. Other patrons who had overheard the radio traffic turned to watch them bolt out the door. "Roger that," Tommy Murphy called into his radio.

"You be careful, Rookie," Melody said, the slightest catch in her voice.

Rick ripped open the driver's-side door of the police cruiser and jumped behind the wheel. He twisted the key in the ignition and jammed the transmission into reverse.

But, because of the street construction and the diagonal parking, traffic was funneled into one busy lane. Tommy ran past the car and held up his hand, his shirt plastered into his body by the wind. A grocery van skidded to a stop. He motioned with both hands for the truck to back up a few feet so Rick could get out of the parking space. Then he hopped into the passenger seat of the black-and-white and snapped his shoulder harness home.

Art Kaplan and a couple of waitresses stood in the doorway of the deli. One of the waitresses raised her hand in a half wave.

Tommy nodded curtly, all business now. Rick stomped on the accelerator and the police car screeched backward into the traffic lane.

Before the car came to a complete stop, Rick pulled it into drive. The cruiser's rear wheels spun in place for a second, then the car leaped forward. Up ahead, a UPS truck was just coming out of an alley.

"On the right!" Tommy shouted.

"Got it!" Rick flicked on the flasher-siren package and made it past the delivery truck. A city bus was stopped at the next corner, backing up traffic all the way to the police car. "C'mon, c'mon." Rick slapped the steering wheel with the palm of his hand. "*C'mon*!"

"There!" Tommy pointed to a broad expanse of sidewalk at the corner in front of a Wells Fargo Bank. A covey of commuters stood in the lee of a glassed-in bus stop, shielded from the wind as they waited for the Crosstown Express.

"You think?" Rick asked.

"Go for it!"

Rick flung the car to the right. Passersby, responding to the whoop of the siren, pressed back against the bank building as the cruiser bounded up over the curb, traversed the sidewalk, and bounced back onto the cross street.

A one-way cross street. The wrong way. They were face-to-face with a taxi. The cabdriver quickly backed up to give the cops room to maneuver.

"Fuckin' city!" Rick cursed as he twisted the steering wheel and powered the car into a U-turn. Then he stood on the gas and careened around the corner of Carmody Avenue, straining up the hill toward Stella's.

The city bus, the construction, the congestion all behind them now, Tommy called it in. "4P99 to Dispatch. We've got a visual on Stella's."

A black kid in a hooded sweatshirt ran outside. Tommy was about to draw down on him, when the boy frantically waved for the cops to follow him. Rick hit the brakes hard and the car sideslipped to a stop at the newsstand.

"Dispatch, we're going in!" Tommy grabbed the shotgun from its bracket and was out of the car.

Rick ripped his pistol from its holster and the two patrol officers, moving forward in a crouch, headed toward the restaurant.

There was a brief spit of static on Jane's walkie-talkie as the elevator doors closed.

"Uh-oh," Jane said to Kenny as the elevator began its descent from the thirty-eighth floor of the Kaiser Permanente Medical Tower in Oakland. She reached into her purse and turned up the volume on her police radio, but that only cranked the static louder.

Kenny's cell phone vibrated on his hip. He checked the readout: *signal lost*. "They're trying to reach both of us at the same time. Something's going on."

"I know. Can't be good." The elevator stopped at thirty-six and a mailroom clerk started to push an overloaded cart aboard. Jane flashed her shield. "Sorry, sir, we have to get to the lobby."

The clerk had headphones on and couldn't hear her. But he saw the badge in Jane's hand and the intensity on her face. He backed out of there.

Kenny jabbed the button to close the door and the elevator continued down. As the elevator passed the twenty-third floor, Jane's radio crackled and Kenny's cell buzzed simultaneously. The elevator slowed at twenty and stopped at nineteen. The doors parted to reveal four women with pillows under their arms, returning from Lamaze class. Jane held up her badge. "Sorry, ladies."

Kenny knuckled the button again.

The elevator picked up speed through the express floors of the hospital and came to a stop at the lobby level. When the doors finally opened, Jane and Kenny burst into the harsh fluorescent world of the first floor and ran through the pharmacy toward the parking lot.

Kenny checked his cell phone's readout. *3H61911*. His call-code—emergency.

Jane called in. "3H58 to Dispatch."

"Lieutenant?" Cheryl Lomax, Precinct Nineteen's dispatcher, asked.

"What's happening, Cheryl?"

"We got a bad one, Jane. Multiple casualties at the Stella's on Carmody. SFPD, CHP, and EMT all responding."

Kenny pulled his keys from his pocket and thumbed the remote. Over in the loading zone, the door locks on his black Explorer popped up. "I'll get the car."

Jane nodded. "Cheryl, what else do we know?"

"Only that the first responders are a patrol unit from Fifteen. They're entering the restaurant right about now. Another two units from Fifteen plus CHP motorcycle units are closing in." Cheryl's voice was tinged with urgency. All of this information was new to Jane, but Cheryl had been on it for a while, monitoring traffic, calling out assignments, trying to reach her lieutenant.

Jane remained calm. "Is Task Force B rolling?"

"Affirmative. Mobile Command, Forensics, Crisis Administration, Fire, and Press Relations all on the way."

The Explorer screeched up and Kenny threw open the passenger door.

"So are we. But we're in goddamn Oakland!" Jane climbed in and pulled the door closed. Then she reached under the seat, found the dome light, and slapped its magnetic base onto the roof of the Explorer.

The red light strobing and the siren wailing, Kenny tore away from the curb. A quick-thinking parking guard raised the arm of the tollbooth. Kenny shot across the sidewalk and whipped into a hard right turn toward Highway 80.

The gray expanse of the Bay Bridge, their only link to San Francisco, seemed a thousand miles away.

"Get down!"

Tommy Murphy waggled his shotgun at the black kid who was standing in the doorway of Stella's.

Rodney Cooper dropped to the sidewalk. "My brother's in there. We didn't do nothin'. Don't hurt him!"

Rick Weymouth sized it up. His instinct told him the kid was telling the truth. "Stay here," he said as he pushed past Rodney and, with Tommy covering him, entered the restaurant.

"...police..." Toni Salazar moaned. Her head was still lying on the top step.

Isaac Cooper knelt next to her, too frightened to touch her. He glanced back and saw two policemen heading toward him. "Here they come," he said. "You hang on."

Tommy and Rick eyeballed the place.

"Holy shit," Tommy said under his breath.

"Check the kitchen," Rick ordered. "I'm going to the victim."

Tommy searched the kitchen, his shotgun prodding in front of him like a spear.

Rick dropped down next to Isaac. "You seen anyone else?"

"No, sir."

"Fine. I need you to go outside and wait for a policeman. Do *not* go home. Just wait. Do you understand me?"

"Y-yes, sir."

"Good. Now go."

Isaac scooted across the dining area and joined his brother outside.

Tommy came back into the dining area. "Kitchen's clear."

Rick brushed the hair off Toni's face. "This one's hit two times I can see." He clutched the shoulder-mic of his police radio. "4P77 to Dispatch."

Melody came on right away. "Dispatch to 4P77. What do you got, Rick?"

"One victim so far. Female Hispanic. Late teens, early twenties. Multiple GSW." Toni coughed, a cloud of bloodred mist sputtering from her mouth. "She's in bad shape, Mel!"

"SFPD backup and EMT are closing in. First ambulance got stuck in construction traffic. Is the site secure?"

Rick looked at the blood trail coming from the lower level. "Just the upstairs."

"…police…" Toni gasped again.

Rick leaned over so Toni could see him. "We're here, honey. We're here."

Tommy Murphy cradled the shotgun in the crook of his arm and undid the safety strap on his holster. "I'm going down there."

"Maybe we should wait for backup."

Tommy shook his head. "Look at this place." He was already halfway down the stairs. "There's gotta be more victims. They'll need help."

Rick realized his partner was right. "Don't do anything stupid," he warned as Tommy reached the bottom step and turned left, passing out of view. He was just about to crane his neck for a better angle when Toni Salazar started convulsing. Her body shook violently, her head banging repeatedly against the floor. Rick slipped both his arms under her and slid her onto his lap. "I've got you, Miss"—he wiped the blood off her name tag with his thumb—"Miss Salazar."

Toni looked up into his eyes and gradually stopped shaking. Then she did something that surprised him: she smiled, her lips rising slightly at the corners. A dribble of blood trickled out of the side of her mouth and streamed down into her hair. Exhaling out of her nose, she relinquished the last of the breath in her lungs, and died.

Just as Rick was about to put Toni's body back on the floor and join his partner, Tommy Murphy came back up the stairs, shotgun dangling carelessly at his side. The first thing that crossed Rick's mind was that Tommy wasn't exercising proper weapon discipline. Somewhere outside a siren whooped and stopped. Then another. The two CHP motorcycle cops who had been at Art's Deli pulled up behind the squad car, simultaneously throwing up their sun visors as they dismounted. Another police cruiser barreled to a stop in the middle of the street.

Tommy reached the sixth step and stopped. He tried to speak, but no sound would come. He tried again, parting his lips, and a flood of vomit spilled out, soiling the front of his uniform shirt.

Rick rose to a half crouch as two cops he recognized from his precinct hurried toward Stella's, their weapons drawn. "What's down there?" he asked his partner.

Tommy looked at his own vomit falling onto his shoes. "Hell," he said weakly. "Hell is down there."

The black Explorer, its siren screaming, tore along the carpool lane of the Bay Bridge.

"Cheryl," Jane called into the mic, "we're at Treasure Island. Three minutes to the city."

Traffic slowed for the curve at Treasure Island, just west of the midpoint of San Francisco Bay. Kenny urged the Explorer forward, forcing the vehicles ahead to cross over the raised double line and out of the carpool lane. The long gray suspension cables whipped past Jane's window, each one bringing them closer to the peninsula.

"Jane," Cheryl's voice came over the two-way, "we just heard from the first responders. Six fatalities. All gunshot wounds."

"Jesus," Kenny muttered. The Explorer tilted forward slightly, entering the last long downhill run toward the city.

"The location is secure," Cheryl went on. "The shooter is either among the victims—too soon to tell—or has escaped."

Jane pressed the mic switch. "Survivors?"

"Negative."

Half a dozen helicopters swarmed over the city—police, fire, and news—showing them the way to the Stella's on upper Carmody. The Explorer crossed the Embarcadero and entered San Francisco. Below the elevated freeway, two ambulances sped along Harrison Street. Farther ahead, a fire-rescue unit, its light rack flashing, merged onto the 101—all rushing to the same terrible place.

Kenny whipped around a slower-moving minivan. When the Explorer settled back into the carpool lane, he reached across and put his hand on Jane's leg. "You okay to do this?"

Jane nodded. "I have to be."

The Explorer raced down the Van Ness off-ramp. Kenny timed it perfectly and caught the green light. Pulling hard on the steering wheel, he threw the car into a sliding left turn and started the long climb up Carmody Avenue.

As they crested the first intersection, they saw that upper Carmody was jammed with emergency vehicles. A young female traffic officer, her white-gloved hands moving in graceful arcs, guided them forward.

As the Explorer passed under the yellow police tape, the young traffic officer smiled at her; Jane knew that this would be the last innocent face she would see for a long time.

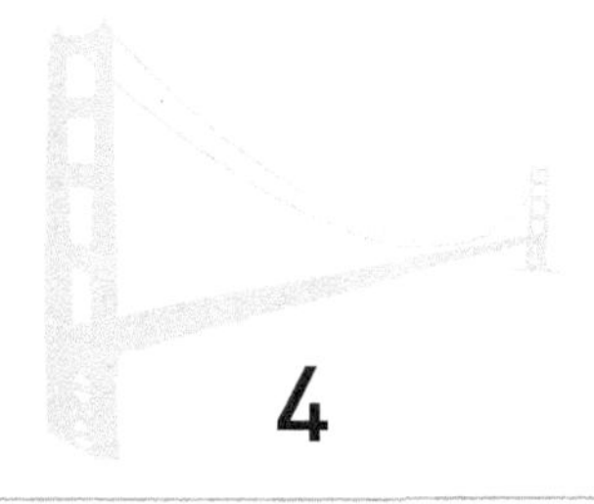

4

Jane stood over Toni Salazar's body.

The young woman's eyes were still open, the overhead lights reflecting tiny specks of electric white.

Kenny approached with Max Batzer, a veteran street cop who had worked with Jane dozens of times over the years. As the supervising on-scene sergeant, it fell on him to coordinate the arrival and dispersal of the responding departments. A Forensics detail fanned out through the restaurant. A videographer finished taping the main level and headed downstairs. Larry Peoples, a crime scene still photographer, took several shots of the ruined cash register, then went to join his colleague on the lower floor.

Emergency medical response teams huddled by the front door, the restaurant's broad windows vibrating in the wind. Many of the EMTs were smeared with blood from checking the victims for signs of life. Soon they would be debriefed and called back to their stations, their services no longer—or never—needed. The victims now belonged to the medical examiner's office.

"Couple a kids called it in," Max said. He gestured outside to where Isaac and Rodney Cooper sat on the steps of the Mobile Command Center. The huge black-and-white tractor-trailer was blocking the main driveway of the Staples across the street. Isaac sipped a Pepsi and talked with a police officer. Rodney squinted into the wind, staring off down the street, suddenly a young boy again as he waited for his mother to arrive.

"This female here," Max went on, "plus five deceased downstairs. Bodies all piled up in a service hallway." He shook his head. "Worst I seen, Jane."

A Forensics tech and a female patrol officer, both with years of experience, came up the stairs. They seemed confused, their eyes lost and unfocused.

Jane surveyed the room. The cops and other personnel went about their work quietly, efficiently. The police photographer climbed halfway up the stairs, then simply sat down, too stunned to move.

"Have someone call the department shrink," Jane said. "We're gonna need his crisis team down here."

"I'll take care of it, Jane," Max offered.

"Also," Kenny said, "when it's safe to touch them, I want you to pull the wallets from the victims. We're gonna need some positive IDs. Bring 'em to me and I'll organize the notification process. I don't want any kid cops screwing this up."

Max made a note and went off to call Dr. Bill Glazer, the department psychiatrist.

Kenny moved closer to Jane. "Ready?"

Jane nodded, her jaw set. "Let's do this."

They went down the stairs together. The photographer heard them coming and rose to make room. "Just changing lenses," he said to Jane, an embarrassed grin creasing his face.

"Do me a favor, Larry?" Jane touched his forearm. "Go out to the canteen truck and get me a water. I think I'm gonna need it."

"Will do, Lieutenant." Larry Peoples climbed the stairs. They both knew what Jane had done—given him a reason, and permission, to leave the building.

Jane and Kenny continued to the bottom step and turned left.

Five bodies lay crumpled in the narrow passageway. A carpet of darkening blood spread beneath them, slick and flat as glass.

At first, the bodies seemed little more than a jumble of limbs and clothing. A flannel shirt here, a sneaker there. But as Jane and Kenny absorbed the scene, the enormity of what they were looking at became more specific.

A man in a clerical collar was at the bottom of the pile. A teenage boy had fallen facedown across his legs. What seemed like a homeless man lay in a fetal position next to the priest's left hand. A well-dressed man, his expensive suit out of place among the modest clothing of the others, was lying on his back, one of his legs on the homeless man's hip, the other over the teenage boy's right arm. A young Hispanic man, maybe a teenager, was slumped in a semiseated position, his head against the wall, blood seeping from a bullet hole high on his back.

"Motherfuck," Kenny whispered.

Max Batzer came down the stairs and walked over to the bodies. He pulled on rubber gloves and, with a quick glance back to Jane, probed the victims' clothing, looking for identification.

Forensics Lieutenant Aaron Clark-Weber came in from the back entrance and motioned for Jane and Kenny to join him. "You okay to be down here?" Aaron was one of the few people in the department who knew Jane was pregnant.

"I can deal; thanks, Aaron. What do you have so far?"

"We're still preliminary here, but a couple of things. You saw the cash register upstairs? After-lunch cash, which is in the hundreds, is gone. So, probable robbery gone bad. Back door is locked and the alley surveillance camera is busted. Looks like it was vandalized weeks ago. Might be pertinent, might not." He flexed his arthritic knee against an ember of pain. "There's a Staples across the street. I've already pulled the tapes from their cameras that face this building."

"Where are the uniforms from Fifteen who called this in?" Jane asked.

"Over there."

Tommy Murphy and Rick Weymouth were leaning against a storage rack filled with condiments.

Tommy's shirtfront was covered with dried vomit, and Rick's stomach, thighs, and arms were drenched with blood. They watched, thunderstruck, as Aaron's Forensics team dusted for prints.

"Poor bastards," Kenny said.

Jane nodded. "The one on the left, the big guy? That's Rick Weymouth. His dad was in patrol when I was starting out. Watched that kid grow up. All he ever wanted was to be a cop."

Kenny shook his head. "Welcome to the brotherhood, son."

Jane shifted her gaze to Tommy. He glanced over and saw her looking at him. His hand went up to his soiled shirt and he turned away.

"I want them debriefed as soon as possible," Jane said. "Then sent home."

A cell phone rang. Beethoven's Ninth. "Ode to Joy."

It couldn't belong to any of the investigators. Crime scene discipline was to put all cell phones on vibrate.

The eerie, persistent sound was coming from one of the bodies.

Max Batzer, who was just finishing the retrieval of the IDs, noticed a flashing cell phone on the belt of the well-dressed male victim. He unclipped it and brought it to Jane.

Jane flipped it open. "Hello."

"Oh…" Charlie See said. "I think I have the wrong number."

"Who are you calling?"

"Terry Unger…but—"

"Just a minute, sir." Jane held out her hand to Max. "Give me that guy's wallet."

Max handed it to her and gave the others to Kenny. Jane opened the wallet and slid out the driver's license. Terrence Boyd Unger's photo showed a younger, thinner version of the man lying in this passageway. She showed it to Kenny, then spoke into the phone. "Sir, what is your name?"

"Charlie, Charlie See. I'm Terry's life partner. Is something wrong? I saw all the police cars going up the hill. Then I turned on the news. Where's Terry?"

"Sir, I'm a police officer and something has happened. I want you to give your address to my colleague and someone will be right over to see you."

Charlie See's voice tightened with panic. "Something happened? *What* happened?"

"It's best if you have this conversation in person, sir. Now I need you to just give us your location and we'll come see you right away. Can you do that for me?"

"Uh, sure."

"Thank you, sir." Jane passed the phone to Max Batzer. "Max, please take care of this one yourself."

There was a rush of activity on the stairs. Everyone in the lower corridor turned at the same time.

Chief Walker McDonald descended the last step, turned left, and stopped in midstride when he saw the carnage. The chief was in full-dress uniform, having just been called away from giving a speech at the Police Academy. His broad shoulders sagged as the enormity of what he was looking at struck home. He turned to Jane. "Lieutenant."

"Chief."

Since Walker McDonald had lost the mayoral primary the previous June, the tension between him and Jane—a tension that had simmered for years—had boiled over. He had asked Jane for support, even offered her an unprecedented Homicide captaincy…and she had refused him on both counts.

Chief McDonald leveled his gaze on Jane. "Anything yet?"

"Too soon, sir. We've got a lot of work to do."

"Suspects?"

"Also too soon."

The chief looked from Jane to Aaron to Kenny. Then he let his eyes fall on the bodies again. He chewed his lower lip. "I've got reporters up the wazoo upstairs. I better go deal with them."

He took a step backward, turned, and quickly ascended the stairway.

Everyone in the corridor caught their collective breath and went back to work.

Jane turned to Kenny. "Let's find a flat surface and I'll help you with the IDs."

But Kenny was looking past her, something unusual just starting to register. Jane followed his gaze and noticed it, too.

Two of the bodies were lying flush against the walk-in freezer door. They knew the bodies hadn't been moved; therefore the freezer couldn't have been searched. Other victims, the killer, an accomplice…anyone…could be inside.

Kenny put the wallets on the storage shelf where Murphy and Weymouth were standing. Then he crossed the corridor and, stepping over the priest's body, tugged on the steel door-latch. It was locked. From the inside.

"Hold the work!" Jane called out.

Two medical examiner's assistants slid the upper part of the priest's body away from the freezer door, taking care not to disturb the position of the other victims.

Several police officers, plain clothed and uniformed, trained their weapons on the door, covering the firemen who were dismantling the latch with a huge pneumatic pincer. Tommy Murphy drew his pistol and inched forward until he was close to Jane, close to the action. He glanced to Rick Weymouth. His partner had his weapon out but was still hanging back on the periphery.

The latch gave way, a fireman catching it so it wouldn't fall on the bodies. Kenny pulled on the door. The rubber collar-seal held fast for a moment, then yielded.

The cops, their weapons level before them, all reflexively crouched.

Jane handed Kenny a hand-mirror. His Glock in one hand and the mirror in the other, Kenny reached into the freezer and pivoted the reflective surface. Waxed boxes of frozen meats lined the walls, a thin mist swirling. Kenny was just about to withdraw his hand and straighten up, when he spotted something.

It took a moment for him to recognize exactly what it was. As the vapor thinned, pushing itself out the partially opened door, Kenny finally made out a human form. It was in a seated position, knees drawn up, in the far corner of the freezer.

It was still.

"I need a paramedic!"

Kenny and a fireman opened the door wide enough for someone to slip through. Jane was just starting into the freezer when Kenny whispered to her, "Not a good idea."

Jane stopped. For a split second, she didn't know what he was talking about. Then she realized that this would be her struggle: the conflict between her professional and her maternal instincts. Everything she'd been trained for, two decades of experience, was pulling her into that freezer. But all of that had been before she was pregnant.

An EMT raced down the stairs. Kenny held out his arm to him, subtly blocking Jane's path. The two men went into the freezer.

Colleen Porter was a heavy woman. Over two hundred pounds.

Her skin was cold and hard, almost brittle. Her nose, ears, and fingertips were somewhere between gray and blue.

Other EMTs pushed past Kenny and examined her body. Someone felt for a neck pulse. Nothing. Another paramedic threw a heavy blanket over her Stella's uniform and vigorously massaged her chest. A cop and a fireman squatted next to Colleen and tried to move her. But the awkward angle and her excessive weight made it too difficult. An EMT started a sodium chloride drip. A couple of other firemen were just passing a backboard into the freezer when Colleen Porter suddenly let out a deep guttural gasp.

Her eyelids opened partway and her eyes darted from side to side. Then she slowly opened her mouth and a long steaming whoosh of air pushed out of her lungs.

A silent scream.

Jane and Kenny stood to the side of Stella's back entrance as Colleen Porter was loaded into an ambulance. An EMT slapped the back of the paramedic unit and, siren keening, it sped off. A tattered orange cat, spooked by the ambulance, leaped out of a Dumpster. It tore across the alley, scaled a fence, and disappeared.

Jane was surprised to see that the sun was so low over the city. It would be dusk soon. "We may actually have a witness."

"If she lives," Kenny said as he stepped down to the black tar pathway that led to the alley.

They were standing in the rear delivery area of the restaurant, a chain-link pen of AC compressors, garbage bins, and milk crates. Wooden slats were woven vertically into the chain-link, providing privacy and the illusion of security. There were dozens of cigarette butts by the stone steps.

A Forensics tech stood on a ladder, dusting the disabled surveillance camera. Another tech was making footprint molds in the greasy pathway. As the siren of Colleen Porter's ambulance faded away, the steady percussive beat of the helicopters came back up.

Jane took Kenny's sleeve. "You notice?"

"Notice what?"

Jane looked around. "The wind stopped."

They were about to reenter the restaurant when Tommy Murphy stepped out. He was carrying the wallets Kenny had left on the storage shelf. "Thought you might want these, Inspector."

Kenny took them from him. "Thanks"—he checked Tommy's name tag—"Murphy."

Tommy brushed at the vomit on his shirtfront. "Sorry 'bout this. I shoulda done better in there."

Jane put her hand on his shoulder. "You did great. Textbook. You and your partner, both."

"Thanks for saying that, Lieutenant. Means a lot to me."

Kenny headed back inside the building, opening the first wallet as he went.

Jane stayed with Tommy. "I need you to do something for me, Officer Murphy."

"Call me Tommy, Lieutenant. What is it?"

"I want you to talk to your watch commander about taking some time to see Dr. Glazer."

Tommy looked down to his shoes. "He the shrink?"

Jane nodded. "And I want you to make sure your partner goes, too." She gave his shoulder another reassuring touch and turned toward the back door of Stella's. As she entered, she saw Kenny using a storage shelf for a work surface, going through the victims' wallets.

She was just about up to him, when Kenny spun around, his right fist clenched around a royal-blue Gore-Tex wallet.

Jane hurried over to him. "What?"

"Bobby!"

He shoved the wallet at Jane and ran toward the bodies. A couple of cops looked up from their work as Kenny forced himself to stop short. He carefully maneuvered around the victims to the teenage boy who was lying facedown across the priest's legs. Then he went down to one knee, his pants leg soaking in the pooled blood, and reached out. His hand touched the back of Robert Farrier's head and gently turned it.

The face of his nephew, his sister's only child, stared blankly back at him. A dark bullet hole below his left eye oozed a stream of blood down to his neck.

Jane leaned in and saw the face of the young boy she had known for years. The face that could not possibly belong to a victim of this awful crime. "Oh, Kenny…"

Other cops gathered in a silent, deferential circle, all work stopping now.

Kenny, torn with grief, rose to his feet. "I've got to find Andrea!" He pulled out his cell phone and dialed his sister's work number.

"You've reached Andrea Farrier's voice mail. I'm either away from my desk or, if it's after four, I'm gone for the day. Please leave a—"

Kenny looked at his watch. Four forty. "Shit. She's left work." He dialed her house and was startled when, after the fourth ring, Bobby's voice came on. "Yo, it's Bobby and Andrea. When the beep beeps, leave a message."

"Andrea…hi, it's me…" Kenny hesitated, then went on. "Call me on my cell…" He hung up and turned to Jane. "We have to find her. She has to hear about this from me."

"What about her cell?"

"She never leaves it on."

Jane pulled her walkie-talkie. "Cheryl, I need an All-Points on an Andrea Farrier. Driving a white 1998 Toyota Camry." Jane knew the car. It had been hers before she met Kenny. They had just given it to Andrea last winter. "License number: 7HBC466. She works at the Teachers' Credit Union on Congress and lives out near the stadium. Could be anywhere in between."

"Got it. Uh, Jane, isn't Andrea Farrier the name of Kenny's sister?"

"Yes, it is."

"Everything okay down there?"

"No, Cheryl. Kenny lost his nephew today."

Everyone in the crowded corridor heard what Jane had said. They stood back, hushed and respectful.

Kenny squatted down again and touched Bobby's hair. "My God…he's our boy."

Jane put her hand on Kenny's shoulder. His body sagged for a moment, then he found a reserve of strength from somewhere deep within and stood up, pulling himself away from Bobby's body. Jane scanned the faces of the men and women she'd worked with for years, all looking at her and Kenny with sympathy. Aaron Clark-Weber stepped up to her. "Tell me what you need."

"I've gotta talk to the chief. Where is he?"

"Still upstairs getting ready for the press."

"Shit," Jane muttered. She knew how much the chief hated anyone or anything getting between him and his moment in the sun. No matter what the circumstances. "Aaron, take over down here. Do not hesitate to come for me if you need me."

"Will do, Jane."

Jane took Kenny aside and put both her hands flat on his chest. "Bobby being down here complicates things. A lot, Kenny. I'm going up to talk to the chief."

"I'll go with you."

"No. You need to take a step back right now, clear your head."

Kenny tensed. "Do not take me off this case."

"That's exactly why I'm going up there. To tell him I'm keeping you on. But you gotta let me know you can do this."

Kenny filled his lungs and let out a long rush of air. "You know I can." He gave Jane a long look, then pulled out his cell phone to try his sister again.

Jane nodded. "Okay if I leave you?"

"Yeah."

Jane squeezed his hand and started up the stairs. Larry Peoples was heading down, cameras bouncing around his neck, and handed her a bottle of water. She smiled her thanks and looked back down to Kenny. He was kneeling near the far wall, waiting for Andrea to answer his call. Jane forced herself to turn away and continued up the stairs.

She was startled by how brightly lit the main dining room of Stella's was. After spending so much time on the downstairs killing floor, it was as if she'd stepped into another world. Vital and active and sunlit.

The chief was by the broad front windows, talking with his press liaison. He checked his tie in the mirror over the booth where Father Cellucci's meal lay untouched. Outside, the press were gathering, nudging for position in anticipation of the chief's statement. Jane noticed that Cameron Sanders, a handsome black man in his early thirties, was front row center. Having just moved over from the *Chronicle* to KGO-TV had its privileges. Jane crossed the room and approached the chief. He noticed her reflection in the mirror and turned to her. "Learn anything?"

"We need to talk."

Jane and Chief McDonald sat in an unused booth across the way, the press liaison hovering nearby.

The chief sat back heavily, absorbing what Jane had just told him. Then, gathering himself and his thoughts, he said, "Please tell Kenny how sorry I am for his loss."

Jane set her unopened water bottle on the table and watched a parade of emergency personnel trudge by in both directions. Each of them filled with purpose and intensity. "Thank you, sir."

"So," the chief began, "now what to do?"

Jane looked him straight in the eye. "I want Inspector Marks to remain on the case." The chief started to respond. Jane kept talking. "I know it bumps into all sorts of protocol, but he's the best homicide cop in the city."

"Forget protocol," the chief said coolly. "There's just no precedent for this."

"Fuck precedent," Jane said. "You ran for mayor on the whole premise that precedent, and City Hall's reliance on it, was what was holding San Francisco back."

The chief offered an empty smile. "And I lost."

Jane tried another way in. "Actually, there are several municipalities where relatives of murder victims have worked the cases. With a high solve rate."

"But they were shithole small towns. That sort of Mayberry reasoning isn't going to get you anywhere." The chief reached across the table and grabbed Jane's water bottle. He unscrewed the cap and took a long pull from it. When he finished, he looked to Jane. She returned his gaze, an immovable force. He'd been in too many confrontations with her and knew from long experience when to relent and when not to. After a moment, he finally said, "Okay, here's the deal—and it's a provisional deal until I hear back from legal—Kenny stays on as long as every step of his involvement, no matter how large or small, is monitored, recorded, and witnessed by another officer in your command. Or by you. There will be no rogue cop bullshit. Got it?"

"Yes, sir," Jane said. "I take full responsibility."

"No, Lieutenant," the chief said as he rose, "I do. And I assure you, you will be on the shortest leash in the history of short leashes." He signaled to the press liaison, then turned back to

Jane. "Anything even close to a fuck-up and I pull his ass...and I fire you. Understood?"

Jane nodded as the chief took another swig from her water bottle and thumped it down on the table for emphasis. Then, reflexively straightening his already straightened tie, he strode outside to talk to the reporters.

5

Jane sat in the back of the Explorer with Kenny, a patrol cop driving them back to Precinct Nineteen. Kenny let his head fall back to the Explorer's rear headrest. "I just...I keep thinking about my sister."

Jane undid her seatbelt and slid over to him, taking his hand in hers. "Of course."

The muscle in Kenny's jaw pulsed. "She's probably in line at some grocery store, or sitting at some Starbucks...and she doesn't know her son is dead." He looked to Jane. "Bobby was a teenager without a driver's license. There are half a dozen Stella's between Andrea's house and the one on Carmody. What the hell was he doing at this one?"

Jane took a long breath; she had been asking herself the same question.

"'Scuse me, Lieutenant..." Their driver caught Jane's eye in the rearview. "Check it out."

Jane glanced out the windshield. The precinct was besieged by news vans, their satellite uplinks telescoping to the sky.

"Take us around back, please."

"Yes, ma'am."

As the black Explorer rounded the corner, Jane turned to Kenny. His eyes were gleaming with grief and anger. Jane realized there was no way around it. No matter what she'd told Kenny, no matter what she'd promised the chief, this case was going to be as personal as they come. For both of them. They'd have to find their way, wade through deep and unknown waters.

A sudden wave of nausea swept up to Jane's throat as she and Kenny climbed the precinct's parking structure stairwell. The harsh taste of metal, as if she were sucking on nails, wrapped around the base of her tongue.

She clutched the handrail and swallowed hard, breathing steadily through her nose. Kenny was one step above and didn't notice her hesitation. The feeling passed through Jane as quickly as it had come and she joined him on the third-floor landing.

"Shit," Kenny said. "I have to tell my parents about Bobby." He pushed open the door.

A sense of controlled chaos pervaded the Homicide bullpen. Every desk was occupied and so many phones were ringing at the same time that it sounded like one continuous high-pitched tone.

Roz Shapiro, a widowed police volunteer in her seventies, sat at her reception desk by the elevators. Nearly a dozen visitors filled the three wooden benches beneath the windows.

Cheryl Lomax monitored the heavy radio traffic at her dispatch console. A large black woman in her late forties with a penchant for outrageous nail polish, Cheryl spoke into her headset to her cops in the field.

Homicide's newest inspector, Mike Finney, typed the incident reports that had just been e-mailed to him. A picture of his baby son was taped to his drafting lamp. Finney had been a severely overweight uniformed patrol officer until Jane had taken him under her wing as the department's administrative liaison. He had shown a talent for the game, and Jane had encouraged him to apply for a recently opened inspector's position. She and Kenny had sponsored him on the condition he go on a diet and pass the proficiency exams. Finney did both.

Now he loved putting on a suit every day, albeit the same one, and carrying the coveted shield of a homicide inspector. Because of his formerly prodigious appetite, everyone had called him Moby. Most, except for Jane, still did. This was his first month on the job.

Inspector Lou Tronick had already been talking about retirement when Jane had first moved up to Homicide. He'd worked every big case in San Francisco from Zodiac to California Street. Methodical and resourceful, he was just the sort of cop Jane could rely on to do the myriad of less glamorous tasks that came with a big city murder investigation. She was glad she'd convinced him to stay.

The TV in the lunchroom played a recap of the chief's news conference to a cluster of empty chairs.

Kenny crossed to Cheryl's desk. She flicked the mute on her mic. "I'm so sorry, Kenny."

"Any word on my sister?"

"Nothing yet. I'll let you know the second I hear."

Jane joined them. "Use my office to call your mom and dad. Want me in there?"

Kenny started to say something, then pulled it back. "You've got enough to do. I can handle this."

"Okay then," Jane said. "I'm going to set up the war room in Interrogation One."

Kenny took off his jacket and dropped it over the back of his desk chair. As he crossed the bullpen, Mike Finney and Lou Tronick rose to greet him. Jane watched her husband hug each of the men, then continue into her office and close the door. One side of the office was a glass wall through which she could observe the squad room. Kenny stepped into the large frame of the window and looked out to his wife, his face etched with pain. Then he reached up and released the blinds.

They fell swiftly, silently, like a wall coming down.

The sun lowered behind a veil of thin clouds, bathing the bullpen in a faint orange glow.

Jane had assembled her Homicide team in Interrogation One. Mike Finney, Lou Tronick, and Aaron Clark-Weber sat on folding chairs in the center of the room. Support personnel—including Administration, Communications, Forensics, and uniformed police—lined the walls.

The names of each of the deceased were written on two blackboards on the far wall.

Terrence Unger.

Antonia Salazar.

Francis Cellucci.

Arthur "Shanty" Rourke.

Nicolas Silva.

Robert Farrier.

There was a blue chalk mark next to each name, indicating that next of kin had been notified. Each name except Bobby's.

Jane looked across the squad room. The door to her office was still closed, the blinds still drawn, and she knew that Kenny was still trying to reach his sister. She turned to her team. "I need somebody to have Robbery send one of their guys over. If this is a busted stick-up, there might be some history."

"I got it, Lieutenant." Mike Finney made a note on his legal pad and picked up a phone. This was his first major case and he was a little nervous about doing well. Keeping yourself busy with the small stuff, Lou Tronick had told him, was a good way to stay focused.

"The alleyway security camera was disabled." Jane turned to Lou at the coffee setup. "See if it was done with any technical expertise or if it was simply vandalized. Could tell us something." She took a rice cake from her purse and nibbled at it, trying to keep her nausea at bay.

Lou topped off his mug and grabbed half a corned beef sandwich. "Will do, Jane."

"Aaron, when can we get something out of you?"

Aaron Clark-Weber flexed his sore knee and raised it to the chair in front of him. "The M.E.'s bringing in a crew to pull an all-nighter. We'll have his initial findings around noon tomorrow, something more detailed the day after."

"I've called City Planning," Jane said, "for a schematic of the Carmody Stella's. I want us all to have an overview of the place. Each of you go down there tonight or tomorrow and walk the scene. See if anything strikes you." She nodded to the support staff along the walls. "You guys, too."

Jane sat on a table and picked up a water bottle. "Look, this is huge, as big and as bad as I've seen since I moved up. The mayor and the chief are all over this, and rightly so. The people of San Francisco have to know that when something like this happens in their city, *to* their city, we're there for them."

She took a long pull on her water and finished the rice cake.

"One other thing. You all know that Kenny and I lost our nephew today..." A female patrol officer at the back of the room swiped a tear from her cheek. "A lot of you remember Bobby from department softball games and picnics. He was a sweet kid who was just at the wrong place at the wrong time. We think. Until we know anything definitive about why he or anyone else was at that Stella's, no one talks to the press. No exceptions. I need all of you—Homicide, Forensics, Administration—to exercise the strictest possible evidentiary, investigative, and interview discipline. And to treat *all* of the victims and *all* of their families with the same professionalism and respect I know you'll show Inspector Marks and me."

There was a sudden flurry in the bullpen.

Cheryl Lomax was hurrying across the squad room toward Jane's office. She knocked once and went inside. A moment later, she and Kenny came out. Jane slipped down off the table and went to the door.

Kenny snatched his jacket off the back of his desk chair. "They found Andrea's car. In her driveway."

Cheryl raced back to her console. "I had patrol check. She's home right now."

Jane turned to the other cops in Interrogation One. Lou Tronick put down his coffee mug and rose. "We'll start the witness and kin interviews, Jane. You go to your family."

Jane pulled her lips into a tight, grateful smile. "I'll be back in an hour." She picked up her bag and ran across the bullpen, just catching up to Kenny at the stairwell door.

6

Andrea Farrier's house was a small two-bedroom bungalow in a humble neighborhood of similar homes in the shadow of AT&T Park. When the Giants were in town, some of her neighbors let fans park on their front lawns for up to thirty bucks a pop. But not Andrea. She thought it was cheesy.

She had rented this house four years ago, soon after her divorce from Bobby's father. Robert Farrier, Senior, a long-haul truck driver, took off one night with another woman and moved to New Mexico. Just like that. It was the last Andrea had seen of her husband, and the last Bobby had seen of his father.

After that, Andrea had a run of bad jobs and bad boyfriends. She had drunk too much and eaten too much. One morning, she woke up with a man she barely knew lying next to her in bed. Another man she didn't know at all was sleeping on the couch. And Bobby was sitting alone at the dinette table eating dry Frosted Flakes.

"So this is my life?" he had asked his mother.

Startled into reality, Andrea changed everything. She stopped drinking and overeating. She got an entry-level job at the credit union—steady pay and good benefits. She stopped dating losers; in fact, she stopped dating altogether so that she could spend more time with her son.

The neighborhood was shrouded in the last gray light of day when Kenny turned the Explorer onto Lafayette Street. Lights were just coming on in some of the houses. A couple of kids were riding their X-treme bikes over a homemade wooden ramp. When the Explorer got closer, they stopped and dragged the ramp over to the side.

"Couple of years ago," Kenny said, "that was Bobby."

"I know, hon." Jane looked into the young faces, flushed and sweaty from exertion. Kids trying to steal every moment from the day before their mothers yelled out the final supper call.

Kenny slowed at a pale-yellow stucco house near the end of the block. Andrea's white Toyota was in the driveway. Beyond it, an old motorcycle lay in pieces in the garage. Bobby had scavenged it somewhere and had been fixing it up against his mother's wishes.

She thought it was too dangerous.

Kenny parked the Explorer behind Andrea's car and scanned the street. "My parents aren't here yet."

Jane watched as one of the bicycle kids raced up and over the wooden ramp and landed awkwardly on a manhole cover. He recovered and whipped the bike around, ready to go again. "They're probably stuck in rush hour. Golden Gate's brutal this time of day." She undid her seatbelt. "Plus, it's better if you tell Andrea by yourself."

Kenny started to get out of the car, then stopped. He turned back to Jane. "Thank God for you."

Jane pulled him into a deep embrace. "Thank God for our baby."

As they walked up the uneven path to Andrea's house, they noticed a soft blue light coming from the living room. Andrea was watching television.

Kenny and Jane quickened their pace, climbed the two steps to the porch, and looked in through the screen door.

Andrea Farrier stood in the middle of the small living room, one arm clutched around her waist, watching the news. She clicked the remote with her free hand, changing from KGO to

CNN and back again. And each time, the news was the same. Cameron Sanders stood in front of Stella's, the KGO logo and the words *Carnage on Carmody* supered on-screen, and spoke of "six confirmed victims in this horrible tragedy."

Kenny reached out and turned the screen door's knob. It squeaked as he opened it and Andrea turned to the sound. "Oh, I thought you were Bobby. He's late for a change." She pointed to the TV as Jane and Kenny stepped up into the living room. "You seen this? Those poor people."

Andrea studied her brother's face and saw the torment in his eyes. "Wait, why are you here? The baby okay? Jane, today was your amnio, right?"

"The baby's fine, Andrea," Jane said.

Andrea took a step back toward the television, fear rising in her throat. "Is Dad okay? He didn't fall again, did he?"

Kenny held out his hands. "Andrea..." He glanced at the TV, then back to his sister.

Until that moment, Andrea had felt that, if she just kept asking questions, she could fend off whatever bad news her brother had come with. Now, suddenly, she couldn't speak. Her hands fluttered, shaking as if they belonged to someone else.

Kenny closed the distance between them. "Andrea..." He took the remote from her and switched off the TV.

Andrea watched the screen go from gray to black, then she whirled and grabbed Kenny's shoulders. "You guys are homicide cops and you just had this major disaster out there. What are you doing in my house?"

Kenny took her wrists in both of his hands and sat on the couch, pulling her down with him. Jane sat on the coffee table, facing her sister-in-law.

Andrea looked from her brother to Jane and gulped back a frightened sob. "Oh God. Please tell me it's not Bobby. Please tell me it's anything but that."

Kenny held both of her hands tightly in his. "I'm sorry, Andy...it's him."

"At the Stella's? He was *in* there?"

Kenny waited for her to focus on his eyes, then he nodded.

Andrea's nose was running, mingling with her tears. "And he's..." She jutted her jaw at the television. "One of them? My little boy is dead?" Andrea pushed him away. "Say the words, Kenny. Tell me that Bobby's dead. Because he's not dead if you don't tell me he is."

Jane put her hand on Kenny's back, stroking him just below the neck. "Andy," Kenny said. "Bobby is dead."

"*NO!*" Andrea's hands flew to her face. Then she dropped them and clenched them and pounded the tops of her thighs. Over and over again. Before Kenny could react, his sister bolted from the couch and raced down the short hallway. She threw open the door to Bobby's room and looked inside...as if looking for her son. "Bobby!"

Kenny ran after her.

As Jane rose, she noticed that the boys outside were standing in the middle of the street, staring at Andrea's house. They'd heard her scream.

Kenny and Jane hurried into Bobby's room.

Andrea held out her hands, palms up, backing away. "I went to work like always. He was sleeping right there like always." She tilted her head toward the bed, the blanket and sheets twisted into a spiral. "I told him to eat something and to dress nice if he was gonna look for a job. He mumbled something like 'All's good, Ma.' So I just went to work. Then we closed early today and I went to have my toes done. I took two fuckin' hours for myself and...and"—she fell to her knees, tears dripping down her chin and neck—"and someone killed my baby."

Bobby's room was a teenage boy's life stopped in midbreath. Motorcycle pictures and a poster of Katy Perry. Underwear on the floor, an empty Mountain Dew bottle next to his hand-me-down computer. A couple of books, stacks of CDs, and a forever-unmade bed. A plastic laundry basket filled with tennis shoes and a half-eaten bag of popcorn. His graduation photo lay unframed and curling on the bookshelf.

This will be the picture, it occurred to Jane, that will be on Bobby's coffin.

Jane and Kenny helped Andrea to her feet. She wrapped her arms around both of them and sagged. "I want to see him."

Kenny looked across his sister to Jane.

"Andrea," Jane said, "that's not a good idea right now."

"Please...I need to."

Kenny put his arms around her waist and half-guided, half-carried her out of Bobby's room. "Andy, if you've ever listened to me about anything, listen to me now. I saw Bobby today. It's not the way you want to remember him."

A car door slammed somewhere outside. Then another.

Kenny walked Andrea back into the living room.

Jane stayed behind in Bobby's room. And suddenly, she was crying. She hadn't even known it was coming. After a few seconds, she realized she wasn't crying for her nephew or her sister-in-law, or even her husband. She was crying for the baby she was carrying.

For the pure tiny heartbeat...and this world she was bringing it into.

Jane sat on a vinyl chair at the dinette table and watched as Andrea's living room filled with people.

She had called the precinct a half hour ago to let them know the final next-of-kin notification had been made. Now the press could run with the story, complete with names and photographs of the murder victims.

Kenny and Andrea's parents had arrived. Their father, Lloyd, a former cop now stricken with Parkinson's disease, sat in the brown Barcalounger, his head and arms trembling. He had fallen a couple of times the past year, and the last of his vitality was diminishing. Jane knew that his grandson's death would undoubtedly hasten his own.

Doris, Kenny's mother, poured water into a large coffee urn someone had brought. It was her way: stay busy, keep moving, and don't let anything or anyone get too close.

Kenny sat on the couch talking with Andrea, a notepad in his lap. If this had been the home of any other murder victim, Kenny would have been taking notes during the survivor's interview. But this was his sister and his nephew, and Jane understood that he was writing down Andrea's wishes for Bobby's funeral.

More people came.

Neighbors that Jane had met over the years. Men just home from work. Two of the boys who had been playing in the street. Women from Andrea's job at the credit union.

Everyone carried something into the house. Pies, donuts, a case of soda. One of the young boys had a single red rose, its stem wrapped in a wet paper towel. He laid it on an end table and, overcome, pushed his way back outside.

Jane's cell phone vibrated.

"Hello."

"Lieutenant, it's Mike Finney. Is it okay to call?"

"Sure, Mike. What's up?"

"We just got the surveillance tape from the Staples across from the restaurant. Thought you'd want to know."

"Thanks. Set up the playback machine and—"

"Already done, Lieutenant. How's Inspector Marks doing?"

Jane looked over to Kenny. He had seen her talking on the phone and knew it was time to go. "He's hurting, Mike. But he'll be okay. We have a lot of work to do. See you soon."

She rang off and stood up. Kenny hugged Andrea and kissed her forehead. Then he went to his father and knelt next to his chair. He took his father's unsteady hands in his own and kissed him on the lips. Rising, he came into the kitchen and hugged his mother good-bye. Even in an embrace, she found a way to keep her distance.

"We gotta get back now, Mom. I'll check in with you later."

"That's fine," Doris said. She lifted a tray of coffee and cakes and carried them to the new arrivals.

Jane took Kenny's hand. "I gotta get back. You take the night with your family."

"No...I'm coming with you."

"How can you go back to work right now?"

Kenny surveyed the tiny house, his eyes coming to rest on Bobby's bedroom door. "Somebody out there just slaughtered six people. How can I *not* go back to work?"

7

Jane stole a look at the blackboards in the war room just as one of the uniformed cops switched off the lights.

There was a blue check mark by Robert Farrier's name. Next-of-kin had been informed.

The Homicide team pulled their chairs closer to the monitor.

"I've backed the tape up to one hour before the murders," Mike Finney said. "But we gotta remember that the camera this came from was set up by Staples to watch their own store. So the angle isn't the most favorable."

Jane looked over the room. There were more than twenty cops and support staff crowded along the walls. It was going to be a long night.

A police volunteer walked through the room offering sandwiches, cookies, and cold drinks. Finney took a turkey sandwich and a Diet Coke. Jane, cursed with noticing everything, was glad to see he was sticking to his diet.

Kenny grabbed a can of ginger ale and held it sideways against his forehead.

Jane nodded to Finney and he pressed Play on the remote.

An off-center black-and-white image came up. The Staples parking lot filled most of the foreground, but the facade and front door of Stella's was clearly visible in the upper half of the screen.

Finney thumbed the remote, toggling between Fast Forward and Play.

"What we're looking for," Jane explained, "is if we can see anyone going in who either was later killed or who doesn't otherwise exit the building—at least through the front door."

A steady stream of customers, hunkered against the wind, entered and left the restaurant. "Okay," Finney said, "this is fifty-eight minutes before the shootings." He slowed the tape as a young man—his black leather jacket billowing like a cape—ran across the street, causing a cab to swerve around him. "That's Nicolas Silva going in." The tape continued at regular speed for a minute or so.

"Okay, Mike," Kenny said, "you can fast forward."

Finney glanced up. "Uh, hang on a sec, Inspector." He looked back to the screen. "There."

Kenny stood up, his arms folded across his chest, and peered at the monitor. "Bobby," he whispered. "So early? He hung out there for an hour?"

Finney nodded. "Apparently."

"Mike," Jane asked, "have you checked the time code on the Staples camera?"

"We did, Lieutenant. We crossed it with the incoming time clock for the 911 call fifty-six minutes later. It lines up perfectly."

Kenny watched as his nephew bounded down the steep hill of Carmody Avenue. Bobby slid his sunglasses on top of his head, their chrome coating catching the sunlight, and went into Stella's.

Everyone in the room fell silent, all eyes on Kenny. He stood there for a few seconds, his jaw muscle bouncing. Then he slowly sat back in his chair, his arms still crossed on his chest. "Keep it going, Mike," he said hoarsely.

The tape advanced quickly, racing along at six times normal speed.

"There's another victim now," Lou Tronick said.

Finney slowed the tape and they all watched as Terrence Unger opened the door to Stella's and held it for a woman and her baby carriage to exit.

"Thank God," someone murmured from the back of the room.

"That's Mindy Sheldon and her five-month-old, Chloe," Finney said. "She's on our interview list. She's pretty shaken up, considering."

A man appeared at the bottom of the screen, his back to the camera. He crossed the street and entered the restaurant.

"That's Arthur Rourke," Lou explained. "Panhandler known as Shanty who hangs at the Staples."

Another man, this one in a clerical collar, came from the uphill side of Carmody Avenue and went into Stella's.

"Father Francis Cellucci," Finney said. "From Saint Vincent's up the street."

A moment later, the elderly Vietnamese man emerged.

"Nguyen Bao," Finney went on. "Been working the newsstand for years. We've got someone at his apartment in Little Saigon as we speak."

Jane watched the people going into the restaurant who would never come out again. A fuckin' Venus flytrap. She looked over to Kenny. He stared intently at the screen, his jaw still flexing.

Lou Tronick dipped a ginger cookie into his coffee. "That's the last ingress or egress until the two skateboard kids arrive. A span of three minutes, thirty seconds."

Finney hit Fast Forward. Then, from the left or uphill side of the frame, Isaac and Rodney Cooper blasted down the sidewalk on their skateboards. They dismounted and kick-flipped their boards into their hands. The team watched as the boys looked at themselves in the broad windows of the restaurant, preening and fooling around. Then they peered inside. They looked to each other and entered the restaurant. Isaac first, then Rodney.

"Here's where they find the Salazar girl," Lou said. "They call 911 forty seconds later."

The video sped forward. An SFPD squad car raced in from the downhill side of the frame. "That's first on-scene, Weymouth and Murphy," Lou continued. "Took them something like four minutes, even though they were taking 10-7M only a couple of blocks away. They, like almost all our responders, got waylaid by the street construction and all that congestion around there. Officer Weymouth did a heroic job of getting on-scene as quickly as he did."

Finney turned off the tape and someone switched on the lights.

"First things first," Jane began. "Who did this, why...and where the hell did he go?"

"Back door?" Finney asked.

"Possibly, maybe probably," Jane said. "It was locked from the inside, but it's the kind that clicks closed when you shut it. Have a team check all the businesses up and down that alley back there. Both sides. See if anyone saw anything."

"I'll take care of it, Lieutenant," Finney said.

Aaron Clark-Weber shifted in his seat. "We've taken dozens of footprint molds from the back pathway and for a hundred feet up and down the alley. But it's a heavily traveled area—delivery people, employees on cigarette breaks, not to mention an ambulance and an EMT crew for that girl we found in the freezer—so I don't hold out much hope of any breakthroughs there."

"Let's check for other, less obvious escape routes too," Jane said. "AC ducts, rooftops, stuff like that."

"What if—" Mike Finney stepped onto thin ice. "What if the killer committed suicide in there? What if he's one of the people over at the morgue right now?" He looked around nervously, then busied himself with removing the SD memory card from the playback machine.

"It's a good thought, Mike," Jane said. "Initial reports indicate none of the wounds is self-inflicted."

"Plus," Kenny added, "that would mean the murder weapon would have to still be on-scene. And it wasn't."

"Oh." Finney made a note in his pad. "Just a thought."

"Remember, guys," Jane said to the room, "the only stupid question is the one you don't ask." She stood up. "Okay, I need you to break up into your task squads and start going over the field reports. There's already a ton of paperwork. I want it all organized by morning so we can get some traction on this thing."

Kenny opened his ginger ale and took a swig. "Hey, Moby, how *is* that girl from the freezer doing?"

Finney slipped the memory card into an evidence envelope. "We found a purse with her ID in the restaurant kitchen. Her name's Colleen Porter. Last I checked, she was still in pretty bad shape. Unconscious, but expected to survive the night."

"Keep me posted on her condition. We need to talk to her as soon as possible."

"You got it, Inspector."

There was a quick knock on the door and Roz Shapiro entered. It was hours after she ordinarily clocked out and Jane was surprised to see her. "'Scuse me, Lieutenant, two things. Someone from Robbery's on his way up, and I kinda have a situation over in reception."

"What kind of situation?"

Roz lowered her voice. "Well, there's this Mexican fellow with a baby says he needs to talk to whoever's in charge. I told him to come back in the morning as everyone's so busy and he said he'd just wait. All night if he had to."

Jane looked across the bullpen. A middle-aged man sat on a bench by the elevators. A one-year-old boy straddled his knee, gnawing on a carrot. Kenny slipped by Jane. "I'm gonna call

Andrea from your office." Jane touched his arm as he passed. Kenny stopped and turned. "Make sure you eat something."

"Thanks. Anything I can do for you?"

"I just need to keep moving."

Jane regarded the man on the bench as she approached.

He was in his late forties, his neck and arms covered with tattoos. There were two tiny black ink teardrops at the corner of his left eye. Prison tattoos. The street wars of San Francisco had been fought on his face.

He wore black engineer boots, tight blue jeans, and a white T-shirt that clung to his broad, sculpted body. There was something kinetically powerful about him, coiled and ready. There was something else about him that Jane couldn't quite identify yet.

The man straightened and started to stand. As he did, the baby dropped his carrot and they both stooped to retrieve it.

"I got it," Jane said. She picked it up and rinsed it off at the water fountain. Then she handed it back to the baby. "Here you go, little one."

The baby wrapped his hand around the carrot and put it in his mouth.

The man shrugged. "Teething." His voice was thin and surprisingly soft.

"Your son is beautiful."

"Nephew."

"He's still beautiful." Jane wheeled Roz's desk chair over and sat down. "I'm Lieutenant Candiotti. Mrs. Shapiro said you needed to talk to someone in Homicide."

"Someone in charge."

"Then that's me. How can I help you?"

The man nuzzled his nose into the baby's neck. The little boy smiled, revealing four new teeth. "Did you catch the guy who killed all those people today?"

"Not yet."

"Any suspects?"

"I really can't answer questions about an ongoing investigation. But I can tell you that we're doing everything we can to solve this crime."

The baby suddenly let out with a delighted squeal.

"*Shh*, Leo," the man said. He looked to Jane. "Sorry."

Jane smiled. "A little baby making beautiful sounds is exactly what we need around here right now." A couple of heads poked out of Interrogation One. "What's your name, sir?"

"I am Edgar Silva."

Jane caught her breath. "Are you related to Nicolas Silva?"

"He...Nico was my brother. Leo here is his son."

Jane reached over and touched his hand. Rough, heavily calloused. "I'm so sorry about your brother."

Edgar looked down to her hand on his. "Thank you," he said, almost inaudibly. "Nico would have been twenty-one tomorrow..." He looked at the clock on the wall between the elevators. It was 12:25 in the morning. "Today."

Jane pushed back in her chair. "Mr. Silva, forgive me, but I'm a cop. I can see by your tattoos that you've done some time. I could go look you up in the computer and try to find you tomorrow, or I could just—"

"Ask me anything, Lieutenant. We both want the same thing." Edgar shifted Leo to his other leg.

"Mr. Silva, is there anyone in your brother's life who could possibly have reason to do this?"

Edgar closed his eyes and rocked his head several times. Then he opened them and turned to Jane. "Yes, Lieutenant. A lot of people." Jane was about to speak, but Edgar went on, his voice hardly more than a whisper. “The life we live in the Tenderloin creates natural enemies. But it also creates loyalties. Deep, long-lasting loyalties. My brother was not the intended victim of these murders.”

“How can you be so sure?”

“Because people out there know they would have to answer to me.” Edgar looked past Jane and stiffened.

Jane turned to see Kenny crossing the bullpen toward them.

Edgar rose, hoisting the baby onto his left hip. “Thank you for your time…and for your kindness. I know you’ll be looking me up on your computer. But remember this: a man is more than his past.”

Kenny joined them. He sized up Edgar with one practiced glance and didn’t like what he saw. “Jane, Eliot Friedman is here from Robbery.”

“Thanks.” She pulled Kenny aside. “How’s Andrea?”

“Totally fucked-up. What’s going on here?”

Jane gestured toward Edgar. “This is Edgar Silva. His brother was Nicolas Silva.” Jane watched both men. An instinctive distrust fell across each of their faces. Neither offered his hand.

“Sorry ’bout your brother,” Kenny finally said. He turned to Jane. “When you’re ready.” He turned and headed back to her office.

Jane started to explain her husband’s behavior to Edgar. But he spoke first. “Doesn’t matter, Lieutenant. I’m an ex-con in his police station. Imagine the greeting a cop like him would get in my world.”

“I want you to take this.” Jane pulled a business card from her pocket. “My cell’s on the back. If you learn anything out there, I want to know about it.”

Edgar slipped the card into the back pocket of his jeans. “Can I expect the same from you?”

His question caught Jane off guard. “I can’t guarantee that kind of cooperation.”

Edgar smiled cryptically. “Then neither can I.” He swung the baby onto his other hip. “*Vamonos*, Leo.” He pressed the call button on the elevator. “Good night, *Senora*.”

“Good night, Mr. Silva.”

The elevator doors opened. Edgar stepped in and turned back to Jane. He nuzzled the baby’s neck again, causing him to squirm and giggle. As he did, his eyes, heavy and haunted with grief, never left Jane’s.

The doors slid closed.

Inspector Eliot Friedman was tired.

There had been a series of armored car robberies on his watch, and he was just coming in from fourteen straight hours of staking out a Brinks truck as it made its rounds from San Francisco Airport to Oakland. He’d had a strike team ready to pounce as soon as the bad guys made their move. But the bad guys didn’t make their move and now he’d have to do it all over again tomorrow.

“First off,” he said, turning to Kenny. “I’m really sorry about your nephew. I got a son that age and I couldn’t imagine.”

Kenny, standing in the doorway of Jane’s office, nodded his thanks.

Jane sat on the arm of her couch, Mike Finney on the guest chair next to her desk. Eliot Friedman paced as he talked, a Starbucks coffee cup in his hand. “I’m so wired on double grande espressos, I ain’t gonna sleep till Chanukah. Anyway, Jane, I did a little research in all my spare time and came up with something for ya on this case.”

He took a long sip of his espresso and grimaced. “Cold.” He tossed the cup into the wastebasket and looked to Jane.

Jane spooned some yogurt into a bowl of Grape-Nuts. “We’re all ears, Eliot.”

"Well, there's been two other robberies at two other Stella's the past month."

Jane looked over to Finney, making sure he was taking notes. "Similarities?"

"Many." Eliot Friedman stopped pacing and sat on the edge of Jane's desk. "Disabled security cameras, herding the employees and patrons to the storage area, and especially the timing. In both the other two, the deed was done just after the lunch rush and just before the cash pickup."

Kenny scratched his back against the doorjamb. "So you're thinking inside job?"

"Has to be." Friedman took a paper clip from the desk and started cleaning his fingernails. "Somebody had knowledge of the…nuance…of these places. Tell you the truth, though, they weren't my cases. Neil Kenyan was lead investigator, but he's in Australia right now on some extradition thing in the Quantas heist. I got a call in to him. So…" He held out his hands. "I'm yours by default. Got any more of that cereal?"

Jane pointed to behind her desk. "Top of the minifridge. Help yourself."

Friedman took the box of Grape-Nuts and emptied it into a soft drink cup.

Finney turned the page in his notepad. "How come, Inspector, we never heard of these robberies at those other Stella's?"

"Actually, you did." Friedman tilted the cereal back into his mouth and chewed noisily. "Paperwork went out. I checked. But they were just piddly-shit robberies. Way below the interdepartmental radar. I mean, really, who cares about some fast food joint getting hit until—"

"Until what?" Jane asked.

"Well…until people start getting themselves killed just because they went out for a burger and fries."

Kenny stepped deeper into the room. "Any theories?"

"Only one. But it's got three parts. A: Inside job. We're pretty sure of that because of the aforementioned nuance stuff. B: Modus is consistent with a drug-user type. The whole quick-hit cash-grab scenario." He finished off the Grape-Nuts and put the empty cup on Jane's blotter. "And three: The guy freaked. Something spooked him and he went postal on those poor fuckers."

Jane glanced over to Kenny. His jaw was going again. Knowing that there was no new information that Eliot had to offer, she rose from the couch, a signal the meeting was over. "Thanks for coming down here so late, Eliot. I'd like you to liaise with Inspector Finney here and get him the witness list from the first two robberies. If your theory holds, could be something there for us."

Friedman pressed his fingertips to his stomach, chasing after some vague pain. "First thing in the morning." He started to leave, Kenny stepping aside to give him room. Then he stopped and turned back. "There a Starbucks or a Coffee Bean around here?"

Kenny shook his head. "Nothing open."

"My fuckin' luck," Friedman said as he headed toward the stairwell door.

Kenny watched him go. "Pleasant guy."

"Good cop, though." Jane crossed to her desk and unscrewed the top of a bottle of vitamin supplements.

"Maybe," Kenny said, "but he's still an asshole." He left the office and went back to his desk. One of the volunteers came up to him and asked something. Kenny shook his head and the volunteer went back into Interrogation One.

"'Scuse me for saying, Lieutenant?" Finney rose from the guest chair.

"What is it, Mike?"

"It's almost one in the morning. Inspector Marks is pretty messed up, what with his nephew and all. And...well, you look pretty beat yourself. Maybe you should think about going home?"

Jane swallowed her vitamins, washing them back with the last of her water, and looked into the bullpen. There were still a few people left in Interrogation One. Roz Shapiro and Cheryl Lomax had left about twenty minutes ago, Cheryl dropping Roz off on her way home like always when they worked late. Lou Tronick was just shutting down his computer. Kenny sat staring at his telephone. Jane knew he wanted to call his sister, that he was hungry for the connection, hungry to share on the most primal level what she was going through. But she also knew that he couldn't make that call at this hour and risk waking her.

"You're right, Mike. What are the chances of you getting out of here too?"

"Chances are excellent, Lieutenant. I wanna go watch my baby sleep. Kinda helps me relax, y'know?"

Jane turned off her desk lamp and picked up her purse. "I know."

She followed Finney out of her office and went over to Kenny. He heard her coming and stood up, his face weary beyond all imagining.

"Come, husband," Jane said, "we're going home."

She looped her arm around his waist and guided him to the elevator. They stepped inside and Jane pushed the button for the parking level.

Then they fell back against the wall and the doors slid closed on the longest day of their lives.

8

Bobby was flying.

He swooped low over the water, the ocean spray bracing his face. The wind whipped the surf into tiers of reaching foam and Bobby turned toward it. He pulled his shoulders back and his naked, slender body soared upward, the cold air filling his lungs. With a confident downward tilt, he plummeted toward the sea.

Down, down, he came. Faster, then faster still. Then he pulled his shoulders back, ready to climb again.

It was too late…the water took him.

There was a slicing splash as he shot into the sea and disappeared.

All was still, the wind stopping and the water smoothing.

And Bobby was gone.

Kenny opened his eyes.

For a moment as brief as the space between heartbeats, Bobby was alive. Then the weight of grief pressed down on Kenny's chest and he choked back a startled sob.

The bed felt different, off-balance, and he slid his hand over to Jane's pillow. She wasn't there. He listened for her sounds in the bathroom. All was quiet. "Hon?" he called as he sat up. He pressed the illumination button on his alarm clock and saw that it was 4:45 in the morning.

As his head cleared of sleep, he heard a faint beeping sound from downstairs and knew that Jane was in the kitchen.

The microwave clicked down to zero. Jane opened the door and removed a covered dish. She peeled off the Saran Wrap and let the steam rise to her face.

"Eggplant?" Kenny said from the doorway.

Jane turned to him. "I'm so hungry."

"And so Italian." Kenny came into the kitchen and opened the refrigerator. A wedge of light fell across the floor. He took out a bottle of apple juice.

"Use a glass, please," Jane said gently.

Kenny pulled two glasses from the shelf over the sink and sat at the small wooden table beneath the window. "Still dark out."

Jane took a couple of forks from the dish drainer and sat down. "Between what happened yesterday and my burning tits, I got maybe an hour's sleep." She picked some cheese from the corner of the eggplant and gave it to Kenny.

Kenny poured two glasses of apple juice. "I had a dream about Bobby."

"Oh, hon. Dream or nightmare?"

"Dream. He was young, maybe ten." He reached up and parted the blinds, looking after some unseen night sound. "He didn't have a very easy life. You know how sad that is to say about a kid? Between his dickhead father and my sister doing the whole eat-drink-binge thing." He let the blinds fall back into place. "I should have done more, *been* more to him."

Jane took his hand. "Ken." She pulled his hand toward her until he looked her in the eyes. "Ken, you were a wonderful uncle and you're a wonderful brother. Andrea went through some major changes and you were there for her. Bobby loved you; hell, he worshiped you...and so do I. You're the best man I know."

Kenny kissed her hand. "It's…it's not like we're naive about violence. But when Bobby can't even walk into a fast food joint without…" Kenny fought back tears. "It's the randomness of it. The world as we know it doesn't seem safe anymore. How can we possibly bring a kid into it?"

"We don't know how random this was."

"Yeah, we do. If it was a fucked-up robbery, then those six people are randomly dead. If, and somehow this seems worse, one of those people was the intended victim, then the five others are also randomly dead."

"All the more reason for us to solve this case," Jane said. "And as for bringing our baby into this world? I went there, too. All night."

"And where did you land?"

"I keep coming back to the same place. This is one lucky kid. We are *so* ready for him…"

"Or her."

"I think it's a him."

"Why?"

"Just a mom feeling."

"I still don't want to know."

"That's your weirdness and you're entitled to it."

Kenny sipped his apple juice. "Remember when I said Eliot Friedman was an asshole last night?"

"Vividly."

"Well, he is. But I was too…and I'm sorry."

A truck rumbled by outside, its lights throwing a silvery arc across the ceiling. Jane chewed on her eggplant. "You get a pass."

"For how long?"

"As long as you need."

Kenny pushed his chair back and rose. He came around behind Jane and put his hands on her shoulders. Reaching up, she took his hands and slid them down to her breasts. Kenny cupped them, feeling their new weight. "Wow."

"No kidding, 'wow.'" Jane leaned her head back and Kenny bent to touch his lips to hers.

They fell into a deep, searching, hungry kiss. When they parted, Kenny nuzzled Jane's lips apart with the tip of his nose. Then he gently blew into Jane's mouth and whispered, "Hey, little one. While you're down there making ears and kidneys and things, your mom and I are doing everything we can to take the bumps out of the road up here."

Jane stood up and pulled Kenny into a hug. "Not all the bumps. Bumps build character."

"As many as I can. Bumps now, character later."

"You're spoiling our baby."

"You can't spoil a baby." Kenny rinsed the glasses and set them on the drainer. "It's five o'clock. Want to go back to bed?"

Jane turned to Kenny, suddenly serious. "I don't want to go to sleep. I want to go to work."

"Good," Kenny said. "So do I."

Andrea Farrier's house sat quiet in its repose, a dark silhouette against the white-yellow of earliest morning.

Kenny drove the Explorer slowly along his sister's street. He touched the brake as he approached her house. "My parents spent the night," he said, nodding to a dark blue minivan parked in front. They continued past a red Volkswagen Jetta. "So did Debbie."

"She's a good friend." Jane studied the neighborhood. All of these small houses with their fences, their struggling patches of lawn, their tiny hopeful gardens. They all looked the same, like an old group photo of some long-ago team. But one of them had been visited by death, a child's death, and it would forever be altered, irretrievably different.

The sweep of headlights played across the Explorer's mirrors.

A rickety old Buick station wagon chugged down the street, its driver flinging newspapers onto driveways, over chain-link fences, and into gutters. The Buick turned right at the end of the block and disappeared.

Kenny tapped the accelerator and the Explorer surged forward. "Bobby's in that paper."

9

Kenny sat on Jane's couch, opening a sympathy card that had been left on his keyboard. He read the message on the bottom and held it out to Jane. "From Finney and Vicki."

When Jane looked up, she noticed Tommy Murphy and Rick Weymouth just coming out of the elevators. They turned right and went up to Roz's desk. Roz listened as they introduced themselves, then pointed down the hall behind them.

Jane stood up quickly and strode across the bullpen. "Hey, guys, wait up."

Murphy and Weymouth turned as Jane caught up to them. "You here for the follow-up debrief?"

Rick Weymouth lowered his eyes. "Yes, I am, Jane, er… Lieutenant."

"It's okay, Rick. You get any sleep last night?"

Weymouth shuffled a bit, standing in place. "None to speak of."

"S'okay," Jane said softly. "Nobody did."

"It's just that…" Weymouth began, struggling to keep his voice from cracking. "Hell, Lieutenant. We shoulda got there sooner."

A door opened down the hall. An administrative secretary poked her head out. "Patrol Officer Weymouth?"

"That's me." Rick Weymouth nodded to Jane, then headed toward the debriefing room.

Jane turned to Tommy Murphy. "He all right?"

"Not really, Lieutenant. I mean, that girl died in his arms and everything." Tommy started to say something else, then pulled it back.

"What is it?" Jane asked.

Tommy looked down the hall to the office his partner had just entered. "Well, Rick and I were talking on the way in? And we think we want to take you up on your advice and go in to see Dr. Glazer."

"I'm glad you're doing that," Jane said. "You guys went through a hell of a lot yesterday."

Kenny came up with a large folded sheet of paper.

"Anything I can do to help," Jane went on, "you let me know."

"Thanks, Lieutenant." Tommy Murphy made his way down the hall.

Kenny watched him go. "That shrink is gonna have one crowded waiting room." He held up the oversized paper he was carrying. "City Planning just sent over the Carmody Avenue schematics."

"Amazing," Jane said. "You ask for something and you get it?"

"Somebody downtown pulled an all-nighter. Case like this, everyone's going above and beyond."

The elevator doors opened and a thin young man with dark skin and a thready mustache stepped out. His clothes were mismatched and cheap, a polyester orange shirt, brown pants, and tattered black tennis shoes. He looked around, timid and uncertain.

Jane watched as Roz leaned forward in her chair. "Can I help you?"

"Yes…I think so. I'm here to see the Homicide police."

"On what business?"

"Inspector Finney called me last night and asked me to come in this morning."

"What is your name, sir?"

"Aram. Aram Hagopian."

Roz checked her visitors log. "And you're here because?"

"I work at the Stella's in North Beach. One of the ones that was robbed before...yesterday."

Kenny dropped the schematic on Roz's desk and grabbed Aram Hagopian by the arm. "Come with me." He led Aram across the squad room and into Interrogation Two.

Jane and Roz exchanged a look that said the same thing. Kenny had been a little rough with this man—if not stepping over the line, then at least getting too close to it.

"Send in a video tech," Jane said as she hurried after her husband.

"Okay, let's do this again."

Kenny stopped pacing and put his hands flat on the metal table. He thrust his chin forward, only inches from Aram Hagopian's face.

Aram sat back in his chair so quickly that it banged against the wall.

Craig Knowles, the department videographer, lifted a headphone off one ear and looked to Jane, waiting to see if she were going to say something.

Jane leaned back against the bulletin board, her arms folded against her chest, and watched.

"I...I already told you," Aram Hagopian said. "I have no information different from what I told the police after the first robbery."

"Think harder," Jane called from across the room. "Did the robber have a limp? A deep voice, a high voice? An accent?"

"I...I was too scared to pay that kind of attention to him. He had a gun in my face. Touching my face." Aram's eyes brimmed with tears. "Please, lady, I didn't do nothing."

Kenny slapped his hand on the table. "And you're still doing nothing! There are six bodies in the city morgue right now because you were too scared to notice anything at all about somebody who threatened to kill you."

Craig Knowles started to reach for his headphones again. But Jane had seen enough.

"Ken."

Kenny whipped his head around to face her. "Jane, the shooter hit two restaurants before yesterday and somebody knows something."

"Maybe so. But it might not be Mr. Hagopian here." Jane nodded to the terrified witness. "Thank you for your time, sir."

Aram Hagopian wiped the back of his hand across his eyes. "I may go now?"

"Yes, sir. You're free to go."

Aram slid out of his chair. He avoided Kenny's glare and crossed the room. Jane opened the door for him and he quickly went out. As he did, Jane noticed several other young people of various ethnic backgrounds in the waiting area. Employees and customers from the two other Stella's.

"I'll have this transferred right away, Lieutenant," Craig Knowles said as he went by Jane. He slung his equipment over his shoulder and started toward the elevators.

Jane watched him go, then closed the door, leaving just herself and Kenny in the room.

Kenny slipped Aram Hagopian's previous witness statement back into the robbery investigation folder. "Anyone else show?"

"They're stacking up out there. Maybe I should do the next couple myself."

"So I was a little aggressive with that guy." Kenny tossed the folder onto the table, his temper smoldering. "This is the big leagues, for Christ's sake!"

"Ken, you're the best cop in the city. The best investigator, the best interviewer..."

"But?"

"But just now, with Aram Hagopian, you were like the anti-cop. Even if he knew something, no way he's gonna give it up the way you were banging on him. Look, you've got every reason to be upset. Hell, it's nothing short of heroic that you're even here. But we can't have this case compromised because a cop lost a relative and, along with it, his judgment. The chief will hang us both up by the nuts."

Kenny sat heavily in the chair Aram Hagopian had been sitting in. "He was flying."

"Who was flying?"

"Bobby. In the dream. He was so young and happy and... safe." He looked up, his forehead creasing with grief.

Jane crossed to her husband and pressed his head against her abdomen. "Listen to your baby."

Kenny snaked his arm around her waist and pulled her to him.

"It's for Bobby and for that sweet little heartbeat that we have to do this right." She kissed the top of his head. "Right?"

"...right."

"Okay then. Let's bring in the next witness." Jane walked over to the door and reached for the knob. As she did, Cheryl Lomax pushed the door open from the other side.

"Just got a call, Lieutenant. That woman from the freezer?"

For one discouraging moment, Jane was certain Cheryl was going to tell her that she had died. "What about her?"

"She just woke up. The doctor says she's ready to talk."

"Hey, Ken, Jane. Hold on a sec!"

Jane and Kenny were just rounding the second landing of the stairwell when Forensics Lieutenant Aaron Clark-Weber called to them. Using the handrail to ease the pressure on his bad knee, he came down the stairs as quickly as he could.

"I've been going over the Forensics prelims and something came up."

Jane noticed he hadn't shaved and that he was wearing the same suit as yesterday. If he had gotten any sleep at all, it was probably on the cot in the lab's storage room. "What kind of something?"

"Well…" Aaron looked from Jane to Kenny. "Bobby had dope on him."

Kenny blew a sigh. "Marijuana?"

"A little bit, yeah. And so did Nico Silva. Except he had kind of a lot. The intent-to-sell kind of a lot. Plus a pretty expensive wristwatch and a matching gold neck chain and bracelet."

"And our shooter," Jane said, "who was there for some quick cash, didn't notice Nico's baubles?"

"Apparently not."

"Why not?" Jane asked, testing her own hypothesis.

"Because the shooter wasn't after these boys," Kenny said, confirming Jane's theory.

"Could be," Jane acknowledged. "But let's stay tough on it."

A uniformed officer made his way up the stairs. He saw his superiors huddled on the landing and hurried past. Taking the steps two at a time, he held on to his gun belt so it wouldn't creak.

Aaron waited until the cop passed into the Homicide bullpen, then turned back to Kenny. "There was money in Nico Silva's pocket with Bobby's prints on it."

Kenny leaned back against the standpipe. "So it's clearly a drug transaction." He looked to Jane. "We have to tell Andrea.

She might know something or someone that could help." He shook his head. "Shit."

Aaron took his car keys from his pocket. "Sorry to be the bearer."

"The truth's the truth," Kenny said. "Thanks, Aaron."

"Where you off to?" Jane asked.

"Back to Stella's," Aaron said. "The…the bodies…are out and I want to do a secondary microscan of the whole place." He continued down the stairs.

Jane turned to Kenny. "If this were any other case, any other victim—"

"We'd move on this dope thing big time. I know, and we should. All that matters is finding the shooter." Kenny pulled out his cell phone and checked the display. "No signal."

"C'mon," Jane said. "We can call Andrea from the car."

"I'm not talking about calling Andrea. I'm talking about calling Edgar Silva. I want him and his hard-time tattoos answering questions in my police station about his drug-dealing little brother."

"Fair enough," Jane said. "But I want in on it."

"Why? You don't trust me?"

"Ken, your emotions are all over the place. If Nico selling drugs and Bobby buying drugs leads to anything, then let's pursue the hell out of it. As a cop, it smells like a good way of going."

"You bet it does."

"But you can't tell me that you and Edgar Silva aren't a bad mix to start with. Add your feelings about Bobby into it and…"

Kenny knew Jane was right. "Fine." He started down the steps, then stopped.

Jane caught up to him. "What?"

"Bobby promised me he was going to stop smoking dope. A thousand times. I'm a fucking cop and my own nephew is getting high? I can't stop thinking I should have done more. About the dope…about him."

"You can do more," Jane said. "Starting now. We have an actual survivor to this whole thing lying in a hospital waiting for good cops to come ask her good questions."

10

"I shouldn'ta even been there in the first place."

Colleen Porter tried to sit up in bed, but she was too weak to deal with moving the wires from the heart monitor. She let her head fall back to the pillow. A pump pushed warm water through the heating blanket covering her bulky body.

"What do you mean?" Jane asked.

"I was subbing…for Marjorie Liu? She calls in sick all the time. And she knows I always need the hours."

Kenny jotted Marjorie Liu's name down in his notebook. "Did you see anyone? Let someone slip in the back door? Did you maybe unlock it yourself?"

Colleen clenched her jaw, trying to hold back the tears. "Yesterday was wicked busy. I was humping like crazy for the lunch rush. Never left the kitchen." She thought for a second. "Don't remember Toni leaving the counter neither. Then, soon as the crunch passed, I ran downstairs and into the freezer for more fries. I'm going back out and I see Toni coming down and I'm thinking that's weird. Then who's watching the upstairs, cuz Toni and I are the only ones working that shift. And then right behind her is this bum from across the street. Shanty? And they're all in this big hurry. And then I can see the legs of Father Francis coming down after him. He's hurrying, too. Way too fast to be normal. Anyway, Toni catches my eye and waves at me like I should go back into the freezer. Her eyes were all scared and big."

"What did you think was going on?" Jane asked.

"First thing in a place like a Stella's is always robbery. But we're trained to just give up the money and cooperate. So this seemed even worse and Toni was scareder than I've ever seen anyone in my life." Colleen lifted an arm and laid it across her face. The loose flesh of her upper arm trembled as she quietly wept. "So now I'm in the freezer," she continued, "hiding in the corner with the door locked."

Jane touched her shoulder, gentle reassuring contact. "What then?"

"There was some talking, but with the freezer motor going, I couldn't tell what anyone was saying."

Kenny made another note. "Could you make out any voices, any words?" He glanced at Jane. "An accent? Any identifying characteristic at all?"

Colleen Porter shook her head. "No, sir. The cooler thingie was going like right next to me. Plus the door is majorly thick. Then I heard this sound. Like popcorn getting made in another room? And then…I realized it was gunshots and I closed my eyes and prayed." Her breathing quickened and grew shallow. "I feel so shitty."

"You're doing great," Jane said. She kept her hand on Colleen's shoulder. "Just a few more questions."

"It's not the questions, Miss," Colleen said. "It's me locking myself in there alone. Maybe if I hadn't of, some of the others coulda gone in too…" She let her arm fall away and turned to look at Jane. "I was so scared and I was so selfish. And now they're all dead." She closed her eyes, tears coursing down her face, falling back to her ears. "Can I sleep now?"

"Sure, Colleen," Jane said. "Is there anyone we can call for you?"

"No. There's no one." Colleen turned her face toward the wall. "But one of my cats is…" And she was asleep.

Jane stood by her side a moment longer, the warm water pump churning away. She looked around the room and noticed something odd. There were no flowers or cards or stuffed animals or balloons.

Colleen Porter was all alone in the world.

Jane and Kenny made their way down the crowded corridor to the elevator bank.

"Monitor me on this," Jane said. "But I think we're working two theories so far."

"I agree." Kenny pushed the elevator call button. "We've got the marijuana deal with Nico Silva and Bobby. A small drug thing that could've blown up in their faces. Over turf. Failure to pay. Over anything. Happens."

"Right. Plus the robbery angle. We have the compromised security camera and two other incidents with the same M.O." Jane took a sip from the water fountain. "And we have a survivor. Shit part of our job is we have to see if she was part of all this."

"I'll have Finney check out the"—he checked his notebook—"Marjorie Liu thing. See if Colleen Porter was really subbing for her."

Jane searched her purse for a packet of vitamin supplements. "I know we have to do that, but all my instincts are telling me she wasn't involved. In fact, when word gets around about a survivor, she could be in danger. I want an armed officer at her door, twenty-four-seven."

"But Colleen Porter doesn't know anything."

"*We* know that. The killer doesn't."

The elevator arrived. Jane and Kenny stepped aside as a patient was wheeled out.

"I'm starving," Jane said. "I need to grab something from the cafeteria."

When the gurney had passed, Kenny put his hand to Jane's back and guided her into the elevator. "Hospital food? You must be pregnant."

11

Jane and Kenny walked past Nguyen Bao's boarded-up newsstand.

A makeshift memorial of flowers and candles had been started by the front door of the Stella's. Someone had placed a framed picture of Toni Salazar against the faux marble wall with a note that said *Always an Angel* taped to one corner. Passing cars slowed, their drivers stealing quick looks before moving on.

The front door was propped open with a small sandbag, investigators and technicians streaming in and out.

Jane and Kenny entered the restaurant. For an instant, the dining area seemed like any other fast food joint. There were people everywhere. Some sitting at tables, going over paperwork or tapping at laptops. Most of them talking, the almost holy reverence of the previous day gone now. But everything else was different. The sounds, the lighting, the smell.

They saw Aaron Clark-Weber at the counter and crossed to him.

"Hey, guys. Just about done here, then the after-crew gets it for cleanup. They're already going at it downstairs."

Jane glanced to the top step of the rear staircase. Toni Salazar's blood was drying in the grooves of the corrugated metal strip. "Anything new coming up?"

"Public place like this," Aaron said, "is pretty much a smorgasbord. We've got *too much* evidence. Probably a couple hundred different hair and fiber samples from employees, customers, delivery people…plus our guys. It'll take some doing, but we'll go through it all."

"What about the weapon?" Kenny asked. "Caliber? Shell casings?"

"Medical examiner's first reports should be on our desks by now," Aaron said. "I'll have them faxed to the van. Decent-sized caliber, though. Looks to me like a .38. As for casings…zero. Which, of course, means one of two things…"

"Either the shooter retrieved the casings after doing the deed," Jane said. "Which is unlikely given how much of a hurry he had to be in…"

"Or," Kenny picked it up, "he used a revolver."

"Jesus," Jane said. "Six victims with multiple GSWs. Which means he had to stop and…reload…" She let the thought drift off, imagining the terror of those still alive while the killer put fresh ammunition into his gun.

Jane looked to Kenny and could tell he was thinking the same thing. Some movement caught her eye and she turned to the front window. A father and his young son were laying a small bouquet of flowers by the door. "Let's set up a surveillance camera on the roof of that Staples over there. Bad guys have a habit of returning to the scene."

Aaron nodded. "Will do."

Kenny was edging toward the stairs, wanting to return to the killing floor.

"Thanks, Aaron," Jane said. She took Kenny's hand in hers and gave it a quick squeeze. "I'm right with you."

Kenny gripped her hand for a second, then let go. As they descended the stairs, Jane watched Kenny's shoulders stiffen and his jaw set. They turned left at the bottom and stopped. A clean-up crew, in full-body hazmat suits, was mopping up the vast blood slick by the open freezer door. They worked quietly, efficiently.

The first thing Jane noticed was how much bigger the corridor seemed now that the victims had been removed.

A man stepped out of the freezer. "Can I help you?" he asked. He was in his late twenties. His navy-blue sport coat and his black pants were supposed to match closely enough to approximate a suit. His short blond hair was spiked with gel and he wore a large silver ring on his left index finger.

"Do you work for us?" Jane asked.

"Depends," he said with an affable grin. "You with Stella's?"

"SFPD."

"In that case, I don't." He offered his hand. "I'm Casey Noveck. Regional supply manager for Stella's Food Services, Incorporated." He held up an electronic wand-like device in his left hand. "I'm taking inventory of the perishables for our insurance claim. Someone left the freezer open all night." He gestured toward the clean-up crew heading upstairs. "There's a job, huh?"

"Not everyone," Kenny said, "can be blessed with a job they love as much as you seem to love yours."

Casey studied Kenny, not sure whether to take him seriously. Kenny held his gaze, giving nothing away.

Jane took a step forward. "Can I ask you something, Mr. Noveck?"

Casey turned to her and there was that smile again. "It's Casey, ma'am. And sure, you bet."

"Could you take us to the back door and tell us company policy about its use for deliveries and stuff?"

"Can do. Follow me." As Casey headed for the back door, he went far out of his way to avoid the clean-up crew. He turned back to say something to Kenny, thought better of it, and continued on. When he got to the storage rack, he zapped a row of condiments with his inventory device. "This stuff lasts forever, all the preservatives and shit. I'm gonna ship it to another store—that's what we call restaurants in the trade."

"I'll remember that, Casey," Kenny said.

Casey Noveck was exactly the type of officious person that drove Kenny over the edge. Jane was relieved that her husband was keeping his temper in check so far. They arrived at the back door.

"Tell me, Mr. Noveck," Jane asked, "what's the procedure with ingress and egress?"

"Ma'am?"

Kenny leaned in. "It's what we call ins and outs in the trade."

"Oh, yeah, right. Simple really. Just like most places," Casey said as he led them outside. "There's a buzzer by the gate. The delivery guy"—he looked at Jane—"or gal, pushes it and, when the security camera's actually working, someone checks the screen and lets them in."

Kenny looked up to the camera. A clipped wire dangled from its base. "And when it's not?"

"Which is only most of the time," Casey said, "someone goes downstairs and physically opens the door."

Jane and Kenny looked at each other. Someone let the killer into Stella's. But who, and why?

"Two possible scenarios," Jane said to Kenny. "Colleen Porter or Toni Salazar let the bad guy in. Which would mean one of the women either knew the killer or had nothing to fear when he presented himself."

"Or," Kenny finished the thought for her, "the door was unlocked. Either on purpose or just because someone was sloppy."

"We need to talk to Colleen Porter again. Maybe some rest and good hospital food has cleared up her memory."

Kenny made a note. "I'll have Finney set it up."

A house sparrow flitted down on top of the chain-link fence. It puffed its feathers for a second, then darted toward the back wall of the restaurant. Jane watched as it landed on a small nest of twigs and lint wedged in the space above one of the air-conditioning units.

She turned back to Casey. "Who else uses the back door? Employees, friends?"

Casey nodded toward the smudged concrete where yesterday there had been a scattering of cigarette butts. They had all been tagged and removed by Forensics. "Some of our workers take their breaks out here. But it's against policy."

A Mother's Hearth Bakery truck bumped its way down the rutted alley. Casey Noveck waved and the driver stopped. "Hey, Casey," the driver shouted over the rumble of the idling engine. "You guys gonna open soon?"

"Up to Mr. Siegler," Casey called. "And he don't consult with me." He turned to Jane and Kenny. "You guys mind if I get back to work? We kinda have a lot to do. Y'know, with this tragedy and all?"

Kenny nodded tightly. "Right, perishables. Thanks for your time. You've been a great help."

"Here's my card." Casey handed him a business card. "It's got my direct dial."

Kenny took the card as Casey stepped up to the back door. It was crumpled and discarded before Casey was even inside.

The truck driver saw Kenny do this and smiled. "He's kind of a putz, but he…well, he's just a putz. You guys cops?"

"Yes, we are." Kenny said. "This your regular route?"

"Since Ninety-five."

Jane looked up to the driver, shielding her eyes from the sun. "You see anything unusual yesterday?"

"This is a Monday-Wednesday-Friday route. Yesterday was Tuesday. City has these traffic congestion rules? No deliveries Tuesdays and Thursdays. They're pretty strict about it, too. Not that you could tell the difference. Traffic's always a mess around here." He lit a cigarette, drawing in a deep lungful of smoke. "I knew that girl Toni a little bit. Good kid. Couple of guys back at the loading dock said a cop lost someone in there, too. Terrible, terrible thing is what it is."

"Yes, sir." Kenny said. "Tragic."

The driver ground the truck into gear and it crept forward. "I gotta get goin'. I'm already late 'cause every stop I got wants to talk about what happened. Good luck to ya. I hope ya catch whoever did this."

"We will, sir," Kenny said as the truck drove away.

Jane pulled her walkie-talkie from her bag. "3H58 to Dispatch."

"Go, Lieutenant."

"Cheryl, let me have Finney."

There was a short buzz of static. Then Mike Finney came on the line. "Homicide, Finney."

Jane and Kenny could hear the pride in his voice as he said this.

"Mike," Jane said, "I need you to do something for me."

"Not a problem, Lieutenant. What is it?"

"I want background checks on all the Stella's employees in the area. Particularly the one on Carmody and the two that were hit before. Look for criminal records, gang affiliations, grudges, and any other agendas you can think of. Good place to start is with their job applications."

"Will do."

"Also Mike," Jane went on, "check out all the suppliers of these restaurants. Anyone with access—delivery people, cleaning people, whoever."

"Y'know, Lieutenant, these kinds of places don't exactly hire Stanford graduates. There's gonna be a lot of stuff turning up."

"Then we'll wade through it. Get some cadets to help you out."

Kenny held out his hand for the radio. "Moby, did you call Edgar Silva and invite him in yet?"

"Tried to. But I can't find him. Where do you want that, prioritywise?"

Kenny glanced at Jane. "At the top. How about Silva's background check?"

"Computers have been down most of the morning," Finney said. "I sent someone from Patrol over to Records to hand-carry it back over. Should be here by the time you get back."

"Thanks, Moby." He passed the phone back to Jane.

"'Scuse me, guys."

Jane and Kenny turned to the voice.

Aaron Clark-Weber stood in the doorway, several sheets of paper in his hand. "Just got the autopsy reports faxed over from the M.E. There's an anomaly..."

Jane looked to Kenny. They knew that one of those pieces of paper had the results of Bobby's autopsy. "What is it, Aaron?"

"Each of the victims was shot twice. Except for the priest, Father Cellucci. He was hit three times. That, plus he has some other wounds that indicate there was a struggle."

"What kind of wounds?"

"Bruises, cuts, that kind of stuff."

Jane dropped her walkie-talkie into her bag. "And nobody else had them?"

"Just the priest."

Kenny pulled out his car keys. "Aaron, call the M.E. Tell him we're going down there." He climbed the two stone steps up to the back door and went inside.

Aaron Clark-Weber looked down to Jane. "This a good idea, him going to the morgue?"

"It is or it isn't," Jane said.

"I'll call Dr. Tedesco," Aaron said as he went back inside.

Jane searched the back wall of Stella's until she found the crevice above the air-conditioning unit again. The house sparrow was sitting on its nest, watching her. It rose up and spread its wings. As it did, Jane spotted the tiny heads of two newborn chicks. Then the sparrow resettled itself over her babies and closed its eyes.

The squad cars were lined up in perfect rows, their windshields reflecting the morning sun back onto the brick facade of Precinct Fifteen.

The building's steel security door was thrown open and Tommy Murphy and Rick Weymouth, late from their debriefing downtown, hurried across the parking lot. Tommy, his duty bag over one shoulder, carried the shotgun in his right hand. Rick popped the trunk and they dropped in their duffels.

"Want me to drive?" Tommy offered. "Give you a chance to catch up."

Rick slammed the trunk closed. "Catch up on what, sleep?"

"Catch up on thinking…talking."

"Thinking is the last thing I want to do right now." He headed for the driver's door. "Make that the second to last."

"What's the first?"

Rick looked at his partner over the top of the car. "Talking." He yanked open his door and slipped inside.

Tommy was just about to open his door when another squad car pulled up. Patrol Officer Candace Wong rolled down her window. "Hey, Rookie," she said to Tommy. They were the same age and had graduated from the Academy together, but nicknames had a way of sticking.

"What's up, Candy?"

"I know you guys were first on-scene at that Stella's yesterday."

Rick got out of the patrol car and joined them.

"It was brutal," Tommy said. "Worst you could think of."

Candace nodded. "So I heard. Anyway, I'm sitting in the ready room." She nodded toward the station. "Reading about 'Massacre at Midday' in the *Chronicle*. And I'm looking at the photos they ran of the victims...and son-of-a-bitch if I don't know one of them." She held up the newspaper. "This one. Antonia Salazar."

Rick took the paper from her and scanned the pictures until he found the photo of the girl who had died in his arms. "What do you mean *know*?"

"I was at her apartment about a month ago on a domestic disturbance. She and her roommate were freaked. Said Toni's boyfriend, Sammy something, was a total cokehead. A total *violent* cokehead. The door was busted in, TV knocked over. The whole deal."

Rick Weymouth leaned forward. "What about Toni Salazar? Was she hurt?"

"Uh-uh. She was at school at the time taking secretary classes and stuff. But Sammy something is cocaine-paranoid and he's convinced she's two-timing him. So he does his macho ransack bit and splits. But here's the thing...before he goes, he backs the roommate into a corner and tells her that next time he sees Toni...he's gonna kill her."

"Do you have the I.R.s?" Tommy asked.

Candace Wong shrugged. "Incident Reports are in the computer and guess what? The system's down for a change."

Tommy put his hand on Candace's shoulder. "How 'bout your field notes?"

"In my files somewheres. Feel like helping me look for 'em?"

Tommy looked to Rick, then back to Candace. "You bet your ass we do."

12

"I had to bring in help from Oakland and San Jose."

Dr. Anthony Tedesco, the county medical examiner, was a small man, nearing sixty, with close-cropped gray hair. "We worked all night, trying to get you as much information as soon as possible." He pulled open the heavy door to the cold-room and turned to Kenny. "Jesus, Ken. I'm so..."

"Thanks, Tony. I'm okay."

The cold-room was a large white-tiled space with several gurneys lining the walls, each with a black rubber body bag on it. The bags were so thick, it was impossible to make out the contours of what they held.

Dr. Tedesco nodded to eight bodies at the back of the room. "Those are the natural causes and accidentals." He crossed to the opposite wall. "These six are from the Stella's."

Jane looked at the autopsy report. "Which one is the priest?"

"Francis Cellucci. First on the right."

Jane and Kenny went to the first gurney. Dr. Tedesco came around the other side. "Shall I?"

Jane nodded.

Dr. Tedesco grabbed the carrying handle at the top of the bag with his left hand and, in one motion, tugged at the zipper with his right.

Father Francis Cellucci's skin had the vague colorless tone of candle wax. Thick black crisscrossing stitches traversed his torso.

Autopsy incisions sewn up without cosmetic consideration. Dr. Tedesco lifted the corpse's left hand. "Bullet entry in the palm, through and through. Suggests a defense wound. Bullet in the shoulder came in at an oblique angle, also consistent with some kind of movement or activity."

Jane looked closely at Father Cellucci's face. There was a starburst hole in the center of his forehead, a speckling of black powder burns surrounding it. "Point blank?"

"That wound is," Dr. Tedesco said. "Not his others." He took a pen from the pocket of his lab coat and indicated a gash on the priest's left cheekbone. "Consistent with being struck by the butt of a pistol."

"And no other victim," Kenny asked, "has any of this?"

"Francis Cellucci is the only one to be shot more than twice, and the only one to have any additional trauma. Also, he was at the bottom of the pile of bodies, which obviously indicates he was the first to be shot. Whether he was already down from the shoulder wound or the blow to the face and then finished off with the point blank…I just can't tell you. But it's something."

"Then our best guess," Jane said, "is he fought back. Tried to defend himself—"

"Or the others," Kenny added. "Could be we have a hero priest here."

"Could be." Jane started for the door. "I want to go back to Colleen Porter. See if we can't jump-start her memory a little." She was almost across the cold-room when she noticed Kenny moving to the second gurney from the left. He reached out, took the zipper between his fingers, and pulled.

Bobby Farrier's hair was damp from condensation. He looked like a sweet, sleeping young boy. There was a small dark hole under his left eye. It looked insignificant, like a blemish.

Kenny touched his nephew's hair. Then he bent over and kissed him on the lips. He hadn't heard Jane return to him, but he felt her hand on his back. He straightened up and turned. Jane started to put her arms around him.

"I'm good," he said hoarsely. "Let's just get out of here."

"Other than hospital personnel? Nobody."

Officer Rudy Medeiros had been posted outside Colleen Porter's hospital room since Jane had requested a police guard earlier in the day.

"Any cards come through?" Kenny asked. "Gifts?"

"Nothing. Only time I ever seen anything like this is if some foreigner gets in a car wreck." Medeiros looked in on Colleen Porter. "But even then, there's a telegram or something."

"Is she getting any better?" Jane asked. "Any more responsive?"

"She wakes up to eat." Rudy sniffed a laugh. "Which, let the record show, she does a good job of. Other than that, she's kind of drifty. Going in and out."

"Thanks, Rudy." Jane stepped into the room.

Colleen Porter slowly turned her head to the sound of Jane and Kenny entering. There was a food tray on the side table, its plate scraped clean. A couple of crumbs remained on a small dessert dish. Colleen parted her lips and took a breath before speaking. "My cat ran away."

Jane stood next to the bed. "When?"

"What day is today?"

"Wednesday."

"A week ago."

Kenny stepped forward. "Colleen, we need to ask you a few questions. Is that okay?"

"I guess."

"Good," Kenny said. "Yesterday before...before it happened. Did you let anyone in the back door?"

"You guys already asked me that," Colleen protested.

Jane and Kenny exchanged a glance. This girl was more *compis* than she looked. "Yeah," Jane said. "We kind of repeat ourselves. Never know what you can learn in Round Two."

Colleen shifted in bed. "Like repressed memory stuff?"

"Exactly," Jane said. "You ever suffer from that?"

Colleen shook her head. "Nah. Saw it on *Oprah*."

Kenny leaned forward. "Any deliveries yesterday? Anyone use the back door at all?"

"Uh-uh. We're not a Tuesday delivery store."

Jane slid the tray table to the side and moved closer so Colleen could see her better. "Did you hear the buzzer ring at all?"

"No. But the kitchen's pretty loud with fryers and stuff. Plus, even though we're not supposed to? We have a radio in there."

Jane pressed on. "So if someone let somebody else in the back way it would have to have been…"

"Toni…"

"Did you see her go downstairs?"

"I didn't. But, like I said, it was wicked busy. She might of, but not that I could see."

Jane drew Colleen's eyes to her own. "Colleen, I need you to do something for me."

"I'll try."

"I need you to think back to when you were in that freezer. I know the cooling system was loud and that you were frightened, but did you hear anything at all that could help us?"

Colleen Porter's lower lip quivered and she closed her eyes. Then she shook her head from side to side, faster and faster. Jane was just about to reach over and touch her, to try to calm her down, when Colleen yelled, "Don't!"

"I'm sorry, Colleen," Jane said softly. "I didn't mean to upset you."

Colleen opened her eyes and found Jane. "No, that's what someone yelled. 'Don't!' "

Kenny edged in closer. "Male or female?"

"Male."

"Was it a young voice?" Kenny asked. "Like a teenager?"

"No, it was a grown-up's."

Jane looked to Kenny. An ember of a clue was emerging. "The only adult men down there were Terrence Unger, Shanty Rourke, and Father Cellucci."

"Mr. Unger," Colleen said, "has this kind of wimpy high voice. No way it was him. Shanty is so raspy from cigarettes and booze, he could never be that loud. And Father Francis…well, he just had the gentlest voice you ever heard." She struggled to sit higher in the bed. "This 'Don't!' was way powerful—"

"But," Kenny suggested, "maybe one of the men was so frightened his voice got stronger, more forceful."

"Could be. But I don't think so."

"Why not, Colleen?"

"Because it was so…so *mean*. It was all like '*Don't!*' As in 'Don't do that!' "

Kenny made a note in his pad. "Anything interesting about the voice? An accent?"

Colleen Porter thought for a moment. "Nah. It was just American." She lay back down on the pillow and looked to Jane. "Can you get a nurse for me?"

"Are you in pain?"

"Nope. Hungry."

Jane and Kenny stood in the back of the oversize hospital elevator.

"So," Jane began to lay it out, "six people are herded downstairs. The bad guy, the evidence suggests, wants to take the money and run. But something happens. Someone does something, he yells *Don't!*, and starts shooting."

"And that someone, the evidence also suggests," Kenny said, "is the priest. He makes a move. The shooter yells, 'Don't!' But the priest doesn't stop. He raises his hand and charges. Now he's shot in the hand. Then the shoulder. He goes down. And he's executed point-blank."

"A simple robbery suddenly gets all complicated, and the bad guy's in way over his head."

"So he murders the five witnesses, one by one." Kenny blew a long sigh. "Stopping to reload as they lay dying. Then he smashes the cash register open, grabs the money, and splits." The elevator reached the first floor. "Is that what happened?"

Jane shook her head in frustration as they hurried across the crowded lobby. "It's sound theory based on witness testimony and physical evidence. But it's only that…theory. And it'll only stick until we have something better to go on. We still have a possible drug thing with Bobby and Nico Silva. Plus whatever else rears its head. This is a huge crime with a lot of moving parts. Anything's possible until we prove it otherwise."

"Speaking of Nico Silva," Kenny said as the automatic doors slid apart and they entered the parking garage. "I still want to talk to his brother."

Jane thought back to her encounter with Edgar Silva. His grief, his civility. "About what?"

Kenny stopped. "Edgar Silva is the poster boy for badness. He's a gangbanger and an ex-con…and that's just from his tattoos. His baby brother's dealing drugs. Who knows what kind of shit he's into?"

"And if he isn't?"

"We move on. You said it yourself…the theory's only good as long as it sticks."

Kenny eased the Explorer out of the parking garage of the San Francisco General Medical Tower.

Moving slowly, he tried to adjust his eyes to the brilliant sunlight. The wailing of approaching sirens reached him and he stopped at the sidewalk. The hospital's emergency room was just across the street and sirens were not uncommon around here.

Looking left toward the ER, Kenny nudged the Explorer down the driveway and into the street.

"Ken, watch out!" Jane yelled.

Kenny stood on the brake just as two squad cars raced up from the right. They came to a skidding stop inches from the Explorer's right front fender.

Tommy Murphy and Rick Weymouth jumped out of the first one and ran up to the Explorer. "Lieutenant," Tommy said breathlessly. "We had our dispatcher call your precinct. Your Mrs. Lomax told us where you were." His eyes were shining with excitement. "We got something. Something big!"

He and Rick leaned into Jane's window. "A cop from our station house," Rick continued, nodding back to Candace Wong at the wheel of the second black-and-white, "recognized one of the victims…Toni Salazar…from a domestic case she worked. She had this druggie boyfriend who threatened her so bad, she had to get a temporary restraining order against him."

Tommy picked up the story. "The computers are down, so we had to go through the field reports by hand. But we found the guy. Name's Sammy Pickett, and he works at the E-Z Pump gas station over at Fell and Divisadero."

Kenny revved the engine. "That's only a couple of blocks from here!" He reached for the gearshift.

"Wait a minute," Jane said. She turned to Tommy and Rick. "This might be a good lead...and it might not. We can't just cowboy in on this guy."

"This is solid, ma'am." Tommy pulled a microcassette recorder from his shirt pocket. "We wanted to be thorough, Lieutenant. So we went to Toni Salazar's apartment and her roommate gave us this tape of Pickett's phone calls to their answering machine. Toni recorded it a couple of weeks ago...just in case." He pressed Play.

"Toni? To-ni! The fuck are you?" Sammy Pickett sounded strung out and pissed off. "I know what you're doing, bitch. And it ain't gonna happen. You dump me and you're dead. And don't think I won't do it neither." There was a brief hiss of static. Then another message. "Toni. You sitting there listening to this call? Making fun of me? You do that shit, I'm gonna fuck you up. Big time. Call me back, baby." Static.

"There's one more," Rick said.

"Okay, bitch," Sammy Pickett spoke in a slow unnatural cadence, as if fighting for control. "I been calling for a week and...nothing. You leave me no choice. I gotta teach you."

"And Lieutenant," Tommy Murphy said, "Officer Wong checked with Pickett's landlord? He moved out this morning. So then we called his boss at the gas station and Pickett's coming by"—he glanced at his watch—"in like five minutes for his last paycheck. Classic stupid criminal flight mode."

Kenny pulled the Explorer into gear. "C'mon Jane. We've got this guy."

Jane took up the dash mic. "3H58 to Dispatch."

"Go, Lieutenant."

"Cheryl, request backup at the E-Z Pump at Fell and Divisadero. Possible Stella's murder suspect. A Sammy Pickett. Look up his vitals in the system and send it out." Jane thought of something else. "The computers back up?"

"Ten minutes ago."

"Good. Send it out. Suspect should be considered armed and extremely dangerous. We're rolling on it now from the Med Tower with two patrol units from Fifteen."

"Officer Murphy found you then?"

"Yes, he did. 3H58, out." Jane dropped the mic on the seat. "Okay, guys, no heroes out there. Just a good clean takedown."

Tommy and Rick scrambled back to their squad car. Kenny stomped on the accelerator and the Explorer leaped forward. Its rear end fighting for traction, Kenny powered into a hard left turn and sped away, the black-and-whites riding his tail.

"That's him with the ponytail."

Tommy Murphy jabbed a finger toward a wiry man with long blond hair standing in the shade of the gas station's canopy. He shook hands with an older black man. "The other guy's his boss, Mr. Turley." Sammy Pickett wore black Levi denims, a tattered Phish T-shirt, and black sneakers.

The Explorer was parked between the two police cruisers in a Ryder truck lot across the street. The massive yellow rental trucks shielded them from view. Jane looked up and down the street. "Where the hell's our backup?"

Turley handed Sammy Pickett an envelope.

"That'll be his paycheck," Kenny said. He slipped the Explorer into gear.

"Shit," Jane said. "Okay, soon as he turns his back to us."

Pickett threw a gap-toothed grin to Turley and started toward an old red Toyota pickup truck near the lube bay.

Tommy Murphy, Rick Weymouth, and Candace Wong looked to Jane. Waiting for her signal.

Pickett folded the envelope into the back pocket of his jeans and closed in on his pickup.

Jane nodded tightly. "Okay, guys, let's do this."

The three police vehicles roared out of the truck lot and blasted across the street.

Candace Wong blocked the west entrance to the E-Z Pump. Tommy Murphy stopped his car in the east driveway. And the Explorer bounded over the curb in the center.

Sammy Pickett whirled around just as Jane and Kenny scrambled from the Explorer, their weapons drawn.

"SFPD!" Kenny shouted as he ran forward. "On the ground!"

"Ken," Jane called, "get back here!"

But Kenny kept striding toward the suspect.

Sammy Pickett didn't move.

Kenny advanced on him. "On the *ground*, asshole!"

Jane covered Kenny from behind the Explorer's open passenger door. Candace Wong was bent over the hood of her squad car, her shotgun leveled at Pickett. Rick Weymouth knelt by the front bumper of his black-and-white, his weapon also trained on the suspect.

A line of three patrol cars careened around the corner and side-slid to a stop. The officers fanned out, forming a secure perimeter. Tommy Murphy worked his radio, coordinating their positions.

As Kenny moved in, Pickett took a step forward. "Freeze!" Kenny shouted.

Kenny noticed Sammy Pickett was sweating heavily and his hands were trembling. He correctly deduced that Sammy's brain was hyped on coke and adrenaline.

Sammy stared at the muzzle of Kenny's Glock. "I didn't do fuck-all," he cried. He jerked his chin toward the Toyota pickup.

"That shit in there ain't mine. Hell, the fuckin' *truck* ain't even mine!"

Kenny's finger tensed on the trigger. "Shut up!"

Jane reached into the Explorer and switched on the loudspeaker. She brought the microphone up. "Samuel Pickett...put your hands behind your head and drop to your knees."

The gas station manager ran into the office and slammed the door closed. "Officer Wong," Jane said over the loudspeaker, "keep an eye on the gas station office. We don't know that guy."

Candace Wong swiveled her shotgun around to train it on the office.

A motorcycle cop pulled up and, his weapon out, crouched behind his bike.

Jane took in the scene. Sammy Pickett was clearly unstable and Kenny was too far out in the open. He continued to close in on the suspect, unnecessarily exposing himself and compromising the equation.

Pickett's eyes darted from the muzzle of Kenny's gun to Kenny's eyes. Then he shrugged and started to raise his hands. Kenny stopped moving forward.

As he did, Pickett spun around and jumped into his pickup truck. He started it up and threw it into reverse, heading straight for Kenny.

Kenny held his ground. Sighting down the barrel of the Glock, he drew a bead on Sammy Pickett's head. He was about to fire when, screaming in from the right side, a squad car rammed the pickup, catching it just behind the engine compartment and sending it spinning. It turned a full revolution, then rolled onto its side, the windshield buckling.

Cops from the perimeter raced in and yanked Sammy Pickett from the battered Toyota. Rick Weymouth dropped a knee between the struggling suspect's shoulder blades and yanked hard on his ponytail. The other officers snapped cuffs on him and dragged him to his feet.

Jane glared at Kenny and thumbed the safety back on her pistol. Then she crossed to the squad car that had smashed into the pickup. "I said 'no heroes.' "

"I'm no hero, Lieutenant." Tommy Murphy said as he climbed out of his badly damaged police cruiser. "Just a cop."

13

"I'm glad the bitch is dead. Fuckin' elated." Sammy Pickett said. "I didn't kill her, but same difference."

He flicked his head to the side, trying to get his greasy blond hair out of his eyes. It fell forward again, cascading down his forehead and over his eyebrows. He reflexively tried to raise his hands, but they were chained to a steel ring in the center of the metal table in Interrogation Two.

Jane sat across the table from him. Kenny stood with his back against the door. Craig Knowles sat at a small desk in the corner, recording the interview.

The public defender, Perry Regan, sat by quietly, biding his time. He'd been doing this twenty years before this damn client was even born and he knew these things had a way of working themselves out. Or they didn't.

"Isn't it true, Mr. Pickett," Jane began, "that you made several threats upon Antonia Salazar's life?"

"Yup."

"And isn't it true," Jane continued, "that you went to her apartment and did great physical damage to the premises?"

"True, true, and…true." Sammy Pickett rocked in his chair, sending it scraping along the linoleum until his shackles brought him up short.

Kenny stepped away from the door. "And Miss Salazar was so fearful of you that she requested and received a TRO against you from Judge Marilyn Cohen just two weeks ago."

"That a question?" Sammy Pickett sneered.

"Statement of fact," Kenny said.

Pickett looked over to him, his eyes narrowing. "Guilty."

Perry Regan shifted in his seat. "Uh…"

"Don't worry, Perry," Jane said. "We're looking for a whole other kind of guilty."

Pickett grabbed his wrist chains in his fingers and pulled himself forward. "Well, Miss, the kind of guilty you're looking for, you ain't gonna get." He blew at a strand of hair that had fallen across his cheek.

Jane ignored him and pressed on. "Why did you give notice to both your landlord and your boss the day after Antonia Salazar was murdered?"

"Because, lady, with her dead, I get the camper."

Jane couldn't tell if this was the beleaguered reasoning of a drug-soaked mind…or the truth. "I'm listening."

"Me and Toni bought this VW camper a couple months ago. We was gonna go live in Big Sur, stuff like that. Then she decides to go back to school to…" He spit the words out. "*Better* herself. Which only means one thing: find someone better'n me. Can you imagine?"

At any time prior to his nephew's death, Jane thought, Kenny would have been all over a straight line like that. "Go on," she said.

"So now she's all in school and working fast food and shit. Like a fuckin' responsible woman. But you don't fool Sammy Pickett for too long. I know she was seeing one of her teachers over at that college. I know 'cause I seen her with him. And I fuckin' lost it." He curled his lips into a crooked grin. "My temper is a bad thing, Miss. But this time, it saved my butt."

"What do you mean?"

"Reason I didn't do them killings at that restaurant? I was at the Social Services building over at Van Ness and Reed at that exact same time. You could check."

Jane glanced to Kenny. "And what were you doing at Social Services?"

"Taking my stupid fuckin' anger management course." Sammy Pickett sat back in his chair. "Court ordered."

Sammy Pickett smirked at Jane as the elevator doors slid closed.

He knew he was in deep shit, but still wanted to throw a little attitude at that bitch lady lieutenant. Perry Regan had explained just how deep the shit was. Possession of a controlled substance while on parole, resisting arrest, and assault on a police officer with a deadly weapon. The deadly weapon being that piece of crap Toyota pickup.

Jane turned from the elevator, took a long drink from the water fountain, and looked across the bullpen for Kenny. He was standing by the windows, talking on his cell phone. Jane knew he was over there trying for some semblance of privacy as he spoke to his sister. The street lamps threw a wash of yellow light through the windows and across his face.

After four hours in Interrogation Two with that jerk-off Pickett, Jane hadn't even realized that night had come.

Tommy Murphy and Rick Weymouth crossed toward her. They had been waiting in reception all these hours to see what would happen with Sammy Pickett. Technically, it had been their collar.

"You guys pulling O.T.?"

"No, ma'am," Rick said. "We called in our log-out when our shift ended." He seemed pale and unfocused.

Jane peered into his eyes. "You okay, Rick?"

Rick Weymouth looked to her, his eyes glistening. "I thought we had the guy, Lieutenant."

"It was good police work on your part," Jane said. "And Sammy Pickett's going to be off the streets for a long time thanks to the two of you."

"But he's not the one."

"No...he's not the one."

Rick started to speak, but it turned into an empty sigh.

Jane touched his shoulder. "Talk to your dad lately?"

"Every night."

Jane gave his shoulder a gentle squeeze. "Tell him I said hi, will ya?"

"Will do." Rick turned to Tommy Murphy. "See ya tomorrow, Rookie."

Tommy gave him a brotherly slap on the back. "Protecting and serving." He and Jane watched as Rick Weymouth trudged toward the stairwell door. "He's all messed up over this, Lieutenant."

"He's in a lot of pain. You gotta make sure he sees Dr. Glazer." Jane turned to Tommy. "How you holding up?"

"I...I keep moving." Tommy held up a sheet of paper. "Speaking of which...here."

Jane took the page and scanned it. "You're applying to Homicide?"

"I never really knew what I wanted from my career. But now, with this case, I want to be where I can make a difference."

Jane smiled. "You'd be the youngest homicide inspector in the department by about ten years."

"'Scuse me for saying, ma'am. But you were the first female lieutenant in the department. Far as I'm concerned, I've got a good role model."

Jane regarded him. "Tell you what, we'll talk about it after this case is behind us. Till then you keep on being a good cop." She glanced at the application again. "What kind of address is that?"

"I live on a boat at the marina. Gas House Cove. Nothing fancy on a street cop's salary, believe me."

"Sounds nice...peaceful."

Tommy Murphy shrugged a smile. "Smartest thing I ever did." He looked at his watch. "I gotta get going, Lieutenant. See you around."

"You take care, Officer Murphy," Jane said. She stepped over to Roz Shapiro's desk and handed her the application. "Two things, Roz. Please put this in my in-box. And please go home."

Roz took the sheet of paper. "Yes to the first. And no to the second. Not until you do, Jane."

Jane saw that Kenny had finished his phone call and was headed for the war room in Interrogation One. "Ken," she called as she strode across the bullpen. "I need to talk to you about what went down at that gas station."

Kenny turned to her, his eyes wet and red. "I just had to tell my sister that we found drugs on the body of the son she's burying tomorrow. You think we can talk about procedure another time?"

Jane took Kenny by the elbow and led him to the entrance of the lunchroom. The TV was on, playing the commercial package before the local late-night news, but no one was in there. "That is *so* unfair of you, Kenny. I loved Bobby, too."

"Then why are you breaking my balls?"

"Trying to talk to my partner...my husband...about an extremely dangerous situation is not breaking your balls." Jane put her hand on his chest. "Look, I love you. I'm having your baby...and I don't want to lose either of you." She grabbed the front of his shirt and brought her face close to his. "But you do something like that again, unnecessarily put yourself in harm's way, and I swear to fucking God, I'll take you off this case myself."

Kenny let his anger cool. "Okay, you're right. I'll do better, be smarter."

Jane leaned forward and touched her forehead to his chest. "Thank you."

"Any chance we can get back to work?"

Jane looked up to him, searching his face for any sign of affection. There was none. "Fine," she sighed. "Let's go in there."

They separated and crossed into Interrogation One.

The City Planning schematic of the Carmody Avenue neighborhood was so large that Mike Finney had to fold it to make it fit on the bulletin board. The Stella's restaurant on upper Carmody was circled in red. The positions of the various responding units were circled in yellow, their roof numbers written in black.

Jane and Kenny entered. "Hey, everyone," Jane said as she crossed the room. "A quick recap, then we'll call it a night."

Finney put the last thumbtack into the corner of the schematic. Then he took a manila folder off the table and handed it to Kenny.

"As you all know by now," Jane continued, "we couldn't file murder charges against Sammy Pickett." She glanced at Kenny. "But it was a good arrest based on good evidence. It just didn't pan out. This may happen again during the investigation. But if and when it does, remember this: it's a process. And every suspect we eliminate allows us to focus all of our resources on finding the real killer." She sat on the table between the two blackboards that held the names of the murder victims. "And I promise everyone in this room: we will find him."

"How do we know it's a him?" Lou Tronick asked. The knot of his tie was pulled down from his neck and his shirt was partly untucked from his pants.

"Because Colleen Porter, the woman who was trapped in the freezer, positively ID'd that the shooter was a male, based on his voice."

Finney started to raise his hand.

"No accent," Jane said, anticipating the question. "Just, and I quote, 'American…and mean.'"

"She give you anything else?" Lou asked.

"That's it for now." Jane pulled her right knee to her chest and stretched the ache from her lower back. "Another thing: I'm sure you've all seen the Forensics report that shows evidence of a minor drug transaction between Nicolas Silva and Robert Farrier." A couple of cops shot a look to Kenny. "Might be something to this, might not. Silva was the seller and had cash, jewelry, and a good amount of marijuana on his person. Farrier, it appears, was a recreational user who had a small amount of dope in his pocket. But we'll pursue this angle vigorously from both sides."

Kenny looked up from the manila folder he'd been reading. "As long as we're pursuing things vigorously, let's start with Nicolas Silva…or more specifically, his brother." He held up the folder. "Edgar Silva has led a recidivistic life—make that life-*style*—of crime. His record runs the gamut from GTA to assault, to drug possession and dealing, to attempted murder. He did a nickel at Shanley in the mid-eighties for possession with intent of *twenty* pounds of crack-grade cocaine." He paused to scan another page.

The others looked to Jane. There was an unmistakable tinge of challenge in Kenny's voice. Jane turned to Finney. "Mike, any luck finding Mr. Silva?"

"Not yet, Lieutenant. We've left word at his house, his mother's house, and the garage he owns with one of his cousins."

"If you have to," Kenny said, "send a unit out to the Tenderloin and pick him up."

Finney fidgeted. "Uh, okay. On what grounds?"

"He's a material witness wanted for questioning in the worst mass murder in San Francisco in twenty years," Kenny said. "That grounds enough for you?"

Mike Finney's face flushed red.

Kenny held up the last page of Edgar's record. "Twelve years ago Edgar Silva was involved in a drive-by in which a seventy-seven-year-old female bystander was killed. Within twenty-four hours, the triggerman was hunted down and murdered. Said triggerman was Silva's brother, Juan, the middle one between him and Nico. Edgar was arrested, but, surprise-surprise, no one felt the civil compunction to step forward and testify." He slipped the page back into the folder and dropped it on the table.

"What if what happened yesterday," Kenny went on, "was a hit? An act of retaliation against Edgar Silva for any of a multitude of past sins, not the least of which was the gunning down of an innocent old lady?"

Kenny's reasoning was sound, Jane thought, but the edge in his voice was unsettling. "It's good theory, Ken," she said evenly. "But isn't it unlikely that a bunch of gangbangers would wait so many years to make a revenge move? And to mimic previous robberies at two other Stella's? Seems a little out there."

The muscles in Kenny's jaw twitched with tension. "If it's good theory, I'm going to pursue it…vigorously."

"Hey, Jane," Lou Tronick said. "Check it out." He pointed through the window to the TV in the lunchroom. Cameron Sanders of KGO News was doing a remote from the Stella's on upper Carmody. Behind him, candles in the makeshift memorial flickered in the breeze. *Carnage on Carmody* was supered on the lower part of the picture.

Jane reached over and turned on the television in Interrogation One. The screen bloomed and resolved to the same image.

"…an arrest this afternoon that proved to be the wrong man. In a related story, Dave Siegler, the chairman and CEO of Stella's Food Services, Incorporated, made a statement to the press earlier this evening."

The picture changed to a close-up of a well-dressed man with black hair that was a little too long and wire-rimmed glasses. He was forty years old and everything about him spoke of power and confidence. Dave Siegler adjusted one of the microphones in front of him and addressed the media. "This is the most difficult day imaginable for our huge family of Stella's employees. This unspeakable tragedy has torn our hearts in two. There is much grieving to be done…and much healing." He paused for a moment. "On behalf of the Stella's family, I am offering a reward of one hundred thousand dollars for information leading to the arrest and conviction of whoever committed this atrocity. We stand willing and eager to cooperate with the San Francisco Police Department in any way we can."

He was caught in a firestorm of strobing flashbulbs. The station switched back to Cameron Sanders. "Mr. Siegler, obviously in great pain, has offered a substantial reward to bring to justice whoever is responsible for this terrible crime." He touched his hand to his right ear, listening to his earpiece. "And tomorrow the funerals begin as the citizens of San Francisco bury their dead. KGO will be there live. This is Cameron San—"

The TV suddenly went dark.

Kenny stood with the remote in his hand. He tossed it onto the table and walked out into the bullpen.

"Okay, guys," Jane said, "thanks for today. Keep asking the hard questions and let's come up with some good answers." She hurried across the room and caught up to Kenny at his desk. "Ken, what is it about Edgar Silva that's set you off like this?"

Kenny turned on her. "Edgar Silva was a known drug dealer. His younger brother followed in his dirty footsteps. If Mr. Silva had been a fine, upstanding, oh I don't know, telephone repairman, then Bobby never would have been at that Stella's." He jammed his Glock into his shoulder holster. "I'm sleeping at Andrea's tonight."

Jane started to go after him, then stopped. She took a moment to absorb what he'd just said. It made sense. It's exactly what Kenny should be doing. The problem was that she was hurting too and there was no room in Kenny's world for them to discuss that. "Okay," she said softly. "I'll bring your blue suit by in the morning." She waited for Kenny to say something. He didn't. "Need anything else?"

"Yeah." Kenny grabbed his jacket from the back of his desk chair. "For my nephew to still be alive."

He walked briskly across the squad room and barged through the stairwell door.

14

That damn baby was crying again.

Aram Hagopian pulled a pillow over his head and tried to coax a little more sleep out of another late morning. He hadn't been to work since the Stella's he cooked at was robbed, calling in sick with his migraines. And now this neighbor kid was wailing like it was the end of the world.

He peeked out from under his pillow. His one-room apartment, too small in the best of times, seemed like it was closing in on him after two weeks of staying in and watching TV.

TV.

That would kill some time. And drown out the racket of that damn baby. He rummaged through the twisted blanket and found the remote. Then he zapped on ESPN. He had watched it for hours last night, seeing the same sports recap repeated every thirty minutes until three in the morning.

He surfed the channels until he found KGO. Maybe the weather was coming on. Always good to know what kind of day it was going to be outside, even if he was staying inside.

That black guy who had been all over the news the past couple of days was reporting from some park. Only it wasn't a park. It was a cemetery.

People were filing into a small chapel. Teenagers mostly, dressed in shirts that were too big and ties that belonged to someone else. Their faces sagging with betrayal.

Then there was that cop who had been so rough with him at the station yesterday. He walked slowly between a woman with a black veil whose shoulders heaved as she sobbed and some old guy whose hands wouldn't stop shaking. Behind them was that nice lady cop.

The camera panned to Cameron Sanders again. He spoke in a low, reverential voice. "...just graduated from Harry S. Truman High School this past June. Robert Farrier was the nephew of Homicide Inspector Kenneth Marks and Homicide Lieutenant Jane Candiotti. In a strange twist of fate, it is this victim's aunt and uncle who are the lead investigators on his murder."

Aram watched as Kenny reached the doorway. The camera pushed in and a coffin could be seen in the background, drawing everyone forward. Kenny clutched Andrea to him as they entered the chapel together.

A camera inside picked up the shot and followed the mourners to their pews. Chief Walker McDonald was already seated in a row near the front. The image came to rest on the coffin, covered in a blanket of white flowers. Bobby Farrier's graduation picture, framed now, stood on an easel next to the coffin.

Cameron Sanders's voice came up over the scene. "Robert Farrier is one of two victims of the Stella's massacre to be buried today. We go now to Saint Vincent's Catholic Church on Gough Street where a funeral mass is being celebrated by Bishop Dominic D'Souza for Father Francis Cellucci. Father Francis was assistant director of the AIDS Hospice in Haight-Ashbury. He, too, was gunned down in the carnage on Carmody."

Aram Hagopian had seen enough. He clicked off the TV and fell back on his pillow. Staring at the ceiling, fighting back the pain of his migraine, he understood that he would have to tell the police what he should have told them yesterday.

That he knew who did this.

Jane watched from the steps as Kenny and Andrea held their father's arms and helped him into the limousine.

Kenny squatted at the curb, talking quietly with his father. Lloyd Marks reached out and put a trembling hand on his son's shoulder, speaking to him with great intensity. Kenny squeezed his father's hand and rose to pull his sister into a final hug. Their mother, Doris, stood to the side and put a tentative hand on each of their backs. They opened their arms and brought her into the embrace, but she was clearly uncomfortable.

Cameron Sanders spotted Jane from the press area and signaled that he wanted to talk to her. She shook her head; now was not the time. Jane had known Sanders for years, from when he was a young reporter on the *Chronicle* to his ascension to KGO. He had always been a resourceful journalist, relentless in his pursuit of a story.

"How's he doing?"

Jane turned to the voice.

Chief Walker McDonald had just come down the stairs.

"Kenny? He's hurting, sir. But he'll be okay."

"Would it be too impolitic of me to indulge in a little shoptalk?"

"Of course not."

"I looked over the I.R.s of the Sammy Pickett arrest. Are you satisfied with the way it went down? With the way Sergeant Marks comported himself?"

It was a typical Walker McDonald trap and Jane wasn't going to fall for it. "Sir, I won't be satisfied until we bring in the killer."

"Nor will I, Lieutenant." Chief McDonald looked past Jane and saw that the press had spotted him. The reporters were rushing forward, Cameron Sanders in the lead, while their cameramen swept up their gear. The chief raised his sunglasses and looked Jane in the eyes. "Next time, do it better. No unnecessary risks. Or I pull both of you off this case." He started toward the press, then stopped and turned back to Jane. "And next time? I expect to be personally informed by you of any impending arrest." He offered a tight smile. "After-the-fact kind of leaves me hanging. You don't want to leave your chief hanging, Lieutenant."

He lowered his sunglasses and moved toward the approaching reporters. "Guys, a couple of quick comments and no questions please...out of respect for the family."

Jane saw Kenny making his way toward her through the courtyard. It crossed her mind how handsome he looked in his blue suit—the same suit she'd bought for him when they'd gotten married.

"How's Andrea?" she asked as he came up.

"Destroyed."

"I'll bet." Jane took his hand. "What was your dad saying?"

"How, now that his only grandson is gone...we need to have a good baby."

"Hey, no pressure there." Jane's cell phone vibrated. She took it from the strap of her purse and checked the readout. *3H77–911.* She showed it to Kenny. Mike Finney was calling with something urgent. Jane scanned the area, searching for someplace she could call in from without attracting the attention of the press.

Kenny understood what she was doing. "This way." He led her to one of the limousines idling at the curb. The reporters watched them pass and nodded respectfully. Cameron Sanders turned as they went by, his innate sense of a story keeping his focus on them while the chief continued to talk.

Once inside the limo, with the doors closed and the tinted windows up, Jane whipped out her phone and called Finney's number.

"Homicide, Finney."

"Mike, it's me. What's happening?"

"Lieutenant, I'm really sorry to disturb you considering where you are and all. But we just got an anonymous call patched over from 911. It was some guy saying he knew who the killer was. And who robbed the other Stella's, too."

Jane looked to Kenny. They both knew, with Dave Siegler posting a huge reward, that any number of loonies would start coming forward. But this caller had said he knew of the other robberies, something the police hadn't put out to the public yet. "Talk to me, Mike."

"He said the bad guy's called Cabbage."

"Cabbage?" Kenny asked. "As in the vegetable?"

"Affirmative. He said he's called that because he...well, he smells. Anyway, I kept him going and got him to tell me the guy's name. Herman Jones. I crossed it with the Stella's job applications I'd collected and guess what. He used to work for them until about a month ago."

"Did you look him up?" Jane asked.

"Sure did. Herman Jones has a long history of violent crime... all drug-related." Finney shuffled some papers. "But here's the thing: his job application shows him to be a model citizen. It even says he was an Eagle Scout and a star halfback on his high school football team. A high school he was kicked out of, by the way."

Kenny leaned in. "Glad to hear Stella's does such due diligence vetting their employees."

"Speaking of Stella's employees," Finney said, "the guy who called 911? We traced it back and it was Aram Hagopian."

"No shit?" Kenny said.

"None, Inspector."

Jane muted the phone and turned to Kenny. "I want to play this one right. Let's bring Mr. Hagopian in and see what he knows and how he knows it. Then we'll move on Herman Jones."

"Agreed. But let's not wait for Mr. Hagopian to come to us. Let's go to him."

Jane turned the mute off. "Okay, thanks, Mike. Good work. We'll take it from here."

She dropped the phone into her bag and looked outside. The reporters were just breaking down their equipment from interviewing the chief. But Cameron Sanders was lingering, glancing toward the limousine. A newshound on the scent. Jane knew he would stay there all day if he had to. An off-duty motorcycle cop held traffic while the hearse and the limo carrying Kenny's family pulled away from the curb. Jane and Kenny's limousine was next in line. It would seem suspicious if they got out and went back to the Explorer. She lowered the privacy screen between the passenger cabin and the driver. "Sir?"

The driver poked his head into the space. "ma'am?"

"Can you take us somewhere? Somewhere other than the cemetery?"

"I'm on a day-rate, ma'am. Anywhere's fine."

"Fucking migraines," Aram Hagopian groaned out loud.

He squeezed his eyes against the pain, setting off a fireworks show behind his eyelids. Climbing out of bed for the first time in two days, he struggled to the counter of the kitchenette. A KFC bucket filled with chicken bones and a congealing glop of mashed potatoes sat in the middle of an empty Domino's pizza box. *Funny*, he thought; he worked forty hours a week in a fast food joint and all he ever ate when he wasn't there was fast food. Maybe it was all the preservatives and shit that gave him these headaches. Plus that goddamn baby crying all the time.

He took an open bottle of Tylenol Gelcaps from the windowsill—the top had been missing for days—and poured himself a fistful. Then he leaned over the sink and, cupping cold water into his mouth, sloshed back the pills. As he straightened up, his head throbbing, he thought he saw a limousine go by downstairs. It occurred to him that someone's either real lost or there's a new pimp in town.

Aram scraped a leftover thread of chicken off a leg bone. He had just put it into his mouth when there was a knock at the door. A casual knuckle one-two like a neighbor coming by to see if he needed anything, him being sick and all.

He crossed the room, making a halfhearted stab at smoothing down the bed as he passed, and opened the door.

Jane and Kenny stood in the doorway, their badges held at eye level. Kenny edged partway into the room, making sure the door stayed open.

Surprised and frightened, Aram took an involuntary step backward. "I thought it was an anonymous call."

"Tough shit," Kenny said as he bulled into the room.

Jane stepped in behind him. "If you wanted to stay anonymous, Mr. Hagopian, you should have called one of the We-Tip hotlines. But you called 911. All those calls are traced." She closed the door. "Please have a seat, sir."

Aram started to sit on the bed.

"Uh-uh," Kenny said. He pointed to a straight-backed wooden chair in the corner. "There's good."

The chair creaked when Aram sat on it, one of its legs wobbling as if it were going to snap. It's what you get when you find a chair next to a Dumpster and bring it home.

Kenny grabbed the edge of the blanket and pulled it onto the floor.

"Hey," Aram protested, half rising from the chair.

"Sit down," Kenny commanded. "And shut up." He tossed the pillows aside. "Can't have a proper conversation if we're all nervous about the possibility of weapons, can we?"

"I don't have any weapons."

Jane stuck her head into the bathroom and turned back to Aram. "Talk to us about Herman Jones."

A surge of fear rose in Aram's throat. "Can't you just go get him and leave me out of this?"

"We're a little less inclined to do that," Kenny said, "given that we already had you in once and you bullshitted us. That wasted our time. And, Mr. Hagopian, you do *not* want to waste our time again." He sat on the edge of the bed, facing Aram. "How do you know it was Herman Jones?"

"Me and him used to work at the Stella's on Pride Street. We called him Cabbage because he always, uh, he..."

"Smelled?" Kenny offered.

"Yeah, like awful. Then he gets fired for being late to work for the zillionth time in a row. 'Bout a week later, this dude shows up with a ski mask and a gun and makes us all go into the back room. I know right away it's Cabbage 'cause of his body odor and his size—he's on the big side. He tells us to lie down on the floor and count to a thousand and no one would get hurt. Then he goes and empties the register. It was right after lunch and we hadn't done the cash-drop yet, so there was more money than usual in the drawer."

Kenny glanced to Jane. The Stella's on Carmody was hit at the same time of day.

"Like I said," Aram Hagopian continued, "Cabbage used to work in that store, so he knew the cash-drop drill pretty good."

"Mr. Hagopian," Kenny began, his voice tight with anger, "why the hell didn't you tell us this before?"

"When Cabbage was robbing us? He knew I recognized him and it was pretty clear what he'd do if I said anything. When we were working together? He was always bragging on how many guns he had and how he wasn't afraid to use them. He said shit like that every day. He was a freak about that stuff."

Jane came deeper into the room. "And why, Mr. Hagopian, did you choose to come forward now?"

Aram started to lean back in the chair, but the back leg creaked and he stayed still. "Because I saw on TV—"

"About the fucking reward," Kenny said. "Hundred thousand dollars could sure change your burger-flipping life."

"No, sir," Aram said. He slumped forward, looking at the worn carpet in the space between his feet. "Because I saw on TV...the funeral of your nephew...and I felt so bad for all those people." He looked up, his eyes filling with tears. "I am so sorry for your nephew."

Kenny stood up quickly. "If you'd had the balls to come forward after the first robbery, Herman Jones would be in jail. And all those people you feel so fucking sorry for? They'd be alive today." He moved closer to Aram, then caught himself. "So don't insult me with your pity, you son of a bitch!"

Jane touched her hand to Kenny's back. He turned to her, his eyes ablaze. "We moving on this?"

"We're moving on this." Jane looked to Aram. "Someone from our precinct will be by to pick you up."

"What for?"

"To identify Herman Jones when we bring him in."

Aram Hagopian winced. "Anonymous?"

"Yes, sir," Jane said. "Anonymously."

Kenny pulled the door open and he and Jane stepped into the dank corridor. The sounds of several televisions broadcasting in several languages filled the hallway. Somewhere, inside or out, a baby continued to cry.

"If this Cabbage guy," Jane began, "is as much of a gun enthusiast as our friend says he is, I want to go in with heavy artillery."

Kenny ripped the two-way off his belt. "I'll call SWAT." He hurried toward the exit door at the far end of the hall.

Jane called after him. "You in control?"

Kenny hustled through the door. "Totally."

Jane pulled out her walkie-talkie as they raced down the steps. "3H58 to Dispatch."

"Dispatch to 3H58. Go, Lieutenant."

"Cheryl, patch me through to Chief McDonald. Tell them it's urgent that I speak with him."

15

"On your go, Lieutenant."

Scott Hicks, the SWAT Team leader, had his crew poised on the staircase of a ramshackle tenement building in the bleakest section of North Beach. Although it was midday, a sparkling San Francisco afternoon, the hallway was dark and musty.

Jane and Kenny were at the bottom landing, the SWAT Team crouched and ready above them. She held her gun close to her side. Kenny's Glock was tight to his hip.

Scott Hicks was in his late thirties. His light blond hair, his pale skin, and his soft blue eyes belied the fact that he was a coldly efficient and utterly ruthless SWAT officer.

Jane took in the scene.

Ten men in black Kevlar body armor with automatic rifles were stacked up on the stairs. Below, in the entryway, were a double baby stroller and a pink bicycle with a faux wicker basket and training wheels. Outside, beyond the SWAT van, the chief's Chevy Suburban idled in a vacant lot.

Walker McDonald sat in the backseat of his command vehicle like a general waiting for news from the front. "Soon as that shitbox is secure," he said to his driver, "I want to know about it."

Scott Hicks switched on the laser sighting mechanism of his M4 assault rifle. The other men did the same, thin red beams slicing the gloom of the hallway. He caught Jane's eye and tilted his head in a question. Ready?

Jane nodded back down to the stroller and bicycle, reminding the SWAT guys that there were children in the building, maybe in Herman Jones's apartment. "All yours, Scott."

The men had been briefed earlier and each knew his assignment cold. This wasn't going to be a polite door-knock maneuver. The guy inside was suspected of killing six people...one of them the nephew of a brother officer.

The battering ram team moved forward.

Hicks whispered "*Go!*" and they charged up the last step and along the hall to the rear unit. The other SWAT members, their rifles up and level, piled after them.

Jane and Kenny came to the next landing and stood back. Strict department protocol dictated that once a SWAT operation was underway, the SWAT Team leader was in charge.

The sixty-pound ram shattered the door to 3C and four armor-clad commandos swarmed inside, their rifles swinging back and forth like scythes, covering every possible angle.

A heavyset black woman, dressed in a sleeveless Garfield T-shirt and bicycle shorts, came running in from the bathroom. Scott Hicks motioned for her to hit the deck. But she didn't move. "I got babies in the tub." She was remarkably calm, as if this happened every day.

"How many?" Hicks demanded.

"Two. They's twin babies."

Hicks motioned for two of his men to enter the bathroom. Five seconds later, one of them poked his head out and gave the thumbs up.

The SWAT Team fanned out around the living room and down the short corridor to the single bedroom.

Jane and Kenny entered the dreary apartment just as SWAT Number Two emerged from the bedroom. "Clear."

The SWAT Team searched the rest of the place, tossing the couch and jabbing into the crawl space in the closet ceiling.

"The fuck you people want?" the woman yelled. She took a step toward the SWAT officer closest to her.

Four rifles pivoted simultaneously, four red laser dots playing on her chest.

"Stand down, ma'am," Scott Hicks ordered.

"Who gonna pay for my fuckin' door?" She took another step forward.

"Ma'am," Scott Hicks said firmly, "you have two choices: go into the bathroom with your babies and one of my men—"

"Or what, motherfucker?"

"Or we throw you down and cuff you until we secure this location. Babies or handcuffs. Up to you."

"They teach you this shit in pig school?" she asked. But her bravado was already slipping away. One of the cops stepped aside, offering her an open path to the bathroom, coaxing her into making the right decision. The woman turned to Jane. "I got babies in there," she hissed. "Shame on you."

Jane held her gaze. "Where's your husband?"

"The fuck do I know?" the woman spit. She pushed past the SWAT officer and went into the bathroom. "You still gotta pay for that door, motherfucker," she said as she left the room.

Kenny slipped his Glock into his shoulder holster. "Mother of the year."

One of the SWAT Team members called from the bedroom. "Got something."

Hicks and four of his men passed into the bedroom, Jane and Kenny on their heels.

A SWAT officer stood on a chair in the small closet, his head and shoulders partway through the access panel in the ceiling. "There's four, make that five, pistols up here. Plus a sawed-off." He jumped down off the chair, his broad shoulders scraping the side of the opening. As he did, a cloud of drywall dust billowed down behind him.

He laid the pistols on the bed and the shotgun across the pillows. "There's a shitload of ammo up there, too." He jutted his jaw back up to the hole in the closet ceiling.

As Jane followed his gesture, she noticed the dusty haze lingering in the room. It hung above them, then suddenly swirled and dissipated. The flimsy curtains danced in the light breeze coming in through the open window.

Jane did a quick catalog in her mind. All of the other windows in the apartment were closed. "Scott...Ken..." she whispered.

They turned to her and saw what she was looking at.

Scott Hicks gave a low, barely audible, whistle through his teeth and his men immediately turned to the sound. He pointed to the window and signaled for two men to go to each side.

As they did, Scott, Jane, and Kenny crouched down, their weapons trained on the window opening.

The men at the window looked to their leader.

He nodded.

One man from each side swung his rifle into the opening. They waited a beat. Nothing. Then their partners poked their heads through the open window. They both recoiled at the same instant.

"Holy shit," one of them said as he stumbled backward. "C'mere boss."

Scott Hicks moved to the window and looked down. The first thing he saw was eight fingernails clinging to the sill. A split second later, as his eyes focused and the impossible became possible, it registered that the fingernails belonged to the man who was staring up at him.

Herman Jones was hanging by his fingertips from a windowsill three stories above the back alley. The toes of his bare feet clung to the protruding brick header of a window of the apartment below.

"How you doin'?" Scott Hicks said.

Herman Jones strained to hold his grip. "I think I want to come in now."

Scott stood back as four of his men leaned out and dragged Herman Jones back into the bedroom. They threw him to the floor and cuffed him. As soon as he was restrained, one of the SWAT guys stood up. "'Scuse my saying, sir," he said to Scott Hicks, "but this guy *reeks*."

The others pulled Herman Jones to his feet. He was in his early twenties, and he wore an Oakland A's jersey and gray Adidas running pants. His shaved head glistened as sweat ran down his scalp and trickled to his mustache. He looked from the guns on his bed to Jane. "Them's plants. You cocksuckers brung 'em in here."

Jane felt Kenny tense up, his body coiling, as he stared at Herman Jones. For a moment she was afraid he was going to do something stupid, maybe strike a shackled suspect. She was about to say something when Kenny found his composure and turned to leave the room. As he did, another member of the SWAT Team came in with two large plastic bags. Water dripped from them, puddling on the bare floor with a dull *plip-plop* sound.

"Cocaine, Lieutenant. Close to five pounds."

"Where'd you find those?" Jane asked.

"Let's just say there was more than babies in that bathtub."

Jane shook her head. "Book the wife and call Social Services for the kids." She turned to Herman Jones. "You're in deep shit, son."

Herman Jones stared at her, a sad veil of recognition falling across his face. He slumped his shoulders and shuffled forward, a SWAT cop gripping each elbow.

Jane thumbed her two-way. "Location is secure. Suspect in custody."

Chief McDonald leaned forward and listened to the radio call. Then he looked through his open window and saw the SFPD support vehicles merge on the tenement.

"Get me Press Relations," he said as he raised his window.

16

"Oh, for God's sake."

Kenny slowed the Explorer as they turned onto Prince Street. The street was jammed with cops, reporters, and bystanders.

Jane sat up in her seat, peering over the top of the squad car carrying Herman Jones to Precinct Nineteen. The chief's Suburban was parked at the curb of the plaza and he was just emerging to a lightning show of camera flashes. On any ordinary day, he would have pulled into the protected parking garage and quietly gone upstairs. But this was no ordinary day and the chief was far from quiet.

The squad car pulled up to the police garage and waited while the sliding security gate cleared. A throng of television and newspaper cameramen swooped in. Bumping and banging the windows of the black-and-white, trying for that one iconic shot that would lead tonight's broadcast and be splashed over the Internet.

Herman Jones, strapped in and cuffed, looked back at them with dull hooded eyes. He sat between Scott Hicks and another SWAT officer, all three of them in bulletproof vests.

Jane and Kenny followed the cruiser into the garage. The reporters scrambled to the grated security fence for a clean shot of the prisoner transport elevator.

"Mr. Jones," Cameron Sanders called as the suspect was helped out of the police car, "why did you do it?"

Herman Jones turned to the voice, everything about his movement indicating he was going to reply. Then he lowered his head and whispered to Scott Hicks, "C'mon guys."

Hicks led him into the waiting elevator. The door closed, reflections of flashbulbs strobing off its stainless steel surface.

There was an odd moment of stillness now that the nexus of all this intensity had gone. Then Chief McDonald cleared his throat and announced, "Forty-eight hours, fellas. Those poor people were murdered something like forty-eight hours ago and we have a suspect in custody."

"A second suspect," a print journalist said. "What about Sammy Pickett?"

The chief didn't miss a beat. "Process of elimination. All part of the job. We've brought Herman Jones in for questioning. We've got witness testimony that might be helpful in this case. That's all for now."

This was followed by a barrage of rapid-fire questions. "Who is the witness?" "Was the motive robbery or murder?" "Are there any more suspects?" "What about DNA?"

Chief McDonald looked past the reporters and saw Jane and Kenny watching him through the fence. Something in him realized that maybe he should tone down the rhetoric just this once. "I'm needed upstairs, guys. Someone will be back down to update you in time for your deadlines." He turned away and strode into the building.

The news crews cleared the plaza, moving toward the media staging area. As they did, Jane tugged at Kenny's sleeve. "Let's go to work on Mr. Jones."

Kenny was just about to turn, when he spotted someone on the edge of the gathering crowd. His sister, Andrea, stood off to the side, her arms clutched around her waist. Still wearing the black dress from her son's funeral, she looked lost and alone.

Jane and Kenny buzzed themselves through the security gate and approached her. "Andy," Kenny said, pulling her into a hug. "What are you doing here?"

Andrea fought to keep from crying. "One of the limo drivers told his boss that something was happening. And he called me." She looked into Kenny's eyes. "Did that guy do it? Did he kill Bobby?"

"Nothing's for sure until it's for sure," Kenny said. "But we feel pretty good about this guy."

Andrea twisted out of Kenny's embrace. "I need you to do something for me, Ken."

"Name it."

"Keep that son of a bitch alive. I want to sit at his trial. I want to be there for his conviction and speak at his sentencing." She let her hands fall to her sides. "And then, when they execute him, I want to watch through the glass and see him die. I need for there to be no mistakes...I need to watch him die." She turned and started to walk away.

Jane caught up to her. "Can we have someone take you home?"

"Mom and Dad will." She nodded to the blue minivan parked across the street. Doris Marks sat at the wheel, watching them. Lloyd Marks dozed in the passenger seat, his left arm trembling in his lap.

Kenny kissed her on the forehead. "I'll be by tonight."

Andrea pulled away and crossed the street. She tugged at the sliding door of the minivan and climbed in. Doris pulled the car into gear and, her eyes staring straight ahead, drove slowly away.

"All our lives," Kenny said, "we'd argue about the death penalty. How it was unconstitutional, imperfect, not a deterrent..." He watched the minivan turn the corner and disappear.

As they turned back to the police station, Jane noticed someone standing between the KGO and CNN news trucks. He seemed out of place, somehow different in shape and size from everyone around him.

Edgar Silva was gazing up to the third floor of Precinct Nineteen. The Homicide floor. Moving only his eyes, he saw Jane looking at him.

"Ken," Jane said, "I left my vitamins in the car. Why don't you start the prelims on Herman Jones?"

"With pleasure." Kenny hurried across the plaza. Jane started to call out, when Kenny turned back to her. "And with restraint," he said as he ran into the building.

Jane watched him go, then turned and approached Edgar. "How did you know?"

"Small town."

Jane was surprised once again at how soft his voice was.

Edgar looked up to the third floor. "He the one?"

"We think so. We'll know better in a little while."

"And if he isn't?"

"We move on."

Edgar brought his eyes around to hers. "But that takes time. Wastes time."

"It's called due process," Jane said. "Everyone gets it."

"Not my brother...not your nephew."

"No," Jane agreed. "Not them...or the others. But it's my job to make the arrest stick. Without that, there's no justice...for anyone."

Edgar nodded slowly, digesting what she'd said. "Your people have been looking pretty hard for me. Does your husband still have a hair up his butt about me?"

Jane thought about mentioning the drugs that were found on Nico's body. But she decided that now wasn't the time. Besides, it might all be proved moot by Herman Jones. She sniffed a little laugh. "Actually? He does." She glanced up to the third floor. "Look, there's a lot of stuff going on right now, and I've got to get up there. I'll be in touch."

Edgar leaned forward slightly. "Or I will." He tilted his head in a gesture of respect and headed off down the sidewalk.

Jane studied him as he walked away. His pain trailing him like a ghost.

"Of *course* my client's prints and DNA were found at the first two Stella's," Jamaal Washington said. "He did, at one time or another, work at both of them."

Herman Jones stared at the chains securing him to the table in Interrogation Two. His attorney, Jamaal Washington—formerly Ernie Washington of Oakland, until he saw the light—tossed his head back, the colored beads on the ends of his dreadlocks clacking into each other.

Jane took a seat next to Craig Knowles at the video monitor while Kenny tried another angle. They'd been going at it like this for more than two hours, with Jamaal Washington either thwarting every approach or refusing to let his client answer even the simplest, most direct questions. As he did, he tried to surreptitiously inch his chair farther away from his client. Cabbage's body odor rapidly became the prevailing aroma in the tiny space.

"How 'bout this," Kenny began. He'd hated this lawyer since they had first crossed swords years ago on a rock-solid murder-one that Washington had gotten reduced to an involuntary. "Mr. Jones, did you or did you not kill Terrence Unger, Arthur Rourke, Antonia Salazar, Francis Cellucci, Nicolas Silva, and Robert Farrier?" He shot a look to Washington. "I can't get any more unadorned than that."

Herman Jones's head rocked as if he were praying. Then he raised his eyes up to Kenny, about to speak.

Jamaal Washington put his hand on his leg. "Don't answer that."

Kenny clenched his fists and drew a sudden teeth-clenched breath. “Why the hell not?”

“Fifth,” Jamaal Washington smirked.

Jane scraped back in her chair. “The Fifth Amendment is only pertinent if your client chooses to invoke it. You’re invoking it *for* him.”

“Then I’d say”—Washington smiled, his dark brown skin glistening—“Mr. Jones has an excellent lawyer.”

“How about,” Kenny said, “we pretend that the murder of six people, and Mr. Jones’s drug and weapons possession, and his attempted flight from arrest, *and* a witness’s testimony putting him at the second Stella’s robbery…have nothing to do with you. Or do you want to keep obstructing and get tossed from this case?”

Jane let the faintest flicker of a smile play at her lips.

The last thing in the world Jamaal Washington wanted was to be bounced from a high-profile, career-defining case like this. Whether or not his client was guilty—he didn’t really care one way or the other—this case promised a lot of face time for an ambitious attorney like him.

Jamaal Washington raised an eyebrow: *touché*. “I’m assuming in advance that your next question will be appropriately phrased.”

Kenny ignored him. “Okay, Mr. Jones, did you or did you not commit the robbery at the Stella’s on Pride Street and the robbery at the Stella’s on Comstock Avenue?”

Herman Jones swiveled in his seat to look at his attorney. Washington busied himself making notes on his legal pad.

“Mr. Jones?” Kenny prodded. “Yes or no?”

Herman Jones’s eyelids drooped as if he were falling asleep. Then he shrugged. “Maybe.”

Jamaal Washington’s head shot sideways. “‘Maybe?’ That’s your answer?”

"Yeah..."

"In my book," Kenny said, "maybe is yes."

Herman lifted his eyes to him. They were empty and resigned. He shrugged, then lowered his head.

Jane quietly absorbed the scene. "Herman," she said gently, "I'm going to ask you something, and you need to understand how important it is. Do you have an alibi for the time when the murders were committed at the Stella's on Carmody Avenue?"

Herman Jones sat still as stone. Then his hands suddenly twitched so badly that the chains rattled against the table. Jane watched as he wound the chains around his fingers, trying to keep his hands from fluttering. His lips parted slightly, the tip of his tongue touching his teeth as if he were about to speak. But he just closed his eyes and shook his head back and forth, beads of sweat changing direction on his shaved head.

"Mr. Jones..." Jane said, "what do you want to tell us?" She glanced over to Craig Knowles at the video setup. He turned up the gain on the volume. Just in case.

"I..." Herman Jones lifted a shoulder to his cheek, trying to wipe the sweat out of his eyes. "I don't got no alibi."

Jane and Kenny looked at each other.

Kenny stepped forward and put his hands on the table. "Mr. Jones, do you understand that, if you do have an alibi as to your whereabouts on the day and time in question, then you at least have a *chance* of beating a mass murder rap? A death penalty rap?"

Herman Jones breathed rapidly through his nose, a wet rasping sound. "Yeah, I understand."

"Then, sir," Jane said, "is it your statement that you still can't come up with an—"

"Damn it, lady!" Herman Jones pounded his fists onto the table. "I don't got no fuckin' alibi!"

Jamaal Washington started to rise. Jane clamped a hand on his shoulder, keeping him in the chair. Herman Jones's outburst was the first crack in his facade and she and Kenny were going to widen it.

Kenny closed in on the suspect, obsessed now, ignoring the smell. "Did you do it, Herman? Did you kill those people?"

Herman Jones stared deep into Kenny's eyes. "No."

"Then where were you? Who were you with?" Kenny pushed the point hard. "Tell me that and you've got an alibi."

Herman Jones strained against his chains, pulling and twisting them until his wrists chafed, the skin peeling pink. He tried to stand, but the shackles holding his ankles to the bolted-down chair held fast. Then he sagged, drained of all strength and defiance. "No alibi," he whispered.

Jamaal Washington ducked away from Jane's hand and shot to his feet. "Lieutenant Candiotti, Inspector Marks, I demand some time with my client."

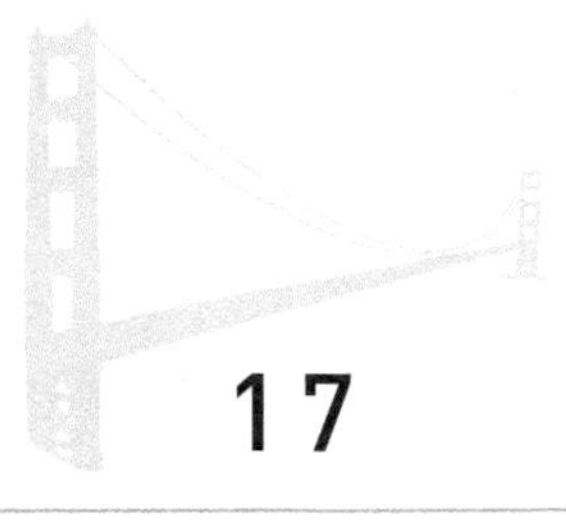

17

Jane and Kenny emerged from Interrogation Two as if coming out of an airlock.

The atmosphere in the bullpen was distinctly different, the air stirring and smelling of coffee. The late afternoon sun gilded the squad room in amber, Roz Shapiro going from window to window to draw the blinds.

Jane looked back to Herman Jones. He sat with his head bent forward at the neck as if it were some great weight he could no longer support. Jamaal Washington was talking intently into his ear, his dreadlocks quivering with each urgent inflection. Herman Jones nodded slowly, occasionally murmuring a low grunt of understanding.

"Why no alibi?" Jane asked Kenny. "Doesn't make sense."

"How 'bout this?" Kenny said as they made their way into the bullpen. "He has no alibi because he's the shooter and he's consumed with remorse or shame…or guilt. Any one of the above will do." He stopped to make his point. "Besides all the stuff we have on him, let's not forget that he was fired by Stella's management. The word *disgruntled* comes to mind. Disgruntled druggie just about fits our profile."

"Just about." Jane noticed Aram Hagopian with Lou Tronick and Mike Finney at the observation window to Interrogation Two. She motioned for Lou to join them. "Did he ID the suspect?" she asked as he came up.

"It's a positive, Jane," Lou said. They turned to watch as Mike Finney escorted the witness to the elevators.

Aram Hagopian walked quickly, his eyes holding on to the elevator doors as if they would save him from drowning in his own disgrace. The doors opened just as he got there and he hurried inside. Without looking back into the squad room, unable to meet the condemnation of Kenny's eyes, he anxiously jabbed at the lobby button and stared at the floor until the doors finally closed.

"Another fine citizen," Kenny said.

Craig Knowles came out of his closet-sized tech lab and handed Jane a flash drive. "Mr. Jones isn't exactly the easiest subject to record. But I got it all. Especially when you got him going."

"Thanks, Craig." Jane turned to Lou. "I need you to take this over to Colleen Porter's hospital room."

"Freezer girl?"

Jane nodded. "Play it for her. See if she recognizes the voice. But go easy on her. She's pretty fragile."

"Who wouldn't be?" Lou Tronick slipped the drive into the pocket of his suit coat and headed toward the stairwell door. Just as he got there, the door was pushed open from the other side and Robbery Inspector Eliot Friedman stepped into the bullpen.

"Hey, guys," he said as he approached Jane and Kenny, a Starbucks cup in one hand, a crumbling scone in the other. He held the scone out to them. "Want some? It's blueberry."

"No thanks," Jane said.

Kenny shook his head. "Tempting, but…"

"Fine." Friedman dumped the scone into the wastebasket next to Finney's desk and scraped at a dusting of crumbs on his lapel. "Got some news for ya on your Stella's arrest. Actually, Neil Kenyan does."

Jane didn't like the tone in Friedman's voice. "I thought he was in Australia."

"He is. S'why we need to use your videophone. He's standing by. Middle of the night for him there. Or it's yesterday. I can never remember." He slurped his cappuccino, a faint milk-moustache tracing his upper lip.

"What kind of news?" Kenny asked.

Eliot Friedman wiped his mouth with his sleeve. "Not good."

The tech lab was so small that there was room for only Jane to sit down.

She sat facing the monitor, the digitized face of Neil Kenyan filling the screen from a similar room at Royal Police Headquarters in Sydney. "Neil," Jane said. "Can you hear me?"

"And see you. Did Eliot tell you what's going on?"

Eliot Friedman leaned in front of Jane. "Leaving that to you, Neil." He stood back out of the way again.

"Okay, here's the deal," Neil began. "I saw on CNN that you brought in a suspected perp on the Stella's shootings. By the way, Jane, please tell Ken how sorry I am for his loss."

Jane glanced up to Kenny. He stood in the doorway, his mood souring at the prospect of bad news. "I will, thanks."

"Anyways, when I saw about the collar, I called one of my guys over at Robbery about the holdback."

"Shit," Kenny muttered.

"You guys kept a holdback?" Jane asked. "On both robberies?"

"'Fraid so, Jane," Neil Kenyan said. "In each of the first two hits, the perp used an employee code to get into the cash register. Then he whacked at it with a screwdriver or something to make it look like he broke in. But the computers in the registers recorded the code, so the screwdriver thing was just a cover. We held that info back so the perp wouldn't know we had narrowed down the cast of characters." The image on the monitor rolled once, then corrected itself. “Actually, your Herman Jones was high on our list, but he’d been out of town when we came knockin’. Then I had to come down here on this extradition, and it just sort of was put on hold.”

Jane leaned forward. “Was the employee code used in the Carmody hit?”

“No, Jane, it wasn’t. So you got a different M.O. and no witnesses to the deed.”

“None living anyway,” Eliot Friedman said. He immediately realized it was the wrong thing to say in front of Kenny and pressed himself back into the corner.

“I’m not saying Jones isn’t your guy,” Neil Kenyan went on. “From what I can tell, he’s a good candidate. Total hard-core loser with a major drug history. But I thought you should know about the holdback as you build your case. Wouldn’t want some overly ambitious public defender blindsiding you.”

“Thanks, Neil. Travel safe.” Jane swiveled the chair around while Craig Knowles disconnected the satellite patch with Sydney.

Kenny pushed away from the doorjamb. “I still got a feeling about this guy.”

“Then we’ll play it out,” Jane said. “Let’s go talk to Dave Siegler.”

Eliot Friedman drained his coffee and put the empty cup down next to Craig Knowles’s keyboard. “Siegler, the Stella’s guy? We tried talking to him about the first two hits. The man’s impossible to talk to.”

Jane started out of the tiny room. “Yeah? Well, I’ve got six good reasons why he’ll talk to us.”

“How can I help you, Lieutenant?” Dave Siegler asked, his voice infused with just the appropriate amount of diffidence.

Jane turned up the volume on her speakerphone. She sat at her desk, her elbows on the blotter, her chin in her hands. Kenny sat on the arm of the guest chair, leaning in.

"This is a call, Mr. Siegler," Jane began, "about cash register codes. Our Robbery Division just told us that, in the first two Stella's incidents, the perpetrator accessed the registers by punching in a designated employee code."

"I was told that too," Dave Siegler said. There was a faint *click* and the static of the call fell away. Then another *click* and it returned. Jane and Kenny knew that Siegler was using the Mute button on his phone to consult with someone—most likely his lawyer.

"When were you told that, sir?" Jane asked.

"After the first robbery."

"Sir, this is Inspector Marks. Did you have the code changed after the first robbery?"

"No, can't say that I did."

Jane raised her eyes toward Kenny. "How about after the second one?"

Click. Silence. *Click*. "Not then either."

Cheryl Lomax appeared in the doorway with sandwiches, drinks, and some late incoming mail. Jane held up a finger: wait a minute. "Why not, Mr. Siegler?"

"The truth? It's too much trouble. Stella's hires thousands of minimum wage employees who can barely speak English. I mean, I have to put *pictures* of the food items on the cash registers so they don't screw up the sales. I change the register code? It'd take these...people...months to catch on. And we just can't afford that."

Jane caught Kenny's eye and mouthed the word *asshole*.

"Sad part of all this is?" Dave Siegler continued.

"What's that?" Kenny asked.

"My sales people tell me no one will go near the Carmody location again. Now I have to close that store permanently. Too bad—it was a good site."

"Shouldn't be too much of a hardship," Jane said. "You still have a hundred and twenty others."

"Hundred twenty-four."

"Thanks for your time, Mr. Siegler." Jane held her hand over the speakerphone Off button.

"I'm here to help, Lieutenant."

Jane pressed the button, made sure the call had disconnected, and rocked back in her chair. "*Such* an asshole."

Cheryl set the food down on the coffee table. "You left out racist. That fella's in serious need of a little consciousness raising." She unwrapped a sandwich and put it on Jane's desk. "Turkey salad. And girl? You better be eating this, with the hours you're clocking and the baby you're cooking." She tossed the mail into Jane's in-box.

Jane let her chair fall forward and reached for the sandwich. "Thanks, Cheryl." She glanced at the mail and noticed that Roz Shapiro had put Tommy Murphy's Homicide application in the box. She suppressed a mild chuckle at the thought of that young kid trying to leapfrog all the way up to Homicide after just three years on Patrol.

"'S'only half of it."

"What's the other?"

"You getting some rest. I been around enough to know that if Herman Jones did this terrible thing, then he can cool his jets all night long. And if he didn't…well, you ain't gonna just go out there tonight and bust the next guy. Hell, you don't even *have* a next guy. Hence, Jane, do yourself and your baby right and get some rest."

Jane bit into her sandwich and smiled. "Thanks, Mom."

"You think I had six kids by accident?" Cheryl said, then added quickly, "Okay, maybe the last two. But I know what I'm talking about here." She put her hand on Kenny's shoulder and gave it a gentle squeeze. "You take care of your family, Ken." She plunked a bottled water down on Jane's desk and left.

Kenny peeled the wax paper back from his sandwich. "Okay, reviewing before I chase you out of here."

"What about you?"

"I'm gonna hang and work on Herman Jones." He pried the lid off his iced tea. "If I can handle the smell. Then I'm going over to Andrea's."

"Where are you sleeping tonight?"

"At home...with my wife."

"Good answer. Okay, reviewing. If Herman Jones did the first two robberies—and we're pretty sure he did—and he used the register codes, then why didn't he use the code at the third one?"

"Maybe he panicked," Kenny offered.

"He doesn't seem like the panicking type to me."

"Me either. But it was a volatile mix of people he had down there. Anything could have happened. Any one of them could have set him off. The priest, Nico, maybe even Bobby. That's why I want to keep grilling him. Also, the longer I keep Herman Jones in that room, the longer I keep Ernie, 'scuse me, Jamaal Washington, in that room and away from the TV cameras."

"Fair enough," Jane said. "Okay, floating a balloon so you don't get ambushed in there. We have hair and fibers from dozens of people at the Carmody Stella's. So far nothing links back to Jones."

"Those kinds of Forensics are only instruments of inclusion," Kenny said. "They're not necessarily instruments of exclusion."

"Right," Jane nodded. "Which brings me back to the alibi thing. Or lack thereof."

"I'll grant that part's a little funky. But if this guy isn't going to alibi-up, then he's protecting someone else. And, if that's true, I want to know who it is."

Jane finished the first half of her sandwich. "You, Inspector, are a good cop."

Kenny rose and came around the desk. Jane swiveled the chair around to face him. She opened her arms and brought him in close. Kenny bent over and kissed her on the nose. Then the lips.

"And you, Lieutenant, are going home."

18

Jane stood at the elevator bank and watched as Kenny returned to Interrogation Two.

Through the open doorway, she saw Jamaal Washington pacing the room like a bear in a too-small cage. Herman Jones sat side-slumped against the wall, his sweaty shaved head greasing an irregular circle into the dimpled acoustic tile, his chained hands motionless in his lap. He raised his eyes when Kenny came in, then looked down and resumed his staring contest with the metal tabletop.

Kenny clicked the door closed, ready for round two.

Jane turned at the soft ping of the elevator arriving. As the doors opened, she was surprised to see Bill Glazer leaning against the back corner of the car. "Hey, Bill. Working late?"

"Aren't we all?" Dr. Glazer was the chief SFPD psychiatrist. In his midfifties, he had neatly trimmed gray hair and habitually wore one of two corduroy sport jackets regardless of the season or the temperature. A pair of stainless-steel reading glasses hung loosely around his neck. Suspended by a tricolored Reggae strap that one of his kids had given him, they looked like a harmonica he was always just about to play.

Jane stepped in and pressed the button for the secure parking level. "What are you doing in my part of the world?"

"I was upstairs meeting with a couple of the nightshift guys who were on-scene at the Stella's shooting. One of them, Mac Steiner, is still so shaky he wants to ride a desk for a while. So

I was helping him with the paperwork." He held up a fistful of departmental files. "Hell, it's easier to take early retirement than it is to take a few days off for psych leave."

The elevator doors closed and the car began its descent. Jane and Bill watched the number panel, caught in an unexpected fissure of silence. The elevator slowed, then stopped at the lobby. The doors parted and Dr. Glazer nodded to Jane as he stepped out. " 'Night, Lieutenant."

"You take care, Doctor." Jane pushed the parking level button again.

Just as the doors were about to close, Bill Glazer turned back and held them open with his free hand. "Jane," he said quickly, "can we have a little off-the-record non-conversation?"

"Of course we can."

Dr. Glazer leaned against the elevator's rubber door bumper, keeping it open. "I consulted on the California Street shootings and these Stella's murders are the worst I've seen since. What they did to the first responders. There's one guy who I know you know and he's kind of messed up and…well, he…"

"Who is it, Bill?" Jane asked, smoothing the way for him.

Dr. Glazer hesitated. "Problem is, naming names is about as unprofessional as you can get."

"First of all," Jane said, "anything we discuss will be held in the strictest confidence. But besides that, if naming a name is going to help someone, then isn't that what professionalism is all about?"

The corners of Bill Glazer's eyes crinkled into a smile. "Okay, thanks. I've been talking to the first two uniforms on-scene. In fact, they both mentioned that you suggested they see me."

"Rick Weymouth and…" Jane searched her weary brain for the other cop's name.

Bill slipped his reading glasses on and riffled through a few pages. "And Tommy Murphy. But Rick's the one who's the more rattled of the two. Keeps talking about how if only this and if only that, they could have gotten there sooner. One of the victims, as I'm sure you know, died in his arms, and he's having a hard time shaking it."

"I remember he was pretty dented that day and then again when he showed for his debriefing. Do me a favor. I kinda know him through his dad. Former cop. Keep an eye on him for me, will ya?"

"Sure thing. But messed up as he is?" Bill continued. "It's the other one I'm worried about."

"Murphy? How come? Seemed like he was coping pretty well."

"That's the problem. He *seems* to be coping. He's got all the mechanisms in place, but there's something evasive about it at the same time. As affected as Weymouth is by the trauma, he's at least dealing. Murphy is what we call disassociating. Sort of floating on the surface of the pain without letting himself get wet. He's obviously a smart guy and he seems like a good cop. I'd just hate for something like this to stop him in his tracks." Bill Glazer took a half step into the car and lowered his voice. "Exacerbating the whole thing? His commander at Fifteen is this Semper Fi asshole, Chuck Hollingsworth. As enlightened as an ape. Let's just say he's less than enthusiastic about cops on his watch doing something as faggy as seeing a shrink." His cell phone vibrated on his hip. He checked the readout. "The wife. She's waiting up."

"Thanks for telling me this," Jane said. "I know it wasn't easy for you."

Dr. Glazer retreated back into the lobby and let go of the door bumper. "It's not about me, Jane." He hoisted the papers in his hand. "It's only about them."

He turned and crossed toward the security desk to sign out, his shoulders heavy and his back bent from all the secrets he carried.

A rush of cool air swept into the elevator as the doors opened at the parking level.

Jane fish-hooked her car keys out of her bag with her index finger and headed down the first row of parking spaces. The garage was virtually empty, just a few vehicles here and there. Some overtime guys and some night-shift regulars still grinding away upstairs.

As she passed Kenny's Explorer, she thought she saw a subtle movement reflected in its rear window. She slowed, craning her neck around to the vast emptiness behind her. There, in the shadow of a concrete pillar, was the partial indistinct outline of a man. Jane stopped, tensing as her eyes adjusted to the contrast of dark and light.

The human form found its definition, and Jane relaxed as she understood who she was looking at. "This is a secure police parking facility," Jane said. "How did you get in here?"

Edgar Silva gave her an inscrutable smile. The light from the overhead halogens glinted off his eyes as he looked down from her face to her midsection. "How far along are you, Lieutenant?"

Most of the people in her own squad room didn't even know Jane was pregnant. "Just finished my first trimester."

"I wish you a beautiful and healthy child." Edgar almost bowed. "Although the beautiful part is a given." He was wearing a tight black T-shirt and black jeans.

"Thank you, Mr. Silva. But, if you're not going to tell me how you got in here, will you tell me *why* you're here?"

"Yesterday was my little brother's birthday."

"Yes, I remember."

"And tomorrow is his funeral."

Jane waited. Edgar Silva was clearly here to talk. She'd let the words come.

"That's two brothers I'll have buried. I don't have any more." His voice was silk wrapped around steel. "Herman Jones didn't alibi, did he?"

In spite of herself, Jane grinned in surprise.

Edgar nodded. "No way he could."

"How do you know?"

"People talk to me. Bad people." Edgar showed a stripe of perfect white teeth. "Used t' be one myself."

"I know all about that."

"Not all, Lieutenant," Edgar said. "Not even close to all. Just what's in my record." A patrol car drove slowly past, two cops going graveyard. Without seeming to move, Edgar Silva turned his face away from them until all they could possibly have seen was the back of his head. A move born on the streets of the Tenderloin.

"Those bad people?" Edgar continued once the squad car had passed through the security gate. "They told me Jones didn't do it. They told me he was somewhere else that day. And while you're doing your process of elimination cop thing? You're wasting time...and the trail is getting colder."

"Where do your people say Herman Jones was?"

"At the docks in San Rafael. Dock Twenty-Eight to be specific. Muling a shipment of coke. Serious weight."

And now Jane understood. If Edgar was right, then Herman Jones was royally fucked. "So," she said, clicking the pieces together, "Jones tells us where he really was that day and rats out the dealer, and then he's dead...and so are his wife and kids."

"And so are his parents and his wife's parents and his cousins and...well, these people tend to be comprehensive."

Jane ran the scenario in her mind. Years ago, when she was just coming up, a family of nine was massacred in a garage down in Daly City. The wife's brother had turned state's against a Mexican drug lord and the family was wiped out, three children under the age of five included.

"Your Mr. Jones," Edgar went on, "doesn't want whoever he's working for going all comprehensive on his wife and babies. So he'll take the sucker's hard fall on this one."

Jane started back toward the door. "I don't guess you'd care to come upstairs while I try this out on my suspect."

"I'm afraid I'll have to decline."

Jane grabbed the doorknob. "But if I get the reaction I think I'm gonna get from Herman Jones, I still need some proof. I can't exactly bring into court the word of…"

"An ex-con?"

"A victim's relative," Jane said. "A relative with a hard-assed agenda of his own."

"I have only one item on my agenda, Lieutenant." Edgar was already backing into the shadows, his features becoming less distinct. "And that is to find whoever did this…and end his life." He was almost gone now, just eyes and teeth and a voice. "You go up there and see what you see with your suspect. It goes down the way I think it will? I'll be at the Dagwood Diner on Pleasant Street." Another step back. "And I'll have something for you."

"I know the place." Jane pulled the door open. "What will you have for me?"

"Proof."

Edgar Silva retreated into the shadows and was gone.

"You disobeying Mama?"

Cheryl Lomax was just forwarding her Dispatch calls to the night shift over at the Hall of Justice when Jane walked back in.

Jane gestured toward Interrogation Two. "They still in there?"

"Going strong." Cheryl handed Jane a note. "Lou Tronick called. That Colleen Porter girl? She didn't recognize the voice on the tape. Said you'd know what that means." She switched off her desk lamp. "Tell me you're back here 'cause you forgot something."

"I need Ken for a minute," Jane said. "Then I'm outta here." She glanced into the war room as she crossed the bullpen. There were maybe a dozen people in there, organizing files, working the phones. Mike Finney looked up from watching the videographer's recording of the crime scene and gave her a solemn nod. There was a glaze of tears in his eyes; probably, Jane thought, a combination of compassion and exhaustion. This case was a hell of a way to break into Homicide.

Jane looked through the observation window of Interrogation Two. Herman Jones was bent over at the waist, his forehead on the metal table. Jamaal Washington was hunched over him, talking into his ear. There was a tech Jane hadn't seen before working the video equipment. Kenny, his tie undone, his shoulder holster empty, stood against the far left wall, waiting for Washington to finish with his client.

She rapped a quick one-two and stepped back. Kenny opened the door, his eyebrows rising in surprise at seeing her. "Thought you were going home."

"I ran into someone. How's it going in there?"

"Brick wall." Kenny came into the squad room and drew the door closed. "Ran into who?"

"Edgar Silva."

"And?" Kenny asked evenly.

"And…he said the reason Herman Jones won't alibi-up is he was muling a mountain of cartel coke up in San Rafael at the same time as the murders."

Kenny chewed his bottom lip, processing. "And he knows this deepest and darkest of secrets, exactly how?"

"I'm not sure. But I want to run his theory by the brick wall in there and see if we get a rise." She reached for the doorknob.

"I hate this shit, Jane."

"Why? Because Edgar Silva is a con or because his brother sold Bobby drugs?"

"Maybe both."

Jane put her hand on Kenny's chest. "Ken, the point is, neither one ultimately matters if we find the killer. You said it yourself: Herman Jones might be protecting someone. Well, that someone could be his own family if his only options are to take the fall or alibi-up and get them all killed." She turned the knob. "And if this turns out to be a bullshit lead, then I promise you I'll do everything I can—break the rules or make new ones—to nail Herman Jones's ass to the wall."

She opened the door and entered Interrogation Two.

Jamaal Washington looked up from the table as Jane and Kenny came in. "When are you gonna let us out of here? This is bordering on cruel and unusual."

Herman Jones was still bent forward, his forehead on the edge of the table.

"I have only one more question for your client, Mr. Washington," Jane said. "He answers truthfully, we call it a night." She looked over the tech's shoulder to make sure he was recording. "Mr. Jones."

"Hmm." Something between a grunt and a growl.

"Mr. Jones," Jane continued, "we've offered you the opportunity to alibi your whereabouts for the time of the Carmody shootings."

"Mm-hmm."

"Sir, we have good information that, at that specific time, you were actually at Dock Twenty-Eight in San Rafael, bringing in a load of cocaine by way of Mexico."

Jamaal Washington started to stand. Jane sat him down and shut him up with a withering look. "Mr. Jones?" she went on, "is that where you were? Is that why you're willing to take this fall?" She advanced on him. "Are you protecting your family?"

Jane sat on a hard folding chair and watched Herman Jones's back as it rose and fell with his breathing. "You take your time, sir." She let her eyes travel along his yellow County jumpsuit to his feet. He was wearing paper prison slippers. A dark wet spot appeared on the top of his right slipper. Then another. Another drop splashed between his feet. Herman Jones was crying. His tears falling from his lowered head to the floor.

"Mr. Jones?" Jane said, her voice just this side of a whisper.

Herman Jones brought his head up slowly and turned to look at her. He blinked his eyes and a rush of tears coursed down his cheeks.

"Sir, this is the last time I'll ask," Jane said. "Will you talk to us?"

Herman Jones dropped his chin forward until it touched his chest. He shook his head and murmured. "Can't."

Jane stood up and looked to Jamaal Washington. "We cool?"

Washington nodded. "We're cool, Lieutenant." His voice was hushed by the power of what he'd just seen.

Everyone in the room, with the possible exception of Herman Jones, understood that nobody was going to be allowed to take a fall on a case of this magnitude. Someone pleading guilty or failing to come up with an alibi wasn't what they were looking for. This wasn't about balancing the books; this was only about finding the killer.

Jane opened the door and stepped into the bullpen. Kenny brushed past her and went to his desk. He unlocked the bottom drawer, retrieved his Glock and jammed it into his shoulder holster. Then he grabbed his coat off the back of his chair.

"Where are you going?" Jane asked.

"With you."

"And where am I going?"

Kenny pulled on his jacket. "Back to Edgar Silva. You got the rise you wanted out of Herman Jones, but we can't exactly bring Silva in to corroborate." He started for the stairwell door. "Therefore you need his source...and I want to be there."

Jane caught up to him. "Ken, listen to me. I bring you along and Edgar Silva is gonna shut down like a dying clam. And then where are we? A prime suspect we're pretty sure is taking a bad rap to save his own family and an informant whose trust we just blew out of the water and who won't take us to the next step. That's a lot of nothing on nothing. And worse than that? We'll never be sure about Herman Jones."

Kenny filled his lungs with air and blew it out in a long frustrated gust. He pulled open the stairwell door and stepped aside. "I'll back off on Silva," he said. "But no way you go to his source without me."

"Fair enough." Jane started for the stairwell.

Kenny caught her hand and turned her to him. "No heroes."

Jane smiled and nodded. "No heroes."

"You were right," Jane said.

Edgar shrugged. "Happens."

"You know my problem, Mr. Silva. I can't very well—"

"Pepe Rodriguez," Edgar said quickly. "He's the next stop on the Herman Jones train."

"Who is he and where can I find him?"

Edgar Silva and Jane sat in the corner booth. He turned his glass of milk in tight circles. The napkin beneath, wet with condensation, rotating with it.

Jane wrapped her hands around a chipped white mug of coffee. She knew she wasn't going to have any caffeine, but something about the smells of the Dagwood Diner made her want to breathe in the steam of real coffee.

"Jose 'Pepe' Rodriguez is about as deep into the drug culture in Northern California as you can get and not be doing hard time down in Shanley."

"Sounds like a charmer. What is he, buyer or seller?"

"Bit of both." Edgar almost smiled, the line of startling white teeth peeking through. "He's DEA."

Jane's eyes widened. "He's a narc?"

Edgar sipped his milk. "Isn't that the point, Lieutenant? You need an unassailable witness to Herman Jones's whereabouts. Who better than an undercover, surveillance happy, danger-junkie cop?"

Jane caught her breath. "'Surveillance happy'? You mean he has video of Herman Jones at the time and place?"

"Digital. Pepe's known in your world as Oja De Aguila… Eagle Eye," Edgar said. "The man lives for his cameras. He's also an arrogant prick, but you should learn to love him. He's all you got." Edgar put the glass back down, lining up its circumference with the circle on the napkin. "Part of me wishes I'd been wrong about all this."

"Me, too." Jane brushed her hand through the steam, bringing it closer. "Then we'd have the bad guy and our only worry would be building the case."

A waitress stood over their table, scratching her forearm. "Somethin' else for yas?" Without waiting for an answer, she slapped a check down in front of Edgar. He flattened a five-dollar bill on top of it and slid it under the chrome napkin dispenser.

"Thank you," Jane said.

"You're a cheap date, Lieutenant." Edgar's voice was soft and thin. "You're welcome."

Jane brought the mug to her lips and touched her tongue to the dark liquid. Although there couldn't possibly have been enough caffeine to affect her or her baby, it felt as if she were crossing some invisible threshold. "I need to tell you something."

Edgar opened his hand, gesturing with his palm. "Go on."

"We found drugs and money, lots of both, on your brother's body. Dealer amounts. And one of his customers appears to have been my nephew."

Edgar pushed his glass away and sat back against the booth. "That the reason your husband has it in for me?"

"Among others."

"In his cop logic," Edgar said, "if I'm a better influence on Nico, then he's not dealing. More than that, my brother was responsible for Bobby being at that Stella's when it all went down."

"Right."

"Where I'm coming from? If someone, maybe even his cop uncle, had even a little sway on your nephew, my baby brother would have been somewhere else, too. Maybe not doing good things, but he'd still be alive. Point is, it's a waste of time to pull these where and when mind trips."

"In your opinion," Jane said, "could the hit at Stella's have been related to Nico's involvement in the drug world?"

Edgar reached across the table and took Jane's coffee mug. "One little taste, Lieutenant, can lead to the next one. Before you know it, you've got a problem." He spooned in a heaping sugar and stirred. "That shooting wasn't about drugs or my brother."

"How can you be sure?"

"Two things. Nico was small-time. No one's going to waste six people and bring the cops down on them for a low-level operator like him."

"What's the other?"

Edgar drank Jane's coffee, draining half of the mug in one pull. "Like I told you before...if it had anything to do with my world, the shooter knows he'd have to answer to me." He finished the coffee and set the mug down on the table. "You go talk to Pepe. Learn what you learn. Then keep pushing this rock up the hill." He slid out of the booth and stood up. "One thing though, I'd appreciate it if you'd keep me informed about what you come up with."

Jane slipped her bag over her shoulder and rose. "I'm not supposed to do that."

"And I wasn't supposed to do this. Any of it." Edgar put his hand flat against the small of her back and guided her to the front door. "Make no mistake, Lieutenant, I will do anything, go through anyone—even you—to get to my brother's killer. The only way I won't be part of the solution is if you get to him first." He pulled open the door. "For his sake, pray that you do."

They stepped out into the cooling night. Jane turned to Edgar. "Let's be clear about something, Mr. Silva. Don't make the mistake of thinking that because I'm a woman or that because I'm pregnant that I, in any way, will be less than ferocious in my attention to this case or the pursuit of this killer. This is as personal to me as it is to you. My job has become my mission."

Edgar rolled down the sleeves of his T-shirt one turn each, his response to the chill of the night air. "When it all hits the fan, Lieutenant, I hope you mean that."

Jane dug her keys out of her purse. "Let's just get it that far."

19

"See Daddy's Beamer down there? The little angels are about to score fifty large of smacko primo."

Pepe Rodriguez sat cross-legged on the roof of an abandoned hardware store. He had a furniture pad spread beneath him, more to protect his surveillance gear than his clothes. After checking the focus on his video, he fired off a half dozen frames with his long-lens still camera. He was in his midthirties and wound tight as a steel cable. The toe of his left Nike high-top bounced nonstop in an adreno-charged *rat-a-tat.*

Jane and Kenny squatted down a few feet away from Pepe, behind the raised facade of the storefront. A walkie-talkie on the ground next to them buzzed a breath of static, then a *click*, then went silent again. A coded signal.

Rodriguez pivoted the video camera hard to the left. "Ah, punctual. I like that in a drug dealer."

On the street below, a black kid, maybe twenty with a skull-tight Oakland Raiders do-rag on his head, rounded the corner at the old bank building. He had a backpack slung over his left shoulder. His right hand was thrust deep in his jacket pocket. "Uh-oh, the mule's packing heat," Rodriguez observed. "The angel cakes better be careful or he could go all worst-case scenario on their asses."

The driver of the BMW flashed his lights once, a swift illumination of the tumbledown row of boarded up windows, then crept forward. "These boys've seen *Traffic* one too many times," Rodriguez clicked off ten more frames.

The car closed in on the black kid. A quick volley of words. A flash of money, a show of merchandise. The exchange.

"Nice," Pepe Rodriguez singsonged as he watched through the video camera. "Now for the coup de." He held something to his mouth and blew. The screeching sound of a bird of prey cut the stillness. The two clean-cuts and the black kid all looked up, turning to find the sound. "Show me them pretty faces boys. Ah...there you go." He pushed in on the lens and captured each kid's face full-on. Then he picked up the walkie-talkie. "Deal is done. Pin the tail."

"Got it, Peps," a static-shrouded voice responded.

The black kid slipped the money envelope into his backpack and turned back up the street. The BMW swung a three-point U-turn, its front bumper just missing a junker Oldsmobile station wagon, and headed the other way. When it reached the corner, the Oldsmobile wagon crept forward, its headlights off, and followed the college kids. "Moving out," came the same voice again.

Pepe Rodriguez squeezed the mic. "Roger that, dude." He turned to Jane and Kenny, flashing a gold-toothed smile. "You were saying?"

Kenny pointed toward the old bank at the corner where the black kid was taking off his do-rag. "What about that one?"

"Him? He works for me." Rodriguez let out a little laugh. "Kids gotta make scratch for college any way they can. The whole socioeconomic thing."

Jane looked down to the bank. The black kid was gone. She turned back to Pepe. "We need your help on the Stella's killings."

"Name it." Pepe started breaking down his surveillance equipment.

"The day of the massacre," Kenny said, "you had cameras going at Dock Twenty-Eight up in San Rafael. We have information that you surveilled our prime suspect at the same time the shootings went down. Which would take him out of contention."

Rodriguez opened two foam-lined metal suitcases. "Don't tell me: he's not alibi-ing 'cause he's afraid of his own little massacre."

"Something like that," Jane said. "We want your tape, so we can know whether or not to move on."

"We push the prosecution button on the wrong guy," Kenny said, "the real killer walks."

Pepe twisted the telephoto lens off the still camera and laid it in its carved-out foam silhouette. "The San Rafael gig was just one cog in a four-year-deep undercover operation. We're talking upwards of a billion dollars' worth of shit coming in, then moving down to LA, up to Seattle, out to Denver…all over the place. This is a highest priority investigation with the highest level of authority. As in federal. There are a lot of careers gonna get made off this one. Accent on mine." He closed the smaller of the two suitcases and latched it. "Sorry, Lieutenant. I'd like to help, but your suspect chose to run with the big boys and this is what happens." He unfastened the video camera from its tripod.

"I've got six people dead, Rodriguez," Jane persisted. "I need that tape."

"I appreciate the dilemma, Lieutenant. But it's yours, not mine." Rodriguez hefted the video camera and turned away from her.

Jane lashed out with her right hand and yanked at his elbow. "Don't you fucking turn your back on me."

Pepe Rodriguez lost his grip on the video camera. It fell to the rooftop, the lens and a piece of its housing snapping off. Rodriguez reflexively pulled his arm out of Jane's grasp and looked down at his shattered equipment. Then he brought his eyes back up to Jane. "S'okay. This shit's confiscated anyway.

Drugheads have better stuff than we could ever begin to afford." He bent down to collect the pieces. "Answer's still no."

Exasperated, Kenny moved in on him, his hands reaching across the void. In a blur of motion, Rodriguez bolted upright and had a chrome .38 snub-nose shoved into Kenny's stomach. "Don't be going all Dirty Harry on me, Inspector. You can't bully me and you can't threaten me. Read my lips: it ain't happening."

Jane put her hand on Kenny's arm. Then she turned to Pepe. "Put that thing away, Rodriguez. This macho violence crap isn't going to get us anywhere."

Rodriguez showed some gold in a thin smile and slipped his weapon into its clamshell at the small of his back. "Nice talking to you guys." He flipped the second suitcase closed, grabbed one in each hand, and squatted down to lift them. As he did, Jane threw a quick look to Kenny, then jammed her heel into his chest and sent him tumbling backward. Before Rodriguez could react, Kenny had a foot on his neck and a vise-grip on his collar. Jane reached behind him and pulled his snub-nose out of its holster. She tossed it aside, the steel gun skittering on the tarpaper and disappearing into the darkness.

Kenny stepped off and dragged Rodriguez to his feet. Pepe looked in the direction of the snub-nose. "That's confiscated, too." He stood up slowly and looked to Jane. "Thought you was all antiviolence?"

"To a point."

"Things're escalating, Lieutenant. To dangerous proportions." Pepe's leg twitched, junkie synapses firing.

"Way your foot's going," Kenny said, "looks like video stuff and guns aren't all you've been confiscating."

"How boring," Jane said, "a narc with a taste for the product. Who's been watching too much *Traffic* now, Rodriguez?" She advanced on him. "Listen up, 'cause this is a onetime offer. Actually, it's not an offer, it's what you'd call a threat." Another step closer. "You don't give me that San Rafael tape, I blow the whistle on your entire operation. Your billion-dollar, four-year gig goes all to shit. The Feds will be…disappointed. Then it's scapegoat time. Accent on you. And your precious goddamn career hits a wall going ninety."

"You do that," Rodriguez seethed, "and both our careers are over."

"Difference between us?" Jane spit the words at him. "Only one of us cares."

Pepe Rodriguez stared at Jane, hatred and rage burning as he played out his options. He sucked on his lower lip, making a tiny clucking sound, and slowly shook his head. Finally, almost imperceptibly, his shoulders sagged.

Colleen Porter was snoring.

The low-dose sedative the nurse had given her to control her nightmares had finally taken effect. The doctors would meet after tomorrow morning's rounds to discuss when to release her. Then they'd have whichever cop was on door-duty get in touch with the Homicide people.

Sarah Mercer had been a nurse in this ward for fifteen years and Colleen Porter was the first patient she'd ever seen who had a policeman outside her door twenty-four-seven. She was also the first patient Sarah could remember who'd never had even one visitor, family or friend. That poor girl. Every time she seemed to be making a little progress, some cop comes by to ask her questions or play a tape for her. And then she'd backslide a little, worrying about this pet or that and not sleeping.

Carrying a cheap glass vase of wilting pink carnations, Sarah came to Colleen's door. Troy Cramer, the night-shift cop, looked up from a month-old *Entertainment Weekly* somebody had left behind. "Sleeping Beauty got flowers?"

"We had a new mom check out early. Third kid and all, she had to get home to her other two." Sarah turned the vase in her hands. "We usually send these over to our nursing home, but"—she looked into Colleen Porter's room—"considering."

"Yeah," Troy said. "Considering."

Sarah passed from the soft light of the hospital corridor into the muted darkness of Colleen's room. As she did, Troy Cramer turned on his chair and followed her with his eyes.

Sarah Mercer had a great butt.

A muffled tone from the nurses' station down the hall chimed midnight. Troy knew that if he were ever going to make his move—he was thinking maybe coffee or something, nothing too forward or off-putting—it'd have to be soon.

He leaned into the doorway and watched as Sarah placed the flowers on the broad windowsill, rotating them just so. She glanced back and caught him looking at her. Troy quickly turned away, his face flushing red. He'd always hated that he was such an easy blusher.

Sarah Mercer jotted the latest monitor readings into Colleen's chart. Then she took up the empty food tray and left the room. "See ya in like an hour."

Troy didn't look up from his *Entertainment Weekly*. "Yeah. An hour."

Sarah made her way down the hallway, the gentle footfall of her tennis shoes sounding like bare feet. Troy stole a glance just as she turned the corner at the elevator bank. Her great butt slipping from view for at least an hour. He let the magazine fall to the floor and leaned his head back against the wall. It was how he passed the time.

Waiting for Sarah.

Troy didn't notice the man step out of the empty hospital room across the way.

The man stood in the gloom between shadow and light and listened as the police officer's breathing found its rhythm and fell into the throaty rasp of sleep.

Edgar Silva crossed the hallway in two steps, passed the sleeping cop, and went into Colleen Porter's room.

"Goddammit!"

Chief Walker McDonald was seething. He sat on a folding chair in Interrogation One, his feet propped on another chair across from him. An hour earlier, Jane had called him at home to come view the DEA surveillance tape, and he had shown up in a gray UC Berkeley sweatshirt, navy blue sweatpants, and sneakers. It was the first time most of the cops in the room had seen him out of uniform.

The video had shown Herman Jones at Dock Twenty-Eight in San Rafael at precisely the time of the massacre. He was part of a four-man crew who were transferring dozens of plastic loading crates from a cargo container into three plain-wrap Ford Econoline vans.

Mike Finney had already verified the time code. There was no getting around it: they had the wrong man.

The chief pinched the bridge of his nose and looked up to the wall clock. Just past midnight. "We are royally fucked, Lieutenant." He dropped his feet to the floor and rose to his full six feet four inches.

Jane stood against the back wall, the chief's bodyguard sitting in the darkened bullpen behind her. There were five or six support personnel still in the war room along with Kenny, Finney, and Lou Tronick. "It's shitty, sir," she said, "but we have to move on."

Kenny rewound the tape. "We could have wasted a ton of time playing this out. It's better we cut bait now."

Chief McDonald swiveled his head toward Kenny. "While you cut bait, Inspector, I have to let the mayor and the press know we fucked up."

Kenny held his ground. "All due respect, sir. It's not a fuck-up to bring in the wrong man with the evidence and the witness ID we had."

Jane knew that Kenny was defending her. "The fuck-up, Chief," she said, "would be to not do everything we could to make our case. And that unfortunately includes coming to the conclusion that we don't have one."

Pressing the back of his fist to his forehead, the chief slowly nodded. "Okay, okay. Granted." He scanned the room, making eye contact. "I know you've all been working your asses off, and I appreciate that. So don't get me wrong here. It's not only the mayor and the press I'm worried about. It's the people of this city. They spend their days watching funerals and they deserve some closure. Not to mention the fact we still have a mass murderer out there." He started for the door. "I gotta make some calls." Hooking a finger to summon his driver, he strode across the squad room and entered a waiting elevator.

"Lou," Jane said, "push some paper and book Herman Jones for the first two Stella's robberies."

Lou scribbled a note on his legal pad. "What about pressing Jones on the drug stuff?"

"We'd have to reveal our sources and that wasn't the deal." Jane shook her head. "Fact of life."

Kenny popped the DEA tape out of the playback machine and handed it to Finney. "This goes into the secure evidence locker. No access without me or Lieutenant Candiotti signing off."

Mike Finney slipped the tape into a white department envelope and put it in his briefcase.

"Okay, guys," Jane said, "welcome to square one. We had good leads and good arrests. But they didn't pan. First thing in the morning, we start digging into the victims' lives. All of them." She pulled on her sweater. "Everyone's got secrets. We have to go into their closets and pry some skeletons loose until we find the right one."

Kenny shrugged out of his shoulder holster and put on his jacket. He kept himself busy while Jane spoke.

"Also, I want the final autopsy reports on my desk as soon as possible. All of them."

"I talked with Dr. Tedesco an hour ago," Finney said. "He said the finals are almost done. He's a little short of help and needs maybe another day."

"Another day's a day too long," Jane said. "I'll call him myself." She scanned the room. "Guys, there's no such thing as a senseless murder. These people were killed for a reason." She went to the door. "Let's find that reason."

Kenny caught up to her as she crossed the bullpen, the soft purr of a dozen computers filling the empty spaces. Jane looped her arm through his. "I don't know if you realize it," she said, "but you did a pretty good job in there of supporting all my arguments about Edgar Silva and the information he brought us." She drew him to her. "You had the chief convinced, and you had me convinced. I'm just wondering how convinced you were."

They reached the elevators. Kenny thumbed the call button. "I was convinced enough to know that Herman Jones didn't do it. Anyone would be." An elevator arrived, its doors sliding apart. "But not convinced enough to change my mind about Edgar Silva. All my cop instincts tell me that man has an agenda and I'm not dropping my guard till I know what it is." He pushed the button for the secure parking level and looked over to Jane. She was lost in thought. "Where are you?"

"Working the logic." She turned to him. "We know now that Herman Jones didn't do it. And whoever *did* tried to cover it up as another in a series of robberies."

"But why?"

"That's just it, Ken. Why bother to copy the robbery M.O. if you were just a thief? Something bigger is going on here."

Kenny absorbed this, then nodded. "You're right. We've got to be all over the other victims. And I want to start with Andrea. Clear Bobby first."

"We can do that. First thing in the morning." Jane let her body fall back against the elevator wall, the give in the wood panel absorbing the impact. "I am so whipped."

"One stop," Kenny said as the doors started to close. "Then home."

"They're all sleeping."

Kenny drove the Explorer past Andrea's house. His parents' minivan was backed into the driveway to shorten the distance his father would have to walk to the front door.

Jane tucked her hand under Kenny's right thigh. "Wanna call her cell in case she's still up?"

Kenny turned to her, a rectangle of light from the rearview banding across his eyes. "I already did."

A silent understanding passed between them that Kenny had to come all this way, this late at night, on the off-chance that there'd be a light on in his sister's house. That Andrea might be awake and might need him. "Let's go home," Jane said softly. "I need you, too."

Kenny touched the back of his first two fingers to her lips.

"Thank God," he whispered.

20

Colleen Porter thought she was dreaming.

There were flowers on the windowsill. The early morning sun bleached the carnations to an almost-white. She must have had a visitor during the night.

Colleen stretched the sleep from her muscles. Whatever the doctors had given her had done the trick. For the first time in days, she felt rested and refreshed.

Her stomach churned with hunger, a rolling gurgle she could feel as well as hear. She wanted to get a closer look at the beautiful flowers; maybe there was a card. Reaching under her hospital gown, she began peeling the heart monitor electrode patches from her chest.

Patrol Officer Troy Cramer waited at the nurses' station for Sarah Mercer to finish her phone call. He was going off duty in twenty minutes and this was probably his last day on this assignment. So, he thought, it's make the move and ask her to coffee or spend the rest of the day wondering what if. The rest of his life maybe. Besides, if she said no and this gig was over anyway, he wouldn't have to face the embarrassment of seeing her again.

"Okay then. I'll e-mail the chart over to your office," Sarah said into the phone. "You're welcome. Bye-bye." She rang off and looked up to Troy. "Wanna get some coffee?"

Before he could answer, Troy felt his face redden and hoped that she couldn't see how deeply he was blushing. "Uh…sure. Coffee's good."

"Great," Sarah smiled. "Just lemme clock out." She swung the desk chair around and rose. As she crossed to the time clock, Troy willed himself not to get caught checking out her butt again.

Neither of them noticed the heavyset woman dressed in a Stella's uniform carrying a vase of pink carnations toward the nurses' station. At the last moment, she turned right and found herself at the elevators. An orderly who was just pushing a food cart into the middle elevator recognized her and held the door open. "Going home?"

"Yeah," Colleen Porter said, breathing in the syrupy breakfast smells coming from the cart. "Going home."

"Pretty flowers."

"Thanks. I've got the best boyfriend in the world."

"Okay, freeze it there."

Andrea Farrier leaned forward in Jane's guest chair and lifted her sunglasses to her forehead. Her eyes were red and swollen from crying and lack of sleep and bottomless misery.

Jane pushed the Pause button on the remote.

"That's Lucas Girard," Andrea said. "Maybe he dabbles in things he shouldn't, but basically he's a good kid. Good parents. Does well in school."

"Almost done, Andy." Kenny ticked off another name on Bobby's funeral list. "Is there anyone on the tape that you *don't* recognize? Any strangers?"

Andrea shook her head. "No. There're some people I hadn't seen in years. But no one sticks out." She touched a tissue to the corner of her left eye. Then the right. "Do you videotape the funerals of all your murder victims?"

"Just the unsolveds." Jane pressed Play. "Was there anything else going on in Bobby's life we should know about? Girl problems, bullies…gang stuff?"

"He was just a typical boy," Andrea said. "Sometimes rebellious; heh, sometimes obnoxious." She looked at the screen again. Her parents coming out of the church. "Daddy got so old."

Kenny watched his father's halting step, the trembling hands. "I know."

"But y'know what? Dad with all his problems and Mom with all hers? They've been there for me every minute since…since it happened. Something to be said for that."

Jane reached from the couch and put her hand on Andrea's shoulder. "It's why I waited so long to get married. I was waiting for the right family to come along."

Andrea held Jane's hand in hers. "I saw you guys drive by last night. With all you have to do, means a lot to me."

Kenny draped his arm around Andrea. "Soon as we figure this out, we'll come by and help you with Bobby's things. Maybe look for a new place if you'd like."

"Thanks, but I want to stay there. It's not so much the memories that hurt. It's the…well, the differences. No underwear on the floor, or loud music, or phone calls too late at night. I still find myself wondering is he covered for lunch? Is he warm enough? Is he safe?" Andrea pulled her sunglasses back down. "He was a wonderful, generous, sparkling kid." Twin rivulets of tears appeared from behind her dark glasses. "No, the memories don't hurt. They…they keep him close to me. Where he belongs." She clutched the arms of the chair and pulled herself up. "I gotta get back."

Kenny crossed to her. "I'm sorry Herman Jones wasn't the one. And I'm sorry we had to put you through all this."

"I know you are, Ken. I know you are." Andrea turned to Jane. "You take care of that baby. It's the greatest thing you'll ever do in your life." She pulled her black linen jacket around her shoulders.

Jane kissed her good-bye. "I will."

Kenny pulled his sister to him. "I'll walk you out."

Andrea let her head fall to her brother's shoulder as they crossed the bullpen. Cheryl Lomax looked up from her dispatch console and was unable to disguise the sadness in her smile. Roz Shapiro pushed the elevator call button and stepped aside. Two uniformed officers stood in the doorway of the war room as Andrea passed. One of them started to whisper something to the other, thought better of it, and watched Kenny and Andrea in silence.

Jane switched off the DVD player and the television abruptly came on. Cameron Sanders was covering another funeral for KGO. He stood across the street from a small California Spanish church. Jane adjusted the volume. "...services for Nicolas Silva," Sanders reported. "The day before yesterday would have been his twenty-first birthday. And today, he will be laid to rest beside an older brother, also a victim of violence, and his father."

The camera pushed in as a clutch of people, each holding the other, emerged from the shadow of the church doorway into the brilliant sunlight of a new San Francisco morning.

Jane saw Edgar Silva, his broad body taller, stronger than the others, help an elderly woman down the steps. Dressed in a black suit, white shirt, and black tie, he stopped at the bottom of the steps and turned to wait for his brother's coffin.

Nico Silva's coffin was carried down the church steps by six young Latino men. As they moved solemnly along the sidewalk to the waiting hearse, Edgar stepped forward and put his hand flat on the coffin, just above a spray of white gladiolas. The bearers paused. Everything, the entire tableau, was suspended for a moment as Edgar bent down and kissed the crucifix next to the flowers. Then he shuffled back and bowed his head.

The six young men slid the coffin into the hearse.

A Hispanic man, dressed in a dark blue suit and black Ray-Bans, came up to Edgar Silva. He kissed the elderly woman on both cheeks, then pulled Edgar into an embrace. As he did, the man in the sunglasses spoke into Edgar's ear, then separated. Edgar nodded twice, his face drawn and grim.

Something about this exchange struck Jane. It could have been just a normal expression of condolence from a friend to a grieving brother. But there had about it the aura of a message delivered.

And a message received.

"I'm Homicide Inspector Michael Finney of SFPD Homicide."

Mike Finney was so proud of his new job, he'd said Homicide twice in the same sentence. "I called earlier?"

"Glad t' know ya." Abe Christian tore the filter off a Marlboro and lit it with the stub of the one he was smoking. He was in his early seventies with bushy gray eyebrows and an ill-fitting too-black toupee. Slapping a key down on the chipped Formica counter, he jerked his chin toward the staircase. "Rourke's room is 2A. Top of the stairs, first on the right. He's...was...paid up till the end of the month, so nobody's been in there since he got himself killed. Might be a little stuffy."

Finney picked up the key. "Thank you for your help, Mr. Christian."

"Yeah, whatever." Abe Christian waved the smoke away from his eyes and jammed his spent cigarette into an overflowing ashtray. A small television sat on the counter next to a stack of week-old *Chronicles* that someone was supposed to recycle. It was playing a rerun of a vaguely familiar nineties sitcom starring some former supermodel. Abe perched himself on his stool, propped his elbows on his thighs, and settled in to pass another day. "Brooke Shields," he muttered, his nicotine-blotched false teeth sliding sideways across themselves. "I'd do her."

Not sure exactly why, Finney nodded. He crossed the small threadbare lobby of the Mark Twain Gentlemen's Hotel and climbed the stairs. A patch of flowered wallpaper had been torn away from the hallway, leaving an incongruous pentimento of clipper ships and schooners.

Finney passed an empty fire extinguisher cabinet and slipped the key into the lock of 2A. He nudged the door open. Abe Christian was right. The air in the room was still, giving off an odor of old wet cloth.

The morning sun threw a latticework shadow of the fire escape across the far wall. Nothing about Shanty Rourke's room was what Finney would have expected from the home of a panhandler. The bed was made, a thin pale-green chenille bedspread taut across the blanket, two pillows lying against an oak headboard. There were three shirts and two pairs of pants lined up neatly on hangers in the doorless closet. A tweed wool overcoat with a patched pocket hung on a brass coat hook. A pair of scuffed work boots and a pair of worn flip-flops sat side by side on the bare closet floor.

Shanty's toiletries were in an open cigar box on top of a small painted two-drawer dresser. Old Spice, a Trac II razor, a toothbrush, Colgate, and a roll-on deodorant. There was no mirror. Finney remembered that there was a communal bathroom at the end of the hall. It's what you get, he thought, for twelve bucks a night.

Finney pulled on a pair of rubber gloves and tugged at the top drawer. It opened grudgingly to reveal two pairs of Jockey shorts, half a dozen pairs of black socks—each neatly rolled into itself—a Gideon's Bible with a Marriott Hotel logo embossed into the cover, drugstore reading glasses, a Fisherman's Wharf ashtray filled with pennies, and a San Francisco Opera Company performance schedule. Finney had learned from Jane that panhandlers frequented the opera and theater district, putting the touch on the high-rollers. He pushed the drawer closed and bent to one knee to open the bottom one.

All that was in the other drawer was a tattered faux-leather suitcase. Finney lifted it out and laid it on the bed. He thumbed the locks and the left one popped up immediately. But the right one didn't budge. He pried at it with the blade of his pocket knife and it finally released. Grasping the top of the suitcase with the fingertips of both hands, Finney flipped it open.

"Holy shit!" he said under his breath.

Unable to tear his eyes away from the suitcase, Finney snatched the two-way from his belt. "3H77 to Dispatch."

Cheryl Lomax came on right away. "Hey, Moby. You okay?"

"Yeah. I need the lieutenant."

"You got it."

There was a brief static break, then Jane came on the line. "Mike, it's me. What's up?"

"I think we just found our first skeleton."

"Cheryl," Jane called as she hurried across the bullpen. "Where's Kenny?"

"Still downstairs with his sister."

"Call him for me, please, and tell him to meet me at the Explorer." Jane was just about to pull open the stairwell door when she noticed Tommy Murphy coming out of the elevator. Dressed in blue jeans and an untucked work shirt, he looked like a college kid.

"I got your voice mail, Lieutenant," he said as he approached. "We're pulling second shift today, so I thought I'd stop by in person."

"Walk with me." Jane opened the door and started down the stairs. Tommy hustled to keep up with her. "I need you to do me a favor, Officer Murphy."

"You bet, ma'am."

Jane stopped at the next landing and turned to him. "You and Rick need to take some time off. A few days. A week even. Rick can spend some time with his family; you can relax on your boat. Decompress. Absorb what you've been through."

Tommy came down another step to the landing. "I appreciate what you're saying. And I'll tell Rick. But I'm okay. Really."

"Okay's not good enough around here." Jane snapped a look at her watch. "Look, if you want me to take your Homicide application seriously, then I need to know that you're a level-headed guy who's smart enough to realize when he's had the wind knocked out of him. You've had some real trauma, Tom. You're allowed to react to it."

"With respect, ma'am? What about you? You've suffered, too. Worse even, with you losing your nephew."

"True enough." Jane started down the stairs again. "For now, other instincts are taking over. Leadership…maternal. But, believe me, when all this is over, after I catch this guy…I'll have a pretty good breakdown of my own."

They reached the parking level. Tommy opened the door for her. "Lieutenant, I—"

"You do this, Tom, and I'll keep your application warm for you." Jane passed into the garage. Kenny was already at the Explorer. "You don't, and I'll be worried about who's coming to me looking for a job."

She was halfway to the Explorer when Tommy called out to her. "Lieutenant? 'Scuse me."

Jane turned back.

Tommy Murphy tried to suppress a smile. "Did you say 'maternal'? As in…" He let his eyes fall to her waist.

"As in." Jane shrugged a smile back to him. "You think about what I said, okay?"

Tommy Murphy started to raise his hand in a salute, then caught himself. "I will, ma'am."

"It's almost sixty-three thousand dollars in ones, fives, and tens."

Mike Finney peeled off his rubber gloves and leaned back against Shanty Rourke's painted dresser, causing the toiletries to clink into each other in the cigar box.

"All this money," Kenny said, staring at the open suitcase on the bed, "and he lives in this shithole?"

"Hey!" Abe Christian said from the doorway, a curl of cigarette smoke stinging his eyes. "This is a fine men's hotel." He inched his way deeper into the room, like a child encroaching on forbidden space.

Jane held out her hand on the pretense of grabbing the doorknob, effectively blocking his progress. "This is a murder investigation, sir. Thank you for your cooperation."

Abe Christian craned to look over her shoulder. "What's going to happen to all that money? I mean, ain't possession nine-tenths?"

"Only if there's a dispute as to its rightful owner," Jane said. "It's pretty clear to us that this money belonged to Mr. Rourke." She began to close the door. "But if our legal department instructs us otherwise, we'll be sure to let you know."

Abe allowed himself to be nudged back into the hallway. "You do that, Miss. I'm here all the time. Day and night. Other times, too."

"Then we know where to find you." Jane shut the door, twisted the lock, and turned to Kenny.

"Legal department?"

Jane shrugged. "A little hope goes a long way."

"Tell me about it," Kenny said. He looked to Finney. "Moby, we need you to dig into the life of Arthur Rourke. Relatives, friends...enemies. See if anyone else knew about this money. See if there's any more. It's possible this whole thing was somebody moving on Shanty Rourke for his money." He looked to Jane. "It's also possible that..."

"That other victims," Jane picked it up, "have other skeletons. If someone as innocuous as Mr. Rourke had such a big secret, what other secrets are out there?"

"2P109 to 3H58."

Jane pulled her walkie-talkie from her purse. "Go."

"Lieutenant, this is Rudy Medeiros over at the Med Tower."

"Hey, Rudy. How's Miss Porter doing today?"

"Well, ma'am...she's kind of gone."

Kenny crossed closer to Jane, listening in. "Gone?" Jane said. "How? When?"

"Alls I know is, when I got here? Troy Cramer, he's the night guy, is tearing the place apart searching for her."

Kenny took the two-way from Jane. "How long ago was that?"

"Like five minutes. But she'd been missing maybe a half hour before that. Cramer waited for me to show up before reporting it. In case she was just wandering the halls or something. He didn't want to push the panic button for nothing. Then we found this orderly who tells us he saw her getting into an elevator. She was dressed in her civilian clothes and said she was going home."

"Okay, Rudy," Jane said. "Put out an APB on her. Check with the taxi companies and send a patrol unit to her house in case she shows up."

"Yes, ma'am. Sorry about this."

"Let's just find her. 3H58, out."

Tuffy was sleeping on the porch swing, the sun warming his fur.

He opened one eye to the sound of a taxi crunching up the gravel drive, then stretched and rolled onto his back, falling asleep again.

Colleen Porter paid the driver and, holding the carnations in the crook of her arm, climbed out of the cab. She was still a little cotton-headed from her time in the hospital, the medication and all.

And she was hungry.

She climbed the two steps up to the porch of her rented Berkeley Hills cabin. The floorboards creaked and Tuffy stirred, rising up and stretching luxuriously. "You came back!" Colleen said, tears rushing to her eyes. She put the flowers on the railing and scooped her cat into her arms. "Oh, Tuffy. We both came home." Holding the screen door open with her hip, Colleen unlocked the front door and pushed.

She hadn't been home for days and the little two-room place looked it. The houseplants were wilted, drooping away from themselves. A couple of fish bobbed upside-down at the top of the aquarium. Others floated listlessly on the current of the air pump.

Colleen let Tuffy drop to the couch as the front door clicked closed behind her. She pulled a hanging fern from its macramé sling, carried it to the sink, and turned the water on to give it a good soaking. Then she reached up and retrieved a can of Whiskas from the shelf over the coffeemaker. Pressing the top of the electric can opener with the heel of her hand, she set the can of cat food rotating. Tuffy scurried into the kitchen area, drawn by the familiar sound.

Dropping to her knees, Colleen spooned the food into the cat bowl and rose with Tuffy's empty water dish. She filled it at the running tap and was just thinking about what she could scrounge for lunch when she heard the floorboards creak outside. Tuffy's head shot around toward the front door, his ears twitching.

Colleen turned off the water and listened. "Hello?"

A shadow fell across the sheer curtains. The backlit silhouette of a man appeared in the small inset window of the heavy oak door. The knob turned. Then stopped. The door was locked.

Colleen moved forward, her uncertainty boiling into dread. "Who's there?"

The man retreated a few steps, his silhouette looming even larger. "Could you open the door, please?"

Colleen gasped, her chest gripped with panic.

She knew that voice.

21

The wooden porch swing had landed upside down in Colleen Porter's living room, spanning the gap between the water-stained brown couch and the coffee table.

Flags of sheer curtain flapped through the gaping hole in the window, catching on triangles of shattered glass.

Colleen Porter's body was on the bathroom floor, on its right side, one shoe on, one shoe in the hallway next to the linen closet. A macramé plant sling was coiled twice around her neck, digging deep into her flesh. Her tongue, swollen and blue, seemed too large to have ever fit in her mouth. The one eye that was visible, her left one, was still open. Light from the small window over the bathtub casting a perfect square of white on its dilated pupil.

"What's the fucking point of putting a twenty-four-seven on her," Jane said, unable to control her anger in front of all the support personnel, "if she can just walk past our guy, leave the hospital, and get herself killed?" She turned to Kenny. "What's the name of the uniform who let her get away?"

Kenny checked his notes. "Troy Cramer. Twenty-year vet with a perfect record."

"Until now," Jane said. "I'll write the file-letter myself."

Aaron Clark-Weber side-slipped into the small bathroom. "Not much sign of a struggle."

Kenny made himself skinny to make room for Aaron. "Could mean the assailant was so strong, he just overpowered her. Or maybe she was so frightened, she couldn't resist." He bumped into the towel rack, one end of it hanging by a loose toggle bolt.

"Don't forget," Jane added as she knelt down next to Colleen Porter's head, "this girl had been in the hospital for a couple of days. And before that, she was found unconscious in a walk-in Deepfreeze. I doubt she had much strength left." She tilted forward on the balls of her feet and let her eyes travel down Colleen's body.

The dead woman's hands had been enclosed in plain brown grocery bags and taped at the wrists by the Forensic techs to preserve any scrape-evidence under her fingernails. She was still dressed in her Stella's uniform. The macramé noose had snagged part of her collar and twisted it halfway around her neck.

Aaron stepped deeper into the room. "That macramé thing? We're pretty sure it came from a plant that's in the kitchen sink."

Jane started to rise, Kenny and Aaron quickly leaning in to help her up. She squeezed her way out of the cramped space and moved down the hallway.

A dozen cops, plainclothes and uniforms, worked quietly in the living room. Two men in black medical examiner's jumpsuits stood inside the front door, arms folded identically across their chests, waiting for the body to be released. A flash strobed from a still camera and Jane noticed Larry Peoples, the photographer from the Stella's murders. He snapped several shots of the ravaged front window and the debris-strewn floor. As he crouched for a better angle, he felt Jane looking at him and raised his eyes to meet hers. He sent a slight nod her way and went back to work.

"One answer," Kenny said as he joined Jane, "is Colleen Porter was the only surviving witness to the Stella's massacre and somebody wanted her quiet."

There was the gravel-crackling sound of yet another police vehicle arriving.

"Another is"—Jane gestured for Lou Tronick to come over—"maybe she was the original intended victim. And that's why all those other people died." She turned to Lou. "I need you to do a deep background on Miss Porter. See if anyone had any reason to do this to her."

"Sure, Jane," Lou Tronick said softly.

Jane looked around. Everyone was moving slowly, as if underwater. They were professional and respectful, as always. But something was different. This latest murder of someone so closely connected to the Stella's shootings was too much, too soon, for them.

The loose floorboards on the porch clacked briefly, wood slapping wood, as someone pounded across them.

An eye-level blur of black-and-white and gray swept past everyone's periphery like something thrown across the room. A cat leaped from the top of the refrigerator where he'd been crouched behind a cow-jumped-over-the-moon cookie jar and rocketed out the front door. He had to adjust his path, zigging in midstride, as a pair of black shoes appeared at the threshold.

"Can't we keep *anyone* alive in this fucking city?" Chief McDonald bellowed from the doorway.

Jane and Kenny rode in uneasy silence across the Bay Bridge, the corrugated blacktop thrumming under the Explorer's oversized tires.

The last time they had taken this route in the middle of the day, they'd been racing to the city after getting the call about the Stella's shootings.

A lifetime ago.

The murders were like an explosion, radiating pain-shrapnel in every direction. Irretrievably altering every life they touched.

Jane looked to Kenny. His jaw muscle pulsed below his right ear and she knew the demons were fighting their way to the surface again. She cracked her window open, letting a soothing slip of fresh air stream in against her forehead. Kenny glanced over, drawn by the sound, grateful in his own way for the distraction from thinking about his sister and his nephew.

"Colleen Porter," he said, "wanted to get out of that hospital. It's almost like it was her fate."

Jane raised the window again, the rush of air and sound disappearing with a suction-like *thwoop.* "Listen to you, talking about fate. I thought in your world everything happened for a reason."

"Maybe fate *is* a reason." Kenny swung left over the raised roadway dots, crossing the double yellow line and into the carpool lane. "I don't know, all my thinking's changing since we got pregnant."

Jane touched his arm. "I love that you see it that way...the *we* part, I mean." She unclipped the two-way mic from the dash, getting ready to gather the troops. "The chief's right, Ken. I was working the playbook by rote and I dropped the ball. Fate or no fate, Colleen Porter deserved better from us." Kenny started to protest, but she talked over him. "I know it's not a perfect world. Believe me. Mistakes get made. But when the mistake is big enough, when *my* mistake is big enough, people die."

Kenny waited for Jane to finish. "It was that street cop who let her walk out of a hospital. This was his fuck-up."

Jane turned to him. "Fuck-ups roll uphill."

The carpool lane ended and the collective urgency of all they had to do came rushing back to them like a suppressed memory.

"I have to do better."

"Arthur Shanty Rourke had no heirs and no will as far as we can find. So the state's gonna get all that money." Mike Finney turned a page in his notebook. "That, plus the fact it wasn't exactly hidden very well, just sitting in a drawer, and was still there when we searched his room, kinda takes money off the table as a motive." He picked at a salad plate, pushing the red onions aside.

"I agree." Jane pressed her fists into her lower spine and arched her back. Through the window wall she saw a couple of uniforms watching TV in the lunchroom. Cameron Sanders was at his anchor desk with a photo of Colleen Porter floating over his left shoulder. "Good work, Mike. But Shanty Rourke could have had other reasons someone would want him dead. Stay tough on this. See what other secrets the old guy had."

Kenny tilted his chair until its back rested against the wall, his toes lightly touching the floor to maintain the precise angle. He stared at the blackboards, the chalk-written names commanding his attention like newspaper headlines. "And Terrence Unger," he added. "And Francis Cellucci..." He turned to Jane. "...and Nico Silva."

Jane sipped her chamomile tea, ticking off the bargains in her mind over what she'd give up for just one more cappuccino. "Everyone, Ken. The secret of this murder is in a secret of one of the victims." She spotted Lou Tronick crossing the bullpen. "We find the first secret, no matter how obscure or well-hidden, we'll find the second one...and then we're that much closer to a solved."

Lou Tronick entered Interrogation One, tossed his coat over the back of a chair, and poured himself a mug of coffee. He broke a corner off what was left of the coffee cake. "I've been excavating the life of Colleen Porter." He dipped the cake into the mug and, stooping forward, quickly brought it to his mouth. "Her story about subbing the day of the shootings checks out. She didn't know until early that morning she'd be working. Talk about your bad timing." He set the mug on the table and opened his case book. "This woman was a total loner. No family, no ex-family, no friends. She did her burger flipping and went home to her animals. Some way to live, huh?"

Kenny let his chair fall forward. "Some way to die."

"Jane, phone call." Roz Shapiro stood at the open door to the war room. "A Lieutenant Commander Hollingsworth from Fifteen. Says it's important."

"How about this, Lieutenant," Chuck Hollingsworth growled into the phone, "I won't come over to Nineteen and recommend that your guys take time off and you stay the fuck away from my people."

Jane sat at her desk, feeling a long day getting longer. "I assume you're talking about Weymouth and Murphy." Roz Shapiro moved from window to window in the bullpen, shutting the blinds against the setting sun.

"You're goddamn right I am. Who the fuck you think?"

In a twisted, unenlightened way, Hollingsworth had a point. Jane shouldn't be suggesting to street cops at another precinct that they see the department shrink or request psyche time without having consulted their commander. But Chuck Hollingsworth was a well-known bullheaded nutjob. The beat cops at his station had even taken to calling him Queeg behind his back.

"You make a good point, Commander. It's just that a lot of cops and EMTs were pretty upset after that day and I was just reaching out to help." It dawned on Jane that she was using the same singsong speech pattern she would use if she were talking a jumper down from a ledge.

"Yeah, well the cops on my watch ain't a bunch of fuckin' florists for Chrissakes," Hollingsworth said, the edge of his bluster falling away as Jane refused to engage. "I'm already budget-crunched and shorthanded as it is. Now I got fuckin' Weymouth taking a fuckin' leave of absence and fuckin' Murphy taking personal time to see the Department shrink. How long before he follows his fuckin' partner and applies for leave, too?"

Even his arsenal of f-bombs was losing its power. It was time, Jane thought, to disarm him completely and get on with her life. "I can appreciate the hardship on you, Commander. But you should know that Weymouth and Murphy's performance that day was nothing short of exemplary. Testament to their training and discipline."

A long pause. "Yeah…well…"

"Commander, I'm sure you're very busy. And I've got a few things on this end that I've got to get back to. I'm glad we had this chance to clear the air."

"Yeah…well…"

Jane hung up, happy that she hadn't been dragged into an exchange of verbal artillery with a simian asshole like Hollingsworth. But even more pleased that Rick Weymouth and Tommy Murphy had listened to her. She made a note on her priority list to bring Chuck Hollingsworth's name up for command competency review at the next fitness evaluation meeting.

"Knock-knock." Kenny came into her office and sat on the arm of the couch. "Left word…again…for Edgar Silva. We don't hear back from him tonight, I'm gonna have him picked up as material."

"It'll never stick."

"Probably not." Kenny rose and started pacing. "But at least then I'd have him." He pulled a slip of paper from his shirt pocket. "Meantime, I've got Finney digging a deeper hole into that panhandler's past and Lou's reinterviewing Antonia Salazar's family. How 'bout you and me go scare up a few skeletons of our own?"

Jane regarded her husband. He was edgy, unable to sit still. "Where do you want to start?"

"With Father Francis Cellucci. Bishop D'Souza's waiting for us at Saint Vincent's. I don't want to step on your Catholic toes or anything, but priests *have* been known to take advantage of their exalted position and cause former members of their flock to become vengeful and wrathful."

"Well put." Jane rocked her chair forward and stood up. She came around the desk and put her hand out, touching Kenny's face. "How you doing?"

Kenny took her hand, kissed her fingers. "All I know is I gotta keep moving"—his voice cracked, the words falling into a hole and climbing back out—"or I'll go crazy."

The gardener guided the huge riding lawn mower over the gently sloping hills. Cutting wide swaths of a deeper green into the light green lawns, he navigated the cumbersome machine around and between the trees and the tombstones.

Andrea Farrier knelt beneath a broad oak tree, the moisture from the dirt of her son's freshly turned grave darkening the knee of her jeans. The steady distant sound of the lawn mower was slightly out of synch with its movements.

She pinched a weed from the edge of the perfect brown rectangle and absently rolled it between her thumb and forefinger. "Grammy and Grandpa went home today. They send their love, sweetie, but they just couldn't come back here. I haven't cleaned your room yet. No big whoop, right? But I'll get to it, I promise." Andrea settled onto both her knees, oblivious to the dirt and the damp.

"The guys came by—Jessie, Lucas, and Jorge—and made a barbecue for all of us. They're good friends, Bobby, and they miss you so much. Uncle Kenny calls all the time, checking in, seeing how I'm doing. He and Aunt Jane are working really hard, trying to find who did this to you."

The oak tree swayed. Nudged by a soft breeze, the dappled pattern of sunlight and shadow moved across the ground.

"Hey, I never told you. Aunt Jane and Uncle Kenny are going to have a baby. We were waiting to break the good—" A sob billowed in her throat, stopping her words, stopping her breath. She gulped it back down and, her jaw quivering, fought to continue. "...the good news to you." Andrea clutched a clump of dirt in her right hand and squeezed, her knuckles turning into trembling pearls. "Oh my sweet...only...baby..." And the tears came, the breeze cooling her face. "What am I going to do? How will I ever—"

The man came up behind her in one swift and silent motion. He brought his forearm around her neck, across her throat, and pulled her to him.

Andrea's right hand jerked open, the dirt from her son's grave spilling onto her shoes.

22

Saint Vincent's was a slowly declining church in a rapidly declining neighborhood. A late-eighties influx of Vietnamese and Thais had consumed all of the available housing in this already marginal section of San Francisco. The population of older parishioners had dwindled to such an extent that the once robust Sunday services were now less than one-third full. Recently, the Catholic Church had begun to consider cutting its losses by selling the building and the attached elementary school.

Tiny flames from the votive candles sent jewels of reflected light bouncing off the framed photograph. A prayer card was propped against the picture. *Father Francis James Cellucci... Child of God.*

Jane and Kenny stood in the hushed portico, the last embers of the setting sun illuminating the stained-glass portrait of the Virgin Mary on the wall above them. Jane genuflected and crossed herself, saying a silent prayer for Bobby and for her baby.

"Lieutenant Candiotti, Inspector Marks?" A young Hispanic priest beckoned from a doorway to their right. He was bathed in a prism of broken colors from the stained glass. "I'm Father Marquez. His Excellency will see you now."

The young priest opened the door to the chancery and stepped aside. Heavy brocaded drapery couldn't entirely hide the wrought-iron security bars attached to the floor-to-ceiling windows. A treacle-tinged veil of pipe smoke floated in from a small room to the left. Jane watched through the glass-paneled doors as Bishop Dominic D'Souza picked up a television remote and muted the Giants game.

Bishop D'Souza sat in a black leather club chair. His shirt was unbuttoned at the throat, his clerical collar protruding from his breast pocket like a white tongue depressor. He puffed thoughtfully on his pipe, cloudy balls of smoke slipping from the corner of his mouth.

A small dark man, the bishop was in his late sixties; most of his passion and much of his greatness now behind him. He wore thick black-rimmed glasses and a signet ring from the Yale Divinity School on the pinkie of his left hand.

Jane and Kenny sat on a royal-blue couch, its rough and abraded fabric as thick as a carpet. "We hate to be indelicate, Excellency," Jane said. "But in order to do our jobs, we have to ask you a few potentially controversial questions about Father Cellucci."

Bishop D'Souza sipped his Diet Coke, the ice cubes bumping in the glass. "You want to ask me about the possibility of an ongoing or previous child molestation as a motive for the shootings." It wasn't a question, but a resigned statement of fact.

Jane and Kenny exchanged a look.

"Yes, Excellency," Kenny said. "We apologize for even—"

The bishop raised his hand. "I appreciate how difficult this must be for you." His eyes wrinkled into a smile. "Especially for a good Catholic like you, Jane. But, given what's happened the last few years, it's an entirely appropriate line of reasoning." He laid his pipe in a crystal bowl and watched the smoke trail off. "It's a question I anticipated myself. I interviewed Father Cellucci's colleagues, even some who have moved away, as well as teachers at our school and the new secular liaison for our altar and choir boys." He sighed. "There's simply nothing there. Father Cellucci was a quiet and devoted member of this church with almost twenty years of service to the community, the AIDS Hospice, and our parish. No one, not one single person, had anything even slightly negative to say about him." Bishop D'Souza chuckled to himself. "With the possible exception of Father Morgan whom Francis consistently beat in handball."

Jane slid to the edge of the couch. "Thank you for welcoming us, Excellency, and for being so candid and gracious."

"Of course, Lieutenant. Anything any of us here can—"

"Dispatch to 3H58."

The radio call seemed to come from another century as it rattled around the chancery.

"Sorry, sir. Excuse me." Jane snatched the two-way from her purse. "May I?"

"Of course."

Jane squeezed the mic. "3H58. Go."

"Lieutenant..." Cheryl Lomax's voice was edgy, unsettled. "Jane, we just got a call from Kenny's sister..." Kenny shot forward, touching his ear to the walkie-talkie's speaker. "Andrea was at the cemetery and she was...attacked."

Kenny pressed Jane's thumb to activate the microphone. "Cheryl, is she all right?"

There was a pause, a cruel endless hiss of static as the connection was momentarily lost. Cheryl Lomax finally came back on. "Yes, Ken. She's shaken up. But she's okay. One of the gardeners chased the assailant away. Patrol units are just arriving on-scene."

Kenny's shoulders heaved with relief. Then he quickly stood up and ran to the door. Jane started after him, then turned back to Bishop D'Souza. "Excellency, we—"

The bishop rose and brought his hands together in a gesture of humility. "Go get the bastard who did this, Lieutenant." He bowed his head. "I will pray for you."

"He wrapped his arm around my neck…but…he didn't squeeze." Andrea Farrier said, almost amazed at the memory. "He just held me in place, asking me stuff."

"What kind of stuff?" Kenny asked. They were huddled beneath the oak tree, the lights from three patrol cars casting an oasis of illumination as evening fell on the cemetery.

" 'What do you know?' He kept asking over and over. 'What do you know?' "

"Did you see anything?" Jane asked. "His clothes, maybe his shoes?"

"No." Andrea shook her head. "Nothing."

"Could you smell him?" Kenny took his sister's hands in his. "Cigarettes, liquor, aftershave. Anything stand out?"

"I…I don't remember." Andrea looked toward Bobby's grave. "I'm sorry."

A young patrol officer approached. " 'Scuse me, Lieutenant?"

Jane stepped away to listen to his report.

"Uh, we just interviewed the gardener?" He opened his notebook. "Zjelko Ivica…I'm not even close to pronouncing it right. Anyways, he didn't really see anything. He was on the riding mower over there." He pointed back over his shoulder. "And the assault happened over in this direction…kind of right in front of the sun, which was super low at the time. He saw some commotion, but the people were just silhouettes to him. Fact is, he didn't even know the victim was a female until he got like real close."

"Thank you, Officer"—Jane read his name tag—"Clason. Good work."

"I'll type this up for ya, ma'am."

A Forensics van worked its way up the winding drive, pushing against the funnel of its own headlights. It parked on the perimeter and two techs got out with footprint mold-making rigs.

Jane rejoined Kenny and Andrea under the tree. "Andy, we're going to have someone take you home in your car. Someone else will follow in a black-and-white and they'll stay outside your house tonight and tomorrow…as long as it takes."

Kenny drew his sister into a hug. "I'm so sorry, Andy."

Andrea nodded her head several times, then straightened, her body tensing. "He was whispering!" she said, the words coming in a rush of discovery. "He *whispered* everything he said to me." She mimicked a male voice. "'*What do you know?*' It was always a whisper." A breeze came up, stirring the leaves of the huge oak. Andrea pulled her collar up. "Like I wasn't creeped out enough."

Jane nodded to a female police officer. The cop stepped forward and took Andrea by the elbow. Jane kissed her sister-in-law on the cheek. "I'm so sorry this happened to you, Andy. We'll get this guy."

Jane and Kenny watched Andrea being led down the narrow road to her car. "Colleen Porter gets killed," Kenny said. "My sister is accosted. This case keeps growing ugly new heads."

Jane moved aside as the Forensics techs carried their equipment toward the ribboned-off patch of grass where Andrea had been grabbed. "It's reasonable to assume that Colleen Porter was killed because she knew something about the murders…or the shooter thought she did. But why come after Andrea?"

Kenny shook his head. "Don't know yet." He started forward, drawn to his nephew's grave. Skirting the crime scene tape, he walked to the opposite end of the large rectangle of turned earth. Then he plunged his hands into his pockets and lowered his head, his lips forming soundless words.

Jane came around the grave and looped her arm through her husband's. She heard Kenny say, "I promise, Bobby…" and then gently tugged him away.

"Now I'm the one who has to keep moving," she said. "Come on, Ken."

"I told Terry a thousand times not to eat fast food. But he ignored me. Said I was keeping him from living in the moment." Charlie See dabbed at his eyes with the bottom of his untucked shirt. "Well, look where living in the moment got him." Sniffing back another tear, he jutted his chin toward a ceremonial urn on the fireplace.

The loft that Charlie See had shared with his life partner, Terrence Unger, was just a few blocks down the hill from the Carmody Avenue Stella's. The place was modest, but tasteful. Not unlike Charlie himself. Rather tall for an Asian man, he was dressed in a blue loose-fitting silk suit over a cream-colored silk shirt. The bottom of the shirt had several moist spots from Charlie using it to dry his eyes.

Jane sat on a brushed chrome stool with a black-enamel tractor seat. Kenny wandered the living room, looking at photos of Terrence Unger and Charlie See.

"Mr. See," Jane began, "I know you've already been interviewed, but we're just doing our follow-ups. Is there anyone in your…Mr. Unger's life, past or present, who would want to do him harm?"

"No, Lieutenant." Charlie See had the faintest trace of a British accent. "Everyone loved Terry." He sighed. "*I* loved Terry."

Kenny sat on a dark mahogany chair, its cushion a beautiful tapestry of a chestnut horse and a rider in a red hunt jacket. "Maybe there was a problem at work." He pushed back in the chair until it balanced on its two rear legs. "Money problems, something like that?"

"That's Biedermeier," Charlie See said quickly.

"Sorry?" Kenny asked.

"The chair," Charlie said. "It's an antique. So, please…if you don't mind."

Kenny eased the chair forward, the front legs once again touching the floor, and rose.

"And no," Charlie continued. "Terry was having a great year at work. What happened at that restaurant wasn't about him."

Jane slid off the stool. "Thank you for your time, Mr. See. We know this must be very difficult for you."

"More than you know, Lieutenant. Do you have any idea how hard it is to meet a good man in this town?"

Jane smiled thinly, thinking to herself that, yes, she knew exactly how hard it was to meet a good man in San Francisco. She joined her husband at the front door. As Charlie See reached for the knob to let them out, Jane noticed the slightest tremble in his hand. She stopped and looked at him. Charlie averted his eyes. "Has anyone," she asked, "been to see you about the…about what happened? Other than cops and reporters?"

Charlie pulled in a quick surprised breath. Jane and Kenny edged their way back into the room.

"Who was it?" Kenny asked. "Who came to see you?"

Charlie stared at his own reflection in the tall window to his right and slowly shook his head. "Please. I can't."

"Why not?" Jane asked.

"Because…he told me not to tell."

Kenny whipped out his notebook. "Then you saw him. You can describe him."

"Actually…" Charlie brought his head around toward Kenny. "I can't. It was late last night. I was just coming back from moving my car. We have alternate side parking every day and I kind of lost track, what with everything that happened. So the elevator comes and the light's out. I reach in to feel for the switch and somebody comes up behind me, puts his arm around my throat, and pushes me inside. First thing I'm thinking is, 'Oh shit, first Terry and now me.' But all he does is ask, 'What do you know? What do you know?' Two or three times real fast."

"And because," Jane said, "the lights were out in the elevator..."

"I never saw what he looked like."

Kenny made a quick note. "Did you call the police?"

"He told me if I did"—Charlie See lifted his shirt to wipe his eyes again—"he'd come back."

"We'll make sure you're protected, Mr. See," Jane said. "But I'm calling for a Forensics team to dust for prints and search the area."

Kenny flipped his notebook closed. "If you'd called us right away..." But he let the thought drift off. The man had been through enough.

"One other thing, sir," Jane began. "When the man in the elevator asked you that question...did he whisper?"

Charlie See released his shirttail, letting it fall around his waist. "How did you know?"

A squad car was parked in the keystone of a streetlight in front of Charlie See's building. The two cops in the front seat, Chris Keiser and Candace Wong, nodded to Jane and Kenny as they came down the steps.

Candace lowered her window. There was a bag of McDonald's French fries between her and her partner. "We've got patrol units at the Mark Twain, at Antonia Salazar's, at Nicolas Silva's, and two at Saint Vincent's. One on either side."

Jane remembered Candace from the Sammy Pickett bust. "Fifteen's got you pulling nights now?"

Candace leaned her head out the window. "I transferred out of Fifteen, ma'am. The command structure there wasn't exactly...

conducive…to advancement, if you know…" She let the thought fall off, both of them knowing she was talking about Commander Hollingsworth. "Besides, I got a kid, and working nights gives me some baby-time during the days."

"Best of both worlds, then," Jane said. "You hear anything from Weymouth or Murphy?"

"Only that Rick's still taking his psych time. He was hit pretty hard, Lieutenant." She offered Jane the bag of fries.

Jane grabbed a few. "I'm just glad he's doing something about it."

The squeal of a woman laughing carried over from across the street. A young couple was going at it in a souped-up Trans Am, its front fender held together by a thick coat of gray primer. The windows were diaphanous with steam. There was a quick flicker of flame, then the orange dot of a lit cigarette. A moment later, the sweet smell of marijuana was carried along the gentle breeze.

"Fucking kids are smoking a joint with a squad car sitting right here," Kenny said. "Some balls, huh?"

Jane looked across to the Trans Am. The couple was going at it again, the car trembling in a familiar cadence. The girl laughed again, her world free of everything but the moment. "When did we get so old?"

Before Kenny could answer, two men appeared at the end of the street. The first thing that registered in Jane's mind was that they were cops. Something about their gait, the way their clothes hung. It took another half heartbeat for her to realize it was Mike Finney and Lou Tronick.

"Something came up, Lieutenant," Finney said as they closed in.

Lou Tronick smiled a greeting to Candace Wong in the black-and-white. "We got those autopsy finals you wanted hurried up? And Moby here did some excellent sleuthing and found an anomaly that might be interesting."

Finney pulled a color Xerox photo from his coat pocket and passed it to Jane. "The report on Francis Cellucci showed he had a tattoo high on his inner thigh. I thought that was a little out there for a priest, so I called Dr. Tedesco at home. He said that one of the junior medical examiners, some guy he imported from San Jose, performed the autopsy on Father Cellucci. So he called that doctor, who told him that he didn't even know it was a priest he was working on."

Candace Wong passed her flashlight through the window. Kenny thumbed it on and trained the beam on the photo. The tattoo was a red numeral four with dark blue wings fanning out on either side.

"Flying four?" Kenny said. "Winged four? What the hell is it?"

Jane turned the photo in her hand. "Don't know. Could be military. Could be gang."

"We messengered it over to Billy Ling at the Gang Smash Unit," Lou Tronick said. "He didn't recognize it right away, but his guys'll work on it tonight and let us know."

"We didn't think of military," Finney said. "I'll get on it."

Jane dropped the photo into her purse. "While you're doing that, Mike, run a crime check on Father Cellucci. All the way back. A priest with a tattoo could be a priest with a past."

Kenny flicked off the flashlight and handed it back to Candace. "Thing is, we don't even know if Francis Cellucci is from the area. He could be from Boston or New Orleans or God knows where."

"Good point," Jane said. "Mike, cross with the NCIC computer. See if you can raise any hits somewhere else in the country." She reached into the squad car and pinched a couple more fries. "Good work, guys."

"Dispatch to 3H58." A male voice. Cheryl's night shift replacement.

Jane retrieved her walkie-talkie. "3H58. Go."

"Lieutenant, we just got a call from one of the surveillance units at Saint Vincent's. A priest, a Father Marquez, said there was someone prowling the premises. Backup is rolling."

Jane looked to Kenny. He was already halfway to the Explorer, keys in his hand. She pressed the mic. "Do we have a helicopter available?"

"Negative. Air One's working a carjack in North Beach. Two's over a traffic accident in the Embarcadero. And Three's down for repairs."

"Peel Two off on my orders and send it to Saint Vincent's."

"But—"

"*Do* it. 3H58, out."

Kenny started the Explorer, ripped it into a squealing U-turn and threw open the passenger door.

Jane ran into the street and climbed in.

Kenny had the car moving, its rear tires fighting for traction, before she could close the door.

23

The sweep of the helicopter's belly-mounted, million candle-power spotlight and the crackle of police radio calls drew people to the windows of the four-story apartment house across from Saint Vincent's.

They stood in their windows—some in bold full-view, others carefully peeking between curtains—as if an artist had constructed an installation of framed live-action models, complete with dramatic lighting.

Jane and Kenny sat in the Explorer in front of a defaced mural of Junipero Serra, monitoring the radio traffic.

"Sky Two to ground..." The powerful beam of the NightSun swung toward the north end of the church and held in place, a brilliant white umbilical. "We've got movement on the roof."

Another patrol unit screeched up, its tires churning blue smoke as it shuddered to a stop. Two uniformed officers exploded from the car and, their weapons drawn, raced into the church schoolyard.

The helicopter's loudspeaker squealed a burst of feedback. "Attention you on the roof. This is the San Francisco Police Department. Lie facedown with your hands behind your—" The loudspeaker fell into an echoing silence and the voice of the same officer came over the police radio. "He's a runner! Going south, now east. Whoa! He jumped! Wait. There he is on the school building. Still going east."

Kenny ripped his Glock from its shoulder holster and threw open his door. Jane pulled her pistol from her bag and was just about to open her door when Kenny leaned back inside.

"No, Jane," he said flatly. "No way you're doing a run and jump."

Jane glared at him. "If I can't do my job, then I shouldn't be here at all!"

Kenny tugged at the action on his Glock, metal sliding on metal. "We can talk about that later. But, right now, I'm not letting you...and our baby...chase down some bad guy in the middle of the night."

"Goddammit, Ken, I—"

"What's the point of chugging vitamins every ten seconds and denying yourself caffeine if you're gonna put yourself and the baby in this kind of danger?" Kenny reached across and held her wrist. "I know it's hard, but it's just too hypocritical of both of us to do this any other way."

Jane tried to pull her hand away, her other hand grabbing for the door handle. But Kenny held on tight. "Listen to me just this once," he said, "and I promise I won't do anything stupid or even vaguely heroic."

Jane saw the relentless urgency in his eyes. She also saw the fathomless depth of her husband's devotion to her. And she yielded to it. "Okay." She released the door handle and tossed him her two-way. "But I want a full play-by-play."

The dashboard radio hissed to life. "Suspect is on the ground. Going northeast toward the basketball courts."

Kenny jammed the walkie-talkie into his back pocket. "This is right," he said. Then he wheeled to the left and tore into the schoolyard.

Jane watched as the outline of her husband's body receded from her. Growing smaller and less distinct until it was finally taken by the darkness.

"Your husband *is* right, you know."

Jane pivoted in her seat.

Edgar Silva was standing at the Explorer's open door. "You have a higher calling now, Lieutenant." He climbed into the driver's seat and pulled the door closed. Jane slid her hand into her bag. "What are you going to do," Edgar asked. "Arrest me? Shoot me?"

"Do I have reason to?"

"Maybe for other things. But not for this."

"How long were you out there?"

"Long enough." Edgar sniffed a derisive laugh. "A hundred cops won't look twice at some Mexican who's just standing still in this neighborhood. And that's the whole problem here. The cops don't look twice."

A radio call came in. "Suspect is at the chain-link."

The helicopter swooped lower and leveled its beam on the far side of the schoolyard.

"Do you know who they're chasing?" Jane asked.

Edgar nodded slightly.

"Who is it?"

"Someone they'll never catch."

"How do you know?" Jane asked.

"Because he works for me." Edgar put his left forearm on the steering wheel and leaned closer to Jane. "Listen to that sound, Lieutenant. It's the window of opportunity slamming closed. I can't let that happen. So I'm doing a little fieldwork of my own. Only without the weight of a badge…and without a net."

The air in the Explorer was warming, a fine film of condensation clouding the windows. "Then it's you," Jane said, "who's been going to the survivors. My sister-in-law, Charlie See, Father Marquez."

Edgar tilted his head in acknowledgement. "Like I said, *fieldwork*."

"You scared the shit out of them."

"Scared people talk." A cop ran by with a shotgun. Edgar turned his head slightly to the right, his face no longer visible to the street.

Jane closed her hand around the butt of her pistol. As long as Edgar was in a talking mood, she decided to go fishing. "What about Colleen Porter?"

"She didn't know anything."

A nibble. "And you know this because?"

Edgar shrugged, his broad shoulders rising. "I asked her."

A bite. Jane started to pull the gun out of her bag, her finger finding the curved steel of the trigger. "You went to her house?"

The radio buzzed. "Suspect is over the fence and into the backyard of that white house just behind the playground."

Edgar looked to the speaker, then to Jane. "No, Lieutenant. At the hospital." He sighed. "I wasn't at her house. I didn't kill her. You know and I know that whoever killed her also killed those people at the restaurant. My brother, your nephew, the others."

Kenny came over the radio, his voice breathless and excited. "Suspect climbed a shed behind the white house and is heading south toward the Village Apartments."

Two police cruisers, their roof lights strobing the night, sped for the area illuminated by the chopper.

Edgar watched them tear around the corner by the front entrance to Saint Vincent's. "Lieutenant, you and I are the same in two very distinct ways. First, we're both, to use your word, *survivors* of this crime."

"What's the second?"

"We're both hunters. But that's where the similarities end because I will stop at nothing to find my brother's killer. And you..."

"Chopper Two to ground. Suspect just went into the underground parking of the Village Apartments."

"3H61 to Chopper Two." Kenny's voice. "We're going in the south entrance. Cover the north and east."

Jane felt a quick stab of fear as she envisioned her husband racing down the oil-slick ramp of a dark parking garage, running headlong toward whatever was waiting for him at the bottom.

Edgar sensed her discomfort. "He has, and you have, nothing to worry about. My guy in there won't hurt anyone. Not even a cop." He smiled. "Besides, he's going to get away."

"You're awfully certain of yourself."

"I know how the game is played," Edgar said. "It's just too bad you don't trust me. We could get a lot done, you and me."

"Which brings us," Jane said, "to our other difference."

"You're part of the system, the police culture," Edgar went on. "With rules and barriers and this pervasive sense of right and wrong."

"Maybe so," Jane acknowledged. "But what part of you can tell me that it was right to terrorize those poor people?"

Edgar held her eyes, solemn and unblinking. "The part of me that one day will kill him." He sat back in the seat, put both hands on the wheel, and stared straight ahead. The muscles in his forearms tensed, taut ropes moving under his skin. "I'm not going to stop, Lieutenant." He turned his head toward her, a smile playing at the corners of his lips. "So what to do with me?"

Jane started to bring her hand out of her bag. Edgar caught her eyes with his, waiting to see what she'd do next. Jane's hand came clear of the purse and she held up the photograph of the priest's tattoo. "Ever seen this before?"

Edgar took the photo from her. "No. It's either not local or it's not current. I can ask around." He started to put it in his shirt pocket. "May I?"

Jane nodded.

Edgar pulled on the door handle, ready to get out of the car.

"I need to ask you something, Mr. Silva," Jane said.

The helicopter banked low, its rotor blast rattling the Explorer as it closed in on the Village Apartments. Edgar dipped his head to watch as it crossed to the other side of the church. "About...?" he asked, still looking out the window.

Jane glanced up to the helicopter, then back to Edgar. "If you and I are going to be trading information, I've got to close the loop on something that I'm still not clear on."

Edgar turned to her. "Such as?"

"Such as that drive-by," Jane said. "About that old woman who was shot." She shifted her weight, closing the distance between them as she pressed her point. "About your other brother's death."

Edgar pushed away from the steering wheel and laid his head back against the headrest. He closed his eyes and sat quietly, falling into some long-ago memory. He took in one last lung-filling breath and let the air slip out his nostrils. Then he turned to Jane. "It had all been spinning out of control," he finally said. "Crack was taking over as the drug of choice and the territory wars were insane. Two, three killings a week. My guys, their guys, anyone who got in the way. It wasn't that life was cheap; it simply had no value."

He chewed on the inside of his lower lip, his eyes on his lap. Another deep breath, another burst of memory. "I had put together a truce with the other three major gangs in the city—the Irish, the blacks, and the Asians. It took two years of backing and forthing. But the killings stopped. From eight or ten a month to zero. Everything was going along fine. You could actually send someone out on a buy or a sell and have a reasonable expectation of seeing him again. I can't impress upon you how revolutionary that was, how different from the usual gangland way of doing things."

"I understand."

Edgar pulled his lips back across his teeth and shook his head as more of the memory presented itself. "Then one night, I remember it was the Fourth of July. Hot as hell. I get a call from Spivey—he ran the black gang—and he tells me there was a drive-by in Chinatown and some poor old lady took a bullet. She was just sitting on her fire escape, beating the heat and watching the fireworks…and she dies in front of her little grandson. Spivey tells me it was *my* crew did the banging and that the Chinese guys—who are pretty ruthless under the best of circumstances—are going to escalate if I didn't make things right, do some house-cleaning of my own. So, in the interest of keeping the body count to a minimum, I brought in outside talent from LA to find out who did this and to take him out."

Edgar looked over to Jane, his eyes brimming.

"Jesus," Jane said, her voice hushed with the realization. "It was your brother!"

Edgar nodded tightly, tears glistening on his lower lashes. "Juan was desperate to get out of my long shadow. He thought a little action against a strong rival would impress people. But he read it totally wrong. And…what happened, happened."

"Would you still have ordered the hit if you had known it was Juan?"

"That's the thing, Lieutenant," Edgar struggled with his emotions, struggled for the words. "Remember I said that crack was the drug of choice back then? Well it was *my* drug of choice, too. I was fucked-up all the time. Best I can say, with the perspective of a clear head and all this time gone by, is…I don't know." His head bobbed slowly as he found the last of the memory. "So I got out of the shit, shut down my operation, and cleaned up my act and my body. No way I was going to let Nico follow Juan or follow me." He turned to Jane. "I was the one who was supposed to die first. Not my two baby brothers."

"3H61 to Chopper Two." Kenny's voice again. "Anything?"

"Chopper Two to 3H61. Negatory, Inspector."

"Widen the perimeter and call for backup," Kenny said. "I'm going back to my unmarked."

Jane and Edgar both knew what that command meant. It was over.

Edgar patted the tattoo photo in his pocket. "I'll shake a few trees."

"Knock a few heads?"

"Whatever it takes." He reached up and switched off the dome light.

Then he opened the driver's door, the inside of the Explorer staying dark, and stepped down into the street. A car pulled up and Edgar got into the backseat. As the car drove away, Jane noticed that it was a Trans Am with a primer-gray fender. The same car that had been across the street from Terrence Unger's apartment.

Out of the corner of her eye, she saw Kenny passing through the schoolyard gate. Jane had two seconds to decide whether to tell him about her encounter with Edgar as she quickly thumbed the dome light switch. Kenny opened the door, the light coming on, and climbed into his seat. "Fucker got away."

"Gave him a good scare, though. We'll get him next time."

Kenny reached over to Jane and brushed a stray strand of hair off her face. "We okay about before?"

"Yeah." Jane took his hand and held it to her chest, conflict welling inside her. If she told Kenny the truth, he'd spend the rest of the night looking for Edgar. If she downplayed it, she could at least think a little longer about how and when to tell her husband what really had happened tonight. "We're fine, hon."

"Good answer." Kenny started the Explorer and pulled the car into gear. "Let's go home."

24

Kenny was awake before first light. Not wanting to disturb Jane, he had shaved and showered in the downstairs bathroom. His plan was to go to the precinct early while Jane slept a few more hours. As he quietly made his way back up the stairs, he noticed the light on in the hall bathroom. He tapped at the door. "Hon?"

"Yeah..." Jane's voice was shallow, more breath than sound.

"You okay?"

"Not especially."

Kenny cracked the door open and stepped partway into the bathroom.

Jane sat on the closed toilet clutching a yellow ceramic bowl in her lap. Her face was pale and sweat-glistened. "Worse than throwing up is needing to and nothing comes." She wretched, her whole body convulsing with the effort.

Kenny took a washcloth from the bathtub faucet and doused it with cold water. He twisted out the excess and spread the towel across the back of her neck.

Jane pressed up into the coolness of the cloth, into his touch. She nodded to the yellow bowl. "Sorry to be using the good stuff. It was the only thing close by."

"Under the circumstances..." Kenny sat on the edge of the tub and massaged her neck through the wet cloth. "Want me in here or do you need some privacy?"

Jane sat up straight and stretched her legs. "Something tells me privacy is going to become a thing of the past." She stood up.

"Besides, whatever I thought was bubbling up, isn't." She took the washcloth from Kenny and pressed it to her face. "It just comes in waves, y'know?"

"They say the worse the pregnancy, the better the baby."

"More Y-chromosome propaganda." Jane crossed to the sink and bent over to run cold water onto her face. When she rose up, she caught Kenny's reflection in the mirror. "I need to tell you something."

Kenny put the yellow bowl on the counter. "Sounds ominous."

"Depends on how you take it."

"This is me listening."

"Last night while you were doing that run-and-jump at Saint Vincent's?"

"Yeah?"

Jane turned to him. "While I was monitoring the chase from the Explorer...Edgar Silva showed up."

"Showed up? What the hell does that mean?"

"He's the one who visited Father Marquez and Charlie See... and your sister—"

Kenny cut her off. "So while I'm off chasing wild geese, you were chatting up the guy who scared the shit out of Andrea at Bobby's grave?"

"He knows we're looking for him and it was his way of making contact." Jane took a half step toward her husband, and he took a full step back.

"In the real world, Jane, when we talk to someone who may be material to a capital case, we do it on *our* terms." Kenny brushed past her and stopped in the doorway. "This is all too complicated: my nephew's dead, my sister's been accosted, and my wife—for whatever reason—is defending some con she doesn't even know."

"I'm not defending him...I'm just trying to tell you what happened."

"*After* the fact!"

Jane relented. Kenny was right. She leaned back against the counter as Kenny started out the door. "And because it's not fucked-up enough," he went on, "I'm now feeling guilty about having an argument with my pregnant wife. I have to sit on my real feelings, so I don't add to your stress."

A truck rumbled by in the street below, causing a loose pane of glass in the bathroom window to rattle. Jane looked to the still-dark window. The first thing she thought when she saw her own face staring back at her was that she looked tired. Not just tired, exhausted. And the day hadn't even started yet.

Just as she brought her gaze back around to Kenny, the phone rang. It was too dark, too early, for that sound to be anything but bad news.

Kenny glanced at her and grabbed the portable from its cradle outside the bathroom door. "Hello? One second, sir." He reached across and held the phone out to Jane. "It's the chief. He doesn't sound so good."

Jane took the phone from him. "Hello, sir." Kenny leaned in to listen.

Chief McDonald's voice was low and strained. "Lieutenant, there's been a suicide. One of our own."

Jane did a quick dreadful roll call in her mind. "Who was it?"

"Patrolman Rick Weymouth. Ninety minutes ago. He left a note on his computer, then shot himself in the heart. First on-scene indicates death was immediate."

Jane gasped, her mind reeling at the loss of yet another young man she'd known for so long. Kenny put his arm around her shoulder and pulled her in close. She swallowed back her emotion and asked, "Does his dad know?"

"His parents and his brother have been notified."

"What about his partner?" Jane asked. Anyone check on him?"

"The police chaplain's on his way as we speak." The chief paused. "I know you knew the family."

"I'll give them a call. Thank you, sir." Jane disconnected the call. "Jesus, Ken," she said as she pressed the speed dial for the precinct.

"Nineteen, Finney."

"Mike, it's me. Do you ever sleep?"

"I could ask the same of you, Lieutenant. What's up?"

"I need you to e-mail me directions to Patrolman Tom Murphy's boat in the marina."

Jane could hear Finney tapping at his keyboard. "You'll have it in like two minutes. Is Inspector Marks available?"

Jane handed the phone to Kenny. "Hey, Moby."

"You know that surveillance camera we set up at the Staples across from the Stella's? There's some stuff on it you might want to check out."

"I'm on my way." Kenny switched off the phone and turned to Jane. "I'm going in. Please give Murphy my condolences."

Jane took the phone from him and held on to his wrist. "My turn to ask…we okay?"

Kenny stepped closer and rubbed the back of his hand along her belly. "We will be."

A thin ribbon of yellow and pink spanned the horizon, the first moments of a new day.

Jane's car bumped along the old wooden parking lot of the marina's Gas House Cove section. She parked near the foot ramp and got out. Sleeping seabirds squatted on the rooftops of the harbor buildings, huddled into themselves and each other. A medley of smells, foreign and familiar, swirled around Jane as, holding on to both railings, she carefully made her way down to the dock.

Finney's e-mailed directions had told her that Tommy Murphy's boat was in slip number eight, second to the end on the right. As Jane walked along the gently swaying dock, she did a quick mental inventory of the area. The faint sound of electric generators emanated from a few of the boats, the ones that people actually lived on. But most of the boats were dark, unoccupied pleasure craft tarped-in against San Francisco's erratic weather.

A fishing boat, seine nets drawn up like an angel's wings, chugged past. Its wake caused the boats at mooring to rise and bob. The dock rose and fell as well and Jane stopped and put her hand against a piling until the motion subsided. As she did, she caught some movement just south of the marina.

A maintenance truck was backing up along the sand; its steady *beep-beep-beep* back-up signal only now just reaching her. Four workmen in orange jumpsuits descended from the truck with rakes and shovels and started retrieving detritus from a delta of debris in front of a huge storm drain. They worked in practiced unison and, Jane noted, they all smoked cigarettes. Probably, she realized, to mask the foul odors wafting from the gaping pipeworks.

Jane continued down the dock to number eight. A modest sailboat, *Sweet Dreams*, gently rolled in its slip, the water making a soothing lapping sound. Soft light bloomed in the portholes. She was about to step across to the gunnel when the hatch just aft of the mast slid open throwing up a wash of light from below.

The top of Tommy Murphy's head appeared. Then his face, drawn and thin. He climbed the last few steps, his shoulders sagging, and held out his hand to help Jane aboard. "Heard the footsteps," he said. "Thanks for coming, Lieutenant. Means a lot to me."

Jane stepped onto the deck. "The police chaplain been here yet?"

"Just left. Seems like a good man." Tommy gestured below. "Want to come down? Get out of the chill?" He stepped aside, the light catching his face. His youth, certainly his innocence, Jane thought, gone forever.

The cabin was close, cramped, lived-in. A rich chicory aroma filled the small space and Jane noticed a well-used Mr. Coffee machine next to the tiny stainless steel sink.

"Made some for the chaplain," Tommy said. "Want some?"

Jane shook her head. "Trying to quit."

"Your baby, of course. How you feeling, Lieutenant?"

"Hangin' in."

Jane sat on a narrow banquette. "How 'bout you?"

Tommy busied himself with smoothing out the blanket on his unmade bunk. "I'm not doing so well, ma'am. I'm kinda all fucked-up, y'know?" He turned to her, tears pooling in his eyes. "Rick called me last night. Like he does every night since the shootings. But he was, I don't know, more clingy or something. Like he didn't want to get off the phone. So I let him talk and he just went off on how inadequate he felt about not getting to the Stella's quicker, and how inadequate he felt about taking a psych leave and how Commander Hollingsworth..." He broke eye contact and looked to a photo of himself and Rick Weymouth goofing like two college kids at an interdepartmental softball game.

"How Commander Hollingsworth...what?" Jane prodded.

"I don't want to be insubordinate, ma'am."

"I came here to help you. It's okay...tell me."

Tommy rinsed a mug, the electric water pump kicking in, and poured himself some coffee. "Commander Hollingsworth wrote a letter of reprimand to Rick's file. He questioned his decision-making under duress and basically accused him of not only screwing up, but then hiding behind a psych leave as a way of avoiding the consequences."

"That son of a bitch," Jane said, her anger rising.

"And what's worse, ma'am?" Tommy went on. "I sorta told Rick everything would be okay and got off the phone. It was after midnight and I just figured we'd catch up in the morning. My partner was calling for help…and I wasn't there for him." He tried to blink back the tears, but they spilled over and coursed down his cheeks.

Jane rose and put a hand on his shoulder. "You are not responsible for Rick's death. He's part of the collateral damage of this whole awful crime." Tommy looked up, his cheeks shiny with tears. "We all are," Jane continued. "But the thing is, we can't act like victims. Because if we give in to that impulse, then we won't find the bad guy. And I will never accept that."

"Me neither, Lieutenant." Tommy tore a paper towel off the roll hanging under the electronics shelf and dabbed at his face. "Thank you."

Jane examined the stacks of electronic equipment. "What is all that stuff?" she asked, trying to divert the conversation.

"The usual mariner's collection: depth finder, GPS, ship-to-shore. That one"—he pointed to a black box crammed between the others and smiled—"is what you call a DVD player."

Jane laughed. "Can't live without that."

"No, ma'am. It can get a little…lonely…out here." He switched on a small instrument next to the DVD player. A bar of tiny lights began blinking in sequence, green to red. "Police scanner," he said. "What can I tell you? I love this stuff."

"Once a cop…"

"It's all I ever wanted, ma'am."

"Like Rick," Jane said.

"Yeah," Tommy nodded. "He told me he knew you a little bit."

"I was friends with his dad in the old days. Talked to him on the way over here. Too many hard phone calls on this job."

Tommy nodded in agreement, as the low chug of another, larger, boat came to them. "That's the *Arabella*," Tommy said as the sailboat rolled in the passing boat's wake. "Goin' after crabs." The boat lifted and fell. A wet suit hanging on a hook next to the yellow foul-weather gear swayed like a pendulum.

Jane felt a surge of nausea billowing in her throat. "Tommy," she said quickly, "I've gotta get to work. But you need to do me one favor."

"You bet."

"Promise me you'll take a psych leave or at least some vacation time. I don't care how short it is, you need a break."

Tommy was suddenly agitated, nervous. "I can't do that, Lieutenant. Commander Hollingsworth will ruin me."

Jane reached for the ladder. "I promise you that I will personally take care of Commander Hollingsworth." The pitching of the boat, the harsh smells of coffee and diesel exhaust, the closeness of the cabin, were all getting to her. She needed fresh air and solid ground.

Tommy recognized her distress and yanked back on the hatch. Cool sea air flooded into the cabin and Jane drank it in. Tommy guided her up to the main deck. "I get seasick myself down there, ma'am. The motion, the stink coming off the storm drain...and I'm not even pregnant."

Jane stepped onto the gunnel and stretched across to the dock. "Well, I sure am...especially today." She pulled the car keys from her purse and looked back to Tommy. He was about to say something, then pulled it back. "What?" Jane asked.

Tommy wrapped his hand around a halyard, his fist tightening until his knuckles were white marbles. "The chaplain said Rick shot himself in the heart. I mean, can you imagine the pain he must have been in to do something like that?"

"It's tough to think about," Jane said. "And I don't want you in that kind of pain. So do we have an understanding, Officer Murphy?"

"Yes, ma'am, we do." He let go of the halyard and reached across the water gap to shake her hand. "Thanks again for coming down here. Means the world to me." He retreated to his sanctuary and pulled the hatch shut.

Jane stood for another moment on the quavering dock. Then she started walking quickly toward the parking lot. And suddenly she was running, sucking in the damp air as her feet pounded up the ramp.

She started the car, jerked it into drive, and clattered across the wooden lot.

On the harbor master's roof, a seagull stood out of its squat, spread its wings, and let an updraft take it away.

Jane turned onto Fort Mason and sped toward the freeway. She wanted desperately to be far away from the smells and unsteadiness of the marina…and equally desperately to be back at work.

Pushing the rock up the hill until all was right in the world.

25

One of the police cadets was stealing a smoke in the stairway of the police parking structure and Jane had to hold her breath as she hurried past.

Pushing open the door to the Homicide bullpen, Jane saw that most of her team was gathered around two TV monitors in Interrogation One. As she crossed the squad room, she noticed a coffee can brimming with ones, fives, and tens just outside the lunchroom. Someone had taped a paper sign to it: FLOWERS FOR RICK WEYMOUTH. Cheryl Lomax came up to her and handed her a scrap of paper. "Got that phone number for ya, Lieutenant."

Jane entered the war room and stood behind Kenny and Finney as they watched the surveillance tape from the Staples. Many of the people who visited the makeshift shrine at Stella's were familiar to them. A female EMT from the first responders laid a small bouquet near the front door of the restaurant. Kids from Bobby's funeral stood near the newsstand, unable to go any closer. Max Batzer, a veteran cop only months from retirement, appeared in civilian clothes. He crossed himself, took off his sunglasses, and wiped his eyes.

The video fluttered for a second as a police car pulled up in front of the fabric store and Tommy Murphy and Rick Weymouth got out. Rick went to the collection of flowers and photographs and knelt on one knee. He lit a votive candle and rose, his shoulders trembling. Tommy put a reassuring hand on his partner's back and pulled him into a hug. Other passersby stopped to witness the wrenching tableau of two policemen so overcome with emotion. Tommy then led Rick back to the black-and-white and they drove off.

A man, dark and thick, with black Ray-Ban sunglasses, turned to watch them leave. The image froze.

"There," Finney said, holding the remote. "There he is again."

"There who is again?" Jane asked.

Kenny turned to invite Jane into the inner circle. "How's Murphy doing?"

"Torn to shreds." Jane peered at the monitor. "Who is that guy?"

Kenny zapped the other monitor on. "Check it out."

Video from Nico Silva's funeral came up. Kenny fast-forwarded to the moment when a man came up to Edgar, embraced him, and whispered something in his ear. Burly and dark, with black Ray-Bans. "Same guy," Kenny said.

"But," Jane offered, "there are plenty of people on the Staples tape who we've seen at other funerals."

"Same thing I thought at first." Kenny rewound the Staples tape and pressed Scan. The tape raced forward. People came and went, their movements sped up and exaggerated. But the man in the black Ray-Bans remained still.

"He's there every day, Lieutenant," Finney said. "Just standing there…"

"Watching," Kenny finished for him. "What we're doing electronically with surveillance cameras, he's doing in person."

Jane looked from one monitor to the other. "What should we do about it?"

"Bring him in," Kenny said flatly. "Him and Edgar Silva."

Jane nodded. "I agree."

Kenny opened his mouth partway, ready to make the argument he'd played out in his mind. But Jane's ready agreement caught him off guard.

"You're right, Ken," Jane continued. "If Mr. Silva knows something, then we need to know it, too."

The door opened. Lou Tronick wheeled in a cart with six large plastic bags on it. "This a bad time?"

"No, Lou," Jane said. "It's fine." Through the door, over near the lunchroom, Jane could see Dr. Bill Glazer, his face flushed with weariness, putting some money into Rick Weymouth's coffee can.

Lou kicked the door closed as he pushed the cart into the room. "They just released the victim's property. Ken, I thought you'd want Bobby's stuff soon as possible."

Each bag had a broad red tag taped to it. Terrence Unger, Antonia Salazar, Francis Cellucci, Arthur Rourke, Nicolas Silva, Robert Farrier. Kenny touched the bag that held his nephew's effects. "Thanks, Lou."

Finney motioned for the other support personnel to give Inspector Marks some time. They filed out, heads bowed. Kenny took Bobby's bag from the cart and put it on one of the work tables. Using his pocket knife, he broke the Coroner's Department seal and spilled out the contents.

Bobby's chrome sunglasses, the blue Gore-Tex wallet, a pack of peppermint Pez, a bus pass, his scruffy tennis shoes. Kenny spread them all out, looking at the pieces of the life left behind by his nephew. He picked up the bus pass and stared at Bobby's picture. "It's like he's trapped in ice," he said. "And he'll never change or grow or age." He reached deep into the bag and pulled out a pale blue evidence receipt. Someone had written down the fact that a small amount of marijuana had been found on Robert Farrier's body.

Kenny quickly scanned the page, folded it, and stuffed it into his jacket pocket. Then he refilled the plastic bag and turned to Jane. "I'm going to Andrea's for a little bit."

"I understand," she said. "While you do that, I'm going to bring in Mr. Silva for questioning." She squeezed his hand. "I'd like your help in the interrogation."

"Wouldn't miss it." Kenny tucked the bag under his arm and left.

Jane watched her husband go, aching to help him and knowing that, for now, she couldn't. She turned to the City Planning schematic of the block that the Carmody Stella's was on. Finney had folded it down to fit on the bulletin board and one of the pushpins had fallen out. Jane retrieved it from under the table and thumbed it back into the lower right corner. Then she stood back and looked at the surveyor's rendering—angular and clean and bloodless—and thought about what Kenny had said.

About how Bobby was frozen in time.

But this building, this city block wasn't. Jane looked over to the monitor where the tape showed a vital, vibrant neighborhood. Altered and bruised, but still thriving.

She turned off the monitors, a static crackle sizzling across the screens. Then she took out the scrap of paper Cheryl had given her and dialed the private line of Precinct Fifteen's commander.

The phone was answered before the first ring finished. "Hollingsworth."

"Commander, it's Jane Candiotti."

"I'm a little busy right now, Lieutenant. Lemme call you back in—"

Jane cut him off. "Commander Hollingsworth, listen carefully because I'm only going to say this once. You will remove your letter of reprimand from Rick Weymouth's file immediately. You will destroy it. There will be no paper trail. Then you will recommend Officer Weymouth for a posthumous promotion to up his pay-grade so his family will be eligible for higher death benefits."

There was a long burning pause. "Anything else?"

"Yes. You will, out of the goodness of your broken heart, insist that Officer Murphy take a leave of absence until he deems himself fit to return to active duty."

"But—"

"Do it, goddamit!" Jane struggled to control her fury. Then she softened her voice and continued. "The other officers in your charge will be impressed by your devoted compassion for the well-being of the rank and file."

"Here's a question for ya, Lieutenant: what if I choose not to be so compassionate and devoted?"

"Then I will instigate such a shitstorm at Internal Affairs that the Pope himself couldn't survive, let alone an ambitious career-man like yourself." Jane took a beat to let that sink in. "Are we clear with each other, Commander?"

"Perfectly."

"Fine then." Jane slammed the phone down and turned to the door.

Cheryl Lomax stood in the doorway, a thin smile rising. "Commander Hollingsworth?"

"The *former* Commander Hollingsworth," Jane said evenly. "When all this is over, remind me to hook up with IA."

"But you just told him if he did what you said, you wouldn't go to IA."

Jane snatched Nico Silva's property bag from the cart and strode across the bullpen. "I lied," she said as she ripped open the stairwell door.

Everyone stared.

In this neighborhood, Jane's unmarked police car may as well have been painted Day-Glo orange.

Old people watched from their porches as Jane cruised by. Teenagers, hopelessly truant and endlessly jobless, glared from the alley-mouths. Young kids playing street games held their ground, suspicion and challenge in their angry eyes.

Jane turned right on Shawcross and parked in front of a fire hydrant. A thin stream of water ran down its surface and puddled in the gutter. The hydrant's seal had been broken so many times by teenagers beating the heat that the fire department had long ago stopped sending crews out to fix it.

An old Hispanic woman sat on the steps of a rundown triple-decker tenement. She was wearing a thin, pale housedress faded to dreary beige after years of laundering, and a pair of unlaced men's brown leather shoes. She shook a cigarette from a pack of Marlboros and lit it with a wooden match. Drawing a lungful of smoke, she let the match fall to the sidewalk. It landed among several other blackened matchsticks, flickered, and died.

Jane grabbed the bag of Nico's belongings and got out of the car. She was about to lock it, when it occurred to her that this might be an affront to the old woman. Leaving the car unlocked, she approached the steps. "Excuse me, *Senora*, I'm looking for Edgar Silva."

The woman fanned the smoke out of her eyes and looked away. Jane squatted down to talk to her. "*Hablas Ingles, Senora?*" The woman's eyes slowly focused on Jane's, then drifted to the plastic bag she was holding. She drew deeply on her cigarette and let the smoke billow out her nostrils. Jane stood up, the pungent smell prompting an unwelcome reflex at the base of her throat.

The front door opened and Jane, shielding her eyes with a lopsided salute, saw a woman in her early forties emerge with a young boy on her hip. "Can I help you?" the woman asked, a wary question etched in distrust. The little boy gnawed on a carrot.

Jane climbed the six steps to the porch. "Is that Leo?"

"You know my nephew?" the woman asked, her face, her body, relaxing. Now that Jane could see her up close, it was clear that she was once quite beautiful.

"Yes, ma'am. I'm Lieutenant Candiotti, SFPD Homicide—"

The woman studied Jane, her dark eyes searching for something. "You the one lost a relative in the shootings?"

"Yes, I am."

"Edgar told me about you. Said you were different than the others." She shifted Leo to her other hip and offered her hand. "My name's Carmen. And that's"—she jutted her chin toward the old woman on the stairs—"that's Celia."

Jane followed her look down to Celia. The old woman sucked on her cigarette, holding the smoke in and then letting it drift from her nostrils.

"It's all she does now is smoke," Carmen explained. "We can't even get her to eat. Burying two sons like that. Won't be long till we lose her, too."

Jane thought of Kenny's father and how Bobby's death would surely hasten his own. "I brought this for Edgar." She handed over the bag of Nico's things.

Carmen hefted Leo up to her shoulder and took the bag. She looked through the plastic and saw Nico's wallet, tennis shoes, wristwatch, and necklace. Turning the bag over, she noticed the pale blue evidence slip at the bottom. "*Pobrecito*," she clucked as she placed the bag on a baby stroller and turned back to Jane. A film of tears came to her eyes. "Thank you for personally bringing this to us."

"You're welcome, Mrs. Silva," Jane said. "I also need to talk to your husband about the…our…case."

"He's in Oakland today…working," Carmen said. "I know you've been trying to contact him. I'll make sure he calls you." Her eyes caught Jane's again and held them. "I promise you that, Lieutenant."

"I appreciate that. But I'm afraid I have to—"

Carmen held up her hand. "I want my husband back too, Lieutenant," she said. "Edgar will get in touch with you today."

The sound of a slowly approaching car echoed down the street. As Jane turned, she knew what it would be. The primer gray Trans Am sat idling in the middle of the street, its driver hidden behind a mask of opaque glass. She looked to Carmen. "Who's driving that car?"

"*Un primo de Edgar*," Carmen said. "One of Edgar's cousins." She nuzzled Leo. "He'll see that you get out of the barrio without trouble."

Jane smiled. "An escort?"

Carmen returned the smile. "As you wish. All I know is Edgar trusts him with his life."

Jane touched Leo's hair. "I'll expect to hear from your husband, Mrs. Silva."

"Today, Lieutenant. *Es una promesa*."

Steering clear of Celia and her cigarettes, Jane descended the steps, crossed the sidewalk, and got into her car.

The Trans Am crept forward, the driver revving the muscular engine.

Jane started her unmarked and pulled away, heading into the sun. The young kids stopped their games and stepped aside.

As the Trans Am followed her out of the neighborhood, the driver, unseen by Jane, pulled the black Ray-Bans down over his eyes.

26

Jane was stuck.

Construction detours and lunch hour traffic had turned the financial district into a bumper to bumper quagmire. She glanced in the rearview. The Trans Am was still behind her, reflections of the urban canyon walls kaleidoscoping off its tinted windshield. On the radio, the local news reported on Rick Weymouth's suicide—each station mentioning that the Stella's shootings remained unsolved.

A city bus, its umbilical cable tethered to overhead power lines, pulled away from the curb. Jane instinctively moved to the right, filling the space it had just vacated. Squinting against the sun, she noticed that she was at the bottom of Carmody Avenue. Just as the light went from yellow to red, she gunned the engine and turned up the steep incline. It was as if the awful crime scene at the top of the next hill were summoning her.

Jane parked behind a U-Haul and got out. The driver of the gray Trans Am cruised past. He tapped his horn, turned onto Ashmont Street, and disappeared. Jane looked around.

This neighborhood that had been visited by such unspeakable violence had, in its way, made its peace and moved on.

Nguyen Bao sat on a wooden stool inside the news kiosk, watching a Vietnamese program on his portable television. Across the street, a new panhandler had taken Shanty Rourke's place. He rocked from foot to foot, jiggling a Styrofoam cup at the customers leaving the Staples. Jane turned back to the Stella's and saw that the flowers and candles and photographs of the improvised memorial were gone.

Two workmen backed out the restaurant's front door, muscling a huge stainless steel frying vat into the sunlight. Another workman, his arms rippling with the effort, hefted the other end of the vat and, with a grunting jerk of his head, motioned for his team to keep going toward the U-Haul.

As they struggled across the sidewalk, one of the men lost his grip and a corner of the fryer crashed to the concrete, its metallic wall crumpling from the impact.

"Jesus *Christ*, guys!" Casey Noveck stormed out of the restaurant, a clipboard in one hand, an electronic inventory wand in the other. "Believe it or not, I hired you to move this stuff, not destroy it." He turned in a quick frustrated circle, then confronted the lead workman. "You insured, huh? You *better* be insured."

The workman stared at him, dripping with sweat and contempt. "Yeah, we insured."

"You fuckin' better be," Noveck sneered and stalked back inside.

The workman looked to Jane. "You with him?"

"Nope."

"Good. 'Cause he's an asshole."

Jane tilted her head, not exactly disagreeing, and went into the restaurant.

All of the chairs and tables and booths were gone. So was the counter and most of the kitchen equipment. This room, the scene of such horror only a few days ago, had been almost completely transformed from a thriving restaurant to a hollowed-out storefront.

Casey Noveck spotted Jane. "You're with the police, right?"

"Yes, I'm Lieutenant Candiotti from Homicide. We met before."

Casey nodded smugly. "I never forget a face. A good trait in my business."

"In any business," Jane said. "I'm gonna go downstairs. Have a look around."

"Help yourself, Lieutenant," Casey called after her. "But you better hurry. This place'll probably be a Starbucks by tonight."

Jane turned left at the bottom of the stairs and stopped.

The killing floor had been scoured clean of any reminder of what had happened here. There was the faint smell of fresh paint and she realized that the walls had already been covered with a new coat of the same industrial white.

The door to the Deepfreeze was open. Jane looked inside. It was completely empty. Shelving, floorboards, even the low bench where they'd found Colleen Porter were gone. Turning toward the back door, she passed the area where the condiment storage racks had been and stepped outside.

The sun, a perfect white disc punched in the sky, hovered at the roofline of the buildings across the alley. A Coca-Cola delivery truck rattled along the cratered roadway. The driver paused at the closed chain-link gate, like a milk-wagon horse making its habitual rounds, and continued on his way.

A brown house sparrow landed on the fence top. It teetered for balance, then flitted across to the air-conditioning unit by the rear door. It stood there, bobbing up and down, chattering loudly. Jane noticed that its nest had been disturbed. The careful weaving of twigs and lint had been pulled out of the sheltering crevice, part of it torn away.

Damn cats, Jane thought to herself.

She heard the commotion before she saw it.

Something burst into her peripheral vision, racing toward her. It was a man. Jane barely had time to register that it was Edgar Silva coming at her before he left his feet and hurtled across the last few yards that separated them.

He thudded into her, just below the shoulder, and sent her sprawling onto a pallet of flattened cardboard boxes. That same instant, the sound of a gunshot boomed in the narrow alley.

Edgar's body clenched for a second, then calmed.

Jane scrambled out from beneath him, her service weapon already out of her purse.

There was a tear in the flesh above Edgar's right eye where the bullet had ripped through his eyebrow. He pawed at the blood that streamed down his face. Then he pointed past Jane to a building across the alley. "There!"

Jane spun around and found herself staring directly into the sun. She squatted down, squinting against the glare, and saw what seemed to be a human form on a roof across the way. A puff of smoke and another bullet caromed off the steel gate post.

Putting herself between the shooter and Edgar, Jane squeezed off four quick rounds. Two of them pocked the brick facade that ran along the top of the building. The figure retreated, running directly toward the sun until he was wrapped in light and gone.

Jane dropped to her knees beside Edgar. He lay propped against the fence, his T-shirt pulled up to the wound on his face. Jane tugged at his hand until he lowered the T-shirt. One eye was obscured by blood. The other was slowly losing focus, drifting aimlessly.

Jane snatched the two-way from her bag and frantically thumbed the mic. "3H58 to Dispatch," she yelled. "I've got a shots-fired and a man down at the Stella's on upper Carmody. He's a friendly. Request an ambulance and backup stat! Shooter still at large." She let the radio fall to the ground.

Casey Noveck raced out the back door. "Jesus, Lieutenant." He ran back inside and then reappeared with a stack of white dish towels. Jane took them from him and applied pressure to Edgar's forehead.

"Did you shoot this guy?" Casey asked breathlessly, keeping his distance from Edgar.

"No, I didn't." Jane worked to stop the bleeding. She glanced over to Casey. "He saved my life."

"How 'bout you, Lieutenant. Are you hit?"

"No, I'm…" Jane saw that Casey was staring at the front of her pants. It was only then that she felt the moisture, the sticky ooze spilling out of her. She sat heavily on the black tar surface, her hands still pressing against Edgar's wound. "Shit."

27

The helicopter floated silently outside her window.

Jane opened her eyes and allowed herself a moment to remember what had happened. The gunshot. Edgar going down. Her own bleeding. The ambulance. The hospital. She felt her heartbeat quicken with a sudden adreno-rush of anxiety about her baby.

Then she remembered the doctor coming to her and telling her that her fetus was safe. That the blood she'd lost was due to a subchorionic hemorrhage, a tiny tear in the placenta. She just needed some rest, he had said, and it would resolve itself.

Kenny had come running in, his face furrowed with fear. And the doctor had repeated everything for him. She had held out her hand to her husband and he had clasped it, kneading her fingers with his. The doctor had slipped out.

Jane had tried to explain. Kenny had said, "*Shh*…later…you rest now." And he had gone outside to make some calls while her eyes grew heavy and sleep had come at last.

Now she was awake again, a gust of memory rushing in. She was drawn to the afternoon sun streaming through the window to her left. Balling her hands into fists, she pushed herself forward on the bed and looked outside.

Miles away, between the hospital and the horizon, a helicopter hovered over the city. Jane knew that it was Air One working her shooting incident in the alley behind the Stella's on Carmody. She wondered who the pilot was. Odds were she knew him.

Pulling the blanket down off her legs, Jane could feel the dry after-sting from where the nurse had washed the blood from her thighs. She put her hand flat on her lower belly, willing herself to sense the fluttering rhythms of her baby. Slowing down her own breathing, Jane whispered a quiet prayer. Then she lay back down again, the hospital bed creaking beneath her weight.

"You call that a nap?"

Jane turned her head. Kenny stood in the doorway. "How long did I sleep?"

"Not even half an hour." He crossed the room, still gripped with worry over what might have been.

Jane sat forward. "How—"

"I'm doing okay," Kenny said as he sat on the bedside chair and took her hand.

"How's Edgar?" Jane asked. She felt his hand go slack. "Ken, no matter what you feel about him, he saved my life today." She squeezed his hand. "And your baby's life."

"His wound isn't life-threatening. An inch in either direction and he's not so lucky. The doctors are pretty sure he won't lose his eye."

"Thank God for that. Where'd they take him?"

"He's here. One floor down." Kenny slipped his hand out of hers. "What do you think happened out there?" His eyes moved to the window, to the helicopter still working the crime scene.

"I know what happened," Jane sighed. "I just don't know why. We get the why—"

Kenny finished for her. "We get the who."

"Right. So let's back it up. Was I the intended victim or was Edgar? Problem is: no one knew I was going to be there. Hell *I* didn't even know I was going to be there until I was on top of the place."

"Not exactly no one," Kenny said. "Didn't someone from Edgar's crew escort you out of the barrio?"

"What are you saying?"

"Look, you've been all over me, and rightfully so, about keeping my cop instincts intact even though my nephew was killed. I think it's appropriate that you do the same. That you ask all the right cop questions regardless of how you feel about anyone who may or may not be involved."

Jane couldn't help but smile.

"What?" Kenny asked.

"You're so right," Jane said, "I can't even argue with you."

"Good answer." Kenny leaned forward in the chair. "So Edgar's people knew you were at that Stella's?"

"Correct. But they have no reason to want me dead. I don't know anything."

"But they don't know that."

Jane let her head fall back to the pillow. "Yes, they do."

"How?"

"Because I've told Edgar what we know. Or more to the point, what we don't know."

Kenny stood up, trying to control his growing agitation. "Why the hell would you do that?"

"Edgar is plugged-in in ways we can never hope to be. If there's the remotest possibility he can help us solve these murders, I want to pursue it." Jane sat up and swung her legs over the edge of the bed. "You say it yourself all the time: we've got to color outside the lines."

"Yeah, but sharing trade secrets on a capital case with an ex-con relative of a murder victim is coloring in a whole 'nother book."

"And why not, Ken? Why the hell not? We all want the same thing here: to nail the son of a bitch who killed all those people. Who killed Bobby. And I don't give a *fuck* how we do it!"

Kenny took a long beat, Jane's anger floating in the room like smoke. "Glad to see," he said finally, "you're listening to the doctor and getting so much rest." He smiled, his eyes lighting up in the way Jane loved. "Let's, for argument's sake, say that Edgar had nothing to do with it. We still don't know who the shooter was gunning for…you or him. But it's obvious that one of you was followed to that restaurant."

"There's another possibility," Jane offered.

"What's that?"

"The shooter was already there."

Kenny chewed on this. "It's good theory, Lieutenant. But why did the bad guy return to the scene of the crime?"

"Because they always do?" Jane shook her head. "I don't know. Could be he was looking for something and I surprised him. Could be he's been there every day and it was my bad luck to show up today. Hell, maybe he works or lives nearby and is there all the time anyway."

Kenny grabbed his notepad and jotted something down. "Might be something to that. I'm gonna have the guys re-canvas the shops and apartments on both sides of that alley."

"While you're doing that, would you get the incident tape from Air One? I want a bird's-eye view of what went down."

"On one condition," Kenny said as he slipped his notebook into the back pocket of his jeans.

"What's that, Inspector?"

"You get some rest…and you kiss your husband good-bye."

"That's two conditions."

Kenny sat on the side of the bed and wrapped his arms around his wife. "Too bad."

Jane walked by the visitors' lounge and glanced in.

Celia Silva was praying hard.

She sat in a slice of sun in one of the hospital's outside smoking areas, a rosary in one hand, a Marlboro in the other. Her eyes closed, her upper body rocked to the cadence of her words of gratitude, thanking a benevolent God who had let her oldest son survive once again.

An old man worked on a jigsaw puzzle of the Golden Gate Bridge. A teenage girl, her head turtled into a hooded sweatshirt, dozed on a pea-green Naugahyde couch. A little boy sat on the floor, his back to Jane, whacking two pieces of Legos together. Jane could tell by his hair that it was Leo. Carmen Silva stood at the window, peeling an orange and looking out at the helicopter hanging in the distant sky. She didn't notice the lady cop pass by the window, making her way toward Edgar Silva's room.

As Jane approached the nurses' station, she realized that she was on the same floor that Colleen Porter had been on. She passed the elevator bank and turned into the first room on the right.

Edgar Silva lay in a pool of light funneling down from an overhead lamp. His head and right eye were swathed in bandages. Jane stood in the doorway, her heart filling with emotion as she looked across to the man who had saved her life.

Sensing her presence, Edgar opened his good eye. "Thought you were the nurse," he said, his voice raspy and soft, "finally come to bring me my food."

Jane stepped into the room. "Should I call for her?"

"Won't do any good." Edgar forced a smile, half of it disappearing into his bandages. "They took one look at the prison-tat Mexican with a gunshot wound and pretty much made up their minds where I fall in the food chain. Yeah, I'm hungry, but I'm not desperate. I can wait."

"May I?" Jane asked, gesturing into the room with her open hand.

"Please...please come in, Lieutenant."

Jane crossed the room and stood at Edgar's side. Even lying in a hospital bed, his body shrouded by a blanket and his head wrapped in bandages, Edgar Silva still seemed powerful, kinetic.

"I think, under the circumstances, we can drop the formalities. Please call me Jane."

"As you wish…Jane. And I'm Edgar."

Jane sat in the guest chair, reaching out to its arms for support.

"Your baby?" Edgar asked. "It's all right?"

"Yes, it's fine. And so am I…thanks to you."

"Glad I was there to help."

"Me too," Jane said. "But *why* were you there?"

Leo's laughter reached them from the visitors' lounge. Edgar looked to the door, then back to Jane. "Carmen called to tell me you'd brought over Nico's things—thank you for that—and that one of my boys rode out of the barrio with you. So I called my *vato* and he said he'd just left you at Stella's. I was close by and needed to talk to you. And the rest is…" He brought his hand up to his bandage and touched the area covering his wound. Then he lowered his hand and pointed to the hospital tray.

Jane rose and poured a cup of ice water. She put in a straw and held the cup out to Edgar. He wrapped his huge hand around hers and pulled the cup closer. Then he took a long sip and sat back again. "*Gracias.*"

"Why did you need to talk to me so badly?" Jane asked as she returned the cup to the tray.

"The reason I was in Oakland?" Edgar began. "I was doing some legwork on that tattoo you showed me. Actually, I was over at Alameda Correctional visiting an old…colleague…who's kind of an expert on that stuff."

"And this colleague, was he helpful?"

"Very."

Jane took a copy of the tattoo from her purse and passed it to Edgar.

He held it up to the light and blinked his good eye into focus. "You see how it's a red numeral four with wings coming out the sides?"

Jane nodded.

"Years ago, before the airport expanded, there was a network of gangs—small-time, but ruthless—in what was then First through Twentieth Streets. One of them was called the Four Birds because they had the run of Fourth Street back then. They were an obscure bunch of punks who basically evaporated when the Airport Commission eminent domained about a hundred city blocks and San Francisco International as we know it was created."

Jane could feel it. The first fissure cracking in the case. Anxious to tell Kenny what she'd learned, she dropped the photo of the tattoo back into her purse and started for the door. "Thank you, Edgar. This helps a lot."

"A question, Jane?"

Jane stopped in the doorway. "What's that?"

"Will you tell me who you got that tattoo off of?"

Jane started to answer, then pulled it back. "I can't."

Edgar nodded. "Here's what I know, Lieutenant," he said, acknowledging the formality that had returned to their relationship. "That tattoo and who it belongs to? You may not realize it yet, but you'll tell me. It's only a matter of when."

He reached up and switched off the lamp. Jane stood half in, half out of the room for another moment. Then she went to the nurses' station to make sure that Edgar got fed, and fed soon.

Jane stood at the taxi stand in front of the hospital and made a call from her cell phone.

"Homicide, Finney."

"Mike, it's me—"

"Hey, Lieutenant. How you feeling?"

"I'm okay, thanks. Any progress on the b.g. check on Francis Cellucci?"

"I've hit a couple of roadblocks, Lieutenant. But I'm all over it. Where does it fall for you prioritywise?"

"It's just moved up to number one. Cross-reference him with known members of an old gang called the Four Birds." Jane pulled open the rear door of a city minivan cab. "Work it hard for me, Mike." She rang off from Finney and speed-dialed Kenny.

"Hi, hon," he answered from the alley behind Stella's.

"Ken, remember that tattoo we got from the priest?"

"Vividly."

"Turns out it's a gang tattoo, the Four Birds from down at the airport. Father Francis Cellucci, the only victim shot execution-style, was a gangbanger in a previous life."

"Holy shit."

Jane could feel the electric connection of a case starting to make sense. There was something to this lead and she wanted to work it fast.

"Wait," Kenny said, "how do you know this?"

Jane pursed her lips, holding back the answer to a question she had known was coming. "Edgar Silva did some research. It's why he was at Stella's when I was there. He'd come to tell me what he'd learned about the tattoo." All Jane could hear over the phone was the percussive *thrup* of the helicopter working the crime scene.

Kenny finally spoke. "Where are you now?"

"In the back of a cab." The driver turned to her as she slid the door closed. She lowered the phone. "Saint Vincent's Cathedral," she told him.

The driver started the taxi and pulled away from the curb. Jane brought the phone back up. "Let's go see Bishop D'Souza. This could be what we've been looking for."

"Feels like something!" Kenny had to shout as Air One made another pass over the alley. "How'd you get out of the hospital?"

Jane clicked her seatbelt into place, taking care to slide the strap off her belly. "The doctors released me a few minutes ago."

"That's good news," Kenny said. "I'll see you in church, Lieutenant."

Jane pressed End and dropped the phone into her purse. As the taxi climbed the hill toward Saint Vincent's, she wondered what the hospital staff would think when they discovered she was gone.

28

It was Five Alarm Chili Night at Saint Vincent's.

Volunteers were setting up tables and chairs in the playground of the church's school. A huge paper banner with a hand-painted thermometer announcing a fundraising goal of five hundred dollars for the school's library had just been taped to the wall of the gymnasium. A corner of it had come away and a light breeze was causing the poster to billow from the bricks.

Bishop D'Souza, his unlit pipe balanced in his mouth, sat on a picnic table between Jane and Kenny. "Not everyone comes into the fold at such a young age like I did." Turning the photo of Father Cellucci's tattoo in his hand, he nodded toward Father Marquez, who was taking a box of paper plates from a station wagon and carrying them over to the kitchen area. "Or like Esteban there. He knew he wanted to be a priest from the time he could first read the wonders of the Holy Scriptures."

"How old, Excellency," Jane asked, "was Father Cellucci when he took his vows?"

"Almost thirty. A bit late, but not unheard of."

"So," Kenny offered, "obviously he had a life before he found God."

Bishop D'Souza put his pipe in the pocket of his robe. "A former gang member seeing the errors of his youth and then finding Christ is not all that unusual." He snicked a flake of tobacco from his lower lip. "But, what is unusual is, often when a former gang member seeks redemption and takes his vows, he goes back to the streets to work with other kids who have lost their way. But Francis only wanted to work for the AIDS Hospice, the toughest calling we have." He handed the photo back to Jane. "It was as if he were seeking penance in the most difficult of the Lord's work."

Jane's cell phone vibrated on her hip. She checked the readout: Finney.

"Pardon us, Excellency." She and Kenny stood up from the picnic table and moved toward the basketball courts to take the call. Jane held the phone up so Kenny could hear. "Hey, Mike."

"Lieutenant," Finney said, an edge of excitement emerging. "I stayed tough on Father Cellucci's b.g. like you said and I think I came up with something."

Kenny took Jane's hand and moved the phone closer. "What do you have, Moby?"

"Turns out Father Cellucci does have a past; only it's buried at the Hall of Records. Looks like he had a pretty significant run-in with the law when he was a juvenile and did time at the California Youth Authority until he was twenty-five."

Jane was way ahead of him. "And because he was a juvenile at the time..."

Kenny picked it up. "His records are sealed."

"Which is why," Finney added, "I've had such a hard time tracking him down in the system. But I just got back from Judge Cohen's office and she's processing a court order to unseal the records due to the special circumstances of this case. It should be waiting for you by the time you get to the Hall of Records."

Jane glanced to Kenny. He nodded appreciatively. "Great work, Mike," she said. "You're making us look like geniuses for bringing you into Homicide."

"Thank you, Lieutenant," Finney said, his voice catching. "I just want Inspector Marks to know how we all feel about him and what he's going through."

"I do, Moby," Kenny said. "I'm a lucky guy."

"Okay, Mike," Jane said, "we're moving on this."

She and Kenny turned to say good-bye to Bishop D'Souza. But he was bounding across the playground, his robes catching the wind, to help with the fundraising banner that had just pulled away from the gymnasium wall.

There were so many fluorescent lights in the small basement registry room at the Hall of Records that it sounded like a swarm of flies were trapped inside.

Lois Galloway had worked in this windowless, airless room for almost twenty years. It was not a coincidence that the most prominent thing at her work station, other than a photograph of her and her husband Sparky on matching tricked-out Harleys at the North Rim of the Grand Canyon, was a Costco-sized bottle of Extra Strength Tylenol.

After verifying Judge Cohen's signature on the court order, Lois handed it back to Jane. "Gimme a sec." She tapped a flurry of numbers into her keyboard and hit Enter.

Jane slipped the court order into her purse. Kenny craned his head over the counter, trying to get a peek at Lois's monitor.

"Mm-hmm. Here we go," Lois muttered to herself as a stream of information appeared on the screen. She reached up and turned the monitor a couple of inches to the left, just out of Kenny's line of sight. He settled back to wait. "Mm-hmm," she grunted again. "Your Mr. Cellucci was a bad boy way back when." She scrolled down farther. "A very bad boy."

A quick Ctrl+P and the printer whirred to life. Eight pages of a single-spaced rap sheet churned out. Kenny started to reach across for it, but Lois intercepted the pages, folded them and put them in a department envelope. "You gotta sign. Here, here, and...here." She held an oversized Disneyland pen out to Jane.

As Jane signed the receipts, Lois looked back to the screen and said, "Huh."

"Find something?" Kenny asked.

"Might could be interesting," Lois said, still staring at the monitor. "Might could not." She turned to Kenny. "Says here that these same records were accessed 'bout six months ago at 3:57 a.m."

"Maybe someone on the night shift was doing some housekeeping," Kenny suggested, trying to draw her out.

Lois Galloway shook her head emphatically. "Not hardly."

Jane passed the Disneyland pen back to her. "Why not?"

"'Cause, Lieutenant," Lois plunked the pen into a Taos, New Mexico, souvenir cup. "We don't have a night shift."

The moment they entered the corridor outside the registry room, Jane tore the department envelope open, pulled out the pages, and handed half of them to Kenny.

They hurried toward the elevator bank, riffling through the pages.

"Jesus," Kenny said, "Father Cellucci sure had a lot to atone for. Look at this: B&E, assault, B&E again, GTA twice..." He turned to the next page. "Make that three times, another assault. Lots of bad stuff, but nothing really of the revenge-provoking variety."

Jane stopped walking. She was staring at the last page of Francis Cellucci's rap sheet. "Ken..."

Kenny turned to her.

"Look at this." She passed the page to him. "At the bottom. His life of crime came to a screeching halt fifteen years ago because..."

Kenny read the last entry and let out a low whistle. "Because they finally put him away after this." He handed it back to Jane. "Good God."

Jane read the entry again. "Wait, did you see who first on-scene was?"

Max Batzer took off his glasses and pinched the bridge of his nose. "Shit guys, I should have put it together."

"It was fifteen years ago, Max," Jane said. "He was a kid."

"Besides," Kenny added, "Francis Daniel Cellucci gave himself up as Frankie Daniels when you busted him."

They were standing between the Explorer and Max's squad car in a vacant lot beneath the Bayshore Freeway. Late-day traffic pushed itself along above them, the thick reinforced pillars groaning and creaking as the occasional big rig rumbled over a seam in the roadway.

Max handed the rap sheet back to Jane. "Until the Stella's shootings, this was the worst I'd seen. And now there's a connection?"

"Looks like it," Jane said. "Walk us through what happened that day."

"Whew…okay." Max ran his fingers through his thick gray hair.

Kenny pulled out his notebook.

"Okay…" Max said again, trying to get some traction on the story. "I was just coming off shift when a 911 came in about a possible home invasion up on Telegraph Hill. I was around the corner and got there in like two seconds. A car, stolen it turned out, beat it out of there just as I pulled up and this teenager vaults off the porch and starts running after it, cussing and screaming. I took him down, cuffed him, and threw him into my black-and-white."

He paused, letting the memory reveal itself. "By then, a couple of other units had shown up and we entered the premises." Max brought his fingers to his mouth and fell silent for a moment. "It was…it was a slaughterhouse in there. A mother and her young daughter had been raped…for hours…then stabbed to death."

"Wait a minute," Jane said. "I remember this case. I was still in uniform when it happened."

Kenny nodded. "And I was in the Academy." Any other time, any other case, and Kenny would have taken a loving jab at Jane about being older than him. But not this time, not this case.

"Guys," Max said, another layer of memory pushing its way through, "there was this kid. This little boy, Brad something. We found him in a closet under the stairs." He shook his head. "It was his mother and sister."

Kenny glanced at Jane. "Any idea what happened to him?"

"I think he just slipped into the foster care system. But I'm not sure."

"We'll try to find him," Jane said.

"Who was the guy you had in the back of your car?" Kenny asked.

"That was Frankie…Francis Daniel Cellucci." Max kicked at a stone in the dirt. It bounced twice and caromed off one of the freeway support pillars. "Son of a *bitch*."

"What about the car that took off when you pulled up?" Jane asked, trying to keep him focused.

"Got away," Max said. A sudden crackle of radio traffic came over his walkie-talkie and he twisted the volume down. "Cellucci was underage and was tried as a juvenile. He always denied any direct involvement in the crimes and there wasn't enough hard evidence to bring him up on a murder one"—he blew a sigh—"so he did an accomplice turn reduced to a dime at CYA."

Kenny turned the page in his notebook. "If he was the accomplice, who did the deed?"

"Xavier Rinaldi," Max said. "'The X' to his gangbang buddies. He was nineteen and clearly the leader of the pack. Lucky bastard killed those poor women back when there was no death penalty. Last I heard, he's doing life without possibility at San Quentin." An ambulance dopplered by on the freeway above. Max looked up to follow its path. When he brought his gaze down again, he had tears in his eyes. "Shit, Jane." His voice was almost a whisper.

"You're a great cop, Max"—Jane put her hand on his shoulder—"and you've been a great help to us."

Max touched her hand. "I appreciate that." He climbed into his black-and-white and rolled down the window. "But I shoulda connected the fucking dots."

Before Jane and Kenny could respond, Max powered his window back up and tore through the vacant lot. Rooster-tails of swirling dust chasing after him like demons.

"Mike, you know how you did the impossible and opened Francis Cellucci's sealed juvenile records?" Jane said into her two-way. "Well, I have an even tougher job for you. Pull this off and you're an official superhero."

"Go for it, Lieutenant."

She and Kenny were deep inside San Quentin State Prison, a place so drab and wretched its walls seemed to sweat misery. Kenny put their weapons into the visiting law enforcement officers safe.

A prison guard, a black man with an old-fashioned Afro and muscles that ballooned against the sleeves of his beige polyester uniform, handed him a receipt. Then he nodded to a tray on his desk. Kenny took two bright orange visitor's badges and peeled the backs off them. He pressed one to his lapel and gave the other to Jane.

"I need you to find me a kid who got swallowed up in Social Services fourteen, fifteen years ago." She patted the orange sticker onto the front of her coat. "Call Max Batzer and he'll catch you up on the details."

"I'll get right on it, Lieutenant."

Jane switched off and handed her police radio to the prison guard. He slipped it into the safe with their weapons, closed it, and spun the dial.

"I got the impossibility of no parole!" Xavier Rinaldi screamed at Jane and Kenny through two-inch thick bulletproof glass. "So lady, lest you gonna play *Let's Make A Deal* with me, I don't got nothin' to tell you."

He glowered at Jane, the scars on his ravaged face tracing crimson tracks across his skin. In his midthirties, with black soulless eyes that danced on the fringes of insanity, he crossed his arms across his chest like a petulant child. A child in handcuffs chained to a waist belt.

"Mr. Rinaldi," Jane began.

The prison guard sniffed a laugh at someone calling this hard-core asshole "mister."

Jane ignored him and pressed on. "Mr. Rinaldi, you raped and murdered two women. There are no deals to be made."

Xavier Rinaldi sat stone still, his eyes boring into Jane. This was his first time out of the hard-time block in six years and Jane was the first woman he'd seen in almost eight—other than that dyke guard who worked nights. He had promised himself that he'd make the most of this, stretch it out to the max. But he couldn't do it. A cryptic grin played across his lips and he slowly started to rise. "You won't deal with the X?" When he was at full height, Jane saw that he had an erection bulging against the khaki pants of his prison uniform. "Then fuck you, bitch!" He whipped his head toward Kenny. "Fuck both you bitches!"

To Jane's surprise, Kenny smiled. "Mind if I take a rain check?"

This threw Rinaldi off-stride long enough for Kenny to ask a question. "Who would want to kill Francis Daniel Cellucci?"

Two guards rushed up from behind Rinaldi and shoved him back into his chair. They stayed close, their hands on their batons. Rinaldi did a quick left-right with his head, then landed again on Kenny. A string of white spittle had formed in the corner of his mouth and he flicked at it with his tongue. Then he narrowed his eyes and said, "Blow me."

Jane scraped her chair back. "Let's get out of here, Ken." She stood up and, without looking back to Xavier Rinaldi, crossed to the prison guard. "Out, please."

Kenny joined her at the cast-iron door as it slid open. "I'm sorry you had to hear that."

"That's not what got me," Jane said as they approached the safe to retrieve their weapons and radios. "We finally get a break in this case and the momentum, the urgency, was just going down the drain in there. We can't waste any more time trying to get a psycho like that to talk." She peeled off the orange prison pass and dropped it into a trash can.

Kenny slipped his Glock into his shoulder holster. "Ol' Mr. X might know something and I've got an idea how we can separate him from the information. But it's coloring way outside certain aforementioned lines."

"I'm up for that," Jane said. "Talk to me."

They passed through the last dank corridor to a revolving door and were buzzed outside, one at a time. Kenny zapped the Explorer with the remote and opened Jane's door. "Edgar Silva. It's not unreasonable to assume he and Xavier Rinaldi might have mutual friends in this shithole. Unsavory and persuasive mutual friends."

He closed the door and hurried around the car. Jane followed him with her eyes, not quite believing what she'd just heard.

Kenny got in and started the engine. "But it would be wrong," he said. "Career-ending wrong. Up to you."

Jane tumbled the ramifications in her mind. The risk she was about to take. The risk she was asking Kenny to take. But there was something more at work here than mere risk. They were closing in on the truth. On justice. "Let's do it."

"Been nice working with you," Kenny said as he handed her the dashboard mic. "I think it's better the call comes from you."

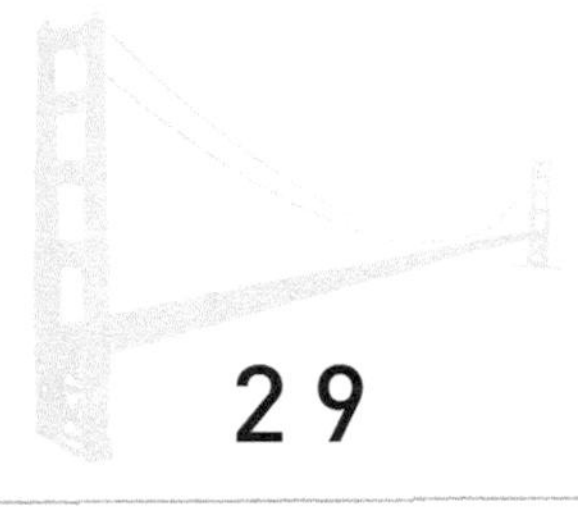

29

"There's a sandwich on your desk." Cheryl Lomax plunked a water bottle onto her dispatch console. "And take your vitamins."

Jane took the water. "Thank you, Mother. Any word from Edgar Silva?"

"Nothing yet."

Through the war room window, Jane could see Mike Finney talking to Kenny.

Someone had moved the blackboards with the names of the Stella's victims next to the bulletin board with the City Planning schematic to make room for more tables in there. Lou Tronick, his perpetual mug of coffee in his hand, was briefing half a dozen new-meat cadets who had been sent over to help shuffle papers for the evening shift.

Jane was pleased; the energy level was still high. Often on big cases like this, there was an initial burst of frantic energy, then everyone would fall into a trough of exhaustion. But her team was still going strong.

Jane twisted the cap off her water bottle and took a long drink. Kenny emerged from the war room and dropped his jacket onto the back of his chair.

"What's up with Finney?" she asked.

"Moby's getting stonewalled on that kid. He looked up the files on that double murder and learned that the little boy's name was Bradley Pomerance. But the dickheads at Social Services are red-taping him to death."

"What about a court order?"

"He's trying. But tonight's the annual Judicial Review Banquet at the Palace of Fine Arts."

"Then he should gate-crash."

The door to Interrogation One flew open. Mike Finney tore across the bullpen, threw back the stairwell door, and bounded down the steps to the parking garage.

Kenny turned to Jane. "I think he's way ahead of us."

Cheryl Lomax came up to them. "Jane…phone call."

"Edgar Silva?"

"No. It's Dr. Berger's office, calling with your…results."

Kenny took her hand and led her to her office. She turned to him. "How much of this do you want to know?"

"Only that my baby's healthy."

Jane sat at her desk, moved the deli sandwich to the side, and picked up the phone. "This is Jane Candiotti."

Kenny stood in the doorway, his back against the jamb.

Jane listened for a minute, then, her eyes warming with tears, looked to Kenny and smiled. She scribbled on her notepad and held it up to him. *Healthy!*

"And the sex?" she asked. "Okay…great…" She hung up, tears falling now.

Kenny stepped into the office, his arms open, a smile beaming across his face. Jane came to him and he pulled her into a hungry hug. "God, this is just what we needed," she said. She squeezed her husband to her, hanging on for dear life. "Just what we needed."

"Lieutenant…" Cheryl Lomax on the speakerphone. "Edgar Silva on two."

"Frankie Cellucci had his share of enemies, Lieutenant," Edgar Silva said. "But then again, who doesn't?"

Jane and Kenny leaned over the speakerphone, their hands flat on the desk.

"Were Cellucci's enemies the killing type?" Jane asked.

"Hard to say. Coulda been someone from when he ran with the Four Birds or somebody coulda had a hard-on…'scuse me…a grudge against him from his time in CYA. People have been known to get disgruntled in a place like that."

Kenny nudged the speakerphone a little closer. "Mr. Silva, this is Inspector Marks."

"Hello, Inspector."

"First of all," Kenny said, "I want to thank you for helping us—"

"We find who killed Frankie Cellucci, we find who killed my brother and your nephew…and we find who shot me in the head. So let's just say I'm motivated."

"What else did you learn?" Kenny asked.

"Apparently there was one guy that got away the night those two women were killed."

Jane put her hand on Kenny's. "That's correct, Mr. Silva. Were you able to get a name?"

"Yeah. Harry Donahue. He's Xavier Rinaldi's half brother and he was understandably reluctant to give him up."

"How about a location?" Kenny asked. "Can you help us out there?"

"Seems that Mr. Rinaldi slipped and fell from the second tier of his cell block. He passed out before our mutual friends could persuade him to offer any more precise information. Hold on…" Jane and Kenny heard another man's voice in the background. "One more thing, Lieutenant. Harry Donahue works for UPS." Edgar fell silent for a second. "Okay, I gotta go. My family's bringing me dinner. That whole hospital food cliché? It's true."

"I just want to go on record, Mr. Silva," Jane said, "that if the information we've just received was in any way coerced out of Mr. Rinaldi either by violence or the threat of violence, then I heartily disapprove."

Edgar chuckled. "The record shall so reflect, Lieutenant." The sounds of Leo and Carmen calling to him came over the line just as he hung up.

30

Harry Donahue's shoulders slumped with resignation when Jane and Kenny flashed their badges.

"Not here, okay?" he pleaded, glancing along the busy UPS loading dock. He had thinning black hair and the wax-colored pallor of someone who'd spent the last decade working nights. He had a wedding ring on his left hand, which he habitually worried with his thumb.

Yellow forklifts bustled from the cavernous warehouse. They crossed the platform, hefting huge plastic-wrapped palettes loaded with cardboard boxes, and disappeared into the maws of the waiting brown semis.

Kenny nodded. "Where can we talk?"

"Lunchroom." Harry Donahue slid his laptop tracking device into the drawer of his rolling desk and turned toward a corner of the building. "This way. Watch out for the forklifts, though. The drivers are on a pretty tight schedule and they're not looking out for visitors this time of night."

A forklift with an oversized load passed between him and Jane and Kenny, obscuring him for a few seconds. Their cop instinct took over and each of them tensed. If Harry were going to rabbit on them, this would be his chance. Kenny hurried around to the back of the forklift, his hand already loosening his Glock from its shoulder holster.

But Harry Donahue was still there.

The forklift bumped up into a UPS trailer and the driver lowered the twin arms. "Machine parts," Harry said. "Just down from Seattle." He opened the door to a small room and stepped inside.

Harry sat on a narrow metal table and offered Jane and Kenny the two steel gray chairs. They remained standing. Junk-food vending machines hulked along two of the walls, bracketing a coffee setup in the corner.

"Mind if I smoke?" Harry started to pull a pack of Camels out of his pocket.

"Actually," Jane said, "I do. Thanks for asking."

"Mr. Donahue," Kenny began, "do you know why we're here?"

Harry leaned back against the wall and drew his right knee to his chest. "I got an idea, yeah."

Jane pulled the photo of the tattoo from her bag and handed it to Harry. "This familiar?"

"Yeah," Harry nodded. "Sure it is."

Jane took it back. "Tell me what it is."

"Four Birds. Old gang from the number streets that got gobbled up when they made the airport bigger."

"Were you in Four Birds?" Kenny asked.

"Yeah…long time ago. A lifetime ago." He looked from Kenny to Jane. "Am I in trouble?"

"Probably," Jane said. "But you can make it easier on yourself." She slid the photo of the tattoo back into her bag. "Did you know Francis Cellucci and Xavier Rinaldi?"

Harry Donahue pressed his lips together, as if to keep the secrets of fifteen years ago from spilling out.

"Sir?" Jane prodded.

Harry let his head fall back against the wall. "Xavier Rinaldi's my brother…" he said to the ceiling. "Half brother. And yeah, I knew Frankie Cellucci."

"You were there that night," Kenny said, a statement, not a question.

Harry Donahue's chin quivered. "I was in the car. Waiting for them..."

"Them?" Jane asked.

"Xavier and Frankie."

"But," Jane pressed further, "the prosecution couldn't put Francis Cellucci inside the crime scene and he got—"

"Away with murder. My brother took the fall." Harry pushed away from the wall and looked at Jane. "Xavier was hard-core all the way and the cops were dying to put him away. The case against him was solid. The case against Frankie was all wobbly. Someone screwed up with the evidence and they didn't want to risk the trial blowing up on them. So they pled Frankie down and dumped him into CYA."

"And the police," Kenny asked, "never came after you?"

Harry shook his head. "This cop car came blasting around the corner, all sirens and lights, and I freaked. I hauled ass out of there. Xavier and Frankie held tough and never ratted me out."

"Code of honor," Kenny sniffed. "All that gang brotherhood bullshit?"

"Look, I had just turned fifteen. I thought they were going in that house to party and I was too scared to even do that. Yeah, I was in the Four Birds. But only 'cause my brother made me do it. After that night, I never did anything wrong again in my life. I've been working here twelve years. Never missed a day. You can check it out. I got a wife and a son." He held Jane's gaze. "I'm not a criminal, Miss."

"That's not for me to decide, Mr. Donahue. But I believe you and, if your story holds, I'll say as much in my report."

"Thank you. Can I say something else, Miss?"

"Sure."

"There was this kid, this little boy, in that house, too. Eight years old." Harry started to reach for his cigarettes, then stopped. "I think about him all the time. My Travis is almost the same age and I..." He shook his head. "What that kid went through."

Kenny flipped open his notebook and riffled through the pages. "Bradley Pomerance."

"Yeah," Harry continued, "Bradley Pomerance. I snuck into my brother's trial—nobody knew who I was—and I watched that kid the whole time. People kept saying how brave he was, how he didn't cry. But all I saw was a little kid going all internal. I mean, he saw what Xavier and Frankie did to his mother and sister and he had no emotion about it. He was just all cold and staring and...silent."

"Did you ever see him again?" Jane asked. "Hear about him?"

"No, Miss. My brother was sentenced around the same time we lost our house 'cause of the airport. My mom moved us down to San Mateo and I kinda had a chance at a new start. I began to do okay at school, hooked up with a new crowd, and got into a J.C. I was all about moving forward, putting the past behind me, y'know?" He looked down to the floor. "Until tonight."

Jane nodded to Kenny: we're done. He tilted his head in agreement.

"Okay, Mr. Donahue," she said. "Here's the deal. You've admitted to being at the Pomerance house the night of the crime. Two women were killed in that house and you didn't give up what you knew about Francis Cellucci. That makes you an accessory after the fact. We can't let that slide. But we're inclined to believe you when you say you didn't know what was going on in there and that you've been scared straight ever since. You want to earn some points with me and help yourself?" She handed him a business card. "Show up at my precinct first thing tomorrow and turn yourself in."

"I'll be there." Harry Donahue took the card and hopped down off the table. "What should I do now?"

Kenny pulled the door open for him. "Go back to work."

As soon as Harry left, Kenny turned back to Jane and started to speak. But she beat him to it.

"It's the kid!"

As Kenny sped through the UPS lot, tractor rigs whipping by, Jane tracked down Mike Finney on the two-way.

"Sorry, Lieutenant," he said. "I was able to get into the banquet no sweat. But the awards are going on right now and the two judges I went up to, Laurenzen and Randa, told me to hang tight."

"No good, Mike. What about Judge Cohen?"

"She's in Sacramento. The governor's antidrug commission or something." They could hear the frustration in his voice. "Tell me what to do, Lieutenant, and I'll do it."

Jane glanced at the dashboard clock: seven thirty. "Mike, what time does the Social Services office close?"

"Five p.m., same as all government departments."

"Meet us at the Social Services Annex on Van Ness in twenty minutes."

Kenny turned to her. "You thinking what I think you're thinking?"

"Nothing is getting between us and solving this case, Ken." She clicked the mic again. "3H58 to Dispatch."

"Go, Jane."

"Cheryl, have Lou put a tail on Harry Donahue. Twenty-four-seven until further notice."

"You got it."

Jane tossed the mic onto the dashboard. "Just in case."

Kenny shot the Explorer past a slow-moving furniture truck and blasted up the on-ramp of the Bayshore Freeway. He slid left across four lanes of traffic and slipped into the empty carpool lane, heading north toward the city.

Pulled along by an endgame they had to believe in.

Yvonne Tracey loved her job. She loved her dark green polyester uniform and her thick black leather utility belt. She loved her pepper spray and her retractable key ring.

But most of all, she loved her badge.

A squat, easygoing black woman in her late twenties, she spent her evenings working the security console at the Social Services Annex on Van Ness. Not so much working as waiting. Waiting for Cesar the floor polisher guy to leave. Waiting for *Love on the Line* to come on her preset podcast. Waiting for *Love on the Line* to end. Which meant she then only had to wait another hour before clocking out and waiting for the number six bus to take her home.

She held the court order for Bradley Pomerance's juvenile records up to the light and read the signature. "Lieutenant Jane Candiotti, SFPD Homicide." Then, her face lit blue by the faintly glowing security monitors, handed it back. "Looks good t' me. But ain't it like usual that a judge or something should sign one of these things?"

"You're exactly right"—Jane checked Yvonne's name tag—"Miss Tracey. But the point is, it's not *un*usual for a homicide lieutenant to sign one also."

"Happens all the time," Mike Finney offered from where he stood just behind Jane and Kenny.

Yvonne regarded him. "And these gentlemen are?"

"My bodyguards."

"Oh." Yvonne started to reach for the phone. "I'll need to see your badge again, Lieutenant. Gotta check the number."

Jane flipped open her shield wallet and handed it over.

Yvonne Tracey examined it closely, turning it in her hand, the facets catching the light like an oversize piece of jewelry. "Nice," she said, dreaming of the day. Maybe she didn't have to make a call. Maybe she had the authority in this go-nowhere shit job to make at least *one* decision in her life. "One floor up, first door on your right." She tilted her head back. "Stairs are just past the water fountain." She passed the badge back to Jane. "But..."

"But what?" Kenny asked.

"Door's locked."

Jane dropped the shield into her bag. "Do you have a key?"

"Yes. But I can't leave my desk."

"How 'bout this?" Kenny said. "You loan the lieutenant the key and Inspector Finney here will bring it back to you. It won't be out of your hands more than half a minute."

Yvonne Tracey considered this, working the problem hard. "Thirty seconds." She yanked the retractable key ring away from her utility belt and unsnapped a key.

Jane took the key from her and passed it to Finney.

"Thank you, *Officer* Tracey." She started toward the stairs, Kenny and Finney flanking her.

Yvonne pulled on her headphones and swiveled in her chair just as the lady lieutenant and her two bodyguards disappeared up the stairs. I could do that, she thought to herself as she dialed in her podcast. The walkie-talkie, the gun, the bodyguards...the whole thing.

Especially the badge.

"Shit," Jane said. "It's password protected."

She had begun a search in the Child Services computer, inputting Bradley Pomerance's name and every year from fifteen years ago until the present. The password request screen had come up every time.

"This one, too," Kenny said from another computer at a nearby desk.

Mike Finney returned from bringing the key back to Yvonne Tracey. "Try one-two-three-four."

Jane and Kenny tapped the sequence into their computers. Bradley Pomerance's Child Services record fluttered onto their monitors. They looked to Finney. He shrugged. "You know how Mr. Siegler puts pictures of food items on the Stella's cash registers because he can't trust his employees to figure anything out for themselves?" He shrugged. "Well, he borrowed that system from the civil service. Or as we former underlings in the police department used to call it: the simple service."

"Your tax dollars at work," Kenny said.

"Jesus, guys." Jane's voice was hushed, solemn, as she peered at her screen. "Looks like Bradley Pomerance was only taken in by one foster family...and that was just for a little over six months."

"Then what?" Finney asked.

Jane scrolled down to the end of the document and looked up. "Then nothing."

31

Jodie Trumbull slipped a slice of apple pie onto Jane's plate.

"I got ice tea. Lipton's. Comes with the lemony flavor already in it." She took two mismatched plastic tumblers from the counter and poured drinks for Jane and Kenny. "No ice, though. Freezer's broke."

Jane and Kenny had demurred the first three times Jodie Trumbull offered them something to eat. That was an hour ago and Jodie had gotten less and less talkative with each refusal. Then a combination of needing to get the information they'd come for and sheer hunger had led them to accept. And that's all it took to turn on the talk-faucet.

A withered woman in her early sixties, Jodie Trumbull's skin had the color and consistency of onion paper. She had too-long gray hair pulled into a forgotten ponytail and wore huge old-fashioned low-slung eyeglasses that dominated her face. Her left arm didn't work quite as well as it used to, the result of a ministroke she had no memory of having.

They sat at a wobbly-legged drop-leaf table in the kitchen area of an illegally converted garage apartment. A thousand-year-old Labrador mix, its face ice-white, grunted and wheezed on a tattered rug, drawing heat from the refrigerator motor.

"Use t' be the day," Jodie Trumbull said as she slowly chewed her pie, "I didn't live so bad as this." Her left hand accidentally bumped her plate and a piece of crust fell to the floor near the dog. He didn't move. "Now I clean people's houses and sleep on a couch." She thrust her jaw to the other side of the room. A brown and yellow fold-out couch was pushed against the wall that had once been the garage door. The dog's leg twitched in his sleep. Jodie regarded him. "But I got my Samson. He keeps me good company."

"He's a sweet pup," Jane said. "Now I need to ask you again about when you had Bradley Pomerance as a foster child. Do you remember when he lived with you?"

"'Course I do," Jodie Trumbull said with surprising force. "Whadaya think? We wasn't one a them foster family factories just took the checks and didn't do the fosterin'. I loved that poor little boy." She looked around. "Had us a real house back then down in Daly City. A room for me and my husband, a room for Brad, a yard, and a garage. For a *car*...not for livin' in. Burt, he was my husband, thought the boy'd like to have a dog for company after what he went through." She started to reach for her ice tea with her left hand, then stopped and picked it up with her right. "Some reason, he never took to the dog, so I ended up taking care of Samson. Hell, poor Brad never took t' nothin'. He was the loneliest kid I ever seen." She clucked her tongue against the back of her teeth. "Lonely's no good. 'Specially not in a kid."

"Mrs. Trumbull," Kenny said, "why was Bradley Pomerance in your care for only six months?"

Jodie Trumbull quickly looked away. Then she bent over to pick up the piece of crust that had fallen. "Well...my husband... see he..." She rose back up and stared off to the middle distance. Kenny glanced over his shoulder to see if she were looking at a picture on the far wall. There was nothing there.

"What about him?" Jane asked gently. "Did he get sick or..."

Jodie Trumbull shook her head. "No-no-no-no," she chanted. Then she turned to Jane, her head cocked at an angle that was just a little off. "He touched him."

Kenny put down his fork. "'Touched him?' Do you mean your husband molested him?"

Jodie Trumbull slowly nodded her head in that same awkward canted angle. "Burt'd had the problem a long time before. But he was all better. For years. We'd had other foster kids, six or eight of 'em, and there never was no problems. But, for whatever the reasons, Burt touched that little boy in all them bad ways...in all them sick ways."

Jane pushed her half-eaten pie toward the center of the table. "How did you find out?"

"The boy ran away. Buncha times. They kept finding him and bringing him back." Jodie Trumbull took off her glasses and wiped them with a paper towel, her face suddenly smaller. "Can you just imagine? They kept bringing that boy back to someone who kept hurting him." She tried to go on, made several false starts, then finally was able to continue.

"There was a caseworker down at Child Services who found it out. Walter Cartwright, a good and kind man. Died a few years back; read it in the paper. Anyways, one day he comes by with the police and they confront my Burt. He denied it at first, all yellin' and blustery. Then he broke down and admitted the whole thing. How he'd go into Brad's room at night and lie with him. Do things to him." A tear splashed onto her plate and she dabbed at her eye with the paper towel. "And in that one day, the day the police came, I went from having my little house and my little yard and my little family...to being alone. They took my Burt away. And they took my Brad away."

"Where's your husband now, Mrs. Trumbull?" Kenny asked.

"He did a couple of years down at Shanley, then got probationed to a halfway house. Mr. Cartwright told me he ran off on them and ended up somewheres in Thailand where people with his problem ain't such a problem." She bowed her head, the tears falling freely now.

Jane reached across and put her hand on Jodie Trumbull's hand. "And what about Brad, Mrs. Trumbull? What happened to him?"

Jodie turned to Jane, her eyes dark craters of pain. "He's gone. Just…gone. I'd call Mr. Cartwright every now and again and he told me Brad kept running away from the group home they put him in. Then one time he just told me he was gone. Maybe living in the streets, maybe left the city. Maybe…dead." She withdrew her hand from Jane's. "Poor little soul."

Kenny folded his paper towel and put it next to his plate. "Do you have a picture of him?"

"Yeah, I got one somewheres." She pushed back her chair and, walking with a slightly halting step, crossed to the sleeper couch. She stooped to one knee and pulled out a plastic storage bin. "Here we go." Pushing up off the bed with her good arm, she brought a curling Polaroid to the table and put it between Jane and Kenny.

It was a photograph of a light-haired boy sitting on the sun-splashed steps of a small bungalow. His lips were curled in on themselves and his eyes, angry dark coins in his round white face, were staring past the camera. There was the elongated shadow of the photographer in the foreground, a man's shadow stretching across the lawn.

"Burt took this one." Jodie Trumbull turned the picture on the table.

Jane glanced to Kenny and they rose. "Mrs. Trumbull, do you mind if we take this?"

"Like I told you, it's my only one."

Jane nodded. "You let us have this tonight, and tomorrow, I'll have copies made. Someone'll personally deliver them to you in the morning. How's that sound?"

Jodie Trumbull kept her fingertips on the picture, pinning it to the table. "I go to work at seven thirty. The Fourteen bus."

"Someone will be by before that," Jane said.

"They'll even take you to work," Kenny added.

"Take me home, too?"

Kenny nodded. "Take you home, too."

"Okay then, but you gotta be super careful with it. It's the only picture I have of…" She bent over to stare at the photo and fell silent.

"Brad?" Jane offered.

"Of my house." Jodie Trumbull slid the photo toward Jane. "You wanna take your pie?"

Jane smiled. "I'd love to."

Jodie retrieved a roll of tin foil from under the sink and wrapped Jane's half-eaten slice. "You could come back anytime." She handed the pie to Jane. "I don't get so many visitors."

"You ever think how lucky we are?" Kenny asked as he drove out of Jodie Trumbull's hard-knock neighborhood. The windows of almost every tiny house flickered with the blue-gray light of their televisions. Ephemeral oases in an otherwise dreary existence.

"Lucky?" Jane turned to him. "How?"

Kenny swung right onto Talbot Avenue, a broad boulevard of factories and warehouses. Endless walls of chain-link flicking by. His face was illuminated by a ribbon of light bouncing off the rearview. "Our baby. I mean, with all that's going on—this case, Bobby's death, our grief—we have this reservoir of hope baking inside you. It's like, I don't know, it's like *religion* almost. Y'know, a place in your head, in your soul, that you go to." He shot her a look, then guided the Explorer up the curling on-ramp that would take them to the Bay Bridge. "Am I making any sense?"

Jane slid her left hand under his right thigh, a gesture so familiar she wasn't even aware of doing it. "It makes complete sense, hon. I go there all the time. You know what this means, don't you?"

"I'm afraid to ask."

"You're finally getting in touch with your feminine side."

Kenny's lips lifted into a soft smile, his first in days. "Speaking of feminine, part of me really wants to know the gender of our baby."

"How big a part?"

The Explorer joined the light late-evening traffic. "Still less than half, I guess." The gray skeleton of the Bay Bridge appeared to the east and Kenny slipped across the lanes toward the arching connector road.

Jane took out the picture Jodie Trumbull had given her and studied it, a slow strobe of passing street lamps intermittently bringing the boy's face into sharp relief. "Ken..."

"Hmm?"

"Everything I know about being a cop tells me we're looking for Bradley Pomerance. But all I know about him is he's a twenty-three-year-old white male that fell through the cracks."

"Here's what else you know," Kenny raised the thumb of his right hand and began counting. "Francis Cellucci was the only victim who was shot point-blank execution style." He lifted his index finger. "Francis Cellucci's juvenile records were illegally accessed six months ago." Another finger. "Francis Cellucci was in a gang." The ring finger went up. "Francis Cellucci was involved in the double rape and murder..." All five fingers were now up. He turned his palm to Jane. "Of Brad Pomerance's mother and sister." The Explorer vibrated gently as it merged onto the corrugated roadway of the Bay Bridge. "We're talking textbook revenge. It's sound theory, Jane."

"That's the problem. It's only theory. What if we're looking for this guy...and he doesn't even exist anymore?"

"It's always just theory until we're proved right or wrong." Kenny raised the thumb of his other hand. "One thing we don't know: given that this is San Francisco, is he even a guy anymore?"

"Please tell me you're kidding."

"Of course I am." The roadway flattened out as they crossed over Treasure Island, the towns of the East Bay a winking bracelet in the foothills. "I'll ask you what you always ask me: what does your gut say?"

Jane held the Polaroid up to the window. Brad Pomerance's face, his eyes looking past the photographer, looking past Jane, bloomed with light as the Explorer passed under the sign for San Leandro. "It's him," she whispered. "It's him."

32

"I need a simple yes or no, Lieutenant," Chief McDonald said over the speakerphone.

Not the way Jane wanted to start her day. She let her desk chair fall back and surveyed the squad room. Cheryl Lomax was talking with someone on her headset. The elevator opened and Harry Donahue stepped out. He went to Roz Shapiro's desk and she sent him down the hall. Jane nodded in satisfaction that Donahue had kept his word and shown up today. She'd remember that. Across the way in the war room, Kenny, Finney, and Lou Tronick were huddled around the playback machine, watching a tape.

"What's the yes or no question?" Jane asked.

"Did you access the Child Services records computer without authorization last night?"

The chief wouldn't be asking if he didn't already know the answer. "Yes, sir, I did."

"And you signed your name to a court order and convinced some poor security guard named Yvonne Tracey that it was all the authorization she needed, risking her job and your career?"

"Yes again."

"And where does this fall in the realm of the rogue cop bullshit you promised to avoid?"

"Not even close to it."

There was a brief span of silence, the static dropping off, as the chief pressed the Mute button to talk to someone else in his office. "Last question, Lieutenant. Are you breaking all these rules because you're moving forward on the Stella's case?"

Jane rocked forward and lifted the receiver, eliminating the implied authority of her boss's voice booming at her over the speaker. "Sir, as far as the Stella's case is concerned, there are no rules...only results. And I'll do anything to get them."

Another brief muted pause, then, "Dr. Chambers over at Child Services was pretty pissed off with me when he heard that his computers had been illegally accessed. He called it 'the most egregious violation of public trust he's ever seen' or something indignant like that. I told Dr. Chambers that I couldn't disagree. And I promised him that I'd get to the bottom of this and write a letter of severest reprimand to your file."

Jane started to respond, but the chief kept going.

"And that's what I've done. It's a good letter too, Jane. Expressing my dismay and outrage that anyone in my charge, let alone a departmental officer, would so flagrantly disregard the... et cetera, et cetera." He sniffed a soft chuckle. "Seems a shame such a good letter was misplaced by my secretary. Now I'll probably have to reprimand *her*." His chair creaked as he stood up. "I've got the mayor in five minutes. Just remember this, Lieutenant: if it holds up in court, I don't give a shit what you do. Get me that shooter." There was an abrupt *click* and the call ended.

Jane pushed back from her desk and rose. As she did, a sudden surge of nausea filled the back of her throat. The metallic taste made her tongue feel foreign in her mouth. Tugging open her middle drawer, she snapped a corner off one of her stash of Ghirardelli chocolate bars and sucked on it until it dissolved. Then she grabbed a water bottle from the minifridge and crossed the bullpen to the war room.

Finney turned to her as she entered. "Lieutenant, I had Baker down in uniforms take Mrs. Trumbull to work. He'll pick her up at five and bring her back home." He handed her a department envelope. "A copy of Bradley Pomerance's picture and his vital statistics. Everything Mrs. Trumbull told you checks out. Though I can't say the lady I spoke with at Child Services was especially thrilled to talk to me."

"Understandable." Jane slipped the envelope into her bag. "The whole Burt Trumbull episode wasn't exactly their shining moment." She broke off a piece of Lou Tronick's chocolate muffin, still trying to smooth down the edges of her nausea. "That, plus they know we were there last night."

"How?" Finney asked.

"Long story."

Kenny glanced back. "We in trouble?"

"Apparently not." Jane peered at the monitor. "That the Air One tape from when Edgar Silva was shot?"

"Yeah." Kenny pointed to the rooftop across the alley from Stella's. "This is where the shots came from." The building had its address painted in large white numbers on the tarpaper roof: 28. Jane's eyes were drawn to the rooftop of the Stella's. It had its address on it as well: 25. "What's next door to the right of twenty-eight?"

Finney unpinned the City Planning schematic from the bulletin board and laid it on the table. "Hardware store. Then, working east, a hobby shop, used clothing place, empty storefront… used to be a bookstore…dry cleaner, appliance repair, Gay Men's Health Clinic…" He reached the edge of the plans.

Jane noticed movement on the tape. A Mother's Hearth Bakery truck drove westward up the long rutted alley, meandering its way past double-parked vans and Dumpsters. It stopped at the police perimeter, idling in place as the driver talked to a uniformed cop. Then it reversed itself all the way down the crowded alley until it was out of sight. "Why's that truck driver fighting his way down that narrow and twisting alley when he can just make a delivery on the street and be done with it?"

"Lots of times," Finney offered, "a truck will service the same type of commercial buildings on both sides of the alley. That way they can work two different streets at the same time. My dad drove a laundry truck when I was a kid. He'd do his drop-offs and pickups at three or four places in one alley without ever having to deal with traffic and double-parking on all those streets."

Jane nodded. "Makes sense, Mike. But you only mentioned one restaurant the whole length of the alley, Stella's. Hardly seems worth all that trouble. Let me see those plans." She crossed to the table and scanned the schematic, finger-tracing the alley. "Dry cleaners and pet stores and video rental places…no other restaurants." She saw that Finney was still flattening down the part of the schematic that had been folded over to make room for it on the bulletin board. "Gimme that, Mike…" she said as she slid it out from under his hand. Pulling the broad sheet of paper closer, she reached over and unfolded the right side, revealing a continuation of the alley's path. "Another dry cleaners, a flower shop, Radio Shack…" Then she saw something.

Jane gathered up the schematic and hurried for the door. "Ken, c'mon!"

Kenny grabbed his coat. "Where we going?"

"To the scene of the crime."

The sparrow's nest was in tatters, wisps of fluffy down caught on the tips of broken twigs. Crushed in two, it still clung to the small space above the air-conditioning unit on the back wall of Stella's.

Jane and Kenny stood at the rear door of the restaurant. A slight breeze caught the detritus left behind by the EMTs who had treated Edgar Silva's gunshot wound and swirled it against the slatted chain-link fence. Jane looked up to the rooftop facade across the way. There were two small divots in the brickwork just below the top edge, scars in the masonry from when she had returned fire.

The wind caught the City Planning schematic and Kenny had to fold the billowing sheet of paper in on itself as they started east down the alley. They passed from sunlight into shadow and Jane pulled her collar up against the morning chill. She pointed to the left. "Hardware store. Incident Report from the day of the shootings says the back door was locked." They made their way past the next door. "Hobby shop. Also locked. That one's the used clothing place. Locked and alarmed. The old bookstore. Back door bolted shut. Dry cleaners. They were closed that day because of a death in the family."

Kenny nodded to the next business. "Appliance repair. No rear access. Gay Men's Health Clinic. Their alley door is always locked."

They followed the path of the alley, checking each establishment against the plans. The narrow roadway, its surface forever pocked with water-filled potholes, veered to the left and they found themselves in sunlight again.

Jane quickened her pace, drawn forward by the instinct that something—an answer, the next clue, another puzzle piece—waited for her somewhere in this alley.

"The second dry cleaners," Kenny pointed out, pressing to keep up. "Back door unlocked after four p.m. The shootings took place at two forty-five. Flower shop. They never use their back door. Radio Shack. All deliveries through the front."

Just past the Radio Shack, on the left, was a tiny parking area. Three regular spaces and a handicapped. A Boar's Head refrigerator truck diesel-idled in front of the blue-striped handicapped spot, its driver just now bumping his two-wheel dolly up the last step before entering a restaurant: Art's Deli.

Jane stopped. "I.R. has Weymouth and Murphy taking their lunch here. Once Melody from Fifteen contacted them about the shootings, it took them"—she checked her notebook, pressing the fluttering pages down with her thumb—"three and a half minutes to arrive on-scene." She looked back up the alley to the shadowed area where it made a right turn, everything beyond it obscured from her view. "It took us what, less than a minute to get from Stella's to here. And we were just walking and talking. Someone in a hurry, someone running, could do it in seconds."

Kenny stepped to the center of the alley and looked in the other direction. Far beyond where they stood, traffic streaked by the narrow opening at the end of the alley. "Okay, obviously Weymouth and Murphy didn't know how close they were. I mean, look at this." He swept his arm up and down the alley. "It's like a hamster maze back here. I've lived in this city all my life and I didn't know that Art's Deli on Liberty Street was so close to Stella's on Carmody Avenue."

"Neither did I," Jane said. "And poor Rick Weymouth was beating himself up over the fact it took him so long to arrive on-scene. He kept blaming himself for not getting to Stella's in time to save Toni Salazar."

"Blamed himself," Kenny said, "then killed himself."

The back door opened and the Boar's Head delivery driver hustled down the steps, his two-wheeler clattering behind him. "How ya doin'?" he said to Jane and Kenny. Then he latched the dolly to the rear doors of his truck, climbed in, and ground it into reverse. The back-up beep droned its one-note warning as he guided the truck toward the alley entrance.

Jane fanned the diesel fumes away with her notebook. "So what's all this tell us?"

"We know from the Staples-cam that the shooter didn't come out the front door of Stella's." Kenny tucked the plans under his arm. "Ergo, he had to go out the back. If he went left, the alley doubles around and ends up here anyway. A waste of time and distance for someone in a hurry."

"So we have to assume he went right," Jane said. "Every door between Stella's and Art's was locked and/or alarmed that day and time. He could have kept going what"—she looked down the alley to where the Boar's Head truck was just slipping into the cross-street traffic—"another five hundred feet...or he could have ducked into the first accessible refuge he came to: Art's Deli. Where two uniformed cops were having their lunch."

Kenny checked his notebook. "Weymouth and Murphy got the call just after Murphy came back from using the bathroom in there."

Jane looked to the frosted window on the back wall of the deli. "Then one of three things could've happened. One: someone hurried through the restaurant and our guys didn't think twice because the call hadn't come in yet. Two: a car sped down the alley and Murphy, in or near the bathroom, heard or saw it go by..."

"What's the third?"

"Weymouth and Murphy didn't see or hear anything and we're still looking for the fucking invisible man."

"Not quite invisible," Kenny said. "We know who he is."

"Only who he used to be." Jane pulled her two-way out of her bag and thumbed the mic. "3H58 to Dispatch."

"Go, Lieutenant."

"Cheryl, I need Finney."

A *click*, a spit of static, then Finney came on the line. "Homicide, Finney."

"Mike, I need you to find Patrolman Tom Murphy and have him come in for a follow-up debrief."

"You got it, Lieutenant. Uh...wait a sec. Cheryl needs you."

Cheryl Lomax picked up. "Jane, I just got a call from Carmen Silva. Her husband's taken a turn for the worse and she can't get the hospital to do anything fast enough. She sounded desperate."

Jane scanned the skyline to the south. The glass walls of San Francisco General, warmed by the sun, glowed like a beacon.

She pressed the mic. "Tell her we're on the way. We're there in five."

Kenny was already running back up the alley. "Wait here," he called. "I'll get the car."

"His fever spiked to one hundred and five."

Carmen Silva paced in the doorway of Edgar's room. "He's been growling in pain for almost an hour now. I went all *Terms of Endearment* on the head nurse, yelling at her to get me a doctor."

"And?" Kenny asked.

"And nothing. Far as they're concerned, Edgar's some gang-bang GSW who can just wait his turn."

"Carmen!" Edgar bellowed, a grizzly in torment.

Carmen rushed into the room, Jane following.

Edgar lay with his back arched, fighting the pain in his head. His hands clutched the rails of the hospital bed, anything to keep from clawing at the bandages. His knuckles bulged like stones trying to burst through his skin.

Jane brought herself into the sightline of his good eye. "Edgar, it's Jane Candiotti. Tell me what you need."

Edgar sucked in two quick breaths through his teeth. "Make…somebody…help me!"

Carmen grabbed Jane's elbow. "Please!"

Jane hurried across the room and was just about to run into the corridor, when Kenny appeared.

He had a doctor in tow who might have thought he was walking under his own power. But Kenny's hand was planted firmly between his shoulder blades, bum-rushing him along. When they got to Edgar's door, Kenny shoved him inside. "The Silva family," he said, "appreciates your coming so quickly, Doctor."

"Breaks my heart."

Carmen Silva closed her eyes and tapped the back of her head against a blood-drive poster, over and over again. She was standing with Jane and Kenny in the surgical waiting area. "The time we wasted." She glanced toward the broad yellow doors that led to the operating room. "Fever means infection. Bad fever means bad infection."

"Your husband is a strong man, Mrs. Silva." Jane touched her shoulder to the wall, standing close to Carmen. "He'll beat this."

Kenny peered through the sliding doors. "Someone's coming."

Carmen stiffened. She whispered a quick prayer and crossed herself.

The doors *whooshed* apart and a doctor in light blue scrubs came out. He pulled down his mask, revealing an impossibly young face. "Mrs. Silva?"

Carmen took a half step away from the wall. "Yes?"

"Your husband's out of danger," the doctor explained. "The infection had a good grip on him. But with an aggressive course of antibiotics and some surgical intervention, we were able to fight it off." He drew a deep breath through his nose and sighed. "You got him to us just in time. But..."

"But what?" Carmen asked, her voice constricted with fear.

The doctor glanced to Jane and Kenny, almost in apology, then turned back to Carmen. "We couldn't save his eye."

Carmen brought her hands to her mouth, her fingers fluttering like twigs. "*Dios mio.*" She lowered her hands to her sides and willed herself to remain calm. Her body stilled, a stoic strength returning. She nodded once, a gesture of acceptance. "When can I see him?"

"Any minute. We're going to bring him up to post-op ICU for observation. He'll stay sedated for a couple more hours. But you can go with him if you want."

Carmen reached down to a wooden bench and picked up her purse. She held its strap in both hands. "I will stay with my husband."

The doors separated again and Edgar was wheeled out. His head was heavily wrapped, the bandages covering both eyes. A nurse hurried ahead and called for the transport elevator.

Carmen squeezed Jane's hand. "Thank you for coming, Lieutenant," she said as her husband passed by. She nodded to Kenny. "And for what you did, sir." Then she went to Edgar's side, walking slowly toward the elevator, her hand on his left shoulder.

The elevator arrived and the transport team pushed the bed inside. Carmen wedged herself in beside him and bent to kiss her husband as the doors closed.

The doctor reached behind and untied his surgical gown. "You family?" he asked Jane.

"Uh, no," she said, still looking at the elevator door. "We're…"

Kenny put his arm around her. "We're friends."

"3H58."

Jane pulled her two-way from her bag. Not wanting to disturb the sanctity of the surgical floor, she and Kenny moved to the elevator bank. The doctor stayed by the security doors, watching them.

"Lieutenant," Finney began, "I called Melody; she's the dispatcher over at Fifteen? I asked her if she had a twenty on Patrolman Murphy and she said that he'd started his psych leave yesterday. Also that Commander Hollingsworth was pretty p.o.'d about the whole thing, excuse my language."

Jane clicked the walkie-talkie. "Don't worry about Hollingsworth, Mike. He's an irrelevant dinosaur."

"Anyways, I got Murphy's cell phone number from his Homicide application on your desk—hope you don't mind—and I left word for him to call you."

"Thanks, Mike."

"Not a problem. Seems a shame, y'know, Lieutenant? Twenty-three-year-old kid going through all this…"

Jane snapped a look to Kenny. He'd heard it, too. "Moby, what did you just say?"

"Uh, I was talking about how sad it is for a young cop like Murphy to be taking psych—"

"No," Kenny interrupted. "You said he's twenty-three. How do you know his age?"

"From his application."

Jane pulled the Child Services envelope Finney had given her from her purse. She ripped it open and, squatting down, emptied it on the floor. Kenny knelt next to her as she pushed Brad Pomerance's photograph aside and sorted through the papers. "Mike," she said evenly, "tell me the birthday on the application."

"Okay…wait. Here it is…January sixteenth."

"Stand by." Her heart pounding, Jane scanned the Child Services printout until she found the DOB entry. She jabbed her finger at it, showing it to Kenny. "January sixteenth!"

"Motherfucker," Kenny said, shooting to his feet, already reaching for his own radio. "Bradley Pomerance and Tommy Murphy are…"

Jane stared at the photograph of the eight-year-old boy sitting on the sunny steps of the bungalow all those years ago. "The same person…"

33

"Toni Salazar kept saying 'police...police...' as she was dying on the stairs." Jane gripped the door handle as Kenny sent the Explorer flying through another intersection. "She wasn't calling for help. She was IDing her own killer!"

Kenny powered the car to within inches of a slow-moving newspaper van. He foot-tapped a button to the left of the brake and the siren whooped from behind the grill. Startled, the truck driver glanced in his rearview and saw the strobing red light on the roof of the Explorer. "What kid is gonna say no to a cop in uniform coming in the back door of a fast food joint?" The truck driver veered over to a bus stop. Kenny gunned the engine and whipped the Explorer into a sliding two-wheel turn down Laguna. "Hang on." The car fishtailed, grabbing for traction, then went airborne as it flew through the intersection at Fort Mason.

Flecks of white glinted off the waters of San Francisco Bay another mile down the hill. Kenny swerved around a cable car and ran a red light, a taxicab skidding sideways to avoid him. "And someone broke into the Hall of Records computer and accessed Francis Cellucci's juvenile crime record. Again, what better cover than a cop in uniform?"

"3H58."

Jane grabbed the dash mic. "3H58, go."

"Lieutenant, this is Hicks. We're at the marina, locked and loaded." Scott Hicks's SWAT Team had just peacefully concluded a domestic disturbance less than a mile from the marina. They were already geared up when the call came in and had deployed immediately.

"We're almost there, Scott. Did Harbor Patrol show up yet?"

"Affirmative."

"Good. See you in two. 3H58, out."

The Explorer banged through another intersection. The sharp angle of the hill leveled off as they hurtled down the last incline. Kenny careened right onto the frontage road.

"So," Jane said, working it out, "Murphy cuts down the alley from Art's, does the deed, and cuts back in something like two or three minutes later. Rick Weymouth has no reason to suspect anything. As far as he's concerned, his partner's in the bathroom like any other cop coming off a long shift in the car."

Kenny slowed slightly as he raced through a stop sign. "Art's has parking in the back and is such a cop hangout…" He tapped the siren at a pack of joggers. They moved up to the sidewalk in unison, like herd animals. "Even if someone saw him, no one would think twice about a uniformed cop going in and out of the deli's back door."

"Murphy probably rehearsed this a dozen times before," Jane said. "Coordinating his lunch with when Francis Cellucci took his break from the AIDS Hospice. Timing how long it would take to go from the deli to Stella's, and back again." She looked to Kenny. "And whoever else was in there was just going to have to die to cover his tracks."

Kenny nodded without looking at her. Bobby had been caught in the collision of Francis Cellucci's vulnerability and Tommy Murphy's rage. "As a cop, he had access to the Robbery reports of the other two Stella's. So all he had to do was find the right time, kill Cellucci, and bury him in such an avalanche of other victims that we'd spend the rest of our lives trying to figure it out."

"The proverbial perfect crime," Jane agreed. "Only problem is, it's a myth, and a cop should know better."

They raced along the fence bordering the marina. The masts of a hundred sailboats swayed and bobbed, riding the ebb and flow of the harbor waters. The concussive pounding of a helicopter dopplered over them and Jane caught a glimpse of Air One just arriving on-scene. Two Harbor Patrol vessels sat at station inside the jetty. The Explorer bumped up into the marina entrance, rattled over the wooden parking lot, and skidded to a stop next to the SWAT van.

"3H58."

"3H58, go," Jane called into the radio.

"Lieutenant, this is Harbor Alpha. The engine on the target boat is running."

Jane sat up in her seat, searching the pier. She spotted a vortex of blue-gray smoke swirling against the afterboards of a sailboat in the second to last slip on the right. *Sweet Dreams*. Tommy Murphy's boat. Then she remembered. "Shit, he has a police scanner. He's monitoring everything we're saying!"

Kenny pressed the mic on his two-way. "All units go to secure frequency Bravo."

Jane started to open her door. Kenny grabbed her elbow. "You stay here. I'll do this."

"Ken, I'm going in." She took his hand and held on tight. "Listen to me. I'm the one who let Murphy get close to us. I'm the one who took him under my wing."

"So what are you saying, it's personal?"

"It got personal when this son of a bitch killed my nephew." She let go of his hand, opened the door, and jumped down to the parking lot. Ripping her pistol from her bag, she strode toward the SWAT Team.

"On your go, Lieutenant," Scott Hicks said into his headset.

He was crouched behind a storage locker, two slips down from Tommy Murphy's sailboat. Jane knelt next to Kenny at the base of the foot ramp leading down from the parking lot. She squeezed the mic on her two-way. "Do it, Scott."

Hicks flicked the safety off his weapon and rose. "Go-go-go!" He hissed into his headset. The eight men of his SWAT Team, their M4s jabbing the air in front of them, stormed Tommy Murphy's boat.

At the same moment, the pilot of Harbor Alpha gunned his twin 350s. The boat bucked forward, closing the distance between the jetty and *Sweet Dreams* in seconds. Harbor Foxtrot held position, poised to intercept any possible escape by water.

Air One hovered just to the north. Its rotor blast whipped the water, causing the other pleasure boats to strain against their docking lines.

The SWAT sergeant reached the hatch just aft of *Sweet Dreams*'s mast. Hicks and two men ran up behind him. Three other men went forward on the boat, their rifles trained on the two master cabin windows. A beat. Eye contact. A quick nod. And Hicks lashed out with his boot. The hatch cover went flying back. Three SWAT Team members, their bulky body armor making them almost too broad for the narrow opening, squeezed their way below.

"One's clear!" came the first report over the radio. "Two's clear!" "Three's clear!"

"Lieutenant," Hicks called back, the idling engine of the sailboat chugging over the radio. "The target boat is secure. No sign of the subject. Somebody want to cut that motor, please?"

The engine abruptly stopped running, the plume of exhaust falling back toward the water. Jane and Kenny hurried down the dock. They arrived at *Sweet Dreams* just as Scott Hicks hopped off the boat. Jane bent over and struggled to catch her breath. Kenny put his hand on her back. "You okay?"

"Yeah, just winded," she panted, then straightened up. "Murphy left the engine running as a lure to draw us in."

Scott Hicks unsnapped his chin strap. "And it worked."

"Air One to 3H58."

"Go…Air One."

"Lieutenant, I got some movement in the water six rows to the north of you."

The SWAT officers were immediately alert, tensing like hunting dogs.

"Scott," Jane said, "ask your guys if there's a wet suit down there. Should be hanging next to the foul weather gear by the chart table."

Scott Hicks spoke into his headset, listened, then turned to Jane. "That's a negative, Lieutenant."

Kenny slid the action back on his Glock, chambering a round. "He's in the water!"

Hicks and his men raced up the dock. They turned right, heading for the wide wind-whipped circle beneath Air One.

"Harbor Alpha to 3H58."

"Go, Harbor Alpha."

"Don't you worry, Lieutenant. We know who we're looking for and what he did. The only way out of here is if this guy swims to Hawaii. And that ain't gonna happen on my watch." Jane didn't answer. "Do you read, Lieutenant?"

Kenny turned to her. She was still pale from running. On top of that, the pitching of the dock and the fumes from the marine exhaust had hit her with a one-two harder than she'd expected. "I…read you…thanks, Harbor Alpha."

As the chopper held steady in its hover, as the SWAT Team scrambled across the connector dock, as Kenny pivoted to follow them…Jane came to a wrenching decision. She held out her hand. "Give me the keys."

"What?"

"Ken, I'm aching as much as you are to bring Murphy in. But there's something bigger than the job or justice or even revenge." She pressed her hand across her belly. "I'll set up a command center at the car and coordinate the radio traffic. You…you go get this motherfucker."

Kenny studied her face. "You sure?"

"I've never been more sure of anything in my life." She took the keys from him. "Go…"

"Air One to Harbor Alpha."

"Go, Air One."

"Something just passed between that schooner and that huge cabin cruiser at the north end of docks nine and ten."

"On it."

Jane stood on the running board of the Explorer and watched as the Harbor Patrol boat, its three-man crew peering into the water, moved to the far end of the marina.

Kenny, Scott Hicks, and the SWAT Team fanned out along the last two docks and did a boat-by-boat search. "3H61 to Air One." Kenny calling the helicopter.

"Go, Inspector."

"I'm boarding *Happy Daze*, that white cabin cruiser with the blue canvas at the end of ten. Keep an eye out."

"Got ya covered, Ken."

Jane strained to see Kenny clamber aboard the enormous pleasure craft at the farthest reach of the marina. A SWAT officer followed him onto the boat and Jane felt a welling of relief that

Kenny wasn't alone. She breathed in the cool sea air, her episode of nausea passing, and thought about the utter commitment to revenge that must have driven Tommy Murphy to this moment.

The puzzle pieces of his life fit together in a chilling pattern of criminal madness. His mother and sister had been killed. He had been abused by his foster father. The system that then failed him so wretchedly was the same system he had wrapped around himself like camouflage. Disappearing, throwing himself into the same cracks that had swallowed up thousands of disenfranchised children for decades. Morally, he had succumbed to his own awful legacy. But physically, socially, he had survived. Some would say, given the circumstances, even flourished.

He had committed himself all these years, Jane now understood, to that one instance of cathartic revenge. Joining the SFPD, going through the Academy training, years as a patrol officer—all had been part of his brutal and calculated design. The dedication and the self-denial, the hate and the anger, were staggering. And the willingness to destroy so many lives in the taking of the one that had drawn him to that Stella's on that day, at that time, marked the true essence of a sociopath.

That was the most disturbing part of all this. Any ember of humanity, of compassion, had long ago been purged from the soul of Tommy Murphy. All that was left had been reduced to performance. A puppet show of a man acting like a human being. Pretending to suffer over the loss of life. Vomiting at the sight of the fallen bodies. Worrying about his partner…

Jane drew a sharp breath of recognition. Rick Weymouth had agonized over his failure to get from Art's to Stella's in time. He had returned to both restaurants several times and he must have discovered their proximity through the warren of alleys behind them. Then he had shared this with the one person he trusted most in life—his partner.

And then his partner murdered him. Muddling Rick Weymouth's death in a haze of suicide notes, departmental reprimands, and his own despair at losing his best friend.

"3H61 to Air One."

"Go, Inspector."

"This vessel is secure."

"Roger that."

"Moving to the next."

Jane squinted across the shimmering marina. The helicopter, the Harbor Patrol, the men scurrying from boat to boat. "He'd have to swim to Hawaii," Harbor Alpha's pilot had said. Exactly what you'd expect of a fugitive so desperate to escape. Head for the water and slip into the black nothingness.

But now Jane had come to know that Tommy Murphy had spent a lifetime of disappearing in plain sight. In the city, on the force, in the same room with her.

There was movement, a lifting of the landscape almost beyond her periphery to the right. She turned away from the search area, drawn by the swirling motion. A sudden turmoil of seagulls rose from the sandy delta at the opening of the storm drain a half mile south of where she stood. They squawked and darted, disturbed by something she couldn't see. Jane reached into the Explorer, grabbed Kenny's binoculars, and dialed in for a better look.

Something low and black was emerging from the foamy shoreline. At first Jane thought it was a harbor seal. But then the silhouette rose and claimed its natural shape. Arms, legs, glistening black skin.

The skin of a wet suit.

Jane threw the binoculars back into the Explorer and cranked the ignition. She slammed her door closed and stomped on the accelerator. The car leaped forward, clattering over the wooden boards of the parking lot. Pounding over the low cement berm at the far end, Jane toggled to four-wheel drive and raced across the beach. Curtains of sand churned from the front and rear tires as Jane pulled the gearshift into low and blasted toward the storm drain.

Struggling to maintain control of the vibrating steering wheel with her left hand, she reached for the two-way on the dash. But the lurching and yawing of the SUV caroming across the uneven terrain made it impossible.

Up ahead, the man in the wet suit raced for the storm drain. When he spotted the Explorer barreling down on him, he turned to face his pursuer.

Tommy Murphy hesitated for a second, locking eyes with Jane, then he started for the drain again.

Suddenly the Explorer side-slipped into a groaning skid, hydroplaning across the wet sand. Sea spray splattered the windshield, blinding Jane as she fought to control the car. It finally shuddered to a stop just as Murphy passed into the maw of the storm drain.

Jane snatched her bag and bolted out of the car. Plunging her hand into her purse, she only had time to choose between her radio and her weapon. She came up with her pistol, thumbed off the safety, and sloshed through the pooling water at the mouth of the storm drain.

"Murphy!" she screamed. "Stop!"

Tommy Murphy kept going, his legs grinding in the muck.

Jane aimed just above his head and squeezed the trigger. Her weapon boomed, the sound and the bullet ricocheting through the cavern.

Tommy Murphy flinched and stopped, a dozen yards deeper into the massive drain than Jane. She strode forward, her weapon trained on his back. The water swirled up to her knees. "Turn around," she commanded, fighting for breath. "Hands where I can see them." The foul smells of the drain and the exertion of the chase had sent her equilibrium reeling.

Murphy raised his hands and peeled the cap of his wet suit back from his head. His hair fell across his forehead and his lips curled in a lopsided grin.

"It's over, Tommy," Jane said.

"The imperfect crime, huh, Lieutenant?" He inched forward.

"They all are." Jane swallowed back the bile rising in her throat and slung her bag over her shoulder. "It's only a matter of finding the mistake. When you killed all those people just to distract us from your real motive, the opposite happened. You focused us to the point of obsession. Nothing was going to stop us from finding you."

"So it seems." Murphy took advantage of the swiftly moving water and nudged even closer to her.

Jane waggled her gun at him. A warning to stop. "In a perverse way, I can almost understand burying the priest under a stack of bodies. But why go back and kill Colleen Porter?"

"She was a live witness." Tommy Murphy shrugged. "I couldn't count on how much she would or wouldn't remember when she finally got it together. It was a loose end I had to..."

"Tidy up?"

"If you will." Murphy moved a little to his left. "You live the kind of life I've had to live, you learn to take care of loose ends."

"And your partner?"

Murphy lowered his arms a bit. "His death appears to have been a tragic suicide, Lieutenant." He shook his head. "Poor guy was so distraught, he shot himself...in the heart."

Jane struggled to control her rising anger. "Bullshit. You killed the one person in your life who turned to you for help."

Tommy shrugged. "He was in the way."

The harsh metallic taste had returned, coating the back of Jane's throat. She spit into the water flowing around her legs. "Life has no meaning to you, does it?"

"You're half right, Lieutenant. Life *had* no meaning. Until the day I killed Frank Cellucci. Since then, I've never felt so alive."

"You murdered eight people! Innocent, everyday people who asked nothing more out of life than the freedom to exist. And you wiped that out." The pistol trembled in her hand. "You killed my nephew."

Tommy Murphy looked at the gun, at the tiny black eye pointed at his chest. "You want revenge, don't you, Lieutenant?" He shifted his weight. "Now you and I are finally connected. You want to talk about being focused to the point of obsession? It wasn't just about solving this case for you. It was about revenge. That's why you stayed up every night. That's why you drove everyone so hard." He nodded his head. "It's okay, Lieutenant. I understand. I planned my revenge for over half my life. It's the only thing that kept me sane."

"It didn't work," Jane seethed. "Because you're not sane."

Murphy came forward. "Why would you hurt your baby this way?"

The question caught Jane off guard. "What are you talking about?"

"We're both standing knee-deep in raw sewage"—he gestured to her soiled clothing, then to his wet suit—"but only one of us thought ahead."

Jane reflexively looked down. The moment she did, Tommy Murphy lunged forward and pushed her into the slimy wall of the storm drain. As she struggled to regain her footing, he was on her. He grabbed her wrist in a police takedown hold. Jane fought to keep from falling face-first into the sloshing water and, as she did, Murphy wrenched her weapon away.

Jane now stared down the muzzle of her own gun.

Tommy Murphy started walking backward, away from the sunlight. Jane took a step toward him. He raised the pistol toward her forehead. "Don't."

"3H58." Kenny's voice sliced through the storm drain. "Jane, where are you?"

Jane shrugged her purse off her shoulder and started to reach inside.

"3H58," Kenny called again, his voice quavering with fear. "Jane, what's your twenty?" A hiss of static. "Jane! Where are you?"

"Don't do it, Lieutenant." Murphy thrust the gun at her face. "Believe it or not, I don't want to kill you. But know this..." He sighted her down the gun barrel. "I will."

And now, Jane thought, it had come to this. The awful choice between taking down this murderer and protecting the baby she so desperately wanted to save. She lowered her head, momentarily overwhelmed by the decision she knew she had to make. Finally she said, "Then you'll have to." Jane narrowed her eyes and brought the radio to her lips. Just as she was about to squeeze the mic, the two-way came to life in her hand.

"Air One to 3H61."

"Go, Air One."

"Ken, I think I see your car just south of here. Hang on. Yeah, it's the Explorer down by the storm drain."

"We're on our way!"

The first sound to come to them was the hammering *whump* of the helicopter. Then the wail of the SWAT van's siren as it raced down the beach. Tommy Murphy took two more steps backward and lowered the gun. "I started from less than zero before, Lieutenant. I can do it again." He tugged the wet suit cap back up over his head. "Besides, I'm not done yet."

"Who else could you possibly hurt?"

Murphy's mouth twisted into a cryptic grin. "There's always someone." He turned away and started slogging up the tunnel.

"Wait!" Jane yelled.

Murphy looked back without stopping.

"Why did you shoot at me at the restaurant?"

Tommy Murphy paused midstep and yelled back over his shoulder. "Because I had to." Then he lowered his head and ran deeper into the tunnel.

Jane started to follow, then stopped. She knew there was no way, in her condition, that she could ever catch him.

A connector tunnel elbowed to the left and Tommy trudged around the corner, disappearing from sight.

Shadows filled the mouth of the storm drain. "Jane!" Kenny called.

Jane turned to his voice and began walking toward him, pushing the thick water with her legs. "In here!"

Kenny and Scott Hicks raced into the tunnel, half a dozen SWAT officers behind them.

Jane pointed toward where Tommy Murphy had escaped. "That way! He's wearing a black wet suit...and he has my gun!"

The SWAT officers plowed past her and followed the path of the storm drain. They paused at the connector and peeked around the corner. Hicks signaled the all-clear. They turned left and were gone.

Kenny lifted Jane in his arms and carried her back to the sunlight. As soon as they were outside, Jane gulped at the fresh air, filling her lungs. Kenny set her down on the dry sand and ripped the two-way from his belt. "3H61 to Dispatch. Suspect is in Flood Control Tunnel Seven heading east from the marina. Be on the lookout for and apprehend SFPD Patrolman Thomas Murphy. Units should respond to all storm drain outlets, manholes, sewers..." He exchanged a look with Jane. They already knew that finding anyone in the endless labyrinth of San Francisco's flood control tunnels was almost impossible.

"Roger on the APB," Cheryl said over the radio. "Ken, is it really Tommy Murphy we're looking for?"

"That's affirmative."

"Jesus."

"Have Press Relations get on this. I want Murphy's face on every TV screen in the city. 3H61, out."

Jane stood up, drawn back to the mouth of the storm drain. Kenny crossed to her and pulled her into a hug. She turned to him, a film of tears pooling in her eyes. "I had him, Ken. I had him…and I lost him. I'm so sorry."

34

"We've alerted the airports, the Bridge Commission, Amtrak, Greyhound, and the rental car companies."

Jane sat in an oxblood leather guest chair in the middle of Chief Walker McDonald's enormous office. Kenny sat on the arm of the matching sofa to her right. Ordinarily, when Jane met with her boss, he would come out from behind his broad desk and join her at the round club table in the corner for a face-to-face.

Not this day.

Chief McDonald tilted forward in his chair. "Go on, Lieutenant."

"It's reasonable to assume, sir," Jane went on, "that Patrolman Murphy rehearsed the Stella's shootings over and over again until he got the timing right. It's also reasonable to assume that he rehearsed his own escape. Our working theory is that he had clothes and money stashed somewhere in the flood control system, and that he's gonna lay low for a while."

"For as long as it takes," Kenny added. "He's a smart and resourceful guy. He monitored us on a police scanner and was half a step ahead the whole time."

The chief slipped on a pair of reading glasses and reviewed the Incident Report. "What did Air One spot in the water that drew you to the wrong end of the marina?"

Kenny looked to Jane, then to the chief. "It turned out to be a long black duffel bag suspended on a line strung between several boats. When the water was agitated by the Harbor Patrol outboards, it slipped along the line, making it look, from the air anyway, like a person moving beneath the surface."

Chief McDonald lowered his chin and looked over the top of his glasses. "And what was in the duffel, Inspector?"

"Junk from Murphy's boat, sir. Old tennis shoes and stuff."

The chief flipped the folder closed, removed his glasses, and looked to Jane. "Lieutenant, word in the corridors is that you're pregnant."

Jane sat back, uncertain where this was going. "Yes, sir. That's true."

"Congratulations. To both of you."

Jane glanced over to Kenny, then faced McDonald again. "Thank you, sir."

"I.R. says there was some concern that your fetus may have been in danger from whatever was flowing down that storm drain."

"It was a concern at first," Jane began, "but we checked it out and the ppb was far below the acceptable limits."

"Still"—the chief touched his fingertips together and studied the pyramid he'd made—"you should see your doctor. Peace of mind and all." He nodded thoughtfully. "It was some good police work on both your parts to ID Officer Murphy and get as close to a collar as you did."

Jane fidgeted in her seat. "Close isn't good enough, sir."

Kenny stepped deeper into the room. "We're going to find this guy. And when we do…" He paused, something close to rage suddenly betraying his voice.

"And when you do, Inspector?"

"And when we do, sir," Kenny went on, "We'll…bring him to justice."

Jane stood up and crossed to her husband. "Anything else, sir?"

"One last thing, if I may." Chief McDonald rolled back his chair and rose. "You'll forgive the indelicacy of this question, Lieutenant. But I think it's relevant considering."

"Considering what?"

"Considering the fact that you had the drop on an unarmed murder suspect and he got away."

Jane felt Kenny's body clench. She touched the back of her hand to his. "What's your question, Chief?"

"Don't adopt a tone, Lieutenant." The chief came around the desk. "It's well within my purview, hell it's my responsibility, to ask if your being pregnant compromised in any way your ability to bring Murphy in."

Kenny pulled his hand away from Jane's. "Sir, I must strongly—"

"It's all right, Ken," Jane said. "I want to respond." She moved toward the chief, glaring across the room at him. "The answer to your question is...yes."

The chief raised his eyebrows.

"I'm a female police lieutenant. A *pregnant* female police lieutenant." Jane pressed her point. "And because of all of that, Tommy Murphy got away. If I had been some twenty-five-year-old male steroid-pumped stud cop, I could've taken Murphy down." She raised her hand and jabbed her index finger at her boss. "But, sir, I am who I am. A cop, and a wife, and a mother-to-be. It's a package deal."

The chief started to speak. "Or..." Jane talked right through him. "If I had been one of your flabby cronies pushing paper up and down a desk for the last ten years, Murphy would've gotten away. If I had been another know-nothing cop who squeaked through the Academy because his old man had friends in high places, Murphy would have gotten away. If I had been any fat-ass rear-echelon cop in this building, Murphy would have gotten away." She dropped her hand. "So if you're implying, or even overtly making some kind of threat…then don't threaten, Chief, show some balls and just do it."

She wheeled around and whipped the door open. "And while you're at it, *sir*, consider this: Patrolman Murphy applied to the SFPD. He went through the Academy and was a cop on the street for three years. In *your* department. Where were the background checks? What kind of vetting was done on the information on his Grade One application? When you start passing the buck, Chief, where exactly *does* it stop?"

Her energy and her patience spent, Jane stormed out of the office.

Kenny stepped into the doorway. "When are you going to realize she's the best cop you have?" He turned his back on the chief and hurried after his wife.

"In a stunning development, one of San Francisco's own policemen has been charged with the Stella's massacre." Cameron Sanders turned to Camera Two in the KGO studio. "Patrolman Thomas Murphy, twenty-three, barely eluded a coordinated police action earlier today." Tommy Murphy's Police Academy picture came on-screen as Sanders continued broadcasting. "In addition to the six lives that were taken at the restaurant, Murphy is now known to be responsible for two more deaths: Colleen Porter, twenty-nine, of Berkeley Hills, a Stella's employee who survived the initial attack by hiding in a walk-in freezer. She was murdered in her home a few days later. And…" Rick Weymouth's Academy photograph filled the screen. "Patrol Officer Richard Weymouth, twenty-six, of Corte Madera, Thomas Murphy's partner and the first responder to the awful tragedy. Officials initially believed

Weymouth had committed suicide. Now sources tell KGO News he, too, was killed by Murphy."

Cameron Sanders paused to listen to his earpiece. "We're going to the Hall of Justice where Chief of Police Walker McDonald has just begun a news conference."

The shot shifted to the chief speaking into a bouquet of microphones in the press room at the Hall of Justice. "…and that this unspeakable crime was committed by a public servant entrusted with the safety of our citizens is doubly distressing. I have been working closely on this case with Lieutenant Jane Candiotti, the lead inspector in our Homicide Department. It is through her dogged determination that we were able to identify Patrolman Thomas Murphy as the killer. And it is with the continued diligence of her and her team of dedicated police officers that we will apprehend him. Further to that, I've ordered a systemwide review of our departmental procedures that might have allowed someone like Officer Murphy the opportunity to falsify his application to the SFPD without proper scrutiny. I am empowering a special committee of—"

Jane zapped the TV off with the remote.

"Heard enough?" Edgar Silva asked. He shifted his weight on the hospital bed, unable to get comfortable. His head was heavily bandaged, both of his eyes still covered. "I know how close you came to getting him, Lieutenant."

Kenny stood in the doorway, just finishing a cell call to his sister. Beyond him, Carmen and Leo sat on the floor of the waiting room working on a well-used monster truck puzzle. Kenny flipped his cell phone closed. "How could you possibly have heard anything so soon?"

Edgar tilted his head toward Kenny's voice. "Degrees of separation."

Jane put the remote down on the end table. "There don't seem to be any."

Edgar nodded. "Not in this case." He let his head fall back. "I lose my baby brother. You lose your nephew..."

Jane glanced back to Kenny. "And it's done by one of our own."

"*Your* own, Lieutenant."

"Yes," Jane admitted. "One of *our* own. But I'll find him."

"Could take forever."

"Then it will."

A sudden gust of a child's laughter carried to them. "Again!" Leo squealed from across the hall.

Edgar cocked his head to his nephew's voice. Then he sucked in a deep breath through his nose, his jaw tensing. A single tear emerged from beneath his bandages and slipped down his cheek.

"Edgar?" Jane moved to the side of the bed. "Are you in pain?"

"Yeah," Edgar said, inhaling sharply, "in my heart." He held out his hand. Jane grasped it. Edgar wrapped his thick fingers around hers and squeezed, his arm trembling. "The only forever," he hissed through his teeth, "...is death."

"I told Andrea the same thing you said to Edgar." Kenny eased the Explorer out of the San Francisco General parking structure. "About finding Murphy, even if it takes forever."

"How's she doing?"

"Like all of us. Numb, disappointed...tired of having this in our lives." He nudged the car into crosstown traffic.

Jane lowered her visor against the late-day sun.

"Some punk reporter called her," Kenny went on. "He'd been doing his homework and saw that we never recovered any shell casings. Rather than come to me, he went to my sister to see if she had any information."

"Jesus."

"Tell me about it. Now all she can think about is, Was Bobby already dead before the killer—Murphy—took the time to reload? Or did her son have to wait, knowing what was coming?"

"What did you tell her?"

"That her son died immediately." Kenny turned right onto Mission. "And she said 'Thank God.'" He looked to Jane, his face drawn with worry. "That's what we're reduced to."

An ambulance screamed through the intersection ahead of them, followed a beat later by a squad car. World without end, Jane thought. She flattened her hand on her stomach, hoping for a connection with the baby pulsing deep within her.

"I've been thinking about something." Jane reached over to Kenny. "When I was in that tunnel with Tommy Murphy, I asked him why he shot at me behind the restaurant. And he said: 'I had to.'"

Kenny stopped at a red light, his gaze instinctively pulled down the path the ambulance had just taken. "But why was he there at all?"

Jane turned in her seat to face him. "It's the gun, Ken. Murphy's service weapon was a nine millimeter semi, like all of ours. Best evidence has the murders being committed with a revolver. Think about it; he couldn't very well hustle back to Art's Deli and have lunch with his partner with an extra gun in his pants."

Kenny picked it up. "Which means he'd planted a gun on one of his dry runs. Then, on the day, he retrieved it, used it, and hid it again."

"And he comes back for it later, but I'm there. He spooks and takes a shot at me."

"That means the gun is still there." Kenny crossed in front of a taxi waiting at the light. He turned right, heading up the hill toward Carmody Avenue. "But where?"

"I have a pretty good idea."

Half of the sparrow's nest was gone.

Kenny stacked two plastic milk crates and, holding on to the drain pipe, stepped up until he was eye level with the air-conditioning unit.

Jane backed away from the wall for a better look. "Now pull what's left of that nest away." Behind her, the sun was just about to pass behind the San Francisco General Hospital tower. An urban eclipse that would signal the end of another day.

Kenny stuck his hand into the narrow space and swept the debris from the abandoned nest out of the way. He peered into the crevice. "Hang on." Then he extended his fingers as far as he could reach and pulled. "Loose brick." Pushing up on his toes and straining to wedge his hand even farther into the hole, he was just able to grab a piece of cloth between the tips of his thumb and forefinger. "Got it." He jumped back down, a cloth-covered bundle in his hands.

Jane carefully unfolded the corners and let them fall away.

There, in Kenny's hands, was a .38 caliber revolver and seven brass shell casings.

"Now we have it all," Kenny said.

Jane looked at the pistol in her husband's hands. The dreadful weapon that had stopped so many lives like thoughts stopped in midsentence. "All," she said, "...except Tommy Murphy."

The sun slipped behind the hospital tower, the shadow of the building falling across Jane and Kenny like a dark veil.

35

Jane's body changed with the seasons.

Her face, her arms and legs, her tummy and back, her breasts. Everything was different. Warm and sturdy. Soft and open. Inexorably preparing for the moment when the baby chose to join her in this world.

For months, all her nights had seemed sleepless. Yet this was the most dream-filled time she could remember. Her baby was in her dreams, doe-eyed and curious and safe. Her parents were in her dreams. Years younger than when they had died; frozen in the timeless snapshot of a daughter's memory.

But the story of her dreams always came around to Bobby.

He came to Jane as a young boy on a scruffy pony in a picture taken before she knew him. He came as the ring bearer at her wedding, fidgeting his way through the ceremony. He came to her as the rambunctious, opinionated teenager who showed up unannounced at her house for a place to eat and a place to crash.

In time, while floating through the other-life of her dreams, Jane began to understand that Bobby's visits were ephemeral moments that always faded away, leaving behind a fleeting after-image of her memory of him. So she struggled to stay asleep, to keep from opening her eyes to the reality of Bobby's death. Soon she would tell herself, even while still dreaming, that Bobby was gone. That she'd wake up and move through another day and draw closer to the time when her baby would come. And Bobby would still be, would always be, gone.

Tommy Murphy came to her once in a dream. He was laughing, without humor, a mocking soundless laugh. His college boy face Dali-dripping into a grotesque, unendurable image. And Jane had startled awake, frightened at what she'd seen and relieved at the realization it had only been another dream.

She had reached over for Kenny. But he wasn't there. He was night-prowling the house again, as he had for months. Never sleeping, he would watch ESPN until he knew the repeat-cycled programs by heart. Then he would take out the photo albums. Pictures of himself with his parents and his sister. Pictures of Bobby as a baby asleep in a wedge of light coming in the kitchen window of some forgotten apartment. Of Bobby taking his first toe-tilting steps on his parents' lawn in Marin. Of Bobby riding his uncle's shoulders at Golden Gate Park. First day of school. T-ball. Hugging Jessica, some long-ago babysitter he had loved. His goofy missing-teeth smile. A guitar. A bike. A prom in a white jacketed tuxedo with a girl he never saw again. In his room with headphones on…

And Jane had found her husband in front of the television watching tennis highlights with the sound off, the photo albums spread on the couch. She had stood over him and taken his head and pressed it to her belly. And he had felt the heat of the growing ember of their child.

Upstairs, they lay the daybed of the baby's room. Kenny spooning his wife, his hands tracing the outline of their baby's body through her skin. As the baby moved to its father's touch, Jane and Kenny's breathing fell into a familiar connected rhythm. Kenny pressed his face into Jane's hair. And to each of them, all three of them, sleep would finally come.

People kept getting murdered in San Francisco.

"Death in the big city," Mike Finney would say when another call came in.

And Jane kept doing her job. Throwing herself into her work with a passion that some whispered might be an obsession. Solving all of the cases. The jealous husband who shot his wife and her lover in a bathtub, the carjacker who killed for a Lexus SUV, the junkie so desperate he snuffed out someone's life for a torn leather jacket, the high school sophomore whose French teacher flunked him.

Jane's solve-rate was unparalleled in the history of the city's Homicide Department. But she didn't care.

Tommy Murphy was still out there.

When she wasn't working, Jane passed the weeks and months—her body filling with promise—taking yoga classes and going for walks with Kenny, her forearms resting on the shelf of her belly as they did laps around their block in San Leandro. Kenny had started taking pictures of her, documenting her amazing transformation. And Jane began seeing Dr. Glazer for regular therapy sessions. He too had been affected by the Stella's shootings, and his counsel and compassion helped Jane through the long days and even longer nights.

But Jane was haunted by the faces of the dead.

They came to her in a hundred surprises every day. The well-dressed man pushing through the revolving door of the Wells Fargo Bank building near the cable car turnaround was Terrence Unger. The young girl sitting outside a Starbucks, a coffee on the small round table next to her laptop, was Toni Salazar. The panhandler jiggling his Styrofoam cup at the Union Square BART entrance was Shanty Rourke. The Mexican kid who worked in the produce section at her neighborhood market was Nico Silva.

And all the teenage boys hanging at the corners and at the arcades, running out of their high schools after final bell and cruising North Beach in their parents' cars—all of them were Bobby.

Jane became aware of an eerie newsworthy aura that evolved around those who had survived or had otherwise been touched by the Stella's shootings. People were fascinated by them and the footnote that followed their life passages—not unlike those left behind by Columbine or Virginia Tech or Aurora.

Dr. Glazer had told Jane to keep talking about it, to talk with Kenny during their walks. To track the stories and remember them until she came to fully understand on a level far beneath her own consciousness, the nuances, in all their subtle detail, of what had happened on that awful day six months ago.

Then, he said, Jane would evolve from someone who had felt so small and impotent in the clutches of grief and in the presence of evil. And the faces of the dead everywhere she looked would become the faces of people just coming out of office buildings and just sipping coffee. The faces of just another bum and just another kid working at a market.

Of just another teenager.

Kenny's sister sold the house she'd lived in with Bobby and moved in with her parents in Marin. She did this, she told everyone, to be closer to her ailing father as he, irretrievably grief-stricken over the loss of his grandson, slowly surrendered to his struggle with Parkinson's disease.

The *Chronicle* ran a short piece on Sammy Pickett, Toni Salazar's former boyfriend. He had served four and a half months in county lockup for the attempted assault of a police officer, Homicide Inspector Kenneth Marks—the newspaper noted that

Kenny's nephew had perished in the Stella's shootings. The day after his release, Pickett had driven Toni's VW camper south to Big Sur. The Highway Patrol Incident Report said that he had apparently swerved to miss a possum scurrying across Highway 1 and gone over a cliff. The van had plunged three hundred feet to the boulder-strewn shore of the Pacific Ocean. It had taken search and rescue all night to recover his body.

Jane heard that Charlie See, Terrence Unger's life partner, had met a man at a survivors of violent crimes support group. They were seeing each other exclusively and had plans to move in together.

Arthur "Shanty" Rourke, it turned out, had a grown daughter living in Portland, Oregon. She came forward to claim the money he had stashed in his room at the Mark Twain Hotel. The state took its chunk, but she still did all right for a waitress minimum waging double shifts in the downtown Ramada coffee shop.

Colleen Porter's landlord sold her belongings and re-rented the Berkeley Hills cabin to a couple from Rhode Island who hadn't heard about her murder.

Herman "Cabbage" Jones was found hanging by the neck in the holding cell of Alameda County Jail. His death was ruled to be at the hands of another.

Jane testified before the Departmental Review Board and Chuck Hollingsworth of Precinct Fifteen was relieved of his command. Hollingsworth then went into a steady liquor-soaked decline. He applied for and was granted a psychiatric leave of absence.

Pedro "Pepe" Rodriguez was awarded the DEA Commissioner's Star of Merit for his work in bringing down a Mexican cocaine cartel. He was promoted to special agent and transferred to El Paso, Texas.

Max Batzer retired after thirty years as a street cop. He took his pension and his savings and bought a Winnebago. He and his wife, Lisa, a breast cancer survivor, began a long-promised tour of the Major League Baseball stadiums across the country.

Casey Noveck was caught stealing inventory from two of Stella's warehouses by electronically rerouting the merchandise and selling it back to the purveyor, who in turn sold it to Burger King. He was dismissed.

Xavier Rinaldi recovered from accidentally falling from the second tier of the maximum security wing at San Quentin. At his own request, he chose to serve the remainder of his life sentence in the segregation block, where he would be locked down twenty-three hours a day and have zero contact with other inmates.

Chief Walker McDonald received a special Mayoral Citation for establishing the McDonald Protocol, a computer networking system that analyzed and verified the applications of prospective Police Academy cadets throughout the country.

Cameron Sanders, after getting so much face time covering the Stella's shootings for KGO, had his contract picked up by the network and moved to New York City.

Harry Donahue pled guilty to being an accessory after the fact for not coming forward with Francis Cellucci's name when the crime was originally committed. In that he was a teenager at the time and in that Jane Candiotti and Kenny Marks spoke at his hearing, the magistrate gave him a three-year suspended sentence and two more years of conditional probation. The far west regional director of UPS pledged that, if Donahue stayed out of trouble, he could keep his job.

Edgar Silva spent another week in San Francisco General Hospital and two more at the Lewis K. Fischer Rehabilitation Center. Soon after his release, he began volunteering twice a week for the city's gang task force, speaking at local high schools and youth centers. At Leo's second birthday party, Edgar dressed up as Cyclops.

Two other businesses tried to make a go of it at the storefront that had once been the Stella's on Carmody Avenue. An espresso bar and a fitness studio. Both failed within weeks.

Dateline did a two-hour special on the Stella's shootings and asked for help in finding Tommy Murphy aka Bradley Pomerance. Thousands of tips came in over the hotline each time the show aired. Tommy Murphy was spotted on a fishing trip in Maine. Or working for the Transit Authority in Chicago. Or had been stabbed to death in a homeless shelter in Louisiana.

Jane and her team, with the assistance of the FBI, pursued each tip and, each time, came up empty.

36

"I heard Saint Vincent's is for sale."

Jane and Kenny were just finishing their walk around the block, the late-afternoon sun slashing through the oak trees. A neighborhood that had been exclusively Italian when Jane was growing up had melted into a mosaic of Asian, black, and Russian families. The people on the street, seeing a nearly full-term woman walking with her wrists folded over the mantel of her belly, always stopped to say hello. To ask boy or girl? I'm not allowed to say, Jane had smiled. To ask about names. Not sure, but we've narrowed it down. To ask when are you due? Any day now.

"Land alone has to be worth a fortune," Kenny said, responding to the news about Bishop D'Souza's church being on the market. He pressed the palm of his hand to the small of Jane's back and guided her up the path to their house. Jane climbed the steps and sank into the overstuffed cushions of the porch glider. Kenny sat on the railing and rocked the glider with his foot.

They sat like that for a moment. Lost in thoughts of time past and time to come.

Jane looked over to Kenny, squinting against the dipping sun. He smiled, his eyes crinkling. She touched his foot. "What?"

"You look so beautiful in this light. So…I don't know… ready." He stood up and headed for the front door. "If we're really in any-day-now mode, I want to take your picture. Could be the last known photograph of you before the big event." He pulled open the screen door and went inside.

Jane sat back, letting the glider sway, as she listened to Kenny bound up the stairs two at a time. A car drove by—a teenage boy going way too fast as far as a certain mother-to-be was concerned.

Kenny clomped down the stairs and pushed through the screen door with his digital camera. He peered through the view finder. "Look at me, honey." Jane tilted her head toward him, still fighting the sun in her eyes.

Kenny turned the lens, fine-tuning the focus, and pressed the shutter button. He looked at the image on the tiny screen on the back of the camera. "Wait. That's no good. My shadow's killing you."

Jane stopped the glider.

Then she brought her gaze down from Kenny to the floorboards of the porch. Kenny's shadow stretched across the space between them like a flattened giant. "Ken…" Jane put her hands on the seat of the glider and pushed herself up. "Ken…the sun behind you. The long shadow. The photograph…"

She brushed past him and hurried into the house. Her purse was on a small table by the front door. She spread it open, reached inside, and pulled out a copy of the old Polaroid Brad Pomerance's foster father had taken on the bungalow steps. Jane turned to Kenny as he came in the door. "I've been carrying this picture around like a talisman. Look at it. The hurt little boy staring past the shadow, to the man with the camera. The man who had molested him…over and over again. Look in that kid's eyes. That's more than pain there…that's hatred."

Kenny took the Polaroid and studied it.

Jane picked up her bag and slung it on her shoulder. "Murphy said he wasn't done yet." She thrust the keys to the Explorer at Kenny and started back outside. "As far as we know, there's only one person left in the world for Tommy Murphy to go after."

"If you're talking about Burt Trumbull," Kenny said, "his wife said he moved to Thailand something like fifteen years ago."

Jane grabbed Kenny by the wrists. "Murphy was obsessed with revenge to the point of insanity. If time didn't matter to him, geography sure as hell won't." She ripped open the screen door. "Think about it: his picture's been on every television screen and newspaper in the country and we haven't had one solid lead. Tommy Murphy didn't fall off the face of the earth…he went to the other side of it."

"Mister Burt Trumbull he dead."

Constable Tran Pradhip of the Bangkok Police Department shifted in his seat. As he did, half of his face slid off the screen of the videophone connection. He found the lens again, corrected his position, and lit a cigarette. He snapped his Zippo lighter shut with an easy flick of his wrist.

Jane sat at the video console in the cramped Com room of Precinct Nineteen. Kenny stood in the doorway, monitoring the call. "What do you know, Constable," Jane said into the microphone, "about the circumstances of Mr. Trumbull's death?"

Tran Pradhip bent forward and opened a manila folder. As he did, all Jane and Kenny could see was the top of his head. He looked up and drew on his cigarette. "Mr. Trumbull live in the Huai Khwang sector of Bangkok. Very appealing to foreigners. Especially Caucasian. Much entertainment of anything you want available. He rent flat in apartment tower where other Caucasian live, too. But he die."

Jane glanced back to Kenny, then turned to the camera. "Sir, how did Mr. Trumbull die?"

"He kill self."

Kenny stepped in and leaned across the console. "Constable, how exactly did Mr. Trumbull commit suicide? An overdose or a hanging? Did he jump from his apartment?"

"He shoot self"—Constable Pradhip looked down to the folder—"in heart."

Kenny whipped a look to Jane: this was it. He handed her Tommy Murphy's Police Academy photo. She held it up to the vid-cam. "Sir, do you recognize this man?"

Constable Pradhip stubbed out his cigarette and leaned in to his screen. "He the son. He very upset when Mr. Trumbull die."

"Do you know," Jane asked, "where he is now?"

"Yah, sure. He live in father's apartment in Huai Khwang. He no troubles. He good boy."

"Problem is," Lou Tronick said as he topped off his mug with fresh coffee, "Thailand won't extradite a criminal wanted for a capital offense to a country that has the death penalty. And the United States has the death penalty big time."

Jane had gathered the Homicide Team in Interrogation One. She put her swollen feet up on a waste basket as she listened.

Mike Finney popped a Diet Coke. "If we can't get the Bangkok Police to bust Murphy for the Stella's murders, can't we at least have them pick him up on suspicion of murdering Burt Trumbull? With our assistance, they could build a pretty good case against him over there."

"That's just trading one problem for another," Kenny said. "Do we really want to take our chances on one of the most corrupt police departments in the world handing our guy over to one of the most corrupt court systems in the world?"

Finney looked to Jane. "Then what are we saying, Lieutenant, Tommy Murphy gets away with murder...again?"

The baby moved. Some hard angular corner of its body pressing downward. Jane winced at the sudden sharp stab of pain and waited for it to pass.

Kenny crossed to her. "Jane?"

Jane pulled in a deep breath and let it slip out her nostrils until the stitch in her groin faded. Then she swiveled in her chair, her eyes tracing from Mike Finney to Lou Tronick to Kenny. "Nobody gets away with murder."

Young Leo was six feet off the ground.

He rode Edgar's shoulders, gripping his uncle's ears, through the crowded outdoor market in the Mission District. A vendor sliced a gala apple in two and, diffidently averting his eyes from *El Patron*, passed half of it up to the little boy. Leo loosened his grasp on one of Edgar's ears and took it.

Edgar Silva wasn't bothered by the furtive glances of the curious around him. He saw what they saw: an old one-eyed warrior with prison tattoos and a toddler straddling his shoulders. He would have looked twice, too.

Stopping at another booth, he crushed a chili under his thumb and smelled its dust. Then he smiled to the young girl behind the table and she coiled a string of the peppers into a plastic grocery bag. Edgar slipped it over his wrist. "Good morning, Lieutenant," he said before he turned around.

Jane and Kenny were waiting for him beneath the awning of a flower stand. "Inspector," Edgar said to Kenny, "your wife seems to be expecting a baby."

"Seems to be."

"My prediction," Edgar said as he passed the other half of the apple up to Leo, "is three more days."

Jane sniffed a little laugh. "We should start a pool."

Edgar reached up and lifted Leo off his shoulders. Just as he did, a man in black Ray-Ban sunglasses separated himself from the milling crowd of shoppers and took the boy. A curt nod, and the man hefted Leo onto his right hip and made his way toward the petting zoo on the far side of the marketplace.

"That little boy," Edgar said looking after his nephew, "that twenty pounds of pooping and teething and *Bob the Builder* is what makes the world right again." He gestured for Jane and Kenny to join him as he walked. "And your baby will do the same for you." A hand reached out from one of the stalls and Edgar accepted a lemon ice. "But something tells me," he said as he scraped his teeth across the crown of ice, "you didn't come all the way down to our *mercado* for the vibrant ethnic atmosphere."

"Something's happened, Edgar," Jane said. "Something we need to talk to you about."

Kenny slipped a tightly wrapped package into Edgar's grocery bag. "In privacy."

Edgar dropped the lemon ice into a trash can and led Jane and Kenny toward a crowded roped-off picnic section. Several families were spread out among the white plastic tables and chairs. Mothers rocked baby carriages back and forth and little kids slalomed between the tables in inexhaustible figure eights. Edgar waded into the crowd, shaking hands, touching babies' faces, tilting his head to the elders in a gesture of humility.

Three young men saw him coming and got up from a table near the center of the food court. Taking their tamales and soft drinks and *churros* with them, they offered their seats to *El Patron* and his guests.

Edgar thanked them with a smile and motioned for Jane and Kenny to join him at the table. "Here," he said as he sat down in the bustling midst of his own people, "here we can talk in privacy."

37

Jane lay awake watching the ceiling change from black to gray.

Morning was coming. The morning of the day her child would be born. All night long, as Kenny snored softly beside her, she had felt her body moving in its final preparations. The tightening and the pulling. The loosening and the calming. The surrender.

She had lain awake in the room that had been her parents' bedroom—in the room in which she was conceived—and massaged her baby through her own taut skin. And in one last primal stirring—something between a tumble and a lurch—the baby had let her know that it was ready.

A tear slipped from Jane's eye and worked its way across her temple to her ear. She had never felt so at peace.

She closed her eyes, squeezing out another tear, and said a silent prayer of thanks. Then she put her hand on her husband's shoulder and turned to him.

"Ken."

There was a quick middle-knuckle rap on the door.

Then another.

A moment later the security chain to the apartment slid free. The door opened to a face-wide crack and Tommy Murphy, bleary-eyed and rumpled, looked out into the hallway. His eyes and mouth fell open at the same time his rum-saturated brain recognized who was standing in front of him.

Tommy Murphy threw his shoulder into the door, frantically trying to close it. But Edgar Silva was quicker, angrier... hungrier. He hurled himself into the door and splintered it off its hinges. Then he bulled his way into the apartment, the sunset burning orange off the Chao Phraya River forty stories below.

"You're doing great," Dr. Berger said. "A quick ten count, then again."

Jane gripped Kenny's hand, their wedding rings touching, and pushed. A nurse wheeled a tall mirror to the bottom of the bed. Kenny wiped the sweat from Jane's eyes with a cool, damp cloth, and she strained one more time, arching her body forward to watch her baby come.

"Here we go. Here we go," Dr. Berger urged. "You're doing great, Jane."

A dark ball of wet fur appeared in the mirror as the baby's head worked its way out. Jane heaved one more time and its right shoulder emerged. She let go of Kenny's hand and sat up. "I can do this, guys." She slipped her fingers under her baby's arm and gently tugged. The other shoulder slid out and, in one great rushing surge, her child was born.

Jane fell back onto the bed, her blinking wet baby wrapped in her arms.

Kenny leaned over and kissed Jane on the forehead. She turned their baby to him.

"He's beautiful," Kenny said, his eyes shining with tears.

Tommy Murphy stumbled backward across the living room, Edgar, a relentless stalking bear, right behind him. Murphy wanted to go to the right, to the bedroom, but Edgar cut him off. He tried running to the left, a short hallway then the kitchen. But Edgar stopped him.

Murphy thudded into the bamboo sliding doors that led to the balcony. Hopelessly trapped, he fell to his knees.

Edgar reached behind and drew the pistol from his belt. He thumbed back the hammer and aimed it at Murphy's face. "Don't!" Tommy Murphy shrieked. Then, as he registered that this was the same revolver he had used to kill all those people in the Stella's, a puddle appeared between his legs, his urine spreading in a flat pool across the polished teak floor.

Edgar strode forward and touched the muzzle of the gun to Murphy's right eye. "*Para mi hermano y los otros*," he spat as he squeezed the trigger. The pistol erupted in his hand, vaporizing Tommy Murphy's eye and sending brain and bullet, blood and skull, exploding onto the doors.

Edgar jammed his boot heel into Murphy's lower jaw, forcing it open. Then he plunged the gun into the dead man's mouth, breaking off the top two teeth, and fired again. The bullet ripped through the base of Murphy's skull. His head whacked against the floor and then lay at an angle impossibly perpendicular to his body.

Switching the pistol to his other hand as he stood over Tommy Murphy, Edgar crossed himself. Then he dropped the revolver onto the floor. It landed heavily, bounced once, and came to rest near what was left of Murphy's face.

He glanced at his watch and, without looking back, left the apartment.

Edgar Silva had a plane to catch.

Kenny was a natural.

Since they'd come home from the hospital, he had changed their baby several times, singing wonderfully stupid made-up lullabies as he cleaned and dressed his new child.

Jane sat in her mother's rocking chair, the same chair she had been breastfed in as an infant, resting in the sunlight that warmed the bedroom window. She had tried to read the *Chronicle* several times but found herself drawn to just staring at her husband and son napping on the bed—the baby lying flat on his father's chest like a cat.

The phone rang. Jane snatched it up before the first ring finished. "Hello."

Edgar Silva sat next to his nephew in the backseat of his Buick. Leo played with a family of small jade elephants his uncle had brought back with him. Carmen drove the car north from the airport, heading back to San Francisco. "Good morning, Lieutenant."

"Edgar, I heard you were away. How was your trip?"

"A perfect blend of business and pleasure." Leo dropped one of the elephants and Edgar bent over to retrieve it. "But the sonsa-bitches customs guys…" Carmen threw her husband a disapproving look in the rearview mirror. "Sorry…the overzealous customs officials searched me head-to-toe when I got back."

"It's a new world out there," Jane said. The baby murmured in his sleep. "Where are you now?"

"Carmen's taking me up to the Hall of Justice. There's a couple of hundred inner-city tough boys waiting to hear this old gangbanger talk about the lessons I've learned and how I turned my life around to become a respectable law-abiding citizen."

"You're an inspiration to us all, Edgar."

"Kind of you to say, Lieutenant. Any good news on your end?"

Jane looked to her sleeping husband and son. "Yes, I had my baby three days after we saw you at the market. Just like you said."

"Congratulations. Mother and child are doing?"

"Just fine."

"And the name?"

Kenny, in his sleep, spread his hand across his tiny son's back.

"Robert," Jane said. "But we call him Bobby."

About the Author

Photo by AP Images, 2011

Best-selling crime novelist Clyde Phillips is the former executive producer of the Emmy-nominated Showtime series *Dexter* and currently serves as executive producer for the network's acclaimed *Nurse Jackie*. He also created the television series *Parker Lewis Can't Lose*, *Suddenly Susan*, and *Get Real*. He is the author of the Jane Candiotti novels *Fall From Grace, Blindsided, and Sacrifice.* A graduate of UCLA and a native of Boston, he lives in Connecticut and on Martha's Vineyard with his wife, Jane. They have one daughter.